To Be Continued

or, Conversations with a Toad

JAMES ROBERTSON

PENGUIN BOOKS

PENGUIN BOOKS

UK | USA | Canada | Ireland | Australia
India | New Zealand | South Africa

Penguin Books is part of the Penguin Random House group of companies
whose addresses can be found at global.penguinrandomhouse.com.

First published by Hamish Hamilton 2016
Published in Penguin Books 2017
001

Set in 9.22/11.98 pt ITC Legacy Serif Std
Typeset by Jouve (UK), Milton Keynes
Printed in Great Britain by Clays Ltd, St Ives plc

A CIP catalogue record for this book is available from the British Library

ISBN: 978-0-241-14685-9

www.greenpenguin.co.uk

MIX
Paper from
responsible sources
FSC® C018179

Penguin Random House is committed to a
sustainable future for our business, our readers
and our planet. This book is made from Forest
Stewardship Council® certified paper.

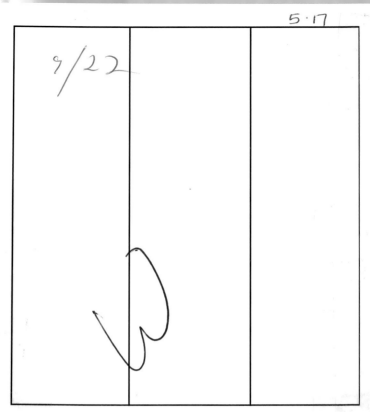

5·17

9/22

This book should be returned/renewed by the latest date shown above. Overdue items incur charges which prevent self-service renewals. Please contact the library.

**Wandsworth Libraries
24 hour Renewal Hotline
01159 293388
www.wandsworth.gov.uk**

By the same author

The Fanatic
Joseph Knight
The Testament of Gideon Mack
And the Land Lay Still
Republics of the Mind
The Professor of Truth
365: Stories

In loving memory of Owen Fraser Stewart (1973–2015).

And for Isla Catherine Isabel Macdonald (born 2015).

do not tell me
said warty bliggens
that there is not a purpose
in the universe
in the universe
the thought is blasphemy

   — Don Marquis, 'warty bliggens the toad'

Author's Note

The geography in this book is not to be trusted.

1

THANK YOU FOR HAVING ME

I am sitting on the upper deck of a number 11 bus, stuck in traffic on Lothian Road, Edinburgh, when I turn fifty.

I check my watch: it is 12.15 p.m. This is it. Exactly half a century ago, I entered the world.

A small cheer rises in me, which I elect to quash.

I am able to mark the occasion with such confidence and precision because, last night, I looked out my birth certificate and examined it closely. Scottish birth certificates specify not only the place and date of birth but also the time. In this, I believe, we differ from the modus operandi of Our Friends in the South. I am uninformed as to what practices prevail in other jurisdictions.

(My chest swelled with patriotic pride when I saw that attention to detail. We may not be perfect, I said to myself, we may fall short of expectations in other departments, but by God we know how to fill out a birth certificate.)

It occurs to me now, in my deflated mode, that we are a nation of record-keepers, not of record-breakers.

Immediately I am ashamed of the paucity of this observation and the feebleness of my wordplay.

Returning to the matter of my birthday, I consider standing up and making an announcement to the other passengers. I could ask them to stop – just for one moment – texting, surfing, reading the free comic disguised as a newspaper, or gazing through the window, as I have something to tell them: 'Fifty years ago, to this very minute, I arrived. I was born. Is that not amazing? I don't remember it myself, but it's recorded fact and I want to share it with you.'

I decide against this course of action. For one thing, I am of a shy and retiring disposition. It would not be a misrepresentation of my character to say that, as a rule, if I am in the vicinity of a parapet I do not put my head above it. Furthermore, proof of my assertion might be demanded and I do not have the birth certificate about my person. It is in a drawer of my father's desk where documents relating to identity, insurance and the ownership of Premium Bonds reside, and have done for as long as I can remember. On the few occasions in my adult life when I needed to produce my birth certificate for official inspection I always asked my father for it, he released it to me, and to that same location it always returned, like a pigeon to its doocot-hole.

This – habit, custom, idiosyncrasy, call it what you will – has been the cause of some ill feeling between myself and Sonya, my – partner, lover, bidie-in, ex- of all the preceding, call *her* what you will. That I did not, during the ten years of our cohabitation, choose to transfer such documents as refer specifically or solely to me from the parental home to hers – the domicile which, until recently, we shared – has been held up by Sonya as exemplifying both my immaturity and a failure to 'commit' to said relationship. There is, no doubt, some truth in the charge. Arguably, however, the fact that I am once again resident in the parental home – which is, legally, also my home, or half of it is, or it half is – and thus in a position to access these papers at my will and leisure (my father being no longer able to perform his role as Custodian of the Family Paperwork), demonstrates foresight, not to mention loyalty to tradition.

There are three other people on the upper deck of the number 11 bus: a woman sitting across the aisle from me, two rows further forward, and two men right up at the front, in the exciting seats, the ones where the future rushes to meet you with worrying questions such as 'Will the bus make it under this bridge?', 'Will it crunch into the back of the bus in front?' or 'Has that smacking branch cracked the glass and will I be held responsible because of my proximity to the scene of the incident?'

It is likely, therefore, that these men already have plenty to occupy their minds, and will not be remotely interested in news of the anniversary of my birth. Nor, in all probability, will the woman. Why should they, or indeed she? Who am I, Douglas Findhorn Elder, that total strangers should care anything about me?

Nevertheless, I do have a small but persistent yearning to tell my news to someone. My mother, for example. 'Hello? Mum? Guess what you were doing right now, fifty years ago?' But I have left my mobile phone in the house and my mother has been dead for two years. A pity, that. Not that she is dead – of course that *is* a pity, even though she reached a good

4

age – but that I can't tell her, can't pass on my congratulations, and my thanks.

'Thank you for having me.'

I would mean it, too, despite everything. In the grand scale of existence, the 'everything' that pertains to Douglas Findhorn Elder is not so very much.

ASKANCE

I would like to talk to someone and receive some positive feedback. Yesterday I spoke to a toad, but all I got in reply was a dirty look. I cannot blame the toad. I was in the garden, digging out some lilies, and I narrowly avoided spearing it with a graip. At least, I hope I avoided it. As I pulled the tines back out of the soil, what I thought was a clod of earth suddenly became animated, wriggling in a wounded kind of way and then crawling under some dead leaves. Fearing that I had stabbed the creature, I cleared the leaves in search of it and touched its back to see if it moved. It did. 'Sorry,' I said, which was when it looked askance at me with a malevolent red eye, before retreating deeper into the vegetation. So I spoke to it from afar. 'Sorry, sorry, sorry,' I said. The toad remained still and invisible, frightened or aggrieved, and possibly injured. I felt guilty but also that I should not interfere further. I pulled a few weeds in a perfunctory manner in another part of the garden and then went inside, where I was overcome by a need to sleep.

THE LATE DOUGLAS ELDER

Fifty is just a number. What is it? It is a 5 and an 0. It is a wee jingle such as one might hear on a radio station the chief characteristic of which is a mood of forced jollity.

Five-Oh. Not long to go.

No sooner have I thought this thought than several other slogans present themselves like messages running along the bottom edge of the screen of my vision. This happens without any voluntary activation by myself of the mental processes, yet to the best of my knowledge they are not slogans that exist outwith my own imagination, and it is therefore a puzzle to me as to how they have got in there:

You will shortly be losing your grip and flying off the not-so-merry go-round of life.

You are going to die. Soon. Soonish. Sooner rather than later.
Sooner rather than later, YOU will be over.
Your immortality warranty is about to expire.

Weighty of authority and dire of consequence though this last proposition appears to be, it does not fill me with dread as I have no idea what an 'immortality warranty' is.

Across my outlook on the world, jogging backwards from right to left, comes another newsflash:

Elder: less time left than already used up.

I consult my watch again. It is true: I am going to be late. I already am late. Not late as in dead: *the late Douglas Elder*. (I feel at my wrist for a pulse, find I still have one.) Late as in late. I am alive, fifty, stuck on a bus, and late for another man's funeral.

The service is due to kick off, if that is not too recreational a term, at 12.30 p.m. I start to get my apologies for being late in early. First I apologise to Ronald Grigson, a former colleague, whose funeral it is, although presumably he is not going to care a button whether I turn up or not. Then I apologise to a pewful of black-coated, horse-faced mourners as I edge along in front of them, causing them to rise and fall like a kind of Presbyterian Mexican wave: more forced jollity. I do not recognise these people and this again is disquieting, for if they are figments of my own imagination then *why* do I not know them? The pew stretches into the far distance and it seems that I am destined to keep disturbing the occupants until I reach a vacant space rumoured to exist at the opposite end several miles away. Why these people cannot all simply shuffle one arse-width along eludes me, but puzzles like this are the stuff of dreams, and if I am not dreaming then I do not know what I am doing.

I do not know what I am doing. This is an accurate statement.

A voice mutters inside my head: 'Sorry. Sorry I'm late. Excuse me. Sorry.' It is my own voice. At least I recognise that.

THE EGG-TIMER OF LIFE

Some minutes pass. The bus nudges forward a few feet. I am getting used to being fifty. It is slightly disappointing. I thought I didn't want any fuss – in fact, I emphasised to Sonya in a phone call that I didn't, and I don't, and certainly I expect none from that quarter – but I feel something is missing.

What can it be? I have all that a man newly turned fifty can reasonably desire, other than a job, a settled relationship and confidence in the future. And a general feeling of contentment. Apart from these trivial absences, I am what you might call living the dream.

Yes, this too is not inaccurate. See, for supporting evidence, the above episode with the eternal pew. I feel that I do not have a good grip on reality. Or that reality does not have a good grip on me.

The phone conversation with Sonya in which I established my preference for a complete lack of birthday fuss took place about a week ago. I called to ask how she and her offspring, Paula and Magnus, were doing, having not seen any of them for some weeks. She was quite chatty, and the news of all three, such as it was, was good. Paula, nineteen, a second-year art student, had started a part-time job in a bar. (This is almost revolutionary, Paula never before having shown the slightest interest in connecting the sweat of one's brow with the possession of a disposable income.) Magnus, twenty-four, who works in IT and seems to have purloined his sister's share of the work ethic while she was asleep and added it to his own, was up for promotion and still enjoying club rugby; and Sonya – well, Sonya was her usual unrelaxed, brittle yet somehow also, to me, I don't know why, endearing self. She made no mention of any life-style changes, such as having met or begun searching for a new significant other to replace the one, i.e. me, she recently ejected from the household, and for this I was, if not grateful, at least gratified.

How can one be attracted to someone to whom one is not attracted?

I don't know, but it happens.

It is 12.20. I am five minutes into my second half-century. Nothing has changed. Everything is different. No it isn't. Yes it is. Thoughts tumble past me like pieces of litter. Through the streaked window of the bus I see them. A gusty wind is blowing. The thoughts whisk, roll, flap, sail by.

I watch them go. It is quite interesting, but also terrifying. I wonder if this is how it is for my father. I see him in his room in the Home, leaning from the beige armchair to grab at passing thoughts, trying to attach words to them.

I see, too, his strong, slashing signature on my birth certificate: *Thomas Y. Elder*. Done with a real pen, in real ink. My father was thirty-three when I was born. That signature represented something in 1964: boldness and energy. He can hardly write his name at all now, let alone dash it off like Zorro with his rapier, and even if he did he would not necessarily recognise it as his own.

Men crash like trees or rot like trees, but they fall at last, one way or the other.

I am not at all sure of my own ability to remain rooted and upright for much longer, or to continue to put my thoughts in order: one thought after another, coherent and connected. The old confidence, never that great, has taken a few knocks of late, and witnessing my father's deteriorating condition does not help. It is as if, hiking across moorland on what I believe to be my own chosen course, I suddenly spot Dad, a hundred yards ahead, sitting on a rock looking lost, and it transpires that I have been following his trail all along without knowing it.

It gives you a jolt, a thing like that. It pings the bell on the egg-timer of life. It brings you face to face with yourself, whoever you are.

This is often not a pleasing experience.

A WALKING ENCYCLOPAEDIA

The bus is at a standstill again. More debris rushes by in the wind – litter or thoughts, one or the other. The world is a jumble of red-and-white-striped barriers, shouting men in hard hats and loud, yellow machinery. As if the road were a patient in the hands of a team of raucous surgeons, it has been opened up and all its internal organs exposed. There is no dignity to it. I feel sorry for Lothian Road – which are six words I never thought I would arrange in that order.

To distract myself from the anxiety caused by being late I engage the woman passenger, or more accurately the back of her head, in conversation. She is occupied with turning the pages of the free comic, so doesn't object.

'I used to make a living from that, you know.'

From what? Roadworks?

'No, wordworks. Arranging words in a certain order. I was pretty good at it, in fact.'

Is that so? What were you, a Scrabble champion?

'No, I was a newspaperman. I was employed by the *Spear*.'

That rag?

'Madam, a rag is what you are perusing now.'

It's all relative.

'Fair point. I concede that the *Spear* is not what it used to be. More than twenty years I worked there. Six days a week, often enough.'

That must have been an awful lot of words, then?

'It was.'

You'll be a walking encyclopaedia.

'A striking metaphor, if I may say so. There's no denying that the words have an effect. After a few years you find that you're seeing your thoughts in the shape of printed phrases, sentences, paragraphs – actual blocks of typography – and then to clarify what it is you're thinking you knock and stretch them into different shapes, so that they fit neatly into the blank space available.'

Is that right? I don't see my thoughts at all. I just think them.

'It's an occupational hazard. You get used to it, but it doesn't make your thoughts any more meaningful. Mind you, in a newspaper context – in the context of actually working on a newspaper – the word-shapes do mean something. They serve a purpose. They tell stories, form opinions, transmit information to readers.'

Och, who reads newspapers these days? It's just rubbish that's in them. This one on the buses, I read it. It's full of rubbish too but at least it's free. When you get to the end you don't feel you've wasted your money as well as your time.

'That's a point in its favour, I suppose. Anyway, where was I? Ah yes, something happened after all those years at the *Spear*. I started to lose the knack. I became incompetent.'

Oh, what a shame! Did you go to the doctor?

'It wasn't really a medical problem. Maybe it was less about my incompetence, and more about my competence no longer fitting the job, because the job had changed. Officially I was a sub-editor, but the demarcation between jobs had been getting very blurred, and for quite a while I'd not only had to sub stories, I'd had to write them as well.'

Sob stories, did you say?

'No, sub. Edit them so they make sense and fit the page. It's a dying craft. The thing is, I was subbing the very book reviews and diary pieces I'd written myself. Even the odd feature – that's a longer article, a kind of short essay. In the old days the trade unions would never have stood for that kind of thing – one person seeing an item through from start to finish – but the old days are over. That's true, isn't it? The old days never last. Hello? Hello?'

But it's no good. I've lost her. If she had eyes in the back of her head they'd have glazed over. Meanwhile, the ones at the front finish with the comic, which she folds and places on the seat beside her. Then she stares steadfastly ahead as if quite unaware of my presence. Which she probably is.

9

Another possibility, of course, is that she is unaware of my absence. That is to say, what proof do I have that I am here at all?

SO I JUMPED

Times change. Technology changes. My competence didn't fit a job I no longer enjoyed doing. There was no satisfaction in putting the newspaper to bed. There should be a parental kind of pride and pleasure in that, but I didn't feel it. I wasn't even putting myself to bed properly. In the old days I came home well after midnight and I was tired but it was a good tired. I felt good about myself and my tiredness. I slid into bed and slept. Maybe Sonya would wake up and we would have a cuddle, or maybe she wouldn't and we wouldn't, but either way was fine, and we would both get a good night's sleep.

When I say 'home' I mean her place. It was my place too – our place – but really it was her place and I just shared her bed and the bills. Most of the contents of the house, including Magnus and Paula, were hers as well, and still are. That's not the point. The point is, the old days were over and I wasn't getting a good night's sleep any more. Not ever. I fell into bed exhausted, I turned and tossed for hours and woke up even more exhausted. Night after night. It wore me down. It wore Sonya down. It wore us both down until we had to deal with it. We dealt with it by me not going to hers after my shifts. I went back to my old home instead, to my old bedroom in my parents' house. When I came in late at night there, at least I never disturbed them because my father slept like a log and my mother was dead. That was another thing. My mother had died a few months before this and my father was lonely. He needed some company and I needed to keep an eye on him, because he wasn't quite himself. He wasn't a lot himself, as it transpired.

With these new arrangements, Sonya and I didn't see each other much through the week. Soon we were getting together only on Sundays. I found all this unsettling. Partly what unsettled me was that Sonya didn't seem unsettled. Except maybe on Sundays.

Meanwhile, back on the good ship *Spear*, the HR people did the rounds with a new voluntary redundancy offer. This happened about once a year. Normally I kept my head down, but this time I put my hand up. I did my sums. I talked to the union rep. I talked to the management. One Sunday I talked to Sonya because we were still, by force of habit if nothing else, a kind of item. Among the things we talked about was my father's failing health. It was more and more obvious that he wasn't right. He was behaving oddly, forgetting things, losing his temper over nothing, not sleeping like a log any more. It had probably been coming on for years, but I hadn't noticed while my mother was alive. Between them they'd managed to disguise it, but that wasn't possible any longer. If I stopped working at the *Spear* maybe I could look after him a bit better, as she had done.

The redundancy offer was not great, but it was better than what was likely to be on the table the next time HR came round, or the time after that when there were no volunteers left. So I took it: a lump sum and – if I don't touch it till I'm sixty – a reasonable pension. And there was a promise from the editor – a dangling-carrot kind of promise but a promise nonetheless – that I might get some freelance work once I was off the company's books. I weighed up the situation: jump, or wait until the ship sank? If I jumped, there was a chance I might land in a lifeboat. Better that than drowning in the engine room.

So I jumped.

GREAT-UNCLE GILBERT

I am not bothered, actually, by the idea that I might not be here. Non-existence would at least remove all other cares. What worries me more is the greater likelihood that I am a living, breathing, corporeal being increasingly disconnected from the environment it inhabits: *in* the world but not *of* it. Six months have passed since I left the *Spear*, and what have I had from the editor? Despite a few emails and phone messages from me to him, only silence. For six months I have not gone out to work. I've seen hardly anything of my Erstwhile Colleagues from the sub-editors' desk, although I know they will be attending Ronald Grigson's funeral because it was one of them, Grant McKinley, who phoned me with the news of Ronald's passing. My relationship with Sonya and her children, if not over, appears to be in its terminal stages. And my father's deterioration means that he and I are now in a different place, or rather in different places, and, while we still utter words when in each other's company (i.e. when I visit him), we don't exactly have meaningful dialogue. For all these reasons, I am feeling somewhat detached.

These are the rational explanations. However, I am also unable to ignore the alternative theory, already hinted at, that I am heading, rather sooner than expected, towards that mystery zone presently occupied by Thomas Ythan Elder.

There is a precedent. Hiding in the foliage of the paternal ancestral tree is a relative who went clean off the rationality rails in his fifties, in *the* Fifties. As a very young man – a boy really – Great-uncle Gilbert was conscripted into the army and spent the last months of the First World War in France. Perhaps he suffered mental and emotional distress as a result of his military experience, and perhaps this was the start of his derailment. After the war he became a primary-school teacher. His favourite subject was arithmetic: indeed, he liked teaching arithmetic so much that he sometimes omitted to teach his charges anything else, which on more than one occasion caused him difficulties with the education authorities. He never married, but lived a solitary, frugal life. Apart from his work, his chief occupation was collecting things. It did not seem to matter *what* he collected, so long as he could count them. One year it was jam jars, the next it was broken clay pipes. He filled a whole trunk with fir cones. He amassed an impressive range of discarded boots and shoes, for the right foot only, and a veritable museum of birds' bones. People were accustomed to seeing him at weekends, scouring the lanes and ditches for whatever new category of amassable items had caught his attention. He had a ledger in which, in a fine copperplate hand, he entered the total numbers of his acquisitions: 557 assorted nails; 260 lengths of string; 37 postcards depicting the Eiffel Tower. Over the years his small home became very crowded.

One Saturday morning he left this home, in Cupar, Fife, and walked to Crail, on the coast, a distance of about twenty miles. His stroll brought him to the North Sea, where witnesses saw him continue straight into the water, fully clothed, pushing through the waves until he was completely submerged. The alarm was raised but Gilbert was not recovered until the next tide brought him ashore at Pittenweem. The pockets of his coat were found to contain seventy-one pennies (five shillings and eleven pence), all dated between 1914 and 1918. If it had only been three and fourpence the message would have been so much clearer. Or would it? Sorry. That's a joke in poor taste.

Although Great-uncle Gilbert wasn't much talked about when I was a boy, sometimes, if my father was in fatalistic mood or my mother wanted to cast aspersions on his pedigree, Gilbert's sad history, in the form of his ledger, was brought forth from the mahogany Cabinet of Morbid Curiosity that stood in a corner of the Best Room, and displayed to me as a terrible warning of what would happen if I took my good fortune and well-being for granted. Gilbert's propensity for counting things had over-whelmed him by degrees as surely as the grey waters had closed over his head. If he had only kept his sums in the classroom where they belonged, tragedy might have been avoided. *Never let your guard down*, the lesson was, *lest the worms of utter confusion enter your skull and turn your brain to sawdust*. My mother (a woman possessed of that excellent Scottish charac-teristic, much admired and some would say encouraged by Our Friends in the South, a total lack of imagination) died at seventy-nine in full command of her faculties. But look at Gilbert! And my father! Did my mother not often say that I took after him in almost every respect? Yes she did!

Oh dear. I peer through the bus window and see a dark, still sea, and no land in sight. Oars, life jackets, plastic containers and other debris float on the surface, and me among them. I have jumped, and missed the lifeboat, or it wasn't there after all. Or did I simply walk into the sea? It is calm now, but for how much longer?

THE ENDLESS PEW OF BASTARDS

The bus surges forward. Evidently the driver has lost patience, seen a gap in the defence and gone for it like a rugby fullback on the burst. Engine roaring like an aeroplane's, the bus sways and jinks along a narrow corri-dor of cones between trenches full of utility pipes and cables. I grab the seat in front of me and cling on. The two men in the exciting seats bounce up and down and the woman with whose tête I have so recently been têt-ing judders, but not one of us complains. Progress! From downstairs comes a ragged, slightly ironic cheer such as the one I previously intern-ally suppressed. A few seconds later the bus is through the junction at Tollcross and disgorging passengers outside the King's Theatre. But it is now 12.30. The coin has been tossed, the funeral referee is about to blow his whistle, and I am not even at the turnstiles.

Off we go again, but within seconds the bus slows to another halt. Ahead of us an articulated lorry carrying a load of immense steel pipes, perhaps – who knows? – destined for the intestinal reconstruction of Lothian Road, is reversing into a narrow side street in order to go back the way it came – and every other vehicle has to wait while this manoeuvre is completed. Should I have got out at the theatre and flagged down a cab? There seem to be plenty of cabs about but experience warns me that this will remain the case only so long as I stay on the bus. The minute I step onto the pavement all the taxis will vanish or turn off their FOR HIRE lights. This is an infallible law, so why invoke it by leaving the bus? There is also the cost to be taken into account. I have become ever more aware of the need to clamp down on extravagances since being de-salaried, which is like being de-bagged when all your money is in your trouser pockets. *The lump sum won't last for ever.* (This is one of Sonya's wise maxims, or if it isn't I never see the words passing across the mind-screen without hearing them in her voice.) *Better the bus fare you know than the taxi fare you don't.* (That's one of mine.)

Meanwhile, I am still making my way along the endless pew of bastards. The pew of endless bastards. No doubt this is symbolic. I see three of my Erstwhile Colleagues looming: Roy Wilkinson, Grant McKinley and Ollie Buckthorn, resplendent in shiny black suits very similar to the shiny black suit I myself am wearing. Roy and Grant join in the rise-and-fall procedure, grinning at me encouragingly, but there is no way, even if Ollie were to rise off his mountainous backside, that I will be able to get past him. Ollie grins too, but far from being encouraging his is the grin of an adolescent prankster, a grin of joukery-pawkery and high jinks. As I approach he lifts his brogue-encased feet and plants them on the shelf for hymn books, while signalling that I am to pass under his legs. Aware that I am causing enough disruption already and that Ollie will be merciless, I have no choice. Down I go on hands and knees into the thin stour of old religion, Ollie's trousered buttocks lapping against my cheek as I tunnel forward. If he breaks wind now I am as dead as Ronald Grigson.

'Sorry. Sorry. Excuse me. Fuck you, Ollie. Sorry.'

Ah. I find I have spoken aloud. Furthermore, I am crouching on a hard floor, among sweetie papers and discarded tickets. I snap out of it fast and regain my seat, but too late. The woman across the aisle has turned, looked quickly at me, then away again. The aisle on the bus, not in the church. Because I am not there yet.

'Sorry,' I say again, to her this time. It is meant sincerely, but the damage has been done. She stands and descends to the lower deck.

THE GAUZY BORDER

This has been happening more and more: getting carried away with, by or in the scenario. It feels odd, but is it? Isn't this treading the gauzy border between reality and imagination, this uncertainty as to which side of that curtain you are on, normal? Some just slip more easily through the gap than others. One moment you're on a number 11 bus going nowhere, the next you're crawling along the floor of a church you've never entered before, with no end to the journey in sight.

Doesn't this happen to us all?

I have too much time on my hands, that's the trouble. Working five days a week, often six, kept me tethered to some semblance of reality, but the rope has been severed. And real life, when it opens up as a void, isn't half as interesting as the imagined version.

Life without the imagined life is, in fact, unimaginable.

That woman might also be going to the funeral. If so, she's as late as I am. Was she in black? I can't remember. I think about following her downstairs and suggesting we share a cab, make a joint late entry together. It could be the start of a beautiful friendship.

I like the idea of a new, beautiful friendship.

But I don't think she would be keen.

ELDER FUCKS UP

Assuming I ever actually get to the church, I'll have missed the opening hymn and prayers but not, I hope, the eulogy. I want to hear the eulogy. It will be my last opportunity to like Ronald Grigson. Not that I actively *dis*liked him, I just never really knew him. He was always rather stand-offish, not much of a team player. I'm not much of a team player myself, but at least I would go for a drink with the Erstwhile Colleagues at the end of a shift. Grigson hardly ever joined us. He was the *Spear*'s business and finance editor, which in the last year or so meant not only editing but also writing most of the contents of the pages for which he was responsible. He always had them signed off before the rest of us were done, and if you read them late into the evening you sometimes felt there wasn't much point in completing the rest of the paper, because according to Ronald the world was likely to end before daybreak or at any rate shortly after the London Stock Exchange opened. For him, every economic cloud had another cloud piling up behind it. He was a glass-half-empty man who, on the occasions when he did come to the pub, usually slipped away before it was his turn to replenish the glasses-wholly-empty. I can't recall Ronald Grigson ever buying me a drink, but I know for a fact that I've bought rounds that included Ronald Grigson. That rankles. I am sitting on a bus trying to attend the man's funeral, and it rankles. Why on earth? What difference does it make if he was a cheapskate? He's dead. He didn't take redundancy, he held out for finishing his career at sixty-five with full pension rights, and look, he's dead, three years short of the target. Woke up one Sunday morning, told his wife he wasn't feeling so good, she went for the papers and when she came back he was away. Heart attack. Whether I liked him or not is immaterial. Sixty-two is way too young for anyone to go.

Sixty-two is only twelve years older than fifty. A blink away. The realist in me knows this isn't worth worrying about. These are merely numbers, and people die all the time. Sixty-two is a damned sight better than forty-two, or twenty-two, or two. Nevertheless. Sixty-two is just around the corner. Over the next ridge. Too close for comfort. To repeat, people die all the time: not comforting at all. And what have I, Douglas Findhorn Elder, done thus far, with my fifty years and nearly twenty-five minutes? Have I even woken up? What if life *is* a dream, a series of pictures that flash in front of you, some with captions, some without? And then, one day, *End of slide show. Click to exit?*

How would you know – until that last message appeared?

The bus is moving again, but it is now 12.40, and even with a clear run through Bruntsfield and Morningside the journey will take at least another ten minutes. Hopeless. ELDER FUCKS UP, MISSES FUNERAL, as a headline in *Life and Work* will never read.

COLLEAGUES

It is one o'clock when I reach the church, an imposing, red sandstone edition surrounded by streets of Victorian terraced houses and detached villas. The church, too, is Victorian, circa 1880, which makes it – like me – late. I approach along a narrow, tree-lined lane, which opens onto a spacious, gravelled apron in front of the church. On both sides of the building are lush green lawns densely populated with gravestones. I don't need to step on the grass to know how thick and springy it will feel – the natural outcome of a long, rich diet.

A hearse, sleek and shiny as a racehorse, is parked on the gravel. One might call it a racehearse. A pale, thin man in a black frockcoat that's far too big for him leans against one flank. He might be polishing it with his tails but he isn't, he is smoking. I make a gesture intended to indicate my legitimate-mourner status as I crunch my way across the gravel towards the set of double doors, which are firmly closed against the day.

'Hih!'

I turn. The smoker has pushed himself erect and is pointing at me. His manner seems aggrieved, even belligerent.

'Gie me the finger, would ye?'

I move towards him. A character actor who has somehow got inside my head speaks on my behalf: 'No, no, my good fellow, you have grasped the wrong end of the malacca.'

'Ye whit?'

'I was just trying to tell you I'm going to the funeral. In there.'

'Ye're late.'

'I know. My bus was held up. Roadworks.'

'Well, dinnae take it oot on me.'

'I didn't.'

'Ye did. Ye gied me the finger, and then ye patronised me.'

'Honestly, I didn't mean it that way. That was somebody else.'

I start back to the doors, and he hurries after me.

'Hih!'

'What?'

'Ye cannae just breenge in,' he says, catching up.

'I'll be discreet.'

'Ye'll need tae wait. They'll be oot in a minute. Listen.'

I stop and listen. A hymn, perhaps the last of the service, has just begun. The organ is playing mightily, and the congregation is far from bashful as it breaks into 'Nearer, My God, to Thee'. Despite the closed doors the music and singing filter into the autumn air. I can see the notes flying heavenward like a flock of starlings.

'That sounds like quite a crowd in there.'

'A full hoose,' my companion replies. He sucks the glow of life out of his cigarette, drops the dowt on the gravel and stamps on it. 'Packed tae the rafters. I stayed oot here tae haud the latecomers back – somebody has tae – but you've been the only one. Naebody else's bus was held up.'

'You can't blame me for that. You're one of the undertakers, I take it?'

'Aye, that's me. Gerry the undertaker. Who'd have thought it would come tae this? The rest of the team's inside.'

'In the church?'

'Naw, no them. My *auld* team. In the jail. I was let out early for good behaviour and I got this job. They're training me but they dinnae think

I'm ready for the actual services yet, so they leave me ootside tae mind the motor. Like a dug. Still, could be worse, eh? They might have tied me up.' He seems altogether friendlier now that we have clarified his role in the proceedings. 'Dinnae say anything aboot me having a fag, will ye? I'm no supposed tae, on the job like.'

'I won't say a word, Gerry.'

'Cheers, pal. Mate of yours was he, the deceased?'

'Colleague. We worked together. Kind of. I didn't really know him.'

'Funny that, eh? All these funerals, and maist folk probably dinnae ken the person that's deid. I mean, *really* ken them. Sometimes no even the faimly. That's what I think.'

'I expect you're right. How long have you been an undertaker, Gerry?'

'Just since last week. I was a delivery driver before. I mean, before before. Suppose I still am.'

'What did you deliver – before before?'

'Och, this and that.' He seems not to want to elaborate. 'Braw singing, eh?'

The singing is undeniably lusty. Loud and celestial, as if from the mouths of a gang of seraphim who also happen to be ardent football fans. And one voice is belting the words out more vigorously and clearly than the rest: the unmistakable bellow of Ollie Buckthorn.

'There let the way appear, steps unto heav'n;
Douglas, my man, where the hell have you been?
Angels to beckon me, nearer, my God, to Thee.'

Surely I can't *really* hear Ollie singing these words? Either my imagination is up to its old tricks or it is warning me, in a subtle way, of the volume of Ollie's greeting should he emerge from the church and find me hovering near the hearse.

'I'll just wait over there by the gravestones,' I say, 'and pay my respects when Mr Grigson comes out.'

'Who's he?'

'The deceased.'

'Oh aye. Your colleague. Well, he'll no be lang. My colleagues will fetch your colleague oot and then we're aff tae another cemetery wi him. This one's full.'

'A full hoose,' I say, eliciting a laugh from Gerry. I retreat to the shelters of the dead until such time as the mortal remains of Ronald Grigson shall be brought forth.

SPEAR CARRIERS

It is peaceful among the lairs. The city traffic is far away, the wind has dropped and the sun is shining. The church doors are opened, and out into this gentle world, for the last time, comes Ronald. I watch the undertakers guide his coffin on a little trolley, the wheels of which, being on the small side, get stuck when they hit the gravel, so they have to carry him the rest of the way. They stow him in the hearse, fold away the trolley, then adopt the classic pose of their profession, solid, respectful, hands clasped in front of their crotches like footballers defending a free kick, all evidence of cigarette-smoking eliminated. Even Gerry gets it right. Part of the training, probably.

The Grigson family is in the vestibule, receiving the embraces, handshakes and mumbled sympathies of the congregation as it files past them. I don't know the Grigsons, and they don't know me. This is not the time to approach from behind, tap the widow on the shoulder and say how sorry I am, especially as I'm not that sorry. What, then, am I waiting for? I am waiting for the Erstwhile Colleagues.

The line-up continues, and while it does I read the names, dates and religious hopes and aspirations of various Victorian worthies, their wives and innumerable children, many of whom, even in this salubrious quarter of Edinburgh, died young. I am suddenly tired, as if all the spent lives whose mortal remains are deposited in this place have risen in a ghostly battalion, invaded my body and then just as rapidly left it again. I am unbalanced, totter, sit down on a flat, tabular memorial – a rougher, older-looking stone than most of the others, its inscription made illegible by moss and weather. The stone is warm from the sun and welcoming, not hard. If I lie down for a nap, will anybody object? Perhaps, but I can also nap while sitting upright. I pull down the shutters of my eyelids. The insides of them are orange with the sunlight. Ah! Ronald Grigson is at peace, and so am I.

My brief sojourn from the travails of the world is brought to an end by a hefty slap between the shoulder blades and a jovial, Dublin-toned cry: 'Hello, you old wanker!' I have been located, as I knew I would be, by Ollie Buckthorn – hence my desire to move away from the immediate vicinity of the main action. I raise the eye-shutters. Here's Ollie, looming over me like two traffic wardens pressed into one, with Roy Wilkinson and Grant McKinley bracketing him like a pair of black-and-white bollards.

'Tempting fate, sitting on that,' Ollie says, lighting a cigarette. 'Either you'll get piles or the ground will open up and swallow you.'

'You're a fine one to talk, smoking in a graveyard.'

'A dangerous occupation, right enough,' Ollie says, inhaling deeply, 'but that's me all over, a risk-taker. It's why I still work on a newspaper, while some timid souls, who shall be nameless in this hallowed sanctuary, took flight at the earliest opportunity.'

'You couldn't take flight even if you wanted to.'

'Ah, you're too cruel. But I'm glad to see the banter has not entirely deserted you since you deserted us.'

There is a comforting familiarity to this sparring, yet I also recall how wearing it could become. I rise to my feet, exchanging handshakes. Grant lights up too. The four of us surround that unreadable stone slab, and it is almost like old times – the *old* old times before smoking was banned inside the *Spear* building – the *old* building – when we used to stare down at a dummy double-page spread and wonder how best to make it work. Then Ollie speaks again.

'So what the hell kept you? The show is over.'

'The bus was held up.'

'Your arse. Who was it, Dick Turpin?'

'Roadworks. What did I miss?'

'A legend,' Roy says, 'if half of what we heard in there was true. Here, recognise this character?'

He extracts a folded order of service from an inside pocket and hands it to me. *A Celebration of the Life of Ronald Grigson* is printed on the front, with his dates, and there's a photograph, but it takes me a few seconds to match this snap to the Ronald Grigson I knew. For this is not the dour, tight-fisted pessimist of the *Spear*, but a laughing, windswept, T-shirt-clad athlete at the tiller of a sailboat. Nor is it a picture of long-forgotten youth. Once I have acclimatised to the sunny features beaming out at me, it becomes clear that the photo must have been taken within the last few years.

I shake my head, and further demonstrate my disbelief by expelling a puff of air through the lips.

'That's who's in the box,' Roy says. 'And what I want to know is, who the hell was the man we used to see in the office?'

'And he was some man, that Grigsy,' Grant says. 'If he wasnae climbing mountains he was sailing across the Atlantic or cycling round Britain and hardly a day went by when he wasnae raising money for good causes. He sang in a choir, he was a great pianist, he loved amateur dramatics. We thought we'd come to the wrang funeral.'

'We tried to get out,' Ollie says, 'but we were stuck in the middle of a pew, and the pews are about a mile long in there, I'm telling you, so we stayed. Then we found it really was Ronald they were on about – or Grigsy, as my Honourable Friend here refers to him. We learned a lot, didn't we, lads?'

'We did indeed,' says Roy. 'It was as if when he got home he changed into his superhero outfit. Especially at the weekend.'

'Never oot of it on a weekend,' says Grant, 'except when he put on a kilt for a spot of Scottish country dancing. Apparently he was in high demand on the Burns Supper circuit, tae. Naebody could surpass his rendition of "Holy Willie's Prayer", according tae his brother, Donald. It was Donald who gave the eulogy.'

'That's a bit odd, isn't it?' I remark. 'Calling your sons Donald and Ronald?'

'The father was a bit of a wag, so Donald informed us,' Ollie says. 'He thought it would be a great wheeze to have rhyming offspring. There are two sisters as well, Phyllis and Dilys.'

'You're joking.'

'He's no,' Grant says. 'And that's where Ronald got his sense of humour from – his father.'

'Now, I know what you're thinking,' Ollie says. 'You're thinking, but Ronald didn't have a sense of humour. Well, not at work maybe, but it was a different story when he was off duty. It seems he came out of his mother's womb cracking one-liners so hilarious the midwife nearly burst her sides. He was the juvenile jokesmith, the class clown, the undergraduate gagster. The grey man we knew at the *Spear* was not the man who entertained his family and friends for six decades.'

'Just shows you, eh?' Roy says. 'You've no idea what happens to some folk when they get home and out of their dungarees. Speaking of which, how are you yourself, Douglas?'

'I'm fine.'

'Retirement suiting you?'

'He's no retired,' Grant says. 'He's resting.'

'You'll be getting under Sonya's feet,' Ollie says. 'Not a bad place to be, if my recollection of Sonya in a short skirt is accurate.'

'Dear, dear, dear,' Roy says. 'Out of order, Ollie.'

'Not at all. She's a lovely girl from any angle. Is she well, Douglas?'

'As far as I know.'

'Oops!' Ollie says, and points at his mouth. 'Extract foot from here.'

'She's fine. We're fine.'

'Has she dumped you?'

'We've not been seeing so much of each other, that's all.'

'She's dumped you.'

'She's busy with work and I've been sorting out my father. He's had to go into residential care.'

'Sorry to hear that,' Roy says. 'I remember you saying he wasn't very well.'

'That's a hard one,' Grant says.

'You do look a bit haggard,' Ollie says. 'You sure you're all right? You've probably been out in the fresh air too much, overdoing the gardening. Isn't that how you retirees fill your days?'

'That must be it, Ollie,' I say. 'Thanks for the sympathy. How's the paper?'

'Dying on its fundament, same as ever,' Roy says. 'Circulation still diving, pages still getting fewer yet at the same time more full of crap – you know the score. Not that that makes our lives any easier. The trouble with folk like you getting redundancy is the rest of us *Spear* carriers have to work twice as hard to keep the show on the road.'

(*Spear* carriers: a term by use of which, for many years, the paper's staff have disparaged or applauded – depending on their mood – their own endeavours.)

'And for no extra pay,' Grant says. 'And you can bet your life when they replace Grigsy it will be with someone they can pay a third of his wage tae.'

'*If* they replace him,' Ollie says. 'Aha! Looks like there's some movement.'

The line-up is over, and now the crowd, which has been milling about making low, funereal small talk, falls silent, rippling back off the gravel apron as two more black cars roll into view from the tree-lined lane and creep up behind the hearse. The minister – an austere, white-haired, long-limbed gent like a silver birch in winter – herds an assortment of Grigsons over to the cars to take their seats within. Then the cortège moves off, tyres spitting stones, and perhaps it is this sound that sparks the next thing: somebody starts to clap. In seconds the entire assembly is joining in. I glimpse a gloved hand waving from one of the limousines

22

as it swings by. Have I missed the presence of royalty? No, surely not, for Grant and Roy, staunch republicans both, are clapping too. Only Ollie – how I love Ollie right at this moment – seems not to be swept up in this mood of the moment.

'What the fuck was that about?' he says loudly as the applause peters out. A man ten yards away turns to glare, then, seeing the size of the speaker, changes his mind.

'A nice touch,' Roy says. 'See the man on his way.'

'He's dead!' Ollie says. 'He's off to the great news desk in the sky. He hasn't won an award. He wasn't Nelson Mandela.'

'Folk want tae show their appreciation,' Grant says. 'No tae him, tae his family.'

'I'm surprised they didn't start throwing fucking roses,' Ollie says. 'Some people watch too much television, that's what I think.'

'Easy, Ollie,' Roy says.

'Don't easy-Ollie me. What do you think, Douglas?'

'I think we should go for a drink.'

'Isn't there a purvey?' Grant asks. 'What does it say in the programme, Roy?'

'The Braidstone Hotel,' Roy answers. He reads out, ' "The family warmly invites you to continue celebrating Ronald's life at the Braidstone Hotel, where they will join you after the private interment." '

'Well, that rules you out, Dougie,' Ollie says, 'because you missed the first bit of celebrating. No tea and fancy cakes for you. Where is the Braidstone Hotel anyway?'

'It's miles up the hill,' Roy says. 'Almost at Fairmilehead. I've never been there.'

'That's too far,' Grant says. 'We'll have to watch our time.'

'Going to work, are you?' I ask.

'Yes, Douglas, work,' Ollie says. 'That stuff most of us waste most of our lives on. You're well out of it.'

'We've left the bairns unattended so God knows what shape the paper will go out in if we don't do a few hours,' Grant says.

'My Learned Friend refers to the fact that the office is overrun with interns,' Ollie says. 'They can do top-ten listicles and Google so-called scientific research into what makes people fancy other people, but anything much beyond that is outside their comfort zone.'

'That's where *we* live,' Roy says. 'Outside their comfort zone, like wild animals in primeval forests.'

'I propose,' Grant says, 'that we repair to a more convenient hostelry to toast our departed brother.'

'I hate to miss a funeral tea,' Ollie says. 'I love the wee sandwiches and the wee waitresses going about manhandling those enormous brown teapots. Oh-oh, look sharp, here comes the Glorious Leader.'

John Liffield, editor of the *Spear*, is picking his way through the gravestones, a dark-haired man with a beak-like nose and sallow skin. Tall and angular, he moves in a jerky, mechanical way that no doubt has contributed to his reputation for being something of a robot. He is the paper's sixth editor in eight years. Having been in post for nearly two of these, Liffield is almost a veteran by modern standards. (The *Spear* has had only twenty editors in its two-hundred-year existence.)

'All right, guys? Thought that was very moving. Thanks for coming along and representing the paper.'

'Oh, is that what we were doing?' Ollie says. 'I thought we were saying farewell to a colleague. Seeing the man on his way. Wasn't that moving, that spontaneous round of applause?' The rank hypocrisy of Ollie Buckthorn never fails to enthral me.

'Very,' says Liffield. 'A moving ceremony all round. Hello, Douglas, didn't see you in there. Mind you, it was packed. Nice of you to come.' His voice is like scraping metal and with every utterance he seems to be trying to wrap up and move on.

'He nearly missed it, eh, Dougie?' Ollie says. 'His bus was held up by highwaymen.'

'Sorry to hear that,' Liffield says, exhibiting his capacity for not listening to people. Then, catching himself, he adds, 'I mean, glad you made it.'

'I didn't really.'

'Absolutely. You're looking well.'

'He's looking terrible,' says Ollie. 'Give him his job back.'

'Oh now, you know I can't.'

'We miss his cheery laugh,' Roy says.

'Almost as much as we miss Ronald's,' Ollie says. 'Good old Grigsy. Help us out here, John. Bring back the one you can. Give us Dougie again.'

'Wish I could,' Liffield says, 'but it's out of my hands.' He keeps glancing round, like a hunted man. 'Guys, I'm going to have to go. Senior-management meeting this afternoon. Various bigwigs up from London. I'd offer you a lift in the cab but . . .'

He leaves the sentence hanging, not because he hasn't thought of an excuse but because he doesn't think he needs to give one. Ollie helps him out.

'Don't worry about it. I fill a taxi on my own. We were thinking we'd go to what my Learned Friend Mr McKinley refers to as the purvey – just for half an hour or so, to show face. You go ahead.'

'The what?' It is apparent that Liffield, a Friend from the South, is not familiar with the term. 'Oh, the reception? Gotcha. Good plan. I've never been to the Braidstone Hotel, actually.'

'You've missed yourself, then,' Ollie says. 'It's lovely. Has an old-world charm to it. Friendly staff, good food. Ronald would have appreciated the choice of venue.'

'Sounds nice. Don't stay too long, will you?' Liffield looks worried. Perhaps he thinks they might never come back to work again. Or perhaps he suspects the London bigwigs are going to sack him.

'It's all right,' Roy assures him. 'We've got things under control. We put in a couple of hours this morning. It was very thoughtful of Ronald, having his funeral at this time of day, before the back shift starts.'

'Mair or less,' Grant adds.

'I'll see you later, then,' Liffield says, gearing up to depart.

'Cheerio,' Ollie says. 'Cab waiting for you, is it?'

For answer, Liffield plucks a slim black phone from his jacket, glances at it, says, 'It's approaching,' and then takes off across the gravel, *crunch, crunch, crunch,* like a man made of Meccano.

I am after him in a second. 'Before you go, John!' I call, loudly enough so he can't pretend he hasn't heard. 'A word?'

He brakes. 'I really need to connect with this taxi,' he says. 'Walk with me.'

I walk with him, quickening my pace to keep up with his long, robotic strides. Mourners are dispersing in all directions, although the main current is towards the tree-lined lane, where we are also heading.

'Do you remember, when I was getting ready to leave, we talked about some possible freelance work?'

'Yes, I do. I'm sorry nothing much came of that.'

'Nothing at all,' I say, surprised at my own boldness. 'Not even a book review.'

'Well, the book reviews aren't down to me. Not my responsibility – not my *direct* responsibility.'

'It wasn't just book reviews. You were quite adamant that you'd be wanting me to write for the paper.'

'Adamant?'

'You said you'd definitely be calling on me for one-off features, opinion pieces, that kind of thing.'

'Did I say that? "Definitely"?'

I sound a little desperate, and I'm not sure that he did definitely use the word 'definitely', but when am I going to get another chance like this?

'I'm not expecting anything regular, but I had a clear understanding that there would be a role for me.'

'A role?'

'I emailed you about it, but you never replied.'

We have reached the start of the lane. Liffield comes to a halt and so do I. We are a little island around which the crowd continues to flow, but I don't think he notices that.

'We're on a very tight budget, as you know, Douglas. I don't think we nailed a *role* down exactly. There's nothing about a *role* specifically written into the terms of your redundancy, is there?'

I very much doubt he knows the answer to this question, but I do: there isn't.

'Eh, not specifically.'

'Well, there you are. It's always tricky, trying to tidy this stuff up afterwards. Different recollections, different interpretations of what was said, that kind of thing. I heard a good phrase for it the other day. You know what it was?'

He waits until I have confirmed my mystification by means of a shrug.

'*Late Expectations*. It's a pun on a novel by Charles Dickens.'

'Really?'

'Yeah. Neat, isn't it?'

'Pithy.'

'Yeah, well, don't be too despondent,' he says.

'I said "Pithy", not "Pity".'

He frowns, then brightens. 'Oh, another pun? Good man. Douglas, I must go, but let's continue this conversation. Why don't I give you a call?'

'Will you?'

For the first time he looks me straight in the eye. 'No, probably not. It'll slip my mind. Come in and see me. I'll have a better sense of what's what after this management meeting. Today's Tuesday. Come in on Thursday.'

'Right, I'll do that.' In a vague attempt to seal the deal I extend my hand, but already he is moving away, as if his metallic parts are being drawn towards a magnet operated by the London bigwigs. He is prevaricating, of course, as who wouldn't in his position? Whatever else is to be discussed this afternoon, one item that will not be on the agenda is whether or not the *Spear* can afford to pay Douglas Findhorn Elder a few quid for the occasional article.

I turn and walk back to rejoin my Erstwhile Colleagues. And very glad I am that everybody else has gone, for the three of them are in a row behind the horizontal gravestone, playing at charades: Grant is strutting on the spot like a camp pheasant, Roy is simulating being sick and Ollie is miming giving a lingual wash-and-wax to Roy's backside. It is only what I deserve, I suppose, for chasing after John Liffield, but for a moment I feel a kind of sympathy for him, as might one rat watching another in a trap.

I am not trapped, needless to say. I am on the outside, looking in. For I have liberated myself.

If I repeat this often enough, I might even come to believe it.

DINOSAURS

'Fifty? Sweet Jesus, Dougie!' Ollie, two large whiskies inside him, collar unbuttoned and black tie wrenched to one side, is all fake shock and commiseration. 'It's over. You're finished, washed up. Driftwood. And only today? God, I feel for you.' He makes a play of seizing my wrist. 'See, this is me feeling for you. Bloody hell, no pulse! Will I call an ambulance? Do you need to lie down? Or' – leering from under his brow like a gross goblin – 'can I get you a stiff one?'

'I shouldn't have mentioned it.' But I did. It slipped out when we were discussing Ronald's early exit from the stage-set of life and establishing, if we were to go in chronological order, which one of us would be next. (Roy, as it happens, followed by Ollie, then me, leaving Grant to switch off the lights and close the doors behind us all.)

'But you have, Dougie boy, you have. It's all over the airwaves now. Headline news. We should sing "Happy Birthday" to you. I'm in the mood for a pagan song after all those hymns.'

'On you go.' Experience has taught me that this is the right approach with Ollie: if you want him not to do something, don't tell him not to do it. Act as if you couldn't care less. Pleading merely encourages him. Condemnation goads him to greater excess.

We have commandeered a small, dark table in a small, dark drinking establishment a stone's throw from Tollcross. Although I can't see a sign actually forbidding celebratory song, it doesn't look like the kind of place where it would be welcomed. Ollie hailed a cab on Morningside Road to get us here. 'The *Spear* will gladly pay,' he declared. 'The sooner we get to a pub the sooner we'll leave and go to work.' In twenty minutes, while the rest of us are still on our first drinks (courtesy of Roy), Ollie has downed those two doubles (the second courtesy of himself) and appears to be just warming up. Since we have missed out on the purvey he has bought up the remaining pies and sausage rolls in the hot cabinet and deposited this healthful feast in the middle of the table. We are supposed to be demolishing it together but so far Ollie has put a good deal more effort into this than anybody else. In the two or three months since I last saw him, he seems to have gone up a couple of shirt sizes.

'Well,' he says, 'maybe I'll save my voice till later. But I insist on buying you a drink. A big fat whisky, how does that grab you? I need another myself.'

'Just a single for me, Ollie. I don't have your capacity.'

'You're right there. My capacity is unique. Roy?'

'Pint of lager, please, Ollie.'

'Same for me,' Grant says. 'Want a hand?'

'I seem to have two on me,' Ollie says, heaving himself up. 'Tell you what, I'll use them to carry a tray. Don't you trouble yourselves.'

He rolls to the bar like a giant medicine ball. Grant sighs as we all watch him go. I know what that sigh signifies: a certain tenderness, a mutual affection that men of our vintage seldom put into words. When you have just attended one funeral, you can't help thinking of the others yet to come.

'He's not mellowed much, has he?' I remark.

'He may have yellowed a bit,' Roy says. 'But mellowed? No.'

'Must be hard to live with.'

'Luckily we don't have tae,' Grant says. 'Mhairi's a tough cookie. She manages him fine. She loves him, daft besom. So do his kids.'

I have never been in this bar before. There are not many other customers. The scattering of old men who constitute the clientele could easily be the remnants of another funeral, possibly one from days ago. They seem to make a virtue of not speaking. Perhaps they're in a competition: who can refrain from cracking a joke the longest? If they regard us at all, it is with indifference.

'So, Dougie,' Grant says. 'Fifty, eh? How does that feel?'

'Bit of a milestone, I suppose. I'm still processing the information.'

Grant is only forty-five. He's looking anxious. 'Fifty,' he says, as if it symbolises a point of no return. Which of course it does. I decide to put him at ease by articulating to him what I already tried to articulate to myself. 'Listen, it's easy to get depressed by this birthday business, especially at a funeral. What's fifty? It's a number. It's nothing special.'

'Fifty's quite special, surely?' Grant insists.

'It's just a number.'

'It's not *just* a number,' Roy interjects. 'Numbers matter. That's all we are, numbers. That's all everything is. Calculations of light and mass and energy. Mathematical equations. Chemical formulae.'

'You're talking tripe,' says Grant.

'I am not,' Roy says. 'It's just over your head, my son. Listen, let's keep it simple. I'm fifty-three, all right? I've got a three-year-old Jack Russell. My third. I've always had Jack Russells – since I was in my mid-twenties anyway. Love 'em. Smart, snappy little bastards. Keep you on your toes. *Eat* your toes if you don't look lively. Dogs – Jack Russells especially, but all dogs – are life coaches. They remind you of the priorities of life: food, sleep, exercise, loyalty and companionship. They get you out the house in all weathers. First thing in the morning, last thing at night and at least one other excursion in between. They give you a routine, dogs. And here's the thing. This is what truly horrifies me. Assuming average lifespan on my part, which is a big assumption if I eat this pie, I mean look at the grease on it, I could be on my penultimate Jack Russell. Do you hear what I'm saying? My penultimate Jack Russell!'

Roy laughs. Grant and I laugh. Short, throaty laughs. We are amused, in a serious, Queen Victoria kind of way.

Ollie returns with a tray of refreshments. 'Unless it was funny, I don't want to hear it,' he says, passing out the glasses. Raising his own aloft, he says, 'Happy birthday, Douglas,' and dashes through a very rapid, not *too* strident rendition of the appropriate song. This earns him some disapproving looks from the auld yins. Fortunately he has his back to them. If he saw the looks he'd sing it again, fortississimo.

'Happy birthday,' Grant and Roy say.

'No cake,' Ollie says, lifting a sausage roll. 'We'll have to improvise.'

Before the glasses go back on the table, I add a second toast: 'And here's to Ronald, wherever he is and whoever he was.'

'To Ronald.'

'One of the last of the dinosaurs,' says Roy. 'Speaking as one myself.'

'Ah now,' Ollie says, 'don't be going down that old road again.'

'Well, it's true. We're dinosaurs, turning out a dinosaur product in a dinosaur industry, and like dinosaurs we're doomed to extinction.'

'Bollocks,' says Ollie. 'We're artisans, craftsmen. And stop knocking the dinosaurs. They were brilliant survivors. They were around for a hundred and thirty million years.'

'Deny it if you like, but the sooner the final blow falls the sooner we'll be put out of our misery.'

'Who's miserable? I'm not miserable. Dougie's not miserable. It's his birthday.'

'Dougie doesn't count.'

'Thank you for that, Roy.'

'I mean, you don't work at the *Spear* any more. You're not a dinosaur.'

'Grant works at the *Spear*,' Ollie continues, selecting a pie, 'and *he's* not miserable. Are you, Grant?'

'Well, I'm not too happy a lot of the time.'

'For fuck's sake!' The pie begins to disappear into Ollie's mouth in chunks. Between chunks he develops his theme.

'I refuse to be consigned to the dustbin of history, and I refuse to be depressed. Just because Grigsy was only sixty-two and the *Spear*'s circulation is about a quarter of what it was twenty years ago doesn't mean we're about to become extinct. We're between eras, that's all. Our skills are still required. If you think yourself into the past, that's where you'll end up – and faster than you expect.'

'I liked the past,' says Roy.

'Not me,' Ollie says. 'I hated history at school. Who did this and who did that – who fucking cares? Keep moving forward, that's my motto. I'm for the future. I'm more modern than any of you. I *am* modernity.'

The pie is now gone. Another sausage roll is next in line for treatment.

'Look at this.' He extracts his mobile phone, an even slimmer and blacker model than John Liffield's. With his cheeks crammed with pastry and grey meat he has both hands free to operate the phone. When he speaks wee flakes of pastry escape back out. 'Wait now, is there a signal in this place? Yes there is! Here we go. See the way that dickhead summoned a taxi out of nowhere? And knew it was coming? You were looking like a lost soul, Dougie. Was it magic? No. Here's how it was done. The *Spear*'s got an account with the taxi firm, Liffield's got an app on his phone, and the app locates him *and* finds the nearest available taxi and brings them together. I've got the very same app here but I'm not linked to the paper's account so I don't use it – hence the receipt acquired from the fellow that stopped for us. However, this sliver of techno-wizardry enables me to manage just about everything else in my life.' His thumbs and fingers fly like fat wee ballet dancers across the keypad as he opens a succession of doors into the many and various worlds of Oliver Brendan Buckthorn. 'Diary here, photo album here, entire music collection here, a library I'll never read one per cent of here, access to all known news media here, entertainment palace in here, porn shop here, only joking, banking, bus timetables, holiday planning, healthcare – but you lads have got all this stuff too, haven't you?'

'Cannae be ersed,' says Grant.

'I've got it, but I don't flaunt it,' says Roy. 'Don't use it much, actually.'

'Dougie?'

'I have a mobile phone, but it's an early model. Clockwork, I think.'

'Well, to hell with you all then. If the world is presented to you on a plate and you choose not to partake of the feast, then I can do nothing for you. Maybe *I'm* the dinosaur that turned into a bird,' Ollie says. 'Maybe I'm a golden eagle and you really are pea-brained reptiles thrashing about in a swamp and choking on poisonous vegetation. It may not look like it, but appearances, as we know, can be deceptive. John Liffield appears to be in charge of the paper, for example.'

'What happens if you lose your phone? Or drop it in the bath?'

'I get a replacement, Douglas. I can lose it once and I'm covered by the deal I'm on. Twice and I pay a penalty. But meanwhile no data is lost. Everything is safe. Everything is stored – up there.' He indicates the ceiling, which looks like it hasn't been painted since the smoking ban came into force. 'In the Cloud. We used to believe in God. Now we believe in the fucking Cloud.'

The whisky is very pleasant. It tastes like a single malt, and I could do with another. I would ask Ollie what he bought us, but he's charging on and now is not the time to interrupt.

'But the thing is, the really amazing thing is, everything I'm telling you, everything I've shown you on this device, *isn't* the future. It's not even the present. Already it's old-hat. Even I'm not keeping abreast of developments, let alone you lot. My kids laugh at me when I say how fantastic it all is. They go, "Yeah, Dad." They are *so* connected to this stuff they don't even notice. My kids and their friends speak, act and think differently from me and Mhairi. And they're not the aliens in this brave new universe. *We* are.'

'So you *are* a dinosaur!' Roy says triumphantly.

'Can I buy you all another drink?' I ask.

Grant and Roy check their watches.

'No, I'm all right, thanks, Dougie.'

'Better not.'

'Ollie?'

'Go on then.'

'What was it?'

'Glen Gloming.'

'Glen what?'

'Gloming.'

'There's no such brand.'

'There is too. At the end of the gantry. Ask your man.'

'If you say so. Sure, lads?'

'Aye, thanks.'

So I go to the bar and right enough there is the bottle and the name on it is 'Glen Gloming', with a stag bellowing at a rising moon on its label. I order a couple of large ones because I am in the mood for it now.

By way of being friendly, I remark that I have never heard of that whisky before.

A grunt is the barman's only response.

'Who makes it?'

The barman is a shifty, hair-creamed character with deep corries under his eyes and a piercing stare within them. He pauses in the act of pouring the drams.

'What kind of question is that?'

'I was just wondering.'

'A distillery makes it. D'ye want it or no?'

I gesture in the affirmative.

He measures out two doubles and places them defiantly on the dark-stained bar. 'Five pound,' he says, daring me to make something of it.

'That's a good price.'

'Is it.' Note the absence of a question mark. 'There's water.' He thumps the jug down beside the glasses.

'Thanks. Can I see the bottle?'

'What?'

'Can I see the bottle? I'm interested.'

'*Whit?*' I seem to have crossed a line. The barman turns to a man I've not even noticed until now, sitting alone in a corner reading a paper. 'Mister G?'

'What?'

'Customer here wants to see the bottle.'

Mister G barely glances up. Maybe he's concentrating on a difficult crossword clue. 'What bottle?'

'The Glen Gloming. Says he's interested in it.'

Mister G puts his paper down. He stands up, revealing himself to be about six times the size he was sitting down. He has dark glasses on even though the corner he occupies is as black as a witch's hat. How he can read the paper at all is anybody's guess, but maybe he doesn't bother, maybe he just stares at it and broods on the wickedness of the world its mere existence represents. He takes a few paces towards the bar. Mister G has sharp hair and a scar indicative of his cheek having been opened up once by a sharp blade. I don't really like to think about what happened to whoever did that to him, but I very much doubt Mr G let bygones be bygones.

'That's good whisky, that,' Mister G tells me.

'Right,' I reply, resisting the urge to inquire what qualifications he has for saying so.

'D'ye mean, "Right, thank you for telling me" or "Right, I don't believe you"?'

'The former.'

'*Whit?*' (There is a pattern emerging here.)

'Believe me, I believe you. I was interested, that's all.'

'Don't be interested,' Mister G says. 'Just fucking drink it. That's what it's for. Got that?'

'Aye. Thanks.'

'You're welcome,' he replies. Something in his tone tells me I am not. The barman puts the bottle back on the gantry, far from my prying eyes. Mister G goes back into his concentrated form in the dark corner, like a really nasty genie retiring to its lamp. And I take the whiskies back to our table, happy to be still alive.

PITCH AND ROLL

Three o'clock approaches. The Erstwhile Colleagues decide they had better go to work semi-sober and capable. Roy and Grant have only had the two pints, and Ollie's eight whiskies don't appear to have made much difference to his general deportment, but the same cannot be said for Douglas Findhorn Elder: five whiskies (Grant insisted on buying me the last) on top of one Scotch pie is not his usual afternoon intake, and he is feeling unlike himself. Then again, it is his fiftieth birthday, and if you can't feel unlike yourself on your fiftieth birthday, when can you?

Roy and Grant move out to the street for some fresh air, while Ollie and I pay a visit to the facilities.

'Hello, Dick,' Ollie says. 'Long time no see.'

I check over my shoulder. No, we are alone in the room, and the cubicle door is not shut. Then I realise that Ollie is talking to himself. Or, rather, to an extension of himself.

'We have a purely touchy-feely relationship these days,' he explains as he steps away from the urinal. 'Unless I'm standing naked in front of a full-length mirror, which I have to tell you is a scenario I try to avoid. Not lovely. When did you last see your do-as-yer-tellt, Douglas?'

'My what?'

'Your welt. Your whang. Your tawse. Your tadger. Your didgeridoo. Ach, but you probably see him every day, your belly elastic won't have burst yet. Mine went years ago. You're looking pretty trim, in fact. How come? You on a diet or something?'

'No, not at all. I try to stay off the pies, and I don't drink much except on special occasions. Birthdays and funerals and suchlike.'

'Today's *really* special then. But why the self-denial? You're a man of leisure. What the fuck are you saving yourself for? Because it ain't gonna happen, my friend. You have crossed the watershed. This is you on the downward slope. Pitch and roll, that's my philosophy. Pitch and roll.'

'That doesn't sound like the fellow who was claiming he was the future half an hour ago.'

'That was somebody else. I'm like one of those weatherhouses with the wee folk with sunhats and umbrellas. Trouble is I don't know who's living in there or who's going to come out at any given moment. Do you get that?'

'Aye. I thought it was just me,' I say, unbuttoning my shirt collar and loosening the tie in solidarity with Ollie.

'It's all of us,' he says, 'but nobody speaks about it. It's the times we're in. It's like that whole carry-on with money.'

'What carry-on?'

'Paper money. The delusional carry-on. We all go around swapping it for things we want or things we think we need, and nobody dares say, "Look at this stuff, it's just bits of paper with squiggles on it." We don't even have to see or touch the bits of paper these days. We just key in numbers on our phones and in some building hundreds of miles away or on another continent a bank clerk types in different numbers or actually nobody types them in, the computers just suck them in, churn them around a bit and spit them back out and that's the financial system. And so long as we all believe in the numbers everything's fine. But suppose we stop believing? All hell would break loose. There'd be nothing there. What are you going to barter with, a printout? But that's all we are really. Numbers.'

We are heading through the bar, back to the real world. 'That's what Roy was saying earlier, when you were getting your round in. "We're just numbers," he said.'

'You don't want to listen to Roy,' Ollie says. 'He knows fuck all about anything. Cheers, my friend!' he calls to the barman. 'Your pies are excellent, by the way. As is your service and the ambience of your charming wee howff.'

The barman glares and his head nods a fraction. I think the words he mouths silently at Ollie may be, 'And don't fucking come back.'

'I never tire of that old-world Edinburgh hospitality,' says Ollie. Then, pausing in the doorway, he turns to me. 'By the way, you never answered the cunningly oblique gardening question I asked earlier. How *are* you filling your days?'

'I've plenty to do. Amongst other things, I try to write something every day. Keep my hand in, you know.'

'What for, if Liffield isn't giving you any work?'

'I'm ever hopeful.' I hesitate, but only for a second. Ollie is an old and trusted, though also crass and infuriating, friend. If I can't tell him, who can I tell? 'Actually, I'm writing a novel.'

He does a very good impression of an aghast gargoyle. 'A novel? God help us! I knew you were ill. That's a mug's game, Dougie. There's enough stories in the world without you adding to them.'

'I knew I could count on you.'

'We need to have a serious chat about this. A novel? Good grief!'

We pick up the others outside. I find myself staggering somewhat as the fumy air of Tollcross hits me. I am fifty years, two hours and forty-four minutes old, and not unpleasantly inebriated.

'That whisky really was good. Did you ever taste that one before?'

'I might have done,' Ollie says. 'On the other hand, I might not. What was it called again?'

'Glen Gloming.'

'Keep a look out for it. You can buy me a case when I turn sixty.'

To save time we walk past the roadworks, and then they hail a cab. They offer me a lift but I'm not going in their direction and anyway will benefit from the walk.

'We'll see you again,' says Ollie. 'In better circumstances, let's hope. Don't be a stranger to us. Oh, and listen. Just watch yourself if you do get any work from Liffield. Make sure he names his price and that he knows what he's paying you for. He's likely to make you rewrite something three times until he recognises it for the thing he wanted in the first place. I wouldn't trust him to piss in the sea and not miss.'

'But one of us will end up subbing it,' says Roy, ever the conciliator, 'so it'll be all right.'

'See you,' Grant says, and they pile into the taxi and it takes them away to the remainder of their shift at the *Spear*. They seem so relaxed, as if the paper will look after itself – but they've already told me that it won't. Then I remember what Roy said to John Liffield: 'We've got things under control. We put in a couple of hours this morning.' That's who they are: professionals, artisans, skilled at their craft. That's who they *still* are.

But who is Douglas Findhorn Elder, no longer late, of this parish?

MY ERSTWHILE STEPDAUGHTER

I make my way down Lothian Road, no more enamoured of that thoroughfare on foot than I was going in the other direction by bus. This time I don't even feel sorry for it. It is noisy and grimy: the traffic is heavy; fast-food detritus spills out of litter bins and is smeared at intervals across the pavement, obliging me to shorten or lengthen my steps occasionally. Furthermore (whisper it), I am an intellectual snob, and Lothian Road has little to offer the intellectual snob. Well, there's the Usher Hall, Lyceum, Traverse Theatre and Filmhouse, so in fact I am talking bollocks. What I mean is, I am not tempted by a sauna, nor to join a gentlemen's club, nor to indulge in a spot of pole-dancer spectatorship. There are bars on or just off Lothian Road – shiny, hard-lined establishments, guarded after 6 p.m. by shiny, hard-lined men in black nylon jerkins – which ferocious types from Glasgow and other points west have been known to avoid, acknowledging their inability to read the signs of impending Edinburgh violence. These places have no appeal for me either. Walking, on the other hand, is good. Walking off the over-indulgence is righteous. I contemplate walking all the way to the Home, another two miles or more, all downhill.

I am diverted, however, by the sight of a familiar figure outside one of those dangerous drinking-places – standing on a spot that doubtless will later be occupied by a bouncer in black nylon. The figure is small, female, in a tight silvery skirt, a loose black T-shirt revealing one bare shoulder, and ankle boots with deadly heels. Her hair, cut very short at the back, falls in a red-dyed fringe over one eye, a style which necessitates a flick every few seconds so that she can see out. Her whole attitude, one of defiance against the world, is further enhanced by the way she is taking abrupt and frequent smoke-sips from the cigarette held like a dart in her right hand. This is Paula, daughter of Sonya: my Erstwhile Stepdaughter you might say if you dared, but she would not thank you for saying it and legally speaking it would be untrue in any case.

She clocks me a moment after I clock her, throws away her fag and disappears through the door of the bar. Could she be avoiding me? Highly likely. Now, Douglas Findhorn Elder in normal circumstances would get the message, swallow his disappointment and move on. But the present Douglas Findhorn Elder is outside a considerable quantity of malt whisky, and it is this that fuels him as he follows Paula through the door into the establishment, which goes by the name of the Lounger. The outside decor – silhouettes of dancers and drinkers on opaque glass, blue lighting over the entrance – makes it look like a strip joint aspiring to be a casino, or vice versa. Inside, the theme is continued: cheap and nasty done up to look superficially sophisticated. It is empty, but far from quiet. Deafeningly loud music, of some techno-synth genre well outside the appreciation range of a fifty-year-old intellectual snob like me, is bouncing off the walls and ceiling, stopping unexpectedly, then starting again, driving me almost against my will towards the bar.

Behind which, Paula is standing. The look of distaste on her face is all too obvious.

'Hello, Paula.'

'Oh. Hiya.'

Swaying slightly, I shout an idiot question at her: 'What are you doing here?' The words come out of my mouth in a rush, tripping one another up, a sort of slurred accusation – as if I have caught her somewhere she shouldn't be. I try again, aiming for a quieter, more conciliatory tone. 'What are you doing here?'

'I heard you,' she says. 'I'm minding my own business. What are *you* doing?'

'I'm on my way home.'

'It's the middle of the afternoon.'

'What about it?'

She assesses me. If she still had her cigarette she'd no doubt take some more of those tiny drags from it while doing so. Paula has long regarded me, unfairly, as standing in some kind of moral judgement over her. Perhaps it's my surname. Now she's doing it to me.

'Oh yeah, I forgot, you don't have a job any more.'

'Actually, I'm on my way home from a funeral. Hence the suit.'

She dismisses the suit with a glance. Then she says, 'Had a few, have you?'

'I have, as a matter of fact.'

'Thought so.'

'Is that a problem?'

'Not for me.'

I half-persuade myself that this is all friendly banter, then try my opening question for the third time. 'What are you doing here?'

'What do you think?' A flick of her head causes the red fringe to bounce. Even her hair is sneering at me. 'I work here.'

'Oh. Is this you starting your shift?'

'Uhuh.'

'Four till midnight, something like that?'

'Something like that.'

The conversation dies. I kick-start it once more.

'There used to be an Edinburgh magazine called the *Lounger*.'

She looks suspicious, as if I'm trying to catch her out. 'Never heard of it.'

'No, it was before your time.' Before mine, too. Eighteenth-century, in fact. I'm ashamed to say I *was* trying to catch her out. 'How's college?'

'All right.'

'Working hard?'

She shrugs. 'Aye.'

'That's good.'

Her intention, with every terse response, seems to be to impress upon me how utterly tedious it is to converse with anybody over the age of thirty, and with me, her mother's partner or ex-partner or whatever I am, in particular. This irritates me. After all, we shared the same house, the same bathroom and kitchen, for a dozen of her formative years. For some of those – the early ones – she appeared to quite like me. Which is probably why she doesn't any longer.

'What do you want?' she asks.

'I saw you outside. I was just passing. So I came in to say hello.'

'Well, now you've done that.'

'True. But since you ask, I'll have a whisky, please. A malt whisky.'

'No you'll no. I'm no serving you any more.'

'You haven't served me anything yet.'

'Any more than you've already had.'

'There's one up there behind you, Glen Gloming, a very fine tipple. Surprised to find it in here but I'll have one of those, thanks. Make it a double.'

'I will not.'

'What'll you have yourself?'

'Nothing. Go away, Douglas. You're embarrassing.'

'Embarrassing who?'

'Baith of us.'

She is right, of course.

'How's your mother?'

'All right. Ask her yourself.'

'I will. How's Magnus?'

'All right, I think.' She pauses, assessing how to get me out quickly. 'Are you and my mum finished then?'

'Not sure. We're having a break. What do you think?'

'It's nothing to do with me.'

'How about that whisky?'

'No.'

She picks up a cloth and wipes something that doesn't need wiping. I consider my options. I am being unfair. I should leave her be. But before I do, something – a protective instinct, I suppose – makes me inspect her, from fringe to heels. This involves leaning over the bar in what might be misconstrued as an attempt to ogle her legs, which is not my purpose.

I am consciously having to remind myself, not for the first time, that Sonya is her mother. There is not an obvious likeness. Paula has a self-awareness that her mother doesn't. She's not as lovely as Sonya, but she is more, well, desirable, and this isn't anything to do with her being nineteen, it's to do with the way she carries herself. What I mean is that Paula seems innately to know that men – women, too, perhaps – will desire her, and secure in that knowledge she both encourages and rejects their desire. And this, especially seeing her dressed as she is in a place like the Lounger, where she is going to be working for the next eight hours, worries me. I am worried *for* her. Both the wide neck of her T-shirt and the way her left breast seems to be constantly on the point of exposing itself contribute to my concern. The partially glimpsed breast reminds me of a comment about Paula which my father, most unfortunately, once made in the presence of her and her mother, which is another story. What also worries me is that I don't have the right to be worried for her, and we both know it.

(Paula's big brother, Magnus, doesn't look anything like his sister, and not much like his mother either. Maybe he looks like Ben, his father: I wouldn't know, never having met the man. Ben left when they were quite young, and now lives in Australia. There is no contact between him and Sonya, and none, as far as I am aware, between him and the children. I could be their substitute dad, and for a little while I kind of was, financially and emotionally, but now I'm not and never will be again.

That's the way it was and is.)

'Well,' I say. 'Better get on. Nice seeing you anyway, Paula.'

'Aye. You too.'

'You look after yourself.'

She rolls her eyes. That's the sort of substitute-dad thing I shouldn't *say*. And then I compound the mistake by doing the sort of thing I shouldn't *do*. I lean across the bar and kiss her on the cheek.

She recoils, anger flashing in her eyes. I have totally blundered, nullifying the hint of warmth with which her last words blessed me. What is doubly unfortunate is that at the moment of transgression a man appears, as if from nowhere, and witnesses it. The bar is an affair of glass and mirrors, with edgings made of a plastic material meant to pass for chrome but which fails to convince by some margin. What I haven't realised is that one of the mirrors is also a door, leading to some inner sanctum. It is through this door that he comes, this man in a dark suit – a much classier number than mine – with a polo shirt buttoned to the neck underneath. The neck is very thick, barely contained by the collar of the shirt. In fact the man is built in much the same way as Mr G up the road, only about three inches bulkier all round, which makes him very impressive indeed, a kind of unanswerable argument on legs. He has a shaven, shiny head, more cone-like than spherical, and thick black brows over lazy, dangerous-looking eyes like those of a snake disturbed while snoozing. I assume he is Paula's employer or at least a working associate. If he were also a close relative of Mr G – Mr F perhaps – I wouldn't be surprised.

'All right, Paula?' he says in a growling drawl, or perhaps a drawling growl, and gives me the once-over, as if it would be a waste of eyesight to look at me twice.

'Aye, Barry.'

'You sure?' Barry says. He is just checking, obviously, because he's thorough like that. 'Didnae look all right.' And a horrible thought occurs to me: that not only might Barry be connected by blood to Mr G but he also might have more than a purely business relationship with Sonya's only daughter.

Perhaps this thought shows on my face, because now Barry does give me a second glance.

'*Whit*?' he barks. You see? The same no-nonsense approach as Mr G's.

Paula raises a hand, patting the air between us, calming the situation. How has it got to be a situation in the space of about five seconds? 'There's no problem, honest,' she says.

'If you say so, darling.'

Again, it's unfortunate he calls her that. Paula has just allayed any reasonable concerns he might have about me, and I am on the point of departing, and then he calls her 'darling'. It spoils the moment. Mixed up with the whisky in me, it reinforces a somewhat negative opinion I'm forming of Barry, and this causes a reaction.

'Aye, she says so.'

I do not so much actually, voluntarily say this as hear myself say it, and I am horrified. It must be the whisky speaking because such behaviour is totally out of character. As already noted, my head and the lower sections of parapets have an excellent relationship. Yet I have just given this bulldozer his own words back to him in a decidedly cheeky, not to say challenging, manner. In addition to hearing my own utterance I see a vision of a gravestone in a corner of that springy-turfed churchyard in Morningside, a stone that bears the following legend:

'What did you say?'

I backtrack fast. 'I agreed with her. There's no problem. Honest.'

'Oh, you agreed wi her, did ye?'

'I did.'

'And there's no problem?'

'None at all.'

'Honest?'

'Honest.'

'And, eh, who asked for your fucking opinion?'

'It's all right, Barry,' Paula says, and she shifts her position very subtly, blocking Barry from coming round the bar, which he is on the point of doing. Barry stares at her the way a wolf might stare at another wolf that has just confessed a preference for berries over raw meat.

'Do you ken this fuck?'

This is a novelty. I have never knowingly been referred to as a fuck before. And on my fiftieth birthday, too!

'Aye. He's a friend of the family.' (I could take issue with her imprecise labelling but the moment passes.) 'He was just going down the street and he saw me.'

Barry bulges everywhere as he takes this in. I've never seen a pressure cooker explode, but I imagine that the second before the lid flies off it might bear a close resemblance to the way Barry looks at this moment.

Then Paula touches him lightly on the sleeve and he goes back to his previous shape, just like Mr G. This only reinforces my suspicion that Paula and Barry are an Item.

'Listen, Gramps,' he says (it's the first time I've been called Gramps, too), 'I don't like people who bother my staff. Especially her. All right?'

Another cue for my exit. All I have to say is, 'Of course, Barry,' compliment him on his caring management skills, and depart. But suddenly the Glen Gloming pipes up again: 'What do you mean, "Especially her"? What's Paula to you?'

I can't believe it! I've just been granted a further stay of execution by bulldozer, and the whisky has put me right back in front of the thing.

This time Paula leaps out from behind the bar, exhibiting a nimbleness of foot which I did not know she had.

'Look, he's a friend of my mum's, Barry, that's all. He's a bit of a tube and he's upset cos he's been at a funeral.'

'A funeral?' Barry roars. 'A *funeral*? I'll gie him a fucking funeral!'

A man who appreciates irony, then. As I think this, I also get an inkling that the Glen Gloming wants to defend me against Paula's slighting reference to my tubularness, so for a brief moment there is a fight within me between a sense of hilarity and a sense of outrage. Then Paula says, 'Just bugger off, Douglas. Now!' and common sense gets the better of the other two.

'Cheerio, then,' I say, and I flee from the Lounger out onto Lothian Road. Once in the open, I pick up speed, skipping food spillages as if they're jumps at Musselburgh Racecourse. Whether Barry pursues me or not, I have no idea, but I don't care. I am oddly exhilarated as I canter down to the junction with Princes Street, where I join with a throng crossing the road and feel that it is now safe to slow down and catch my breath. This exhilaration is either the thrill of having lived dangerously and survived, or the last of the lunacy unleashed in me by five Glen Glomings. I suspect the latter, and make a mental note that should I ever come across the brand again, I will not breenge in but, as they say, ca' canny.

EVERYBODY HAS CAKE

I arrive at the Home at about 4.30 p.m. Before entering the premises I spruce myself up a bit, straightening and tightening the tie, tucking in the shirt, smoothing the hair and generally making myself look less like a drunk man who has just narrowly escaped being crushed to pulp by a wrecking machine. Actually I feel completely sober: the run followed by the long walk has had a beneficial effect.

Two members of staff are finishing doing the rounds with a tea trolley. I give my name and explain that I have come to see my father, Tom Elder. One of them says, 'He's in his room. I'll take you down.' Her name, according to the badge on her uniform, is Muriel. I've not met her before.

'Please don't bother. I know the way.'

'It's no bother. He's not long gone there. He's had enough of the day room for today.'

Or the day room has had enough of him. 'Was he being difficult?'

'A wee bit loud, that's all. A bit agitated. It's not that he's difficult. He's himself.'

'He just wants some peace, I expect.'

'Well, you do, don't you? And there's not a lot of it about.'

We are passing the open doors of residents' rooms. Some are empty, some contain residents: a woman in a bed with its safety rails up, a little old child; a man in a chair looking through his window; another watching television. Somewhere nearby another television is on very loud, but this one has the sound muted: peace. The man watching the screen glances in our direction. Recognising his snow-white hair, I pause and call his name.

'Jimmy! Hello, Jimmy!' Then, remembering that he is stone deaf, I wave at him. When Dad first arrived, Jimmy took a shine to him: another man, physically in reasonable shape, among the Home's mainly female population. They sat together at mealtimes, and Jimmy tried, without much success, to get Dad to play card games. They didn't converse much because of Jimmy's deafness, but there was something between them, a silent camaraderie. More recently, that has gone.

Jimmy looks over but doesn't wave back. His gaze returns to the screen. I catch up with Muriel, who has reached Dad's room.

'Here we are. Do you want a tea or a coffee? Tom, there's someone to see you. It's your son, David.'

I correct her. 'Douglas, Muriel.'

She looks at me oddly. 'Douglas Muriel?'

'No, just Douglas. You're Muriel.'

She laughs. 'Oh, so I am. Honestly, my brain's mince. It's supposed to be my day off, you see, but I swapped shifts because it's my niece's wedding on Saturday. Sorry. Tom, your son, Douglas, is here to see you. Did you say you wanted something?'

'No, but yes, a coffee would be great, thanks. Milk, no sugar.' I am still trying to work out why swapping her shift would make her forget her own name.

'Coming up. Make yourself at home.'

'Thanks.' She heads back towards the trolley. I go over to Dad's armchair and give his cheek a kiss.

'Hello, Dad. How are you doing today?'

He stares at me from his armchair, then with his fingertips touches the spot where the kiss landed. In spite or because of Muriel's introduction he could be trying to work out who I am, or he could know that but be wondering where I've been all this time, or he could be trying to remember the son David he doesn't have, or he could be genuinely probing for a genuine answer to my question. How *is* he doing today? Is this what is responsible for the furrowing of his brow? I sit down on the second chair in the room, one of those flexi-backed plastic jobs, and wait.

'What day is it?'

There is a table next to his chair, with a mug of coffee and a plate with two biscuits on it, a plain one and a chocolate one. That will be the ration. The room is not big, in fact it is pretty cramped, but there is a window looking out onto the garden and at least it is his own space, with photographs of him, Mum and me on the wall, and a few other familiar objects dotted about. The idea is to make the Home feel more like home. He doesn't seem to notice, or to care much.

The Don't Care Much Home.

'Tuesday, Dad. It's Tuesday.'

'Aye, but what day is it? Isn't it a day?'

'What *date*, do you mean?'

'No, not that. What the hell do I need that for? What bloody use is that? What *day* is it? Is it a *day*? *Is* it a day?'

He never used to use swear words, not even mild ones. He prided himself on *not* swearing. This wasn't because swearing offended him, he once told me, his boy, but because it represented a loss of control. It was counterproductive, if what you wanted to do was get your message across. And what else was language for, if not that? Swearing distracted your listener from the information you were imparting. I was thirteen at the time. I accepted his argument until one particular day when we were together in the shed, building a bird-table. Dad sawed a bit of wood in the wrong place, making it too short for its purpose, and just as he realised what he'd done the saw jumped and took a bite out of his left hand. And all he said, through clamped teeth, was 'Drat!' *Drat?* For a few seconds, I remember, I mused on the etymology of that word (I looked it up in the dictionary afterwards – that was the kind of boy I was; and I have made a mental note just now to look it up again, to remind myself – that's the kind of man I am) and then I saw that Dad had turned pale and was trembling, and that blood was gushing from his hand. He wrapped his handkerchief round his hand to staunch the flow, and went off to fix the wound. 'Don't touch anything,' he said as he was leaving. And I was disappointed: his self-restraint wasn't admirable. It was, in the circumstances, quite unreasonable. A full deployment of the foulest possible language would, in my adolescent opinion, have got the message across much more effectively.

Latterly, however, Dad has been sprinkling some of his voiced thoughts with expletives. When he gets 'agitated' they come in increasing strength and number. And other aspects of his nature, unanchored, have risen to the surface of his new life: forceful observations his sense of decorum would once have firmly suppressed. Some of the other residents of the Home find all this difficult. So Tom Elder goes to his room. He volunteers or is persuaded to go. This is better for everybody. But he can't be left alone for long, unless he falls asleep. Awake, without someone to watch over him, he is a restless searcher for undiscoverable things. He focuses on what he cannot see and, usually, he then trips and falls.

Muriel knocks and comes in with my coffee and two plain biscuits. That will be the non-resident's ration.

Dad eyes her as if he has never seen her before in his life. I sense that he has an urge to interrogate her about her intrusion, but he holds it back while she asks if he is okay and if we need anything else. When she has gone he transfers his gaze to me, then deliberately looks again to the door.

'She wants watching, that one.'

'Muriel? What's she done?'

'Nothing. That's the point.'

'What's the point?'

'Biding her fucking time, isn't she?'

'For what, Dad?'

He doesn't answer this. Whether he can't or chooses not to I am not able to determine. Then he repeats his earlier question. 'Is it a day?'

'I'm not with you.'

'Aye you are.'

'I mean, I don't understand what you're getting at. Yes, it's a day.'

'It's something else. Not day. Is it a –' His fingers grab at the air, trying to pull the word free. 'Is it a – a show? You're all got up for something. The suit and . . .' He makes a rapid, repeated clutching motion at his throat with thumb and forefinger.

'Tie?' Such a small word, easily misplaced. I hate ties.

'Aye. Tie, fucking tie. What for?'

'I've been at a funeral. Fellow from the *Spear*. Not a close colleague, but I thought I'd better put in an appearance.'

46

'Spear?'

'The paper, Dad. Where I worked.'

'Is this you going to work then? In the suit and – tie? At the – paper!' He shouts the word in his triumph and I hate to disabuse him.

'No, I don't work there any more. Remember? I left. I finished.'

He's not satisfied. 'What's the other bastard thing? Not a show. Party. Party?'

'Funeral. I've been at a funeral.'

'There's another thing. Weddings, funerals, weddings, funerals . . .'

'Christenings?'

He jabs a finger at that. 'Close!'

'Birthdays?'

'Aye, aye, that's it.'

'Are you remembering that?'

'What?'

'That it's my birthday?'

'What?'

'Today. Today's my birthday.'

'Today? Ah.' All the muscles in his face slacken. 'Knew there was something.'

'Actually, there's nothing.'

'What?'

I am doing it all wrong, of course. It doesn't make it easier, me speaking in riddles, which is how it must seem to him. I'm not speaking in riddles, I'm just speaking, but the way I frame things is not helpful. Various leaflets, medical professionals and websites agree on this: I should be cueing him up, making simple statements or asking simple questions that prompt simple yes or no answers. If only life were like that.

I really don't want to patronise my old dad.

'Nothing's happening about my birthday. I'm not celebrating it. No party, no presents, no nothing.'

'Och, that's a shame.'

'I don't want anything. I don't need a thing.'

'No . . . ? No . . . ?' The grappling starts again. He can't get whatever it is. Then he sees the plate, pokes one of the biscuits. 'Like that.'

'Food? No cake, you mean?'

'Aye, cake!' And this time we are both triumphant because between us we've hooked and ringed the word, and thereby the concept.

The concept of cake.

'No cake. No candles. But I had a pie earlier, in the pub.'

'That's fucking terrible.'

'You're right. It was.'

'Everybody has cake.' He stops, perhaps to consider the truth of this statement. Then: 'Cold, isn't it?'

'It was sunny earlier. It's gone off a bit now. It's not cold though.'

'Aye it is. Winter's coming. Make sure you wrap up.'

'I will.'

'How old are you?'

'I'm fifty.' We are in sync. For some brief spell – and it will be brief – our words and thoughts touch when they meet, kiss rather than collide.

'*Fifty?*' Utter disbelief is in the frown and downturned mouth. 'That's old.'

'It's not as old as you.'

'True.'

'It's just a number, Dad. I'm not bothered by it.' How effortless it is to lie to my own father.

'Good.' After a few seconds: 'Where do you stay now? Do you stay here?'

'No, I'm at home. In our old house. Your house.'

'And what's your mother saying about it?'

'About me being there? Not much. She's fine about it.' I decide to try a kind of joke. 'And Sonya is too, I think. Glad to see the back of me.'

'Good. Me too. When's she coming in?'

'Sonya?'

'Your mother. Who the fuck's Sonya?'

'Sonya's my friend. My *girl*friend, remember? I moved out and lived with her for a while, but then I came home again, to give you a hand when you started forgetting things. Remember?'

He adopts a narrow-eyed look of cunning. 'Aye.'

'Really?'

'Aye.'

'Can you remember Sonya's children's names? You've met them a few times.'

'Who?'

'Sonya's children. Do you remember their names?'

The sly look intensifies.

'It's not a trick question. I'm just interested to see if you can remember.'

His lips tighten. He puts a finger to them, stares at the ceiling then back at me. He has no idea who I mean. Defeat fills his eyes. He shakes his head.

'Magnus is her son, Paula's her daughter. I just saw Paula, up the town. Bonnie lass. Remember?'

Why do I keep saying that? *Remember, remember.* As if I'm deliberately rubbing in to his wounded mind the fact that he can't.

And, on the subject of rubbing, why go on about Paula? It was to Paula, in the presence of her mother, that Dad made one of those forceful observations which were once so out of character, namely that he would like to rub his face all over her breasts. Unforgivable, really, however much he couldn't stop himself. Paula and Sonya haven't seen him since.

'Paula.' He sounds the name but it doesn't give him anything. Probably just as well. 'Do they stay in our house?'

'No. Just me. I moved back. It was difficult. And then you moved here. It was better for everybody.'

'Better for you, aye.' Sometimes he seems to see everything totally in focus. 'Not so good for me.'

'It's nice here.'

'It's a shitehole.'

'No, Dad, that's not true.'

'Fucking is. When's your mother coming in?'

'She's not coming. She's not here any more.'

'Well, where is she? What's the time? She should be coming. Where is she?'

'Dad.' I pause, to make sure he is paying attention. 'She's dead. She died two years ago.'

It is a terrible thing, to have to keep breaking this news to him. It is terrible that he has to keep receiving it.

'Dead? But you said . . .'

'I know. I said she was fine about me being back home. I'm sorry. Misuse of tense. I thought it was easier. I was wrong. Drink your coffee.'

Dad looks at the mug as if it has only just materialised. He picks it up, spills a little coffee, slurps some. I lean forward to wipe his chin with a paper napkin, ready for further action if required. Sometimes when he learns that Mum is dead he starts to cry. This time he is annoyed with her.

'That's what she says. Drink your coffee, drink your coffee. Like a . . .'

With his free hand he makes a flapping motion.

'Parrot?'

'Wee-er.'

'Budgie?'

'Aye, like a fucking budgie.'

I laugh.

'What?'

'What you said.'

'What did I say?'

'You'd never have said "a fucking budgie" before.'

'Before what?'

'Never mind.'

'*Never mind?* Poor thing. I dinnae like birds in cages.' He is starting to get upset, raising his voice.

'Forget it, Dad.' *Forget it, Dad!* Jesus! 'It doesn't matter.'

'You can say that. You're no a budgie.' And suddenly *he* laughs. So that's all right, and I can join in. Then we sit in silence for a minute. Outside the window, uncaged birds are tweeting important or trivial messages to one another. Someone in another room is laughing at some other remark that might or might not be funny. Further away, down the corridor, a human is shouting. 'Leave me alone!' she shouts. I think it's a she.

'Drink your coffee, drink your coffee,' Dad repeats, developing his budgie routine. 'Do you get that?'

'Not any more. Not at the moment, I should say. With Sonya it's usually, "Could you not have put that somewhere else?"'

'What?'

'She's very tidy.'

'Who is?'

'Sonya.'

'That's terrible.'

'It's because they want things to be organised. They're more organised than we are.'

'Who are?'

'Women.'

My father groans. 'Don't listen to them. What's your mother saying about it?'

Before I can remind him that she's not saying anything about anything any more, he carries on.

'They're aye plotting something. Don't let them boss you about. This is what happens.' He finger-jabs his own chest. 'It's all women here, ye ken.'

'They treat you well, Dad,' I remind him. 'They look after you. And there *are* men here. I just saw Jimmy down the hall. You like him.'

'Bastard.'

'I thought you two got on?'

'Bastard.'

'Suit yourself. And there are men on the staff as well. It's not all women.'

Dad hunches his shoulders, a form of protest. It's something I do, the very same movement. I could be looking in a mirror. Did I learn it from him without learning it?

After a further silence I begin to make the usual stirrings preparatory to departure.

'I'll need to go, Dad. Got to get on.'

'Get on a bus?'

'No, I'll walk. Got to get on with things at home.'

'What things?'

Why not tell him? What is there not to tell? 'I'm writing a book.'

'You? What about?'

'I don't really know. It's a novel. I'm making it up as I go along.'

'Why?'

'Well, how else would you do it?'

'Do what?'

'Write a novel. I don't know any other way. Do you?'

He gives me the look of contemplation, the one that might be full of deeply considered opinions or a complete void.

I prompt him. 'No ideas?'

'Shite.'

'Aye, probably. Tell you what, if I ever get it finished I'll bring it in and read it to you. Then you can tell me what you really think. Is that a deal?'

He chuckles. 'Aye, deal. Want my advice?'

'Yes, please.'

He nods. I wait.

'Only thing is,' he says.

'What?'

He leans in conspiratorially. 'Eh?'

'You were going to say something. "Only thing is," you said.'

'Only thing is, don't listen to them.'

'Right. I won't.'

'I'm older than you. I should know.'

'Aye, Dad.'

'*I'm* Dad. I'm your dad.'

'Yes, you are,' I say, staring across heather at my father sitting on a rock.

EXAMPLE OF A LISTICLE: TEN REASONS WHY HAVING YOUR PHYSICALLY AND MENTALLY INFIRM FATHER LIVING AT HOME WITH YOU BECOMES TOO MUCH TO COPE WITH

1. You turn your back for a minute: he falls over.
2. You pick him up off the floor, put him in his chair and ask/tell him to *stay* put while you make him a cup of tea. When you return he is on the floor, having tried to get to his feet again. And fallen over, again.
3. He is always looking for something he has mislaid. He has mislaid everything. Everything in the house is therefore in constant turmoil. Even when he finds what he was looking for, it often turns out not to be what he was looking for. He then usually tidies it away where neither he nor you can find it when it is next something he *is* looking for. In fact he tidies everything away. He tidies things away very untidily. And in no order. He is very fastidious about this. He creates chaos perfectly.
4. While your back is turned, and even though you have recently supplied him with one, he decides to make himself a cup of tea. This involves him opening a tin of baked beans and emptying the contents into the electric kettle, then putting the kettle on the hob and turning the gas on. Fortunately the kettle does not catch fire as he fails to ignite the gas. Fortunately, too, you are alerted to what he has done by the smell of gas just before he tries to light a candle in the belief that the smell suggests that there has been a power cut.
5. He sometimes mistakes radiators for urinals, even though there are no urinals in the house. Problematic though this is, at least it doesn't upset the neighbours, unlike his occasional venturing onto the street to micturate against their cars.
6. You cannot leave him alone in the house, but taking him out with you is extremely difficult, owing to his newly acquired predilection

for using language that some find offensive, and the likelihood of his making loud comments concerning other people's appearances, which on one occasion led to both of you being ejected from a supermarket by security staff and asked not to return.

7. He sometimes wakes in the middle of the night, gets dressed and prepares to go to work at the builders' merchant where he was employed as a warehouseman for thirty years. When you hear him moving about noisily in the kitchen and go down to dissuade him, he becomes angry, then distressed, then bemused. By the time you get him into bed again you are exhausted and yet unable to go back to sleep yourself.

8. He needs to check that everything is safe, secure and in good working order. This may simply be a case of going round the house switching on all the lights or opening all the windows. Sometimes, however, it means lifting carpets to examine the floorboards, attempting to deconstruct furniture, or testing the strength and flexibility of plastic coat hangers. The garden shed has become a locked depository for dangerous tools and equipment, and you are obliged to keep the key on your person at all times and deny him access to it. Ironic, given his previous occupation.

9. You find it increasingly difficult to manage his difficulties – keeping track of the days and hours, maintaining regular routines, remembering names, remembering what happened yesterday, remembering what is supposed to happen tomorrow, and so on. In fact *his* difficulties are becoming more and more like *your* difficulties. You fear that if this goes on much longer your mind will start to adapt itself to his way of doing and seeing things. You will, in other words, slip almost unknowingly into the place he is in. This terrifies you, not least because you might not recognise that it has happened.

10. When you stop to think about all this, you realise that you are as isolated, in some ways, as he is. Caring for your father, if 'caring' is the word, has blighted all your other relationships. You resent his domination of your days. You sometimes feel sorrier for yourself than you do for him. You are brought out of this guilt-ridden, self-pitying condition by a crash in another room. He has fallen over again.

'DRAT!'

'A minced oath (early 19th century). Derived from "Od rot 'em!", "Od" being a reduced form of "God". Cf. "Od's bodikins!", "Gadzooks!", "Strewth!", "Uksake!", etc.' [Source: *Tanner's Cornucopia of Inconsequence*, 3rd, revised (1965), edition.]

STORIES

If someone tells you that there are already enough stories in the world, they are missing the point. The point is, the world *is* stories. Here's one more.

CONVERSATIONS WITH A TOAD:
CONVERSATION #1

Left hand clutching a glass, a bottle of red wine tucked under the corresponding oxter, Douglas Findhorn Elder opened the back door of what was half his and half his father's house – the house in which he had grown up, which he had never really left and which, one day perhaps not too far off, would be wholly his – and stepped into the blue night. Stars and the sodium vapour of many street lamps contested the sky above him, but the garden was dark with October darkness.

His movement triggered a security light set on the wall of the house, and this illuminated the stone slabs of the patio or – as it had always been known in the family – the *sitootery*; or – as his father used to observe with dry wit on wet days – the *raindaffery*.

Douglas stood on a small bright stage in a sloe-black arena and breathed in a portion of the gentle breeze. Tens of thousands of his adoring fans could be out there but not one of them was visible to him.

A slight swell of Rioja rolled in his gullet and he belched softly.

To his surprise an answering rift, suggestive of imitation or even mockery, came from a spot close to his right foot.

Douglas looked down and smiled. He could not help smiling, for what he saw was pleasing to him. Squatting on one of the slabs was a large, jowly, brownish-backed, creamy-breasted toad, well covered with warts.

There is something appealing about a toad, especially one that strikes the attitude of a fat monk disturbed while at prayer.

'Good evening,' Douglas said.

He did not anticipate that much would follow this opening remark. A few platitudes from him, a blank glance or two from the toad, and they would go their separate ways – he to his bed, and the toad to its, presumably after a night of foraging for snails, worms and other comestibles. Douglas felt that the toad had acquitted itself well merely by belching with such excellent timing. He expected nothing more from it.

He was therefore astonished when – in a low, dark, yet sonorous and somehow commanding voice – the toad spoke.

'It *is* a good evening,' it said. 'And mild, for the time of year.'

Douglas bent down.

'Did you just speak?'

'Did *you* not?'

'Aye, but . . .'

'Aye, but what?'

'But you are a toad.' Even to Douglas, this sounded lame and inadequate. For if a toad has spoken, not once but three times in succession, then its toadness is already one of its less interesting features.

The toad hunched its back. No creature, of any species, can match a toad when it comes to looking disdainful.

'Your point being?'

Douglas swayed slightly, removed bottle from oxter in order to be able to raise glass to mouth, and took a drink. It occurred to him that he might have had more wine than he thought, and that the toad might not really be there. Or *he* might not be there. Conceivably, neither of them might be there. However, the Cartesian paradox suggested by this possibility was of such magnitude and complexity that he, for the moment, did not feel mentally adequate to address it.

A period of silence ensued. When Douglas checked again the toad was still present and still, apparently, waiting for an answer.

'What?' Douglas said.

'What do you mean, what?'

'You're looking at me.'

'*You're* looking at *me*. And it is rude to stare.'

'I wasn't staring.'

'You have changed tenses, from which I infer a sense of guilt. You may not be staring now, but you certainly were, and you know it.'

'You were staring at *me*!'

'I was not. I was dazzled when you put the light on, that's all. I simply happened to be facing in your direction.'

'The light comes on by itself.'

'Well, you should have it repaired.'

'That's what it's meant to do.'

'Dazzle me? Charming!'

'When anybody or anything above a certain size moves in this area, it comes on. It's a security device. I'm sorry that it dazzled you.'

'So am I. As a security device it is flawed, since it would appear to offer no protection against the smaller bandit or housebreaker. Still, I accept your apology.'

'Fine. Acceptance accepted.'

They had reached, Douglas thought, either an impasse or an accommodation. Carefully, so as not to cause further offence, he stepped round the toad and set the wine bottle on the patio's cast-iron table. He sat on one of the two matching chairs and raised his glass.

'Your health,' he said. The toad took a few lumbering steps towards the back door, examined a weed or two between slabs, then turned and lumbered back to its original position.

A thought occurred to Douglas as he watched.

'Did we . . . ? That is, have we . . . met before?'

'Where might that have been?'

'Over there, in that flowerbed. Yesterday. I was digging out a clump of lilies –'

'Why?'

'Because it's autumn, they're long over, and there are too many of them. They're taking over the whole garden.'

'There can never be too many lilies,' the toad said. 'However, continue with your story.'

'I was digging out the lilies, and something happened. My graip had a close encounter with you, if it was you.'

'Your what?'

'My graip. Garden fork. Or you had a close encounter with it. For a moment I thought I'd impaled you or amputated your leg. But you dived into the undergrowth before I had a chance to make sure.'

'That you'd amputated my leg? Again, charming!'

'No, that I hadn't! Which, clearly, I haven't.'

'You seem very certain of that.'

'Well, you have your legs. A complete set. So, unless it wasn't you . . .'

'It wasn't.'

'Oh.'

Although the toad's expression hardly altered, a slyness seemed to invade its features.

'You know something about it, though, don't you?' Douglas said.

'News gets around. It was a cousin of mine.'

'Is he all right?'

'*She* is fine, no thanks to you. You missed her' – holding up two digits almost closed together – 'by that much. She is still in shock.'

'I am so sorry.'

'So you should be. It scares the daylights out of you, something like that. And when I say "daylights" I don't mean "daylights".'

'It wasn't intentional. I hope she makes a full recovery. Would you give her my apologies?'

'No.'

'Why not?'

'We are not on speaking terms. But I'll make sure she's told.'

'That's kind of you.'

'Humff!' the toad said, and made a small, ungainly hop, landing a foot closer.

'Two chairs, one bottle, one glass,' it said. 'Why are you drinking on your own?'

The security light went out. Douglas said, 'Do you mind? Close your eyes,' and waved his arm to bring the light back on again.

'If you are patient your vision will adjust to the night,' the toad said. 'You will be able to see me perfectly well – if that's what you wish to do. Of course you will also have to sit still. Whereas I . . .'

It stood on its back feet and stretched itself against one of the table legs, like an athlete warming up. Then, with the laborious care of an expert rock-climber, it began an ascent of the table.

'Want a hoist?' Douglas asked.

'No. It's good exercise.' Left hand, right foot, right hand, left foot, the toad made steady progress and quite evidently needed no assistance. 'You haven't answered my question.'

'Why shouldn't I drink on my own?'

'I'm not judging you. There used to be other people here, that's all. An old woman and an old man. And you weren't around so much. Then the old woman disappeared.'

'She died. That was my mother.'

'Then, recently, you've been here more. You used not to show up for long spells, but in the last few seasons . . .' The toad left the sentence unfinished as it negotiated the overhang of the tabletop with impressive skill. It settled beside the wine bottle, breathing hard.

'I used to come and go a bit. But now I'm back, you're right. A permanent fixture, you could say.'

'The old man was the permanent one. Your father?'

'Aye.'

'I quite liked him. Not that we ever met, or spoke . . . like this. He seemed content, self-contained. There was no sign of violence in *him*. But he's been absent lately. What's happened? Dead, too?'

'No. He's in a home.'

'Is this not his home?'

'It is. It was. But he couldn't stay here. So he's gone to *a* home. A *Home*.'

'Either I am being obtuse or you are being obscure. Please explain.'

'My father is ill. He is suffering from various afflictions. Memory loss, confusion, dizziness. He struggles to articulate his thoughts and feelings. He doesn't always know who he is or where he is. He gets depressed. He falls over a lot. He no longer has full control of some bodily functions.'

'Like my cousin when you attacked her with your . . . graip?'

'I didn't attack her. I didn't see her till it was too late. She happened to be in the wrong place at the wrong time.'

'She was in bed! It was mid-afternoon. She was in exactly the *right* place at exactly the *right* time.'

'Toad time.'

'It would be odd if we kept any other kind.' The toad then said something that to Douglas, dredging up the Latin he had studied for a year or two at school, sounded remarkably like 'Suum cuique'. He must have misheard.

'To each his own,' he said, just to check.

'Precisely,' the toad said.

'Well, I must say, you have an impressive command of English,' Douglas said. 'And not just English.'

'You have a very good command of Toad,' the toad said.

'I'm not speaking Toad.'

'Yes you are. Never mind. Where were we? Your father. Not a well man, by the sound of things. All these ailments – did they arrive simultaneously?'

'They crept up on him over a period of time, like saboteurs, setting off little explosions, disrupting lines of communication and generally causing fear and alarm.'

'How dramatic.'

'It isn't really. It's horribly tedious.'

'Curable?'

'Taken as a whole, no.'

'But if he's so ill, why isn't he here and why are you not looking after him?'

There was a hard, cool edge to the cast-iron table. Douglas gripped it.

'I can't. I tried, believe me, but it became impossible. He's better off where he is. He's safer, apart from anything else. He became a danger to himself while he was here – and to others. Me, in particular. He set things on fire – mostly by accident. He fell over and couldn't get up. He went out leaving the doors and windows wide open and was lost for hours at a time. I couldn't go out without taking him with me, and that usually ended in disaster.'

'Disaster? You exaggerate, surely. How many times can an excursion end in disaster if those involved are not seriously injured or killed? Has anybody been seriously injured or killed?'

'No, but it's been close.'

'Had you sliced off my cousin's leg or decapitated her, that would have been a disaster, for her at least. Has your father lost a limb, or his head? I can see you haven't.'

'Near-disaster, then. And it wasn't just when we were out. Even here, in the house or garden, I couldn't turn my back for five minutes without something going wrong.'

'So now he is in *a* home, and you're *at* home? Is that why you're here drinking wine by yourself?'

'No. Well, yes, in a way. Don't look so critical.'

'I already said, I don't judge. You people do what you do, we do what we do. If a toad is ill, he stays at home until he gets better or dies. It's logical.'

'It used to be like that for us, but not any more.'

'Why not?'

'Because life is more complicated. And people are living longer.'

'Toads aren't. We live long enough already.'

'Good for you.'

'Good for us, yes. When you said, earlier, that you came and went, where did you go?'

'I was in a relationship. I still am, I suppose, but it's been a little rocky lately, so maybe I'm not. Anyway, I went to Sonya's. That's the name of the woman I was in a relationship with.'

'Sonyas?'

'No, Sonya. My partner. Erstwhile. Ex. I lived with her and her two children. They're grown up now.'

'I don't recall ever seeing these people of whom you speak.'

'You wouldn't have. They didn't live here. I lived there.'

'Where?'

'With them. In their home.'

'*Another* home?'

'Yes, Sonya's. In another part of the city. As I said, life is complicated.'

'Complicated, but interesting,' the toad remarked. 'Incidentally, the security light went out some time ago. That, too, I find interesting. Don't make a sudden move.'

Douglas made a gentle, slow move and refilled his glass. 'I hadn't noticed,' he said.

'That's what I find interesting,' the toad said.

The nodules of its skin seemed somehow to catch the starlight, or the street-lamp light, and thus to glitter. When it turned its gaze on Douglas the eyes were revealed as amber discs slashed horizontally by black pupils. There was something beautiful and intelligent about the toad. Despite its curt manner, Douglas felt that here was somebody he could confide in, a fellow creature he could really talk to.

'And another reason for taking a drink tonight,' he said, 'is to celebrate. Today is my birthday.'

'I take it you mean an anniversary of your birth. Which one?' the toad asked.

'The fiftieth.'

'In years? Hmm. Not much to celebrate, that. Not much of a celebration either.'

'Good enough for me. Do toads celebrate their birthdays?'

'We don't even notice them. Age is approximate with us. Years don't matter, only seasons.'

'That's a healthy attitude. Humans could learn from it.'

'It's not an attitude, it's reality. It wouldn't work for humans.'

'Why not?'

'Different reality. How, if you were going to, would you *really* celebrate, as you put it, your birthday?'

'Well, I could ask some friends to join me, and have a party.'

'Do you have some friends?'

'A few.'

'And if you did, what would happen at this party?'

'Well, there might be a cake, with candles on it representing the number of years. Sometimes people give you presents. Or they send you cards with messages in them.'

'Messages?'

'"Happy birthday", "Many happy returns", "Eat, drink and be merry", that sort of thing. But presents and cards don't matter to me. They're more for children, really.'

'Did you receive any presents? Or cards?'

'I was bought some drinks. And I had one card. From Sonya.'

'What was her message?'

'She wished me a happy birthday. Well, no, she didn't, because that was already printed on the card. She just signed her name. No other message. I suppose that *was* her message.'

'And that was everything?'

'That was it. Oh, I did get a birthday communication from the National Health Service, inviting me to take part in the Bowel Screening Programme.'

'What is that, a film festival?'

'Not exactly. The idea is to check for signs of bowel cancer every couple of years from the age of fifty until you're seventy-four. The earlier it's detected, the sooner it can be treated, and this increases your chance of survival.'

'Why not start the checks when you're a child, then?'

'Because older people are much more at risk.'

'But the checks stop when you're seventy-four?'

'I know it sounds illogical. They must reckon you're as likely to die of something else by then.'

'And what happens in this programme?'

'You do three tests to see if you've any symptoms.'

'Tests?'

'You provide three samples. I haven't read all the instructions yet. I think it's going to be difficult.'

'Oh, the tests are difficult?'

'Not in that way. I mean, awkward. There's a kit due to arrive any day now. Don't worry about it.'

'*I'm* not worried. Well, let me add to the messages you've had from Sonya and the National Health Service. Happy birthday.'

'Thank you. I'd offer you some wine, but I don't suppose you do.'

'Do what?'

'Drink wine.'

'I don't drink at all,' the toad said. 'However, I am not averse to alcohol. I can't take too much, but then who can? Splash a bit on the table there.'

The deed was done. The toad crawled across and poised his rump over the pool.

'Many happy returns,' the toad said, and settled into the wine.

'Thank you,' Douglas said. 'To your liking?'

'Very absorbing,' said the toad.

'And now,' Douglas said, 'I have some questions for you.'

The toad inclined its head.

'First of all, and don't take offence, am I right in believing that you are a *Mister* Toad?'

'As opposed to what? A Doctor Toad? A Rear-Admiral Toad? MacToad of that Ilk?'

'Are you a *male* toad?'

The toad clapped a hand on top of its head and drew the fingers down over its nose. 'For heaven's sake. Do I look like a female toad?'

'I don't know.'

'No, I do *not* look like a female toad. Female toads are bigger and fatter than males, and there are other anatomical differences, beyond the obvious ones, with which I will not tax the limited capacity of your brain. Your next question?'

'If, as you say, toads live long enough, how long is that? I read somewhere that a common toad can live as long as forty years. You yourself, judging by your observations of my family, appear to have been around some considerable time.'

'A remarkable thing about humans,' the toad said, 'is their arrogance. If you knew anything at all, you would call us *uncommon* toads. That is the remarkable thing about *us*. We are all uncommon. Each of us is an individual. That's why we lead solitary lives, except in the spring. Ah, the spring!' There was a pause, during which he (for so he must now be designated) appeared to inspect his hands and feet and possibly to count his fingers and toes. 'Forty!' he said at last. 'I would be a *very* uncommon toad if *that* was the best I could hope for.'

'Then our estimates are inaccurate?'

'Wildly so! Look at the pace we go at, compared with you. Barring accidents or foul play, sir, there is little doubt that I shall outlive you.'

Douglas was tempted to dispute this assertion, but he had a third question for his amphibian acquaintance. 'If we are going to continue this relationship,' he said, '– which I should very much like to do – it would be easier if I could address you by name. Do you have such a thing as a name?'

The toad didn't exactly stamp one of his feet, but he shifted his weight with irritation. Douglas noticed that the pool of wine had diminished considerably.

'Do you ever stop being patronising? How would we function as a community – even a community of solitaries – if we didn't have names?'

'And yours is?'

'You couldn't pronounce it. Not a chance, even with your proficiency in Toad. Call me . . . let me see . . . call me Mungo.'

'Did you just pluck that out of the air?'

'I did. Like a gnat. It has a ring to it. Mung-oh. Mungo. Call me that.'

'Very well. My name, which appears on my birth certificate, is Douglas Elder.'

'Dugliselda?'

'No, Douglas Elder. It's two names.'

'Douglas Fir would make more sense.'

'You're not the first to have cracked that joke.'

'What joke?'

'You should call me Douglas.'

'Douglas. But you have two names. If you have two names, I'd better have two as well.'

'So what will your second name be? Mungo what?'

'No, I don't like it. Mungo Mungo.'

'You can't just use the same name twice.'

'Why not? Mungo is my first choice. I like it very much. I cannot imagine any name to match it, except another Mungo. Ergo, Mungo Mungo.'

'Actually I have three names. Douglas Findhorn Elder.'

'Three? I could go on adding Mungos, but Mungo Mungo Mungo is excessive. Even I can see that. What is the significance of your middle one?'

'It's the name of a river. It's a tradition in the Elder family to have

Scottish rivers in our names. My father is Thomas Ythan Elder. *His* father was Donald Garry Elder. And so on.'

'Rivers are good, although sometimes perilous. I shall be – appropriating your family tradition – Mungo Forth Mungo. A local touch.'

'That's very good. You could go far with a name like that.'

'Perhaps, but it's October. I usually settle down for a long sleep about now. Mind you, I have always wanted to travel. Like my namesake, Mungo Park, although I wouldn't wish to go as far as he did.'

Douglas was again surprised by the toad's erudition. 'How do you know about Mungo Park?'

'In the same way that I know about David Douglas, after whom I believe the aforementioned fir is named.'

'But what way is that?'

'You forget what I said before, about our longevity. Knowledge acquisition and transference go on all the time. How else does one learn to survive?'

'You didn't seem to know much about birthdays.'

'Not so important, nor so interesting.'

'Aye, but – with respect – what possible use to you, a toad, or to your survival, is knowledge of long-dead Scottish explorers?'

'"With respect",' said Mungo, 'is a phrase generally employed to preface remarks of a disrespectful nature. Your question is no exception to this rule. I might just as well demand of you whether your supposed knowledge of the so-called "common toad" is relevant to you or to *your* survival.'

'Well –' Douglas began, but Mungo interrupted.

'Do you or do you not subscribe to the view that all knowledge is potentially valuable, and that its value, potential or realised, cannot be determined by the superficial assessment of its perceived utility at any given moment?'

'I'll have to think about that,' Douglas said. It seemed too grand and complex a proposition to be unscrambled so late in the garden of October darkness, especially after the best part of a bottle of red wine.

'Do so,' Mungo said. 'I already have.' And in one untoad-like leap he left the table and landed somewhere in the night. Douglas could not have sworn to it, but he was fairly sure he heard a groan following the faint impact of Mungo's touchdown.

Douglas shivered: the air was a little chillier now. His glass was empty. So was the bottle, almost. He picked up both, and stood unsteadily. If a man cannot stand unsteadily at the end of his fiftieth birthday, he thought, when can he? The security light came on. He was on the bright stage again. Of Mungo there was no sign.

It was possible, Douglas thought, that his senses had completely failed him and that he had imagined the entire evening. It was possible that every word of their conversation had taken place inside his own head.

It was possible. But he did not think it likely.

[To be continued]

HEFT

'Come in. Sit down. You want a drink? Tea? Coffee?' John Liffield asks.

'I'm fine,' I say.

We are in his room in the *Spear*'s latest building. Like my father, the newspaper changed residence recently, a move brought on by reduced circumstances and new maladies similar to his – depression, loss of circulation, diminution of certain faculties and functions leading to confusion, inarticulacy, lack of balance, et cetera. The grand old edifice in the heart of Edinburgh that once housed the *Spear* is now a hotel, and the paper's editorial and commercial departments operate out of a bland 1970s block in a western suburb. Former editors enjoyed fabulous views of the city centre, and gravitas and purposefulness oozed from the oak-panelled walls of their offices. The vista from Liffield's room is of parking spaces, three large bins on wheels for recyclable waste, and a scrubby patch of grass bordered by a hedge full of unrecycled waste – chocolate-bar wrappers and drinks cartons, mainly. Inspiring, it is not. I worked in this building for a year. I am glad, on balance, that I no longer do.

Liffield's desk is big and very tidy: lots of clear space interspersed with piles of papers that look as if they have been methodically sorted and processed. Sonya would appreciate it. A mug decorated with the words I'M THE BOSS sits within Liffield's reach. He reaches for it, takes a gulp. 'Yuck. Cold,' he says. 'You're probably off the coffee now, are you? Easier to cut down when you're not in this environment.'

'No, I still drink coffee.'

'Me too. I used to be able to drink it all day, all evening, gallons of it, and still fall asleep as soon as my head hit the proverbial. Not any more.

Now, if I drink coffee after about three in the afternoon, I'm awake all night. My legs are jumping like fish in the rain. Do you get that?'

'No, I don't get that.'

'Lucky you. Maybe it's just a phase. Water?' He walks over to the cooler that stands in one corner – his own personal cooler.

'No, thanks, I'm fine.'

He fills a plastic cup, brings it back to the desk. 'It was good to see you on Tuesday. Not good circumstances, obviously, but there you go.'

There Ronald Grigson went, actually. I don't say this. Instead, I ask if the meeting was successful.

'Meeting?'

'You had to leave right after the funeral for a management meeting. Bigwigs up from London.'

'Oh, that. It was fine.' I find it interesting that we all say this, all the time. I'm fine, we're fine, it's fine. It seldom is. It's usually cloudy. Sometimes the rain is coming down in torrents. But saying it's fine is code for: whatever it's doing, let's pretend it isn't. Like Ollie's money carry-on. Or one of his brolly-bearing wee characters coming out of the weatherhouse saying, 'I'm fine. We're fine. It's fine.'

'So the *Spear* survives to be chucked another day?'

'Things aren't *that* desperate yet, Douglas.'

'No?'

'No.' He says this quite sharply. 'Anyway, I said to come in for a chat, and here you are. No sooner out the door than you want back in, eh?'

'No I don't.' I say this quite sharply.

'But you want to write something for us?'

'That's what we discussed.' I can see that, from his perspective, I must be coming across somewhat negatively. I shift up a gear. 'Yes, absolutely.'

'Well, as it happens, I have an Idea.' Elbows on desk, he brings his fingertips together, to form an airy hand-cage in which the Idea is exhibited. I can't spot it, but Liffield is peering intently at something in there.

'Context,' he says. 'This year. This historic year for the nation. *Our* nation. Decision time. Destiny. We have a responsibility, I think. Agreed?'

I haven't a clue what he is talking about. He seems to be reading from the jottings on an invisible notepad. Bearing in mind Ollie's advice not to agree to anything prematurely, I do the first half of a nod, raising my eyebrows meaningfully.

'Who has a responsibility?'

'We do. The *Spear*. The Voice of the Nation. The nation has spoken but now we must channel what was said and say it afresh. Shape what is said next. Voice what *happens* next. I want the *Spear* to drive forward what this whole thing has been and continues to be about, whatever that is. You with me?'

I do the second, downward half of the nod. Very slowly. I need to check something.

'Are you talking about the referendum?'

'Of course.'

'The referendum on Scottish independence?'

'What else? The one on whether we exit Europe isn't due for ages, if it ever happens.'

'Okay. It's just that the independence referendum was five weeks ago. The nation, as you point out, has spoken. Quite decisively. Against independence.'

'True. But it's not *over*, is it? Anybody can see it's not over.'

He sounds like a disappointed Yes voter. As if he wants a replay.

'But the *Spear* came out decisively for No. You won. So I'm confused. You're not about to take a new, post-referendum position on the referendum, are you?'

He looks shocked. 'No! Well, not exactly. But if we're to shape the future, we have to be cognisant of the mood of the people. We have to reach out to those we previously disagreed with. Bring them on board. Persuade them that we're on their side.'

'Even if you aren't?'

'We will be. I'll level with you, Douglas. I said things aren't desperate, but that's not to say they aren't tough. They are tough. You know that. Tough, but not desperate.'

'Not *that* desperate,' I can't help interjecting. 'Yet.'

'Exactly. The prospects for our industry are not rosy. Here at the *Spear* we've been losing readers year on year' – he hesitates, as if he's just recognised the opening lines of a poem and is half-minded to draw it to my attention – 'but now we think we're getting down to a hard core. People who'll always want a daily newspaper. But what do they want it for? Not for news! Who gets their news from a newspaper these days? I don't! Those days are gone. What these hardcore readers want is opinion. Lots of it. The cut and thrust of debate. Provocation and outrage. The daily chit-chat. Let me tell you something: the referendum was good for us. Our sales steadied, they even picked up a little. People were engaged. So now we want to hold on to that hard core, and to grow it. And here's something else you already know: talk is cheap. Filling the pages with opinion is a damn sight easier than filling it with real news – I mean real, original news stories. Gathering stories from scratch is expensive. Recycling stories from the internet and other media is free. To put it bluntly: *more chat, less facts.*'

'Fewer.' The grammar pedant in me can't resist. Liffield's slogan doesn't even rhyme properly.

'If you say so. The bottom line is, we can make a profit on that model. We can survive and prosper. We need to take the news out of newspapers.'

This, then, is what Tuesday's management meeting was about, and the invisible notes he is reading are from that meeting. As he has just admitted, though, he is hardly telling me anything I don't already know.

'But to pull in as many readers as possible,' Liffield continues, 'we need to soften our editorial position. Blur it, if you like. You're right, the referendum result was decisive, but not *that* decisive. Forty-five per cent voted for independence. If the latest opinion polls are remotely accurate, if another referendum were held tomorrow Yes might just sneak it.'

'I doubt it,' I say. 'Opinion's a fickle beast.'

'Whatever. But tell me this. Even if the polls are wrong, why would we alienate nearly half our potential readership anyway?'

'How about out of principle?' I suggest. 'You genuinely don't think independence is a good idea, and you said so and will go on saying it. Or has the *Spear* had second thoughts?'

'Let's say we're alert to the possibilities. Circumstances change. One of our rivals – the only paper that came out for Yes – has seen its circulation leap.'

'So?'

'So, this tells us that all these pro-indy people are *really* engaged, and that they can be wooed.'

These pro-indy people: a phrase suggesting that they are distasteful to him; that he would prefer to keep them at a distance but knows he can't. It is time, I feel, for a recap.

'Let me see if I'm getting this right. The referendum generated a lot of popular interest in politics, and the *Spear*, like other papers, was a beneficiary. This has slowed the decline in your sales. You want build on that experience. You can't afford to do real news but you can do lots of opinion and the core readers you're left with seem to be happy with that. The company is happy because that model is profitable. And you're happy because it's easy to recycle stories from the internet, even leaving aside the question, where does the internet get most of its stories if not from newspapers?'

'Leave that aside.'

'Okay. A newspaper isn't a newspaper if it doesn't take a line on the big issues of the day, but you want to keep on board the readers you've got, and gain some more, presumably poaching them from rival papers. To do that you have to blur the *Spear*'s editorial position. Be all things to all men. Is that what you're saying?'

'And all women. Don't forget the women. You've got it, Douglas.'

'And as far as Scottish independence is concerned, you need to blur your position on that too?'

'Basically, blurring is good. We have to get away from the binary choice that the referendum represented: on the one hand, Yes; on the other hand, No. Life's not like that.'

'Aye it is.'

'No it isn't. I'm not interested in how people voted five weeks ago. The referendum is history and we have to move on. And the *Spear* can be at the forefront of that moving-on-ness. No more black and white: we can occupy the grey area. We need to be for as well as against.'

'So when I mentioned principle, I was a bit wide of the mark?'

'This isn't about principles, it's about survival.'

'And that's your Idea?'

'No, that's the context.'

'We're still on context?'

'Context is crucial. Now, the Idea. Over the next few months I want to take Scotland's temperature. This is where you can have a role. I want to do a national audit, a cultural and intellectual stocktaking. Who are we? What are we? Why are we? To be or not to be? Stands Scotland where it did?'

'That tired old horse.'

'That's Shakespeare for you. One cliché after another.'

'That's another tired old horse.'

Liffield leans forward, aiming an accusatory finger at me. 'You sound tired yourself, Douglas. A tad jaded, if I may say so. You want to hear the rest?'

I nod, yes please. Partly I am keen to hear how bad it is. Partly I want a glimpse of what my role might be. Two days earlier he was saying I didn't have one.

'The Idea is to home in on *ideas*. The Idea of Scotland. That's what the series will be called. Interviews, profiles, essays. Big themes. Science. The Arts. Law. Education. Religion. The Land. Lifestyle. All seen through a tartan lens.'

'A what?'

'It's a figure of speech.'

'Is it? It sounds a bit limiting. A bit pro-indy, even.'

'Got to capture the territory first, Douglas, that's how I see it. Big themes – and big names, too – but reassuringly familiar. Don't frighten those horses you mentioned. And when I say big names I don't mean politicians. They've been hogging the limelight too long. I don't mean celebrities either. Who cares what a pop star or a tennis player thinks? Delete that, of course we do. But for this series I'm looking for more gravitas, more heft. Know what I mean?'

Indeed I do. I can see the gravitas oozing from the non-existent oak panelling. As for heft, it's a word I hate. Book reviewers use it to describe tedious literary novels that they feel obliged, the tedium notwithstanding, to admire. I've used it myself. Context, as the man said, is crucial.

'Who do you have in mind?'

'Professors of this and that. Historians who don't bore their readers to death. Scientists who splash around in stuff the rest of us don't even recognise as stuff. A theologian or two. Same as the scientists, only different. High Arts people like composers and film directors. Business colossi.'

'Colossi?'

'I mean people who've been around the block a few times, not just been dragons on *Dragons' Den*.'

'I thought that was how they got to be dragons. They've been around the block a few times.'

'Those turds? They put bets on sales pitches. They don't *make* anything. They're not going to change the way we think about our existence, the way scientists and artists can.'

This is the first really interesting thing he has said. I acknowledge this with a full up-and-down nod.

'That's good.'

'It is, isn't it? A writer or two, obviously, but not your usual crime, sex and swearing mob. Writers of books that are likely to last beyond the current decade. Where will all this Tartan Noir be in a few years?'

'People still read Sherlock Holmes.'

'Yeah, but he was a genius. I mean writers who write serious books.'

'Books with heft?'

'Exactly. Literature. The stuff you don't read for fun. And not just fiction. Philosophy. It would be good to have a philosopher in the mix, don't you think? There must be one or two knocking around this country somewhere.'

'I'm not sure. The last time I checked, some of our finest universities were trying to close down their Philosophy departments. Not cost-effective.'

'I'll have someone look into that. Anyway, I'm going to run these pieces on a regular basis – once a week if possible. Some of them might be in two parts, perhaps four thousand words in total – it depends on the subject matter or the person we're profiling. After a year we'll pull them all together into a book: *The Idea of Scotland*. I think it'll take. A Christmas bestseller. This is where you come in. I have a number of people in mind to do the interviews and/or write them up, and you're top of my list. You up for this?'

I wasn't even *on* the list on Tuesday, but John Liffield seems to have deleted Tuesday.

'Why me?'

'Because you know what you're doing. Like those dragon people, you've been around the block. The kids in here these days, we've taught them to cross-check information on websites but they don't know how to do human interaction and make it work on the page. Anyway, I can't spare them, I've got a paper to put together and that requires them to be at their keyboards. Whereas you can be out in the field, working away undisturbed. It'll take you as long as it takes you. Don't worry, I'll pay you a decent fee and any reasonable expenses. I want these pieces to stand up in years to come. I want people to say, "The *Spear* led the way."'

Another rhyming couplet. I'm not sure if he noticed it. He hasn't specified the decency of the fee, but it doesn't matter. I know I am going to agree. From a position of deep suspicion and doubt, I have moved to one of doubt and shallow enthusiasm. I don't think much of the Idea – I am unenthused by the prospect of a prolonged bout of national navel-gazing of the kind he is proposing – but even so I can see the potential for some interesting articles. And for some long-term earnings for Douglas Findhorn Elder.

'It's a big plan,' I say. 'And there was I, thinking the *Spear* was economising.'

'We are. That's why we made you redundant, you and the others. It's staff costs that kill us. Now you're freelance we can afford you. We're getting slimmer and fitter all the time.' He stands, drops his plastic cup into a bin and fetches himself more water, using a fresh cup. He must be worried about infecting himself. On the way back he appraises me, like a doctor or a tailor. 'You're not looking so bad yourself. Thought you looked well on Tuesday. Wasn't so sure a few minutes ago. Must be the light. *Are* you fit?'

He sits down, leans forward again, palms down on the desk. He might be preparing to leap across and wrestle me. Apart from the dark hair, yellowish complexion, long, sharp-cornered body and almost everything else about him, momentarily he bears a striking resemblance to Vladimir Putin.

I assure him that I am fit, although actually the word I use is 'fine'.

'Good. Ready for your first assignment, then?' The metallic rasp of his voice becomes somehow more Slavic. An orchestra plays a few chords that conjure vast, sweeping plains and wild horses.

'Sounds exciting.' I am wondering if I should stand up, put my palms on my side of the desk and crouch in expectation. 'Where are you sending me?'

With these words I seem to have accepted the mission.

'The back of beyond, and then some,' he says, sitting back with a smile. 'Guess who I want you to interview?'

I shake my head. I don't know anyone at that address.

He pauses, no doubt for dramatic effect. He is glowing with savage anticipation, and sweat glistens between his upper lip and his huge, sharp nose.

'Rosalind Munlochy.'

I can't help it. I disappoint him.

'Who?'

POSSIBLE NOVELISTS

'Who the fuck is Rosalind Munlochy?' is Ollie Buckthorn's way of putting it.

I couldn't leave the *Spear*'s premises without dropping by to observe the Erstwhile Colleagues at their toil, but after a while they tire of my idle chatter and Ollie offers to escort me off the premises. He shows me out via a fire exit at the rear of the building. I update him on the interview while he pollutes the air with a cigarette.

'That was what I wanted to know. I had this vague notion that I'd come across her, but I couldn't think why. I thought she might possibly have been a novelist.'

'We'll talk about possible novelists in a minute.'

'And it turns out she was. And a poet. And a politician – MP for somewhere in the Highlands after the war.'

'What war?'

'Second. World.'

'That's a while ago. Are we talking about the 1940s?'

'We are.'

'What breed of politician?'

'Radical socialist. She was in the Labour Party.'

'Ah,' Ollie says. 'In those days you could be both.'

'But before that she was a communist. And a nationalist before that. Or possibly after. Liffield wasn't certain.'

'He's having you on. Rosalind Munlochy? There's no such person.'

'Oh, there is.' I proffer a folder of printouts and photocopies which Liffield has given me. 'He's dug up quite a bit of stuff about her from the archive. We checked online too. According to Wikipedia she was a Liberal.'

'That could be true. They're a funny lot, Highlanders. Any Tory tendencies in her profile, just to complete the set?'

'I don't know. She seems to own some land up there, so maybe.'

'Up where?'

'I'm not quite sure. I need to check on a map. The surprising thing is, she's still alive.'

'Why is that surprising?'

'Because she's very, very old. She was born in 1914.'

'How propitious. Or should that be ominous?'

'Take your pick. John Liffield's certainly treating it as one or the other. He says it's Meant To Be. In this year of years – the centenary of the First World War, the year of the referendum – here she is, not gone but forgotten, and it's *her* centenary too. The birth of the modern age – the age of industrial war and mass communications – she's the live link, the woman who holds the two ends of that hundred-year story in her crooked wee hands. Rosalind Munlochy, Mother of the Nation. Liffield was almost lyrical at the prospect of reintroducing her to her people. There might even have been a tear in his eye.'

'Like I said,' Ollie says, 'he's taking the piss.'

'No, he's serious. I'm going to do this big profile of her, in two parts. I'm planning to go up there to interview her next week.'

'Up where again?'

'Wherever she is. I'll find it. She's away in the wilds but that's part of the adventure.'

'Adventure? Have I just woken up in an Enid Blyton book? What currency is Liffield paying you in, lemonade?'

'Very funny.'

'Let me rephrase that. And the fee is?'

'Pretty decent actually. All reasonable expenses. You know.'

'So you didn't discuss it.'

'Oh, it was discussed. I just haven't pinned down the details yet.'

'In other words, you don't know what he's going to pay you.'

'Come on, Ollie. I have to show willing – and a bit of flexibility. If this works out there could be a lot more in the pipeline.'

Ollie grinds the end of his fag out with a ferocious heel. 'What are you, some kind of overgrown intern? Whatever happened to workers' solidarity? Fixed rates of pay? No, don't tell me, it's the times we live in. Well, at least if you go gallivanting off looking for this Munlochy woman you'll be too busy to waste any more time writing a novel. You weren't serious about that, were you?'

'I was. I am. As a matter of fact, Ollie –'

'Don't!'

'Don't what?'

'Don't speak about it. And don't, whatever other favours you may be looking for, ask me to read the opening chapters. I'm not giving you any feedback. I refuse to encourage you, not one tiny bit.'

'What's your problem?'

'*My* problem? I don't think I've got a problem, Dougie. You're the one writing a novel. Here you are with twenty-plus years of journalism under your belt, an ability to string sentences together in a coherent and effective manner, reality knocking at the door saying, "Hello, let's talk about me", and you want to indulge yourself with an excursion into the La-La Land of contemporary fucking fiction. What's going on?'

'What have you got against fiction? You've a whole library on your phone, you said. Don't tell me there's no fiction in it.'

'Oh, there's plenty of fiction. The virtual shelves are bulging with fiction. *Classic* fiction, Douglas. Fiction from before Rosalind Munlochy was born, and then a few bits and pieces up until she takes her seat in the

74

House of Commons – *if* she ever did. *That* stuff is worth reading, there's a mountain of it, and – a fact not to be sneered at – if it's out of copyright it's downloadable for free. Jane Austen and Anthony Trollope and George Orwell. Those people knew how to fashion a paragraph! What we don't need is you or anyone else from the fucked-up, smug, postmodern apology for a society that we have the misfortune to inhabit adding their hard little pebbles of constipated shit to the pile. And note that I say "shit", by the way. "Shite" is too good a word for it.'

It is not unusual for Ollie to shift into rant mode. This one is moderate to rough, as the shipping forecast might put it. I should let it go but I don't.

'For a man so modern that you make the rest of us look like sludge-eating dinosaurs, you seem a wee bit embittered, Ollie Buckthorn, and, if I may say so, a wee bit behind the times.'

'Up yours.'

'And I wasn't going to ask you to read what I've written, anyway.'

'Good.'

'Because you wouldn't like it.'

'You're right. I wouldn't. What *were* you going to say?'

'Just that I am finding the whole process quite cathartic. Liberating, even.'

'Fuck's sake.'

Another thing about Ollie is that he often winds himself up more than the person he means to wind up. And then it's over. This is such an occasion. He stands looking incredibly disappointed by life in general and me in particular, shoulders heaving and jowls juddering, and for a few seconds I think I may be about to witness a medical episode. Then a big, cheesy grin spreads across his face and he reaches out and wallops me in the chest with his big, meaty right paw.

'You're an arse, Elder.'

'You're entitled to your opinion, but I say opinion is a fickle beast.'

'It is that. You're still an arse. Right then, that's settled. I'd better get back to work.'

'So had I.'

'Ha! Cheerio, then.'

'Cheerio. I loves ya, Ollie,' I say, doing my Popeye impersonation.

'Fuck off,' he says, doing his Ollie impersonation.

Douglas Findhorn Elder opened the back door of what was half his and half his father's house – the house in which he had grown up, which he had never really left and which, one day perhaps not too far off, would be wholly his – and looked out into the night. Rain with the consistency of a fine, soft mesh was falling. No stars could be discerned and the light of numerous street lamps in the neighbourhood struggled to do more than add a yellowish-grey, dirty tone to the October darkness. Douglas did not step out onto the patio or – as it had always been known in the family – the *sitootery*; or – as his father used to observe with dry wit on wet days and nights such as this – the *naechancery*. He had no intention of sitting at the watery cast-iron table on either of the watery cast-iron chairs. Furthermore, mindful of the entertainment of the evening before last, he did not wish to trigger the security light and thus distress, should he be out and about, his recent acquaintance the toad, Mungo Forth Mungo.

Douglas had come to the door in the hope that Mungo might be there and that they could renew their conversation. He had done the same the night before – had even wandered the garden with a torch, but not a sign of any toad had he found. He had gone to bed that night, sober and disappointed, and almost persuaded that he must have dreamed the whole thing.

Then, tonight – just a few minutes earlier, in fact – he had been sitting at the kitchen table, typing, when he heard a faint but persistent scratching at the door. He had ignored it at first, then decided that a cat on the prowl must be responsible. It was surely not possible that the sound could be connected with a common toad going about its normal nocturnal business. Or even an uncommon toad. He had continued to type, and to read back what he had written on the screen of his computer.

Suddenly a dreadful fear had struck him: if it *was* a cat, going about *its* normal nocturnal business, it might be a cause of some annoyance or even danger to Mungo. And so, telling himself that he was merely playing games with himself, he had opened the door and called out, like the medium at a seance to which nobody else has turned up, 'Is anybody there?'

Somebody was: Mungo was there! Enough light from the back lobby spilt onto the nearest stone slabs to reveal the toad in the middle of some strenuous exercises. He rose on all fours, puffing out his chest, then stood briefly on his back legs and performed an even more impressive pectoral expansion before returning to his standard squatting position. He repeated this performance several times, breathing heavily.

Douglas felt a corresponding swelling of his thorax, which he attributed to the pleasure of seeing his batrachian amigo again.

'Good evening, Mungo,' Douglas said, when the toad had finished.

'Oh, it's yourself,' Mungo said. 'I didn't see you.'

But Douglas was convinced that the toad's amber eye had spotted him and that Mungo was pleased to have had his exertions witnessed.

'I was just limbering up,' Mungo explained. 'One has to, to obviate stiffness and stimulate agility, both physical and mental.'

Two, Douglas thought, could play at this game. 'I thought perhaps you were adopting an intimidating posture for the purpose of self-defence,' he replied. Only that afternoon he had read, on the internet, that this was what toads did.

'Why would I be doing that?'

'A cat might have been bothering you.'

'A cat? Bother me? I don't think so. Much more likely that I would bother a cat. They don't like my . . . perfume. Humff. They wouldn't need to like it if they kept their distance.'

'I once saw a dog upset by a toad,' Douglas said. 'The dog wanted to make trouble, or perhaps just to play, but it couldn't do either. It started frothing at the mouth – a reaction to the toad's . . . perfume, presumably.'

'Dogs are cleverer than cats,' Mungo said.

'The received wisdom among humans, generally speaking, is that cats are cleverer than dogs.'

'Well, that's human wisdom for you,' Mungo said rudely. 'Cats think they are clever, but they never learn. That dog you saw, I bet it learned. Dogs have been learning for untold generations. They even learned not to be wolves – but of course there was a price to pay for *that*. Collaboration,' he added, with a meaningful stare.

The toad sounded to Douglas like some Scotch comedian of bygone days, a Willie McCulloch or a Rikki Fulton or perhaps a Chic Murray. He had not picked up on this peculiarity on Tuesday, but it was unmistakable now: the broad vowels with a hint of narrow irritability; the see-through bravado. It brought to Douglas's mind a schoolmaster with a gambling addiction; a grocer with a grudge against his customers; or, in this case, a gymnast with a prejudice against cats.

'Collaboration,' Douglas said. 'That's a word with connotations. Mostly negative, historically speaking.'

'Which is why I used it. But that's your problem, not ours. You have history. We have aeons.'

Douglas, somewhat irritated by Mungo's insistent assertions of superiority, changed the subject.

'Not such a nice night,' he said.

'On the contrary, it's a wonderful night. Delightful temperature, a good steady drizzle, and plenty of food about. What more could one ask for? You're not coming out?'

'No, it's too wet for me. I just wanted to see if you were around.'

'Well, I am. Very much so.' He took a few, almost jaunty steps to demonstrate that he was. Just like Chic Murray, Douglas thought.

'May I suggest,' Mungo said, 'that if you're not coming out, I could come in for a while?'

'You'd be very welcome.'

'Just to see how the other half lives. I don't suppose I'll like it much,' the toad said, as he clambered over the lintel. The back-lobby floor was laid with large, earthy-red tiles. 'Oh, but this is very pleasant after all. Which way?'

'Turn right. That's the kitchen,' Douglas said, following him in.

The kitchen floor was covered with black-and-white-lino squares like a chessboard. Mungo, a lugubrious bishop, moved diagonally across it. He came up against the kickboard under the sink unit and stopped.

'Much better than I expected,' he said. 'Any wine tonight?'

'There's a bottle open. I was letting it breathe while I was working. Do you want some?'

'A splash.'

'Do you mind if I put it in a dish? Otherwise it'll stain the lino.'

'So?'

'I'd rather it didn't.'

Douglas found a small, shallow-lipped dish, such as might be used for butter or the extinguishing of cigarettes, and poured red wine into it. He placed it on the floor and Mungo made his way towards it.

'This is rather demeaning,' he said, shuffling into position over the dish but not lowering himself onto it.

'Think of it as like taking a bath,' Douglas said. He poured himself a glass and sat down at the kitchen table. The computer purred its gentle and continuous electronic purr; the cursor flashed its insistent flash.

Mungo was now sitting on the dish and Douglas had a sudden, disturbing vision of his father, trousers round ankles, in similar circumstances. He looked away quickly, and with a single keystroke inserted the two dots of a colon into the sentence he had been composing before he went to the door: thus.

'I seem to have interrupted you,' Mungo said.

'On the contrary,' Douglas said, 'I was just finishing. That's it, done. The truth is, I wanted to see you. I *needed* to see you. I couldn't quite believe, when I woke up yesterday morning, that Tuesday night – well, that Tuesday night had really happened.'

'Do nights – or days – sometimes not happen for you?'

'You know what I mean. That we met and talked.'

'Let's assume that we did, and take things from there. It will make things simpler. What are you doing?'

'I'm writing. Do you know about writing and reading?'

'I *know* about them. We don't *do* them. No need.' His tongue lashed out and reeled in a small spider that had been making its way along the kickboard. 'Ours is an oral culture. What are you writing?'

'A book. You know about books, too, I suppose?'

'You can suppose that I have a wide knowledge of many things. What kind of book?'

'Well, I'm only at the start of it. It's the story of a man who goes on a journey to the back of beyond. He is sent there on a mission which looks straightforward enough but unexpected things happen to him along the way. He has all kinds of adventures but to be honest I'm not sure yet what form these will take. If you were to ask me how the story ends the answer would be I don't know. In a way that is my reason for writing it: to find out.'

'You mean, it is a work of fiction?'

'It is, but loosely based on real events and characters, although of course there will be a disclaimer denying that, should the book ever be published.'

'That would be a lie then, the disclaimer?'

'Well, yes, but then a novel is one big lie from start to end, if you think about it.'

'I see. And is this your first big lie, or have you always told them?'

'I have always been a writer, but this is my first book. I have spent much of my life working in the sphere of journalism, editing other people's writing, and penning occasional articles of my own. I enjoy literature, travel and fine wines. I live in Edinburgh with my partner, Sonya, and her two children. I'm sorry, Mungo, I got carried away there. I was composing a blurb about myself.'

'A what?'

'A blurb. A kind of mini-biography, to go on the dust jacket of the book. I was projecting into the future. It'll probably never happen.'

'Like Tuesday night. I understand. I will disregard the part about Sonya and her children, which from our previous conversation I deduce is also a lie. Or should I say a wish, projected into the future?'

'I'm not sure about "wish". It's a possibility. A possible fresh start.'

'But you don't wish it.'

'I'm not sure what I wish. I'm seeing Sonya tomorrow. Maybe I'll have a better idea then.'

'Your home or hers?'

'Neither. I sent her a message earlier and we've arranged to meet for lunch near her place of work.'

'Do you have one of those?'

'No, I used to have, but I stopped going there six months ago.'

'That would be the sphere of journalism you mentioned?'

'It's not actually a sphere. It's an ordinary building with corners. The newspaper I worked for is called the *Spear*.'

'The *Spear of Journalism*?'

'Just the *Spear*. In its early years it had a reputation for poking the Victorian establishment in painful places. Inevitably it became part of the establishment but it still gave a sharp jag to folk who needed it from time to time. Unfortunately, its glory days are past. It's been losing sales and staff for years. They offered me a redundancy package and I took it. I was surplus to requirements, but now the editor wants me to write for the paper again.'

'He's going to serialise your novel?'

'No, he doesn't know about the novel. Nobody does, except Ollie.'

'Who's Ollie?'

'A friend. He still works at the *Spear*.'

'Then Ollie could serialise it?'

'Not his decision, but even if he had the authority to run it, he wouldn't. He doesn't think I should be wasting my time writing fiction. How do you know about serialisation?'

Mungo's upper body shifted in a particular way. Douglas was beginning to read correctly what these gestures meant. Many toad movements resemble a shrug, but this one really was a shrug.

'I just do. I know what a redundancy package is too, and what "surplus to requirements" means. Our methods of acquiring, storing, retrieving and passing on information are much more sophisticated than your books and computers. Clever though such tools appear to be, they have a deleterious effect on the user. We don't have them and so we rely on our own brains. Consequently we use a vastly greater percentage of them than you do of yours. And, as I said, we live to a good age. Which is a long way of saying, I know about these things because I know about them. Where were we? Ah yes, the editor of the *Spear* wants you to write something that is not your novel. What?'

'I'll tell you in a minute. That's why I've arranged to meet Sonya. I need to tell her about it too because I'll be going away for a couple of days.'

'Why does she need to know that? I thought your relationship was over.'

'I'd prefer to think of it as between phases. I hope it isn't completely over because I have a favour to ask her.'

'Oh? What's that?'

'I need to borrow her car.'

Douglas gave Mungo an inquiring glance. It was all that was required.

'Yes, yes, I know what a car is. Monstrous things. You used the word "disaster" in a flippant manner the other night. If you want to talk about true disasters, put "cars" and "migrating toads" in the same sentence. Absolute carnage. Why do you need a car?'

'Because it's a long journey I'm going on, and a car will make it a lot simpler. There's a woman I have to meet.'

'Another woman? Are you in a relationship with her as well?'

'No. I've never met her before. She's called Rosalind Munlochy.'

Mungo chewed the name over two or three times, sounding it from alternate sides of his mouth. His verdict, when it came, was positive.

'Impressive. She could go far with a name like that.'

'I don't think she's going anywhere. I'm going to her, to interview her.'

'Why?'

'To ask her opinion about things. To see what she's done in the course of a long and varied life. To find out who she is.'

'So, pretty much the same process as writing a novel? Is there any point?'

'That *is* the point, Mungo.'

81

'I see. Any more wine?' The toad raised himself while Douglas refilled the dish, and then Mungo said, 'So what do you know about her already?'

[To be continued]

EXTRACT FROM NOTES FOR AN AS YET UNWRITTEN
BIOGRAPHY OF MRS ROSALIND MUNLOCHY, NÉE
STRIVEN, BY MR DOUGLAS FINDHORN ELDER, AUTHOR;
COMPOSED PARTLY FROM SUNDRY PAPERS PROVIDED BY
MR JOHN LIFFIELD, EDITOR OF THE *SPEAR*, FOR THE
PURPOSE OF ENABLING MR ELDER TO PREPARE FOR AN
INTERVIEW WITH MRS MUNLOCHY; PARTLY FROM HER
AUTOBIOGRAPHICAL WORK *SOME LIFE*; AND PARTLY FROM
INFORMATION GATHERED IN CIRCUMSTANCES BEYOND
THE SCOPE OF THE PRESENT WORK, TO WHICH THE
READER IS CONSEQUENTLY DENIED ACCESS

On the first day of November 1914, when the Battle of Ypres was raging and the true, ghastly nature of modern warfare revealing itself to the world, Rosalind Isabella Striven was born into an ancient family which had long held lands in Argyll and Perthshire, though by the time of her birth these were reduced to a few hundred acres around an old family house in Glentaragar.

The Strivens, who are of aristocratic stock, have borne their name with serious, literal intent for at least the last three centuries, and there is no reason to suspect, though the historical record is faded, that they have not always done so. Not for them the irresponsible existence of absentee landlords, living off rents and inherited wealth in the fat South for nine months of the year, and descending on their Scottish domains only for the fishing of spring and the shooting of late summer and autumn. A Striven who does not strive is not a Striven in the eyes of other Strivens, whose family motto is *Strive Ane, Strive A'*. Even when the work in hand may simply hasten disaster, Strivens do not cease: they would rather be industrious than indolent. Whole septs of them came out with the Earl of Mar in 1715, and dashed energetically back and forth at Sheriffmuir, achieving little forbye the forfeiture of their estates. In 1745, having re-established themselves, half of them came out again with Prince Charles Edward Stewart, while the other half stayed at home, managing their farms with great diligence and guarded loyalty to the House of

Hanover; and it was afterwards said that this division was the outcome of a rapidly convened family conference during which the menfolk agreed to disagree, at least in public, for the duration of hostilities, with a view to preserving the future for as many Strivens as possible, whatever the outcome. But as on this occasion fortune did not favour the brave, who were either killed in battle, executed, exiled or transported, it came to pass that the farming Strivens found themselves, several months after Culloden, conveniently sundered from titles associated with the Jacobite Cause yet in possession of a great deal more property than they could ever have reasonably hoped to own.

They spent the rest of the eighteenth century draining fields, clearing stones, building dykes, planting trees, rotating crops, breeding cattle and sheep and generally improving their estates. They did not shirk from hard physical labour but in time they came to sweat and toil less and to supervise and delegate more, and this gave them additional time in which to improve their minds by hard mental study. A great library was accumulated, and generations of Strivens read their way along its shelves, which contained very many works of practical utility, political economy and natural history, and very few of fiction, poetry or theology.

Although Strivens, male and female alike, did fish, shoot and stalk, some becoming experts, they treated these activities as useful endeavour, not as recreation, and killed only for the pot. Other sports, such as football, swimming, boxing, shinty, athletics and mountaineering, were encouraged for their promotion of fit, healthy bodies and alert, agile minds. No Striven, however, has ever taken up the game of golf.

If they did not mistreat their tenants neither were they sentimental about them: when, for reasons of efficiency and cost, they found it necessary to relocate families, they moved them as short a distance as possible, built better accommodation for them and supported them while they acquired new skills or new trades. An almost radical streak – or a strong commitment to fair play, at least – ran through the Strivens, and they despised those neighbours who ruthlessly cleared their lands of people to make room for sheep. A Striven in the House of Commons was fiery in calling for Land Law Reform in the 1880s, and his wife was active in the cause of Women's Suffrage in the 1890s. These were the grandparents of Rosalind Isabella, and no doubt their strong and active characters – they both lived until the 1920s – were an early influence on her own.

Other relatives – cousins, uncles and siblings – were geographers, scientists, judges, physicians, and campaigners in the fields of public health and housing. Rosalind's father was that rare exception among the modern Strivens, a soldier: this was somewhat frowned upon because, though he strove as hard as any other Striven, the military life was not thought to be a very *constructive* occupation. He redeemed himself, however, by taking a special interest in military engineering, including the building of earthworks, tunnels and trenches, which *was* very practical between 1914 and 1918. He rose to the rank of Lieutenant Colonel, exhibited enough independence of thought to express dismay, in a guardedly loyal way, at how the war was being conducted, and pleased everyone by surviving the entire four years, only to drown in 1924 while swimming in the sea near Oban.

The death duties resulting from his premature demise led to a further reduction in the acreage in Glentaragar, and the selling of a townhouse in Belgravia. His widow, although not a Striven by blood, had so thoroughly become one by nature that she declined to exchange, as she could have, the uncertain difficulties of a Highland life for a more comfortable one in London, and strove – with some success – to run what was left of the Glentaragar estate for the good of her children and the local community. Her children – Rosalind, her three older brothers and one younger sister – thoroughly approved of her resolve. They even loved her for it, although Love was not much mentioned among Strivens in those days, as it smacked of being a distraction from Industry and Achievement.

Rosalind learned to read (newspapers and the Bible) when she was four, to ride (horses and bicycles) when she was six, to swim (lochs and the ocean) when she was eight, to shoot (guns and arrows) when she was ten and to smoke (cigarettes and a pipe) when she was twelve. All of these skills she acquired at Glentaragar. She learned other things at her boarding school in Edinburgh: French, Latin, Mathematics, Botany, History, Geography, Music, Drawing, Literature and how to be a lady, the last of which accomplishments she discarded as soon as she walked through the gates of that institution for the last time, aged seventeen. It was the summer of 1932, the Great Depression was deepening, unemployment and poverty were everywhere, and the fragile economy of the Highlands was near collapse. Rosalind came home to Glentaragar, looked around and did not at all like what she saw. After three days she packed a suitcase, said farewell to her mother and took the sleeper to London.

[To be continued]

Friday morning. I consult the online telephone directory. No residential number in the West Highlands is listed under Munlochy, Striven or Glentaragar. I have an address from John Liffield, but it is so vague as to be almost useless: Glentaragar House, Glentaragar, Argyllshire. I bring a map up on-screen and hunt around the countryside until I find the glen, and when I home in on it I see a small black square identified as 'Glentgr Ho.'. I print off the right section of map and match it to the equivalent page of a road atlas. It is hard to see how any inhabited mainland location could be more difficult to reach than Rosalind Munlochy's place of residence. Main roads shrink to B roads, B roads to unclassifieds (presumably with passing-places), and one of these, eventually, turns into what appears to be little more than a track ending at the house. Just running my finger along the twists and turns that lead round lochs and hills and across rivers and burns makes me travel-sick. Sonya had better be in a receptive and generous mood. I am really going to need a car for this journey.

We are due to meet at one o'clock in a café near her office, which is in the university area of the city and handily close to the Central Library. En route to our appointment, I visit the library's reference room, where I hope to find an old edition of the paper telephone directory for the Argyll area. I am in luck: a librarian retrieves the relevant 1980s phone book from a backroom and this trusty old volume contains an entry under 'Munlochy, R., Glentaragar', with a four-digit number which, to be functional in the twenty-first century, only requires to be prefixed by another two digits and a new area code. I write down the details and am just about to leave when I think it may be worth checking if the library has any of Munlochy's books in its lending stock. To my deep joy it does – a short memoir published in 1966 called *Some Life*. I borrow it and, feeling rather pleased with myself, make my way to the café and my assignation with Sonya.

Sonya is employed in an educational consultancy firm. The last time I checked she was its Administration Officer, but this could easily have changed in the interim. Periodically the firm attaches a new title to her job, although her duties have never changed in all the time I've known her. Broadly speaking, the pattern of her working life is as follows: her employers – two men and a woman, all partners in the business – spend their days in a continual stream of meetings in which they consult with or are consulted by other people who, like them, inhabit the field of further and/or higher education. Whenever the partners emerge, singly or en masse, from one set of meetings, they swing by Sonya's desk and dump a load of paperwork on it, and she sorts it out for them. By the time she's typed up notes, filed reports, made new appointments, cancelled old ones, scheduled meetings and drawn up agendas for same, the consultants are swinging by again with another load of paperwork. This has been going on since before the start of the present millennium. I am not sure that the process didn't begin when the trio, all of whom used to be academics, heard the Prime Minister of the day utter the mantra 'Education, education, education' and took it as a clarion call to stop actually teaching and start talking about it instead. I have an image of them taking one 'education' each with a view to seeing how long they could keep passing them round without dropping them. Fortunately, Sonya is a very methodical and tidy person, so the cycle of activity I have described is meat and drink to her. She seldom complains that she is put upon, overworked or underpaid, whereas if her job were my job I would long ago have fed the three consultants, head first, through the enormous paper-shredder beside her desk. It is odd that she is so uncomplaining: my experience of her in a domestic setting is quite different.

Furthermore, the Sonya of admin and desk-tidying has a past. Don't we all? (Well, I don't, not really: I have a kind of lump of time that suddenly congealed into fifty years.) As a student, Sonya (so she has told me) was a keen member of the Drama Society. She acted a little, danced a little, even sang a bit. In the summer holidays she worked in bars and cafés and took parts in Edinburgh Fringe shows of one kind or another. There have been hints – never really elaborated upon, at least not to me – of a wild, even bohemian lifestyle. It was, so I understand, during the last of her student summers that she met the man who would become the father of her children. He was a member of a troupe of artistes appearing at the Festival Fringe. I suppose that is quite bohemian, but it ended, as my mother would have predicted had she known about it at the time, in tears.

When I arrive at the café Sonya is already seated, reading her *tablet*. (In olden days Scottish witches used to do this, tracing people's fortunes in the sugary lines of the hardened fudge-like substance they made in their cauldrons. I jest. Sonya is engrossed, I assume, in a newspaper or book.) She seems relaxed. I approach quietly, like a television naturalist, and am able to observe what a fine-looking woman she is, especially when unconscious of being under observation. As I watch, she lifts a hand to tuck a strand of her long, dark hair behind one ear, and I am reminded both of the delicacy of that ear and the slenderness of her fingers. If I were in my shoes I would have to question the sanity of having so disappointed such a woman as to cause her to ask me to move out of the home we shared for ten years. But I am already in my shoes and already questioning my sanity, so there isn't much point.

'Hello, Sonya.' These words leave my lips right at the moment when a nasty suspicion enters my head: that she is *not* engrossed in her reading material and *not* unconscious of my approach, and that she deliberately did that thing with her hair, ear and fingers in order to trigger the very pang of self-doubt upon which I have just decided not to dwell.

'Oh, Douglas, it's you,' she says, bookmarking (not, obviously, with a real bookmark) whatever she was reading, and closing the device.

'You weren't expecting me?'

'Yes, but not on time.'

Deciding not to rise to this, I do the opposite and sit down. It is true that my timekeeping has not always been up to Sonya's standard, but factors beyond my control – roadworks on Lothian Road, for instance – have usually been to blame.

'Reading anything interesting?'

'A very bad novel,' she says. 'I don't know why some people bother.'

Again, I resist the urge to respond. It is entirely possible that Sonya is simply saying what she feels at this moment, and not being antagonistic. Then again, she could be referring to my own literary aspirations, for although I have told only Ollie of my current engagement in the craft of novel-writing, it would be less than honest of me not to admit that there have been previous attempts. These, regrettably, have never progressed very far and, while Sonya's critical terminology is less explicit than Ollie's, it has always been clear to me that she has as little time for my fictional dabbling as he does. Sonya, an admirable woman in many respects, and capable of fair-mindedness and generosity (I sincerely hope, when it comes to vehicular matters), is however not hugely tolerant of failure. Even honest but insufficient application sometimes does not cut the mustard with Sonya, and her face has a particular way of showing disapproval which, while hard to describe, is impossible to mistake.

(In olden days English witches used to cut the mustard, which they made in their cauldrons, with herbs, spices and other ingredients – the usual stuff: eye of newt, toe of frog, et cetera – producing a hot, evil-smelling concoction with supposed magical properties. I jest again.)

I lift the menu from its position between the salt and pepper shakers. 'What do you fancy? My treat.'

'I've already ordered,' Sonya says. 'I must be back at the office by a quarter to.' She flashes me a toned-down version of the full disapproval display. 'You have to go up to the counter.'

This is not an encouraging start. She is not bringing to the occasion the positive spirit that I require of her. The text-message exchange seemed friendly enough so I am not sure what new thing I might have done (or not done) to displease her. No doubt I will find out soon enough.

The café offers a variety of soups, pasta dishes, sandwiches, toasties, panini, and so forth. It really doesn't matter to me what I choose, except that I want to eat at the same pace as Sonya. That is, I don't want to order a sandwich if she is having three courses, nor do I want to have the sea-food linguine with a mixed salad and crusty bread on the side if she is going to gulp down a bowl of soup and make her exit. However, asking her what she is having and then copying her is not likely to shift her opinion that I am weak-willed and indecisive.

I decide to be decisive.

'Sonya, I'm going to level with you. I'm not prepared to sit here nib-bling at a cheese-and-ham toastie while you work your way through a full lunch. I came here to talk, and I need your complete attention. The con-sumption of unequal quantities of food is hardly going to establish a favourable context for an open discussion of the state and status of our relationship, and what's more –'

She interrupts me. 'Douglas, I'm not having a full lunch. I'm having a sandwich.'

'Good. I'll have something similar.'

I do not jest: I lie. Not one word of the above exchange takes place. Sonya never eats much. I go to the counter and order a cheese-and-ham toastie and an apple juice. The man serving wants payment up front. From this I deduce that Sonya has already paid for whatever she's having, thereby eliminating any leverage my buying it might have given me when we come to negotiations about the car. Things are not going well.

'And I'm not discussing our relationship in a public place,' she says when I return to the table, as if she has been having a conversation with me in my absence. Perhaps she has. It's something I do, after all.

Alternatively, she might simply be reading my mind. Maybe that's what she has downloaded onto her tablet.

'So what are we here for?' This comes out rather more bluntly than I intended.

'I don't know what you're here for, but I'm here to be friendly,' she says, squeezing the last word out between her teeth. 'And just for the record, wasn't it you who texted me?'

'You're right. I apologise. I wanted to see you. It's been a while.' I count two beats. 'I miss you.'

'Do you?' She gives me a flattered – or at least less acidic – but rather pitying look. 'I wonder if you do. I think, on balance, the present arrangements are better for both of us. I wanted to see you too, Douglas, or I wouldn't have said yes. In time, if we both continue to want to, we'll be able to do this more often. It's about respect, really, isn't it?'

'I've always respected you.'

At this moment a waitress arrives with Sonya's meal. I was right: she's ordered a sandwich, a brown-bread item crammed with so much lettuce, shredded beetroot, tomatoes and other healthy produce that most of the contents are already spilling vigorously out onto the plate. And a smoothie of sunset tones, mainly deep reds, pinks and purples.

Not until the waitress has departed does Sonya reply: 'Well, I'm glad.' I wait for a reciprocal expression of respect, but it isn't forthcoming. 'Anyway,' she says, sweeping some imaginary crumbs from the table, 'enough of that. What have you been getting up to?'

'I've been getting up to fifty.'

She pauses in the act of lifting one sandwich quarter to her lips. 'I'm sorry?'

'It was my birthday on Tuesday.'

'Oh, of course. I hadn't a clue what you were talking about. Did you get my card?'

'I did, thanks.'

'Did you do anything, in the end?'

'Not a thing. I ate a pie and drank some wine.'

'Oh, Douglas!'

'It's all right. I said I didn't want a fuss.'

'Yes, you insisted. I took you at your word.'

'That was the right thing to do, Sonya. Honestly.'

'It just sounds a bit . . . dismal.'

'Not at all. I had a very jolly time. The pie was poor but produced no ill effects. The wine was good. It came later.'

'That was it?'

'No, no, far from it. These were only two of the day's highlights. I also got stuck on a bus and took in a funeral. Oh, and Ollie Buckthorn bought me a mystery dram.'

'Hmm.' The disapproval mask slips on again, and she concentrates on eating her sandwich. Sonya has met Ollie only two or three times. He did not make as good an impression on her as she did on him.

'I heard about the funeral, actually,' she says. 'From Paula.'

'Ah yes, I was going to say I bumped into her. She was just starting her shift.'

'At the pub, yes. I told you she'd got a job, didn't I?'

'You did. You said a bar job. You didn't say which bar.'

'Does it matter? She's gone out and found herself some paid employment for the first time, and she's sticking at it. I think it's commendable.'

'Have you ever been in the Lounger?'

'No.'

'I have.'

'From what Paula said, you didn't need to.'

This, then, is the source of the displeasure: Douglas, a bit tipsy in broad daylight, has caused embarrassment to her daughter and by extension to Sonya. Secretly I am quite pleased. It means she still feels a connection.

'It was my birthday. Aye, I'd had a drink, but I wasn't drunk. Anyway, I'm concerned about Paula working in a place like that.'

'Why? She can look after herself.'

'Couldn't she have got a job in Tesco or somewhere?'

'Oh, don't be so boring, Douglas. Everyone works in a bar at some stage when they're young. It's a rite of passage.'

'I didn't.'

'Well, quite.'

'I just don't think it's a good place for Paula to be.'

'How can you say that on the strength of one short visit? If it's not right she'll find something else. It's experience anyway. She says she's enjoying it.'

I remember Barry. 'Has she got a boyfriend?'

'I'm not sure. It's none of my business. Why?'

'I just wondered.'

'Well, it's none of your business either.'

The waitress returns with my food. My cheese-and-ham toastie, compared with Sonya's sandwich, looks old-fashioned and morally suspect, and my apple juice looks, yes, boring alongside her smoothie.

'So what else have you been doing?'

'Oh, this and that. I've been offered some work, actually.'

'Gosh, you and Paula both?' (I ignore the wee dig.) 'That's good. What kind of work?'

'For the *Spear*. They want me to write a feature or two, do some interviews. John Liffield, the editor, had me in yesterday. He seems serious about upping the quality of the paper's content.'

'Well, about time! Who are you going to interview?'

'Have you ever heard of Rosalind Munlochy?'

She shakes her head. For the first time since entering the café, I have an advantage over her, knowledge, as they say, being power. I immediately begin to abuse that power. I find myself not quite telling lies, but exaggerating, elaborating. I talk to Sonya about what a major national figure Munlochy is, or would be if she hadn't suffered such scandalous neglect. In spite of her impressive array of achievements, her critically acclaimed writings ('Have you not heard of her memoir, *Some Life*?' – waving it at her), her political career and activism, her feminism and all-round progressive credentials, she has been almost entirely forgotten. Now, though, the wheel has turned full circle, and she is going to be famous again, because by good fortune she is still alive, and about to enter her one-hundredth-and-first year. And it has fallen to me to interview her and write about her, and thus pluck her from obscurity.

Why do I say all this? Bluntly, because Sonya is more likely to lend me her car if my mission has an aura of cultural significance about it. That, at any rate, is the theory I am working on.

'Perhaps,' she says, gathering fugitive crumbs and salad debris with a lightly moistened fingertip, 'Rosalind Munlochy doesn't want to be plucked from obscurity. She may like it there.'

'I intend to establish whether that is the case this evening. I hope to speak to her on the phone.'

'How do you know if at her age she can even come to the phone, let alone hear you or be heard on it?'

'If she can't come to the phone, the phone can surely be taken to her. I have no reason to believe that she is mentally or physically so incapacitated that she can't have a conversation.'

'She's a hundred!'

'Ninety-nine. Perhaps we should be thinking of age as approximate. Years don't matter, only seasons.'

'That's rubbish.'

'Is it? It's been well established by behavioural ecologists that other species, if they conceive of time at all, think of it not as linear but as a circular progression of seasons. And why not?'

'Douglas, you just made that up. Anyway, we are not "other species".'

'Aren't we? Think of my father. Man or ape? He notices the time of year – he sees winter coming – but he doesn't care *what* year. And even though he's seventeen years younger than Rosalind Munlochy, I bet she's in better shape than he is.'

'You can't possibly know that.'

'It's highly likely. She's had boundless energy all her life. Dad had energy once but he used it all up fetching boxes of screws and lengths of pipe for joiners and plumbers. No reserves. It's a genetic thing, probably. There's high-octane blue blood in her veins, dirty diesel in his.'

'You are so full of crap, Douglas. How is your father, by the way?'

'Much the same. As before, I mean. That is, he has his ups and downs. When I saw him on Tuesday he had some of each. I'll drop in on my way home this afternoon.'

'Give him my best wishes.'

'I will. He might not remember who you are.'

'Really?'

'He didn't on Tuesday.'

'I should go and see him myself.'

She's been saying this ever since he went into the Home. I know she isn't going to go. So does she. Only Dad doesn't know, and he doesn't care. They never got on that well. Relations were always polite but strained. He didn't – probably the right tense, since he has forgotten who he is – like Magnus much; thought he had, as he put it, a good conceit of himself for no good reason. And then, when he was becoming ill, he made that lewd remark about Paula's breasts, and that pretty much put an end to communications between Sonya and Tom. That he couldn't help himself only made it worse, because that implied that what he had said was not just offensive but sincerely meant.

I suggest to Sonya that while a visit from her would be kind, it wouldn't necessarily be appreciated. She shouldn't feel under any obligation.

'I won't,' she replies, and this time her smile is warm and, I assume, genuine. Now, surely, is the moment to make my pitch. I clear my vocal cords with a sip of apple juice.

'Rosalind Munlochy does live quite a long way from here. Up in the wilds of wildest Argyll. Very difficult to get to on public transport. Almost impossible, in fact. I was wondering, do you think I could have the car for a couple of days?'

Note the subtle use of the definite article. This is because 'the car', a Volkswagen Polo in a rather fetching shade of red, is actually a shared asset. We paid for it together, and I am still a named driver on the insurance. Admittedly, we bought it quite a few years ago, and its value has plummeted in the interim, but nevertheless there is a principle at stake. The trouble is, the car has always lived outside Sonya's house, it is the car in which Magnus learned to drive and which he also uses from time to time, and a myth, which I should have challenged in its infancy, has morphed into an article of faith: that it really belongs to Sonya. Until now, this has never bothered me. I never need the car around the city. I don't even particularly like driving. But it would be very convenient to have the use of it for my proposed excursion to the West Highlands.

Give Sonya her due, she doesn't prevaricate. She comes back at me without a second's hesitation. Not, unfortunately, in quite the way I hoped.

'I'm sorry, Douglas, it's out of the question. Magnus needs it this weekend – he has an away game, and it's his turn to drive some of his teammates.'

'How is Magnus?'

'He's fine.'

'Give him my best wishes.'

'I will.' ('He might not remember who you are,' she doesn't add.)

'I wouldn't want to interfere with his rugby plans. I was thinking I could take the car next week some time. I'll work around your schedule.'

'Oh.' Again, she barely falters. 'No, I'm sorry, I need the car next week. We have a couple of out-of-town presentations to make and a lot of materials to transport. I've volunteered to drive. It will make a change to get out of the office for a day or two.'

'What days would those be?'

'What days were you thinking of going?'

'That depends on Mrs Munlochy.'

'Oh, that's too vague, Douglas. No, I'm sorry. You'll just have to hire a car.'

93

'I'd been hoping I could avoid that expense.'

'Won't the paper cover you?'

'Fuel costs but not car hire. The budgets are all shot.' I suspect this is true, but I haven't actually asked John Liffield because there is another problem, which Sonya has either forgotten about or doesn't think is a problem. A year ago, driving through the Borders visiting various locations for an article on tourism, I was pulled over for speeding – only 10mph over the limit, but that was enough. When they inspected the vehicle – Sonya's car, our car, the car, call it what you will – the police discovered that one of the tyres had insufficient tread on it. As a consequence, I have six penalty points on my licence. I've been checking, and thanks to those points I won't be able to hire a car from most rental firms, and the ones that might do business with me will charge extra premiums or impose massive excesses on the insurance. Basically – and I don't want to say this to Sonya, whose instinct is always to reinforce a defensive position once she has adopted it – if she doesn't help me, I am stuffed.

She sucks the last of her blood-and-bruises-coloured smoothie from the bottom of her glass. It is her way of drawing a line under that part of our conversation.

'So you can't help out next week? What if I postpone the interview till the week after?'

'And then how long would you want the car for? That's no good either, Douglas. Sharing a car when we live independently, in different parts of town, isn't going to work.'

'Is that what we're doing now? Living independently?'

'Now?' she says. 'You moved out months ago.'

'At your request.'

'It was a mutual decision, Douglas.'

'I didn't put up a fight, if that's what you mean.'

'No, you didn't. But then, that's not really you, is it? You don't ever put up much of a fight. And let's not forget the other reason why you went back to your parents' house. Or rather, why you never officially left it. Money, Douglas. Didn't that play a part?'

Three times in the space of half a minute she has used my name. This is a sign. I affect an affronted tone, partly to distract myself from the element of truth in her hurtful observations.

'If you are referring to the fact that I part-own the house, then you are being unfair. The fact that my parents transferred half the title to me ten years ago is fortunate in the present circumstances, I accept that, but the present circumstances didn't exist back then.'

'You were planning for them, though, or something like them.'

'I didn't plan for anything, but as things have turned out, you can't deny that it was a wise decision. Otherwise, as you well know, the authorities would treat the entire house as part of Dad's assets and it would have to be sold to meet his care costs. Then you'd be stuck with me whether you want me or not – which, evidently, you don't.'

'If you'd ever demonstrated that you really wanted to make a commitment – to me, to us – sorting out your father's care costs wouldn't have been a problem,' she says. 'We could have worked it out. But you never did make that commitment, did you?'

'I always paid my share of our bills. Yours and mine, I mean.'

'Exactly. You're always calculating. There's always been a credit column and a debit column in your head. You're like an old-fashioned grocer.'

'It's how the world works.'

'One house against the other. Theirs against mine. Yours against ours. That's not commitment, that's accountancy.'

Sonya, you are beautiful when you are mean, is what I am thinking.

'I thought you weren't going to discuss our relationship in public,' is what I say. As soon as I do I regret it, for it gives her a perfect cue to leave.

'You're right,' she says, 'but actually that wasn't about our relationship, it was about you.' She gathers her coat and bag. 'Anyway, I have to go now.'

'Wait!' This comes out a little too loudly, and with a hint of desperation in it that I really don't intend.

'What?'

'Dogs or cats? Which, on the whole, would you say are cleverer?'

'I don't know what you're talking about,' Sonya says, returning to a familiar refrain, but this doesn't stop me plunging on, or even breenging in.

'Most people would probably plump for cats, but if you think about it, dogs are more adaptable. They learn, and they don't forget what they learn. And also they collaborate.'

I don't know what I am talking about either. Sonya stands, gives me another of the pitying glances, this one laced with a little revulsion, and says, 'Cats, every time. Goodbye, Douglas. It was nice to see you, I think.

I'm sorry about the car, but I'm sure you'll sort something out. Now I must go.' She bends as if to kiss my cheek, thinks better of it halfway down, bobs up again and swishes out of the café.

I have eaten only half of my toastie and even that was too much. I knock back the last of my apple juice and leave too. Outside, the loose pages of countless bus and train timetables are falling from a ponderous, grey sky.

A TWELVE-POINT INCIDENT

'Oh, Mr Elder, you'll be in to see your father. Could I have a quick word?'

Beverley Brown, the Don't Care Much Home manager (although I usually think of her as a shade on a paint chart: I was once in the York-shire town of Beverley on a dull autumn day, which probably accounts for it), comes out of her office as I enter the building. She ushers me in and closes the door behind us. This is ominous.

'Please have a seat, Mr Elder.'

'Call me Douglas. Is something wrong?'

'Not really, but I do want to talk to you about your father's behaviour.'

So something *is* wrong.

'As you know, he can become quite distressed sometimes. Agitated. Not himself.'

'That's why he's here, though, isn't it? Because he's not himself.'

'Yes, I suppose you could put it like that.'

'I did.'

She throws me a look. 'Well, anyway. We feel we've got to know Tom – your father – very well in the time he's been with us. Now, when he's in one of his calmer moods he's absolutely no trouble at all. He's very amenable. That's when he is most content, most at ease with himself. Would you agree?'

'No. We can't be sure of that. He might be most content when he's stirring things up. Which I know he does from time to time.'

'Don't apologise.'

'I didn't. Has he been agitated today?'

'Yes, rather. And I wanted to tell you that before you saw him. You'll probably find him . . . not very communicative. Quite sleepy. And what I should explain is that it is our policy to manage our residents' behaviour with care and consideration, and to work with them to help them through any difficulties they may be having. It is absolutely not our policy, as far as possible, to medicate in order to calm somebody down. However . . .'

'However, sometimes you have to.'

'If they are a danger to themselves or to others.'

'I understand. Believe me, I know what he can be like.'

'Often all that's required is a mild sedative, a settler.'

'Not a chemical cosh, then?'

'Certainly not. Who do you think we are?'

'A good question. I often ask it myself. "Who do I think we are?"'

'I'm sorry?'

'Don't apologise. There's no easy answer. "My name is Legion, for we are many."'

'Mr Elder –'

'Douglas. Please go on. I interrupted you.'

'The difficulty is persuading someone to take medication when they are in a confused or, shall we say, non-cooperative state of mind.'

'I see. What was my father doing?'

Beverley Brown refers to a page in a ring-binder lying on her Beech Blond desk. I realise that Dad's misdemeanours have been written down. A record of all the drugs they give him is also supposed to be kept but, being one who cowers behind parapets, I've never asked to see it. I wonder how many bad-behaviour penalty points he has accumulated, and if there is an upper limit which triggers an automatic ban on – well, on what? Physical movement? Continuing to be himself, whatever or who-ever that is? Life?

'Well, he didn't want any lunch. In fact, he didn't want it so much that he threw it against the wall.'

'Oh dear.' (Six points at least.)

'Something had clearly upset him.'

'Clearly. What was it?'

'Scotch broth, and mince and potatoes. Quite a lot ended up on him.'

'I meant, what had upset him?'

'Ah, if only we knew. He came along to the dining room readily enough but when he got there he seemed to think he'd come for something else. Not a meal, I mean.'

'Well, that can't be unusual, surely?'

'No, but he thought he'd had a trick played on him and he didn't like that. Then he refused to leave. He is surprisingly strong when he doesn't wish to move.'

97

'It is surprising, isn't it? He's not that big a man. Was he shouting?'

'Oh yes.' (Another three points.)

'Swearing?'

Beverley allows herself a smile. 'Spectacularly.' (Three points redeemed for creativity.)

'Lashing out if anyone went near him?'

'I'm afraid so.' (Wipe out the previous deduction.)

'What happened next?'

'He fell over. I'd come in to help and he took a swing at me – please don't worry, Mr Elder, I'm very good at dodging – and lost his balance. He didn't hurt himself but it took the wind out of his sails for a minute and that enabled us to get him into a wheelchair and along to his room. But he was still quite distressed so we did give him a sedative. I just wanted you to be aware. He's been dozing since then.'

'By my calculation that's a nine-point incident.'

'I'm sorry?'

'Don't apologise. I'd say you handled it pretty well.'

'Oh. Thank you,' she says, turning Gratified Pink.

The kind of scenario she is describing is not unfamiliar to me. I remember that occasion when Dad decided he was going to lift all the carpets in the house to check that the floorboards were properly nailed down. When I said he didn't need to do that he thought I was saying *he* wasn't needed. I probably spoke more sharply than I should have because he had a claw hammer in one hand and a long-bladed screwdriver in the other, and had already made a start in one of the bedrooms. It was a tense moment. In the end, after the hammer had missed my head and gone through the window, we had a kind of wrestling match on the bit of carpet he'd managed to prise up.

'Mr Elder?' Beverley Brown's voice brings me back to the present.

'I'm sorry. I was reminiscing about a twelve-point incident we had, not long before he came here.'

'We don't operate a points system,' Beverley says sternly.

'Perhaps you should introduce one. A bit of competition among the inmates. Sorry, residents.'

The thing is, once I had him in a bear hug, or he had me in one, we just clung on to each other, grunting and gasping, and then we both started laughing. All we could do was lie there, clutching each other's sides. Apart from the broken window not too much damage was done.

'I don't think so.' Beverley Brown rises. 'Thank you for your under-standing, Mr Elder. I appreciate it.'

'Please call me Douglas, Beverley,' I say.

'Douglas Beverley?' she says. No she doesn't, but she does regard me with curiosity, as if sizing me up as a future client. If I were in her shoes, that's what I'd be doing. She opens the door and lets me out and I begin the long walk to Dad.

The other thing about the carpet-lifting episode is that after the laughter came the tears: floods of them, first from him and then from me, because we knew that our lives were changing and there was nothing either of us could do about it.

And yes, Beverley is right, he is very sleepy. He is the least violent, obstreperous, stubborn old man you could ever hope to meet, snoozing away his autumn days in a clean jumper and a Moderation Beige arm-chair. When I kiss him he opens his eyes and stares at me with knowing unknowingness, or possibly unknowing knowingness or some other vari-ation on a theme by Donald Rumsfeld. I am not at all convinced that he recognises me.

'What's up, Dad? Did you get angry at something, earlier?'

He raises a hand and tries to point – at me, I think – but the finger wavers and the hand drops again.

'What was it? You didn't fancy what they were giving you for lunch?'

He mutters something. His eyelids flutter. I lean in closer.

'What's that?'

Another mumble.

'Sorry, Dad. Could you say that again?' I put my ear right up to his lips, and he speaks, and what I can just make out is:

'Drink your coffee.'

'Ah.' I move back. 'You don't like being told what to do, is that it?'

No response. Maybe he doesn't like being told he doesn't like being told what to do. Then his eyes close again, and I wonder if he has even heard me. I doubt he takes in what I say next, either: that I have to go away and that he won't see me for a few days. Sonya sends her best wishes and might put in an appearance. (Some chance! Even though she can come by car and park in one of the visitor spaces.) Zero response to that, too. So I tell him to be good and kiss him goodbye, and leave him be.

Before I head off I seek out Beverley Brown and inform her of my planned absence. I have previously informed the Home of my mobile number in case of emergency. They already have my landline number and, because I haven't updated the information, still have Sonya's as well. They have all the information *they* need, and – once I have spoken to Rosalind Munlochy and consulted the online bus and train timetables – I should have all the information *I* need. How lucky we are, compared with Dad! How cursed is his life without information and the capacity to act upon it in a rational manner!

Notice the irony. For all I know, there is a whole world spinning within the confines of that skull, a multiplex, surround-sound experience compared with which the wildest possibilities of the outside world are mere pale flickerings. And in the middle, seated in an armchair marked Director of Operations, is my father, Thomas Ythan Elder.

FURTHER EXTRACT FROM NOTES FOR AN AS YET UNWRITTEN BIOGRAPHY OF MRS ROSALIND MUNLOCHY, NÉE STRIVEN, BY MR DOUGLAS FINDHORN ELDER, AUTHOR; COMPOSED FROM SUNDRY PAPERS, INFORMATION GATHERED IN CIRCUMSTANCES BEYOND THE SCOPE OF THE PRESENT WORK, ETC. COPYRIGHT. ALL RIGHTS RESERVED. THE MORAL RIGHT OF THE AUTHOR WILL BE ASSERTED IN DUE COURSE

London in 1932 was, as it ever has been, a heaving mass of human activity, a city of endeavour, opportunity, inequality, wealth and squalor. Greater London at that time had a population of more than eight million – including numerous strivers, idlers, grafters, plodders and visionaries, with the vast majority simply trying to make a living and have some cash left over at the end of every week. While unemployment levels soared in Scotland, Wales and the North of England, London and the South fared better. Light, modern industries less adversely affected by the global slump were located there, and new factories and businesses catering for a growing consumer society continued to be established throughout the 1930s. But London, too, had its slums and desperate poverty, and radically different political groups clashed often on its streets. A few weeks after Rosalind alighted from the sleeper and went to stay with a cousin in Bloomsbury, contingents of National Hunger Marchers arrived from all over the country and were greeted by a crowd of a hundred thousand in Hyde Park. Thousands of police were mobilised against them by Ramsay MacDonald's National Government, and violence ensued. Rosalind and her cousin – a music teacher who lived a mildly bohemian life among other musicians and teachers – had gone to support the marchers, and were caught up in the trouble, which continued across central London for several days. The cousin took fright and retreated to her flat, but Rosalind was exhilarated by the experience and stayed out on the streets. She fell in with a thoroughly disreputable, therefore thoroughly attractive, set of socialists, anarchists, writers and artists, joined the Communist Party and began to write poetry and fiction herself.

Over the next two years she immersed herself in political campaigning at both local and national levels, devoting much of her energy to opposing the rise of the British Union of Fascists. Her first novel, *The Hindered*, was published by Victor Gollancz in 1935 when she was just twenty. It failed dismally, but despite this Gollancz published her controversial polemic, *What Must We Not Do?*, the following year. In this short work she attacked moral authoritarianism and advocated free love, contraception and the right of women to control their own reproductive systems. She also had a volume of poetry published by the Buff Coat Press of Putney.

Rosalind moved between the world of her family connections and that of her intellectual and political engagement in London. Thus during her childhood and young adult years she knew or rubbed shoulders with a wide range of people from many walks of life. Among them were Robert Bontine Cunninghame Graham (after whose late wife she would name her first daughter), Sydney and Beatrice Webb, C. M. Grieve ('Hugh MacDiarmid'), Neil M. Gunn, Rebecca West, George Bernard Shaw, Beatrix Potter, Duncan Grant, Aldous Huxley and Vita Sackville-West.

Although she left the Communist Party in 1936 and joined the Labour Party (believing that only the election of a genuine Labour Government offered a realistic chance of establishing socialism in Britain), she had married the communist poet Guy Merriman (b. 1905) the previous year. This intense, sometimes tempestuous relationship produced a daughter, Gabriella, in 1936. In 1937 Guy went to Spain to fight for the Republic: he was killed in the failed offensive on Zaragoza that September. His body was brought home by a fellow member of the International Brigades, Ralph Elphinstone Munlochy (b. 1903), and was buried in Highgate Cemetery.

Ralph already knew Rosalind slightly. He was the eldest son of Lord

Munlochy, one of Scotland's senior judges, who despite his established position approved of his son's political stance against the rise of European fascism. Rosalind and Ralph, consoling each other over the loss of her husband and his friend, became lovers. In 1939 they married, and left London to run a farm on land owned by Ralph's father in Easter Ross.

Until this time, Rosalind had continued to use her own name of Striven for all purposes except legal ones, but she now adopted the surname Munlochy – 'as an act of appreciation, not as an act of surrender', she wrote to a friend. They managed the farm together until 1942, when Ralph returned to London to work as a liaison officer with the Free French Forces. That same year Rosalind's mother was incapacitated by a stroke, and Rosalind left Easter Ross for Glentaragar House to care for her and to help her sister, Jemima, run what remained of the estate.

Of her three brothers, the eldest was a Professor of Physics at Oxford, the second a cartographer in South America and the third a civil servant in the War Office. None of them had any interest in Glentaragar, and after Jemima married an Australian cattleman in 1946 and emigrated to Queensland, neither did she. Rosalind thus became the de facto inheritor of the house and land when her mother died in 1947.

Before this happened, however, she had succeeded in having herself adopted as Labour candidate for the local constituency in the General Election held in July 1945. The Labour Party had never come close to winning the seat in the past, but her opponents' votes were split between a Unionist, an Independent and a National Liberal, and Rosalind slipped through the middle and was elected with a majority of 147, much to the horror of local religious leaders who abhorred many of her opinions. By this time she and Ralph had two children, Gregory (b. 1940) and Georgina (b. 1942), half-brother and half-sister to Gabriella. Ralph wholeheartedly supported his wife's new political life and remained at Glentaragar for the next five years, running the estate and looking after the children and Rosalind's mother while she divided her time between Westminster and the constituency.

Despite all this activity Rosalind had found time to write two more novels, *Wild Hyacinth* (1941) and *Unto These Be Given* (1944), which had received mixed reviews. Printed in small runs owing to wartime paper shortages, they have never been reissued.

Her parliamentary career was brief. Despite being part of Labour's landslide majority, and despite the energy and ambition of Attlee's first government, she found the House of Commons a stultifying environment, dominated by men, and preferred to concentrate on local issues, such as crofting and grazing rights and the improvement of rural housing. She also championed access to further and higher education for women, and worked closely with Tom Johnston, Secretary of State for Scotland, on the hydro-electrification of the Highlands, although she did not accept that all modernisation was necessarily beneficial. 'So much supposed economic improvement,' she said in a House of Commons speech, 'turns out to be neither economic nor an improvement.' She was also a vociferous advocate of Scottish Home Rule even though that longstanding policy had been dropped from Labour's election manifesto.

At the 1950 General Election Rosalind lost her seat to the Liberal candidate, and indeed was narrowly beaten into third place by the Unionist. She described her defeat as a 'Liberal liberation', and remained on excellent terms with that party's local representatives for many years. In 1952 she resigned from the Labour Party and was briefly a member of the Scottish National Party. In the 1960s she was an Independent Councillor on the County Council. Criticised for being a political butterfly by Baron Ross of Marnock (William Ross, Secretary of State for Scotland under Harold Wilson), she responded, 'It is better to have wings and fly than to remain forever in a cocoon.'

[To be continued]

EMPLOYEE OF THE MONTH

'Hello? Is that Glentaragar House?'

A brief interlude follows. Not exactly a silence. It is as if my question has to travel through a disused railway tunnel or along a narrow lane overhung with trees before arriving in a gloomy hallway.

'It is.' The voice sounds surprised by its own confirmation. It is very faint and could belong to either a man or a woman.

'Would it be possible to speak to Mrs Rosalind Munlochy?'

After a slightly longer interlude, the voice replies, 'It would.' There is a definite West Highland intonation and a measured slowness to this short phrase.

'Thank you. My name is Douglas Elder. I'm a journalist. I work for the *Spear*.'

Silence. I listen for the sound of the receiver being laid down, or of retreating footsteps, or of a door banging, or of a few words explaining to a third party that a Mr Elder of the *Spear* is on the telephone, but nothing happens. And after a minute I begin to doubt that the person at the other end of the phone has gone away at all. I am pretty sure I can hear breathing.

'Hello?'

'Hello.'

'You're still there?'

'I am. And you, too?'

'Yes. I am waiting to speak to Mrs Munlochy.'

'Oh, you want to speak to her?'

'Yes, I thought you were away to tell her.'

'No, no.'

'Well, how was she going to know I was waiting?'

'She wouldn't know that. You should have said.'

'I did say.'

'You only asked if it would be possible to speak to Mrs Munlochy.'

'To which you replied that it was.'

'No. I said that it would be. That is a different matter.'

'Well, may I speak to her now, please?'

'No, I am sorry, she is not available.'

'And to whom am I now speaking?'

'You are speaking to me.'

At this point I lose patience, which is something a journalist seeking an appointment for an interview should not do.

'And who the hell are you, for God's sake?'

'That is a big question, especially the way you have phrased it. A very big metaphysical, not to say ontological, question.'

I take a deep breath. 'Look. No, scratch that. Listen. My name is Douglas Elder, I am a journalist working for the *Spear* newspaper, and I wish to arrange to come to Glentaragar House some time next week in order to interview Mrs Rosalind Munlochy. Would you please convey that message to her?'

Again, silence.

'Are you still there?'

'Yes,' came the reply. 'Douglas. Elder. Journalist. Not Douglas Fir, then?'

'No! What are you doing?'

'I am writing down your request. What about?'

'What do you mean, "What about?"'

'What is it you wish to interview Mrs Munlochy about?'

'Well, everything. Her life. Her views on politics, culture, and so on. Just a general interview.'

'A wee chat?'

'No, not a wee chat! An interview, a formal interview.'

'I was just checking. I was using shorthand, you see. Very well, "formal interview" it shall be. I will pass the information to Miss Munlochy, who looks after Mrs Munlochy's diary.'

'*Miss* Munlochy?'

'Miss Coppélia Munlochy, yes.'

'Is she there?'

'Who?'

'Miss Munlochy.'

'Oh yes.'

'Well, could I please – no, please ask her to come to the phone so that I can make the arrangements directly with her.'

'That will not be necessary, as I have written it all down now. You are coming for an interview. Life, politics, culture, and so on. No chat. Yes, I am sure it will be fine. We will see you next week, then.'

The voice now sounds more masculine, though still soft and slightly high-pitched, and it seems to be floating away down that long tunnel. I am suddenly anxious that the call is not terminated.

'Yes, but what day will I come?'

'What day suits you?'

'I don't know. You see, I don't know how long it will take to get to Glentaragar. I am in Edinburgh.'

'Edinburgh? My goodness. Well, that will take you a while, yes indeed it will. If you were coming from Fort William, or Oban even, that would be far enough, but Edinburgh – well, well! What day is it?'

I feel like I could be having this conversation with my father. 'Today? Today is Friday.'

'Och, but you should manage fine to get here by next week in that case. Shall we say Tuesday?'

'Are you sure?'

'Three days should be ample, even from Edinburgh.'

'Yes, but I thought Miss Munlochy would need to consult the diary.'

'In theory, yes, but there is never anything much in it. Tuesday will be fine, I am sure.'

'I'd better give you my number, in case it isn't.'

'Och, that will not be necessary.'

I utter my next words with great deliberation. 'I would rather that you add my number to what you have already written down, and pass it to Miss Munlochy. Just. In. Case.'

'If you insist.' The speaker – I am now convinced that it is a man – sounds put out, as if his intelligence or his probity has been questioned, a suspicion not without foundation. Slowly and distinctly I read out the eleven digits of my mobile phone number, and slowly and indistinctly he repeats them. I picture a white-haired, crook-backed retainer – a gardener or butler perhaps, the last remaining servant – laboriously copying the figures out in thick, soft-leaded pencil.

At last it is done. 'You have my number now, so that either Miss Munlochy or Mrs Munlochy can contact me if for any reason Tuesday is no good.'

'It will be fine,' is the reply.

'And what is your name? You have been so terribly helpful.' As if I might put him up for Employee of the Month, when really I just want to know who to blame when everything goes wrong.

'My name is Corryvreckan,' he says, at which moment I understand that I am dealing with a lunatic. 'We will expect you on Tuesday.'

'Oh, there is one other thing –' I start to say, but this time the line does go dead. I was going to ask about nearby bed-and-breakfast accommodation. I contemplate another call in the hope of getting through to one of the Munlochys, but am too dispirited to make the attempt.

CONVERSATIONS WITH A TOAD: CONVERSATION #3

Douglas Findhorn Elder opened the back door of what was half his and half his father's house – the house in which he had grown up, which he had never really left and which, one day perhaps not too far off, would be wholly his – and looked out into the night. The moon was a not quite circular disc of pale luminosity in the October darkness. Its big face shone benignly on the stone slabs of the patio or – as it had always been known in the family – the *sitootery*; or – as his father used to refer to it on wintry mornings or evenings – the *skitery*. This was no such evening, the temperature still being unseasonably warm, but Douglas was not tempted to set foot upon that sometimes treacherous surface in any case. His single purpose was to ascertain whether his bufonidian acquaintance, Mungo Forth Mungo, was present and, if so, to invite him inside for a small soaking of wine.

'Beautiful, isn't it?' came the low and, to Douglas's ears, sweet croak of the toad, from some black spot not far from the patio.

'Ah, Mungo,' Douglas said. 'Good evening. Where are you?'

'Here,' Mungo said, unhelpfully.

Douglas peered but saw nothing. He found his heart fluttering with intense anticipation. That he should be communing with a toad!

'What is beautiful?' he asked.

'The moon, of course,' Mungo replied, as he hauled himself into view over the lip of the patio.

'Were you under there?'

'Where else?'

'That's your home?'

'And that's yours. Why this perpetual astonishment at the idea that I lead a normal, regulated life?'

'I apologise.'

'I accept.'

Douglas took a step beyond the door in order to get a clearer view of the moon, and the security light came on.

'Sorry.'

'It's all right. Stand still and the full splendour will be restored in due course.'

In due course it was. Man and toad, they stared together into the sky. It occurred to Douglas that, although he had often admired the moon, he had never before realised quite how lovely it was.

'To think,' said Mungo, shuffling closer, 'that each one of us has one! Amazing, isn't it?'

'It is,' Douglas replied. He did not wish to be irritating, but he was confused. 'One what?'

'Moon,' Mungo said dreamily.

'Do we? Where?'

'Where what?'

'Where is it – where are they – kept?'

Mungo stroked his chest with the splayed fingers of one hand. 'In here.'

There was something different about him. He seemed, in the moonlight, ragged at the edges. Had he been human, Douglas would have said he was in need of a haircut.

'You have a moon inside you?'

'Naturally. What did you think I meant?'

'I wasn't sure. Not as big as that one, presumably?'

'Oh, much the same size. And it changes shape in the same way, over and over again. Sometimes it doesn't appear to be there at all, but it is. It is always there.'

'I see.' Douglas considered how to pose his next question without causing offence. 'Is this peculiar to toads, or does every living creature have a moon in its chest?'

'Since you ask the question, I assume that you don't feel it yourself, then?'

'No.'

'Ah. That's such a shame. It's a wonderful feeling.'

'*You* feel it?'

'Oh yes. I told you before that we are uncommon. Perhaps we are even more uncommon than I thought.'

'Yet you lead a normal, regulated life.'

'Even the commonplace is uncommon. It has only to be recognised as such.'

'There is a legend, among us humans, that you keep a jewel in your skull.'

'Well, it's easy to see how that arose. A moon is a kind of jewel, after all.'

There were moments when Douglas felt that neither he nor the toad could have spoken. Yet this discussion was taking place in spite of that feeling. He tried to be awake, and found that he already was. Therefore he could not be dreaming.

'Would you like to come in?'

'I would,' Mungo said, 'but I have some business to attend to first.'

'Take your time. I'll go ahead and open a bottle of wine.'

Leaving the door ajar, Douglas went inside. On a chair in the kitchen lay a bowel-screening kit, which had arrived in the post that day. He transferred it to the worktop, not wishing Mungo to spot it and ask awkward questions about what, from the information he had so far read, was going to be an awkward procedure. He prepared a dish of wine for the toad, poured himself a glass, and waited.

Mungo did not appear.

After twenty minutes, Douglas went to look for him.

The toad was crouched on the tiles of the back lobby, arching his vertebral column and apparently either resisting or exerting some considerable force.

'Are you all right?' Douglas asked. He could see the rapidity of the toad's palpitations.

'I'm . . . fine.' Mungo continued to strain at something. Douglas wondered if he was constipated. Then he peered a little more closely. Mungo was splitting in two, right down the middle of his back. And he was pulling at each arm, first with one hand, then with the other, as if trying to brush something off or remove a pair of lady's evening gloves. And plucking at his throat too, like a man trying to loosen his tie.

'Mungo, are you sure?'

'Yes, yes,' Mungo said. 'It's all coming along nicely.' He was now peeling great flakes from his arms and chest and stuffing them into his mouth with hardly a pause. 'Last of the season. Late this year,' he mumbled, and began to shrug himself out of the rest of his skin.

Douglas watched, fascinated. Mungo was like a worker ridding himself of his overalls at the end of a shift, the difference being that he was eating the overalls.

When he had finished, he belched and sank down into himself. A soporific silence descended. After a few minutes Douglas was startled to discover that, although still standing, he had fallen half-asleep. He looked down at Mungo, whose eyes had glazed over. Had the toad somehow mesmerised him?

'All right now?' Douglas asked quietly.

Something happened to Mungo's eyes: the clarity came back.

'More than,' he said, in what was hardly more than a whisper. 'Very nutritious, toad skin. And not just for toads.' He fumbled around his body. 'Look, I missed some. Want to try it?'

Douglas hunkered down. Mungo was holding a tiny scrap towards him, something less in volume than one of the many bits of dead flesh he had chewed from his own fingernails. Yet he felt an inner revulsion and it must have shown on his face.

'Are you a vegetarian?' Mungo asked.

'No.'

'Then you are being unreasonable. I can think of much less palatable things to eat.'

Still Douglas hesitated.

'Some would consider such an invitation a great honour,' Mungo said. 'And to refuse it, a great insult.'

What possible harm could it do? Delicately, Douglas took the offering and put it on his tongue. Was there a momentary hint of something acidic? He couldn't be sure. He swallowed.

'I have heard,' Mungo said, 'that in some human societies people will pick toads up and lick them. There's something in us that gives them a kind of . . . kick. I've never seen this revolting practice – revolting for the toad, that is – but I don't doubt that it happens.'

'Perhaps some of your moonlight gets into them,' Douglas said.

'That could be it. I understand there is a sect in a place called Arizona that goes by the name of the Church of the Toad of Light. About your offer of wine – I'm feeling quite full. Don't let me stop you, but if you don't mind I'll watch – as you did just now.'

They went into the kitchen. Douglas was surprised at how fast Mungo could move when he chose to, and this despite his recent meal.

'How was your meeting with Sonya?' Mungo inquired when they were settled, Douglas at the table and the toad wedged against the kickboard below the sink unit.

'Not so good,' Douglas said. 'She says her son needs the car. And then she needs it. In short, I can't have it.'

'What will you do?'

'Travel by other modes of transport. Buses and trains. A taxi may be necessary. I'm going to investigate the options later.'

'This is in order to find this other woman. What is her name again?'

'Rosalind Munlochy.'

'Last night you said it would be a long journey. Where to?'

'The other side of the country, and further north. The Highlands.'

'Ah, the Highlands.'

'You've heard of them?'

'Yes. I've heard they are beautiful. Will it be cold?'

'I doubt it. It's so mild everywhere.'

'Hmm.' Mungo's expression glazed over again.

'Did something happen to you just now?' Douglas asked. 'Your eyes changed.'

'Changed?'

'Became, I don't know, less focused. But now they are as they were before.'

'I was thinking. When I think deeply it is as if I go underwater. When

I go underwater my eyelids slide into place. They're transparent, so I can see where I'm going. That's probably what you're noticing.'

'Like goggles?'

'No. I have no control over them. They operate automatically, like your security light. How is your novel coming along?'

'I've not made any progress since yesterday,' Douglas said. 'I'd hoped to do some writing this evening but I was distracted by a difficult telephone conversation.'

'Would you care to tell me the outline of the plot?'

'Are you interested?'

'Why would I not be?'

'Nobody else is.'

'Who is nobody else?'

'Sonya. And my friend Ollie.'

'Well, perhaps it's not to their taste.'

'That's likely, but to be honest I haven't shared much of my work with them. I've not got very far with it.'

'Tell me about it, as far as you have got.'

'Very well.' Douglas refilled his glass while he collected his thoughts. Then he cleared his throat and began.

'The story is about a man who goes on a journey to the back of beyond. Douglas Findhorn Elder is sent on a mission which looks straightforward enough, but unexpected things happen to him along the way. Ostensibly he is a journalist whose task is to secure an interview with Rosalind Munlochy, a woman of immense wealth, power and influence who runs her complex business empire from its secluded headquarters in the Scottish Highlands. An air of mystery surrounds Munlochy, who has not been seen in public for many years and is said to have become a recluse owing to the devastating effects of a wasting disease on her appearance. In fact, Elder is a member of the British Security Services, and Munlochy is suspected of being the criminal mastermind behind a fiendish plot to destroy human civilisation by releasing a deadly virus, after which most of the planet will be transformed into an enormous wildlife park. Elder has to uncover and then disrupt Munlochy's plans, if necessary by assassinating her. Having gained entry to her heavily defended redoubt in Glentaragar, Elder finds that Munlochy, far from being disfigured by disease, is healthy, beautiful and seductive. A deadly sexual and intellectual game of cat-and-mouse ensues, from which there can be only one victor. After three days –'

'Douglas,' Mungo said.

'What?'

'Douglas, this is – how can I put it? – absolute pish.'

The author blanched. 'Oh, you think so, do you?'

'I know so. As we discussed previously, books don't have any appeal for me, but even I can tell that the narrative you have just outlined has neither artistic merit nor even the advantage of an original plot-line. How much of this drivel have you actually written?'

'Not much.'

'Well, that's a blessing.'

'I'm still at the sketching-out phase.'

'If I were you, I wouldn't bother moving to the colouring-in phase. Not unless I wanted to be a laughing stock in literary circles. I assume literary circles are what you wish to move in?'

'Not really.'

'Well, what do you want? Money?'

'No.'

'Fame?'

'No. I just think I have a book in me. They say everyone does.'

'Leave it there, is my advice.'

'You're worse than Sonya or Ollie.'

'I'm merely honest. "The toad's tongue grows from the front of his mouth, and so he cannot lie." Do you know that old proverb?'

'No.'

'That's because I just invented it. Please don't take offence at my candour.'

Douglas sighed. 'I don't. You're right. I knew it was pish myself. The whole idea, I mean. No doubt that's why I've only written a few hundred words.'

'That much?'

'You're probably doing me a favour by being so frank.'

'I am.'

'May I ask you something?'

'You may.'

'How do you know all this human stuff? Literary circles and plot-lines, and so on?'

'As I said before, we acquire knowledge differently from you. It's very informal. I've really no idea how I know it, but I do. We've been around a long time, and we've been around *you* a long time too. One of my ancestors – don't ask me which, I have no interest in genealogy – spent much of his life in the apron of a woman who was held to be a witch by the idiot peasants who surrounded her. I expect a lot of it comes from him. He had a narrow escape when they burned her. He'd gone for a nap under the kindling and only just got out in time.'

'You know,' Douglas said, 'if you had a bunnet on your head –'

'A what?'

'A bunnet. A flat cap. Tweed or tartan design. If you had one on your head you would be a dead ringer for Chic Murray. I don't suppose you've heard of Chic Murray?'

'Oh, come on, Douglas! Everybody's heard of Chic Murray.' Mungo had no eyebrows, but he did have a bulging gland full of bufotoxin set behind each eye, and now the left one appeared to rise slightly. 'Do you really think I'm like him?'

'I do.'

'Well, I'm flattered. But, Douglas, something else about this so-called novel of yours. *You're* in it. You appear to be the principal character. Yet this is a work of fiction?'

'It's only a name. I thought I'd use my own until I thought of a better one. It's not really me, that character.'

'I understand authors often say that, usually disingenuously. In this instance, it is true. He certainly isn't you, by the sound of him. But he *could* be. Have you thought about that? You could ditch that ludicrous plot and come up with a better one. You wouldn't even need to use your imagination, you could simply let art imitate life. Your novel could be thinly disguised autobiography.'

'Then it wouldn't be a novel.'

'Of course it would. That's all fiction is, isn't it? And suppose you did go down that road, as it were. Might there be – I mean, there might be, depending upon how it developed – room for other characters based on, well, real-life acquaintances of yours. Don't you think?'

'Mungo,' Douglas said.

'What?'

'Are you angling for a part in my novel?'

'Am I –? Ha! Preposterous idea! No, no, no! I meant Sonya, or this fellow Ollie, or your father. But since you mention it, the Highlands in their autumn colours would, I imagine, be rather romantic. And it is so mild! I'm not in the least bit inclined to hibernate. I have always wanted to travel,' he added wistfully.

'So you said before. Have you any idea what I mean when I talk of "a long journey"?'

'I wasn't proposing to crawl.'

'Are you proposing to come?'

'If I'm invited, I might consider it. Who else is going?'

'Nobody. Just myself. It's a working trip, not a jaunt.'

'I see.' Mungo studied the lino pattern for a moment. Then he said, 'What about your father?'

'What about him?'

'You can't leave him, surely?'

'He'll be all right.'

'But wouldn't it be good for him to get out of that place you've put him in?'

'No, Mungo, it would not. And it would be very bad for me. How would I manage to interview Rosalind Munlochy *and* stop my father getting into trouble? That's assuming I was able to get him to Glentaragar without incident, which would be impossible.'

'There you are, talking about things being impossible again. Next you'll be saying the whole expedition will be a disaster.'

'It would be if my father came along.'

'You are very hard on him.'

'I am not.' Douglas found himself growing heated. 'Look, taking him with me is out of the question. It was bad enough having him here in the house while I tried to write. I couldn't turn my back on him for five minutes.'

'You said that before.'

'Well, it's true. No wonder I've not made any progress.'

'Aha! Now we approach the crux of the matter. You consigned him to that home place for your own selfish ends – so that you would have peace and quiet to fulfil your literary ambitions. What a despicable way to treat your own flesh and blood! What vanity!'

'Don't talk to me of vanity! You're the one who wants to be immortalised in a novel!'

'I put it to you,' the toad continued, suddenly adopting the look of a corpulent QC, 'that your father is not the only casualty of your scheming. Is it not the case that you also engineered the break-up of your relationship with Sonya so that you could reoccupy your parents' house, oust your father from it and thus create the ideal space for gratifying your desire to write fiction?'

'That is absolute nonsense. You don't know a thing about it, you, you – toad!'

During much of this exchange, as Douglas's voice had begun to rise in volume, the toad had remained pressed up against the kickboard, but towards the end he had moved into the centre of the floor, and had raised himself on all fours in a provocative manner. Now, he relaxed again and wiped something indefinable, and possibly non-existent, from his right eye.

'Excellent, excellent,' he said. 'That was splendid, Douglas. Much better than that Secret Service rubbish you were spouting a few minutes ago. This is the stuff of real literature – the ordinary life made extraordinary. It's shaping up beautifully. Now, when are we leaving?'

Douglas stared at him. 'You were winding me up?'

'Yes, yes. Never intended that your poor old father should come along on our trip. Quite impractical.'

'You made me lose my temper.'

'Well, you can see the dramatic potential, can't you? But never mind about that now. When do we go? Tomorrow? The next day?'

'You want to come with me?'

'Thank you, I'd love to. "Haud me back," as I have heard it said hereabouts. We'll not get away tonight, I assume, as you will need to research our transportation options and make the necessary arrangements. All I will require is a large pocket, so make sure you wear a decent-sized jacket or coat. I'm very flexible when it comes to sleeping accommodation – can kip down almost anywhere – and although my bladder does sometimes get very full I will do my best to relieve myself in places and at times that don't cause you embarrassment. I know how fussy you humans can be when it comes to waste disposal. Well, I shall leave you to it, Douglas, and return to my humble abode perhaps for the last time for who knows how long. How exciting! Good night.'

Mungo almost broke into a run as he left the kitchen. Douglas stood up and pursued him. 'Wait!'

'Yes, indeed, you'll need to open the door for me,' Mungo called over his shoulder, without easing his pace.

'I will,' Douglas said, 'but it's not that.'

'What's not what?'

'I can't take you.'

Mungo halted at the door. 'Why not?'

'Because I can't. I can't be responsible for you. What if something happens? You might get lost, or squashed –'

'Or murdered with a graip, or picked off by a passing crow, or I might catch my death of cold. Douglas, these things could happen here, at any time. I'm old enough to make my own decisions. I won't be any trouble, and I won't blame you for any trouble there is. Not unless it's your fault. Take me with you.'

There was no arguing with him. He was smaller than the size of one of Douglas's fists, but in the end the man could not refuse the toad. The door was opened, Mungo slipped out into the moonlight, and Douglas returned to his computer to investigate the various ways of getting from the city of Edinburgh to Glentaragar House, Glentaragar, Argyllshire.

[To be continued]

VARIOUS WAYS OF GETTING FROM EDINBURGH TO GLENTARAGAR, AS GLEANED FROM NUMEROUS WEBSITES, MAPS, BUS AND TRAIN TIMETABLES AND ONE LONG SATURDAY-MORNING TELEPHONE CONVERSATION WITH A HELPFUL WOMAN IN THE TOURIST INFORMATION OFFICE, OBAN

1. Drive. If you are unable to drive, do not own a car, own a car but do not have access to it, or are not able to hire a car owing to the penalty points on your driving licence, then this method will not be available to you.
2. Walk or cycle. These methods are unrealistic given the time and distance involved.
3. Hitchhike. It is a very long way, the weather conditions may not be conducive to standing at the roadside for long periods, and in the closing stages of your journey the limited availability of passing vehicles may prove a particularly challenging barrier to success. This method is also not advised if your time is restricted.
4. Take a train or a bus to Fort William (via Glasgow in both cases) or a train or a bus to Oban (via Stirling by bus, via Glasgow by train). On arrival at one or other of these destinations transfer to a local minibus service (see 5 & 6, below) for the next stage of your journey. It is possible to alight at a number of stops along either of these routes and await a local service bus connecting to the aforesaid minibus service (see 5 & 6, below) for the next stage of your journey. However, this is not advised as these connections are

116

infrequent and unreliable, and indeed non-existent at weekends and on Wednesdays.

5. From Fort William, catch the local minibus service (see 4, above), which runs on Tuesday and Friday mornings via Loch Glass and Glen Araich to Glen Orach, returning on Tuesday and Friday afternoons. If using this service, alight at the Glen Araich Lodge Hotel (see 7, below, for the next stage of your journey).

6. From Oban, catch the local minibus service (see 4, above), which runs on Monday and Thursday mornings via Glen Orach and Glen Araich to Loch Glass, returning on Monday and Thursday afternoons. If using this service, alight at the Glen Araich Lodge Hotel (see 7, below, for the next stage of your journey).

7. It may be possible (this information acquired informally, and with no guarantee as to its accuracy, from the helpful woman in the Tourist Information Office, Oban, who had it from a colleague to whom she referred for advice) to arrange a lift from the Glen Araich Lodge Hotel (see 5 & 6, above) to Glentaragar, should you make known to the hotel reception desk your desire to reach that destination, and should any vehicle be travelling in that direction. Alternatively it may be possible to borrow or hire a bicycle from the hotel.

    7.1. N.B. The Glen Araich Lodge Hotel is not open all year round. Its seasonal opening hours are not readily identifiable and (again, this information acquired off the record) are said to be irregular, and to vary according to the whim of the management.

8. If wheeled transport is unavailable, follow the unclassified road on foot westward from the Glen Araich Lodge Hotel (see 5, 6, 7 & 7.1, above) for approximately two miles, to the junction at Fairy Bridge. Take the left fork and follow the road for a further two miles, where an unadopted road is reached. This leads after half a mile to Glentaragar House.

    8.1. N.B. This road is not suitable for caravans and some other types of vehicle.

    8.2. There are no suitable landing facilities for helicopters or aeroplanes at or in the near vicinity of Glentaragar House.

The phone rings out for an age when I call on Saturday morning, and I am on the point of giving up when somebody answers – somebody, I am relieved to hear, who is not the Corryvreckan character with whom I previously spoke. Again, there is that slight time lag before the voice – female, and of indeterminate age and class – reaches me.

'Glentaragar House.' Clearly she feels no obligation to identify herself.

So we begin again. 'Good morning. My name is Douglas Elder. Am I speaking to Miss Coppélia Munlochy?'

'You are. It was you, wasn't it, who telephoned last night about an interview with my grandmother?'

'Yes, it was. I'm delighted the message got through. To be honest I am quite surprised that it did.'

'Oh? Why?'

'Well, when I spoke to somebody who called himself – I think it was a he – Corryvreckan, I wasn't sure that he was . . . that he had . . .'

'That he had what?'

'Taken down all the details.'

'Corryvreckan is an absolute stickler for details,' Miss Munlochy says a little frostily, and I imagine her in a certain way. 'I conveyed your request to my grandmother and she said, I quote, "If Mr Elder can be bothered to come all that way to see me then I can be bothered to speak to Mr Elder." So that's all right. We are expecting you on Tuesday on the bus from Fort William. Are you telephoning now because you have changed your plans?'

'No, not at all. I have just spent the last hour or so trying to work out the simplest way of reaching you.'

'You can spend a lot longer than an hour doing that, Mr Elder. The fact is, we aren't very simply reached.'

'So I've discovered.'

'How were you thinking of travelling?'

'By train.'

'To Fort William? That would be your best option. You will need to take the first train from Glasgow on Monday, the half-past eight, stay in Fort William that night and come on to Glentaragar on Tuesday.'

'That's my intention.'

'Be sure to get on that train. There are later ones but that is the best one to take. In case of cancellations.'

'Thank you, I will. The reason I'm phoning again is because I wondered if you could advise me about accommodation. It does look as if I will have to stay for a night or two if I am to interview Mrs Munlochy in depth.'

'Or if she is to interview *you* in depth.'

'I'm sorry?'

'An interview is a two-way process, is it not?' Again, I imagine Miss Munlochy in a certain, not very positive, way. 'Yes, you will certainly have to stay.'

'I'm assuming that the Glen Araich Lodge Hotel is the closest place where I could get a room.'

'Oh, I wouldn't make that assumption at all. Have you tried contacting the hotel?'

'Yes, but there is no answer.'

'That's perfectly normal – for the Glen Araich. I think a better idea is for you to stay here.'

'That's very kind. I don't want to impose on you.'

'It's more of a necessity than a kindness. Don't worry, you won't be an imposition. You must take us as you find us. If you arrive here on Tuesday, you'll be able to leave on Thursday. That means you must take the bus *from* Fort William when coming, and the bus *to* Oban when departing. Will that be an inconvenience?'

'It may be complicated, but it won't be inconvenient.'

'Good. There isn't really an alternative. Do you know this part of the world at all?'

'No, I'm afraid not.'

'Well, I would come prepared for all eventualities – including the weather. Is there anything else?'

'Well, there was one thing. Does Mrs Munlochy keep in good health – given her age, I mean? Is there anything I should know beforehand? Is she hard of hearing, for example?'

'Hard of hearing? Not at all. My grandmother keeps very well. Of course, she tires a little sometimes, but who doesn't? The bus should let you off at Glen Araich about midday. I shall see if Corryvreckan is available to bring you on to the house. It's a bit of a walk otherwise.'

'That's very kind.'

'Again, Mr Elder, it is really more of a necessity.'

Once more I imagine Miss Munlochy. It is most unfair of my imagination but I can't stop it conjuring up a cliché – a tight-lipped, dowdy, tweed-and-twinset-clad woman, old before her indeterminate time, dutiful, embittered, lonely – but that's as developed as the cliché gets because at this point in the conversation I become aware of furious rattlings of the letter-box flap in my front door, interspersed with energetic stress-testing of the door's wood and long bursts of pressure applied to the bell.

'Miss Munlochy, you will have to excuse me. Somebody appears to be trying to break down my door. I'd better go and find out what's happening.'

'Yes, you had,' she says. 'Now, don't forget, will you, to be on that eight-thirty train from Glasgow on Monday?'

'I won't. I must go.'

'Until we meet, then,' she says, 'goodbye,' and she hangs up before I can say goodbye back – which for some unaccountable reason leaves me momentarily bereft. The din outside continues. Imagining that fire or flood must be engulfing the house or that some emergency is unfolding in the street, I hurry to the door and open it.

'Oh, you're in?' says Ollie Buckthorn. 'I thought you were out. Any chance of a coffee?'

'Jesus, Ollie, I couldn't have got here any faster. Stop ringing that bell or you'll break it. And do you have to bring that inside?'

He is wheeling a bicycle past me which he proceeds to prop up against one wall, beneath a painting of snow-capped mountains, purple heather and hairy cattle, an example of the Scotch Realist School much admired by my mother.

'I do,' he says. 'No padlock, and I hear this part of town is awash with disreputable characters who can't resist the opportunity of an unsecured bike loan. But don't worry, it's dry outside. The tyres will have hardly any muck on them. What about that coffee?'

'Aye, all right, all right. I'll make some fresh.'

'Wouldn't want it stale,' he says, and bowls ahead of me straight through to the kitchen, as if he has done the route countless times. No doubt the residual smell of breakfast toast is a clue. In fact he has never been here before, as our friendship has been maintained purely in the workplace and sundry social venues such as pubs and cafés. I put the kettle on to boil.

'I got your address from Grant,' he says, draping his rump over a wooden chair. 'And as it was such a lovely morning, and my day off, I thought I would seek out my former workmate Douglas and see what he gets up to at the weekend now he's an idle layabout.'

'Rich from you, that,' I say. He is wearing filthy old trainers and a faded blue tracksuit with white stripes. The muddy bottoms of it hardly extend to his plump hairy calves, the sleeves are rolled up to his elbows, and a T-shirt that has come adrift below the top reveals rather more of Ollie's girth than I care to view. With his sweaty red face and wild hair, he is a picture of neither sartorial elegance nor sporting physique.

'At least I got on my bike and pedalled, as Jesus exhorted the sick fellow,' he says. 'Or was that Norman Tebbit? I've been thinking, Dougie – thinking and worrying.'

'What about?'

'About you. Have you set up this interview with the Munlochy dame yet?'

'I was in the process of doing just that when you started demolishing the front of the building. You interrupted me in the middle of a conversation with her granddaughter. Whose name, by the way, is Coppélia.'

'Is that significant?'

'Just unusual. It's the name of a life-size doll in a French ballet. There's also a mad old servant called Corryvreckan.'

'In the ballet?'

'No, at Glentaragar House, which is where Rosalind Munlochy lives.'

'Ah, you've located her? Corryvreckan: isn't that a whirlpool up the west coast somewhere?'

'It is. Top end of the Isle of Jura.'

'That's not where this Glentaragar House is, is it?'

'No, it's on the mainland, but as far as I can make out it's about fifty miles from anywhere. Can't find a picture or anything else about it online, but I've been invited to stay for two nights.'

Ollie looks concerned. 'You'd better take a big ball of wool with you so you can find your way back. Or leave written instructions here in case you don't. Life-size dolls and mad old servants named after whirlpools? It sounds as safe as a bag of snakes.'

'It'll be tedious and staid, and the biggest health hazard will be damp sheets. Potentially good background copy for the article, though.'

'What a pro you are. Got anything to eat? A bacon roll or a cheese omelette, something like that? I haven't eaten since breakfast.'

'It's only half-past ten.'

'Ah, but this cycling lark plays havoc with the old calories. Even just a biscuit would help.'

I fetch out an unopened packet of digestives and Ollie sets about processing them with the efficiency of an assembly-line robot. Between bites, and gulps of coffee, he quizzes me more about my impending excursion to Argyll, but I sense that this isn't the real reason for his visit, and indeed it is not.

'Now, I said I was going to have a word with you about this novel-writing carry-on, Douglas, and that's what I'm here to do. You can talk to me, you know. Don't hold back. Tell Uncle Ollie all about it, from the beginning.'

'I don't need counselling, Ollie. Everybody has a book in them. I just want to see if I can write mine. It's that simple.'

'No, no, no. I don't care about that. Tell me about the novel itself. How does it start?'

'Hang on a minute. On Thursday you point-blank refused to hear anything about it.'

'I was too hasty. We go back a long way, old chum. If you've decided to write a novel, I should at least give you some moral support, even if I have to be the one, finally, who says, "Elder, it's no good. Give it up and go back to the day job. Deal in facts, my boy, not fairy tales."'

'You'd say that, would you?'

'Perhaps not in those exact words but, yes, I would. Home truths. That's what friends are for. So tell me, what's the basic premise? What's your pitch? Imagine I'm a literary agent or a publisher.'

I am touched by his change of tune. 'Well, if you genuinely want to know . . .'

'I do, and what's more I have big money to spend if it's the right book.'

'The thing is, I've been doing some restructuring. You pick up bits of advice, feedback, and it makes you see things afresh. Everybody's got a different take.'

'What? You've not been sending your book out to other agents, have you? That's a serious breach of protocol.'

'No it's not.'

'It is.'

'It might have been back in that golden age of the classics you were going on about the other day, but not any longer. Anyway, I've not sent it to anyone. I haven't even written it. And you're not a literary agent, you're Ollie Buckthorn, eating my biscuits.'

'Role play, Douglas, role play. Who's been giving you advice? Not Sonya, I sincerely hope. Delightful girl though she is – to look at, anyway – she wouldn't know a potential bestseller if it bit her ankles.'

'No, not Sonya. Do you want to hear an outline of the story or not?'

'Fire away.'

'Well, it's about a man who goes on a journey. He is sent to a place he's never been before, on a mission which looks straightforward enough, but unexpected things happen to him along the way. You wouldn't know this from the opening, though, because everything seems so normal. In the opening scene this fellow is sitting on a bus, thinking about the fact that it's his birthday and he doesn't care and neither does anybody else. He's having a kind of existential crisis, haunted by doubts about whether there's any purpose to life and so forth. He's male and middle-aged, which is what has triggered these morbid thoughts. He realises that he has less time left than he's already used up. His immortality warranty is about to expire. You get the picture. Anyway –'

Ollie raises a hand like a policeman on point duty. 'Hold it there.'

'What?'

'What was that thing you mentioned just then?'

'His immortality warranty.'

'Right you are.'

'Anyway –'

'Sorry to interrupt you in mid-flow, but it all sounds quite Kafkaesque.'

'Thank you.'

'It's not a compliment, it's a nightmare. Did you say this all takes place on a bus?'

'That's correct. A number 11 Lothian bus, as it happens.'

'Oh dear God, no. You're off entirely on the wrong foot.'

'How so?'

'A middle-aged man on a bus, having morbid thoughts about his birthday? How many pages does this go on for?'

'Quite a few. I know when you put it like that it doesn't sound –'

'Quite a few? You mean more than one? What's keeping him there? Has he committed a crime? Robbed a bank, perhaps? He's given the police the slip for the time being but he has this sack full of money and now he's sweating over what his next move is going to be – is that it? Or is he a good guy on the run, and if so who's after him? Is there a bomb on the bus? Has he put it there and now can't get off because his foot has become trapped under the seat in front? *That* would be something to worry about. What's *happening*, Douglas?'

'Actually the bus is stuck in traffic and it's going to make him late for a funeral.'

'Aha!' Ollie strikes his forehead with his fist. 'I see where this is coming from. You've fallen for that old trap set by teachers with no imagination: "Write about what you know." This isn't fiction, Douglas, this is autobiography *disguised* as fiction. Quite different.'

'Some would say that's what fiction mostly is.'

'Well, they're idiots. Fiction is heroes and villains, explosions and car chases, and sex in high places – aeroplanes and the Oval Office, that is, not trees.'

'Oh, like Jane Austen and Anthony Trollope?'

'I'll ignore that. Fiction is the places most of us never get to go, the things we only ever dream of doing. It isn't sitting on a bus feeling miserable about the ageing process.'

'That's your view. Somebody else would say the precise opposite, and that if I go along the populist lines you're describing I'll be a laughing stock.'

'Well, you'll never please a snob.'

'Who's a snob?'

'You tell me. This fount of wisdom you've been consulting.'

'I've not been consulting anyone.'

'Protecting your sources, eh? Well, whoever they are, they sound like they've got a ramrod up their respectable arsehole. It's up to you, of course, whose advice you follow, but I'd have thought the views of a dear old colleague such as I might count for something.'

'Erstwhile.' I am not expecting this. It pops out by accident, and not a drop of Glen Gloming in sight.

'What's that?'

'Worthwhile. Your views are. Very much appreciated. What I still don't understand is why you're interested now.'

'I just want to help,' he says, demolishing another digestive. 'What strikes me most about your protagonist is his banality. He needs livening up. As you've just admitted, you're harbouring a misconception as to what this fiction game is all about. Autobiography in disguise, I think was how you put it.'

'No, that's how you put it.'

'Well, let's not split hairs over who said what. Now listen carefully, and don't take this the wrong way. As a fellow human being, Douglas, you're one of my favourites, and I'm seldom happier than when in your company, but – how can I put this? – you don't exactly fill a room with your presence when you walk into it. An author whose preferred mode of existence is loitering in the wings can't just take his own personality, dump it centre-stage in a false beard and expect it to sparkle. And an author is what you're aspiring to be, isn't it? Your readers are going to see the failings of this character straightaway, and they won't sympathise with him, they'll despise him. Whereas if you have someone with a bit of panache as your main attraction, someone who thrills the readers, keeps them guessing as he leaps from one sentence to the next, someone larger than life who's roaring drunk one minute, single-handedly foiling an international consortium of arms dealers the next, then rushing off on his bike to rescue some children from a burning building –'

'Ollie?'

'It is I.'

'You want to be in my novel, don't you?'

'What? Why would I want to be in a novel? I despise modern fiction. My life is overflowing with excitement as it is. Mhairi keeps begging me to ease off on the high achieving. Less is more, Ollie, she says. Only this morning she was warning that if I didn't pace myself I'd burst. "You big balloon" – those were her very words. However, if you thought there might be mileage in using me as some kind of model for your hero I'm not going to stand in the way of your art. I won't sue you for libel or plagiarism – not unless you say something really offensive. I won't even object if you give him my name.'

'Oh, that's a relief. For a moment there I thought I would have to come up with something original. Any other reason for your visit this morning?' I am, it is fair to say, a little pissed off with Ollie.

'Loyalty, Douglas, loyalty, which I'm sorry to say seems to be in short supply on your side of the relationship.' Somehow he manages to say this in an Ollie-like way that I don't find offensive. There is a twinkle or a strobe effect or something happening in his eye. 'Actually, there is something else. Has John Liffield been in touch with you about your interview with La Munlochy?'

'Not since I saw him, no. Why?'

'He said that he forgot to discuss pictures with you. He can't afford to send a photographer all that way, so would you ask for a couple of historic images of her – as an MP or author or local laird or whatever. If nothing doing, take a few snaps with your phone and we'll do what we can with them. How antique *is* your phone?'

'I believe it can take photos, but I've never tried it.'

'Well, see what you can get from her or her minders.'

'Anything else?'

'Yes. Liffield said if I happened to bump into you to mention how essential it is to get a particular bit of information out of her. In the course of a comprehensive, in-depth, wide-ranging review of her life and achievements, you've to find out how she voted in the referendum.'

'Liffield said that?'

'Absolutely. And I was to make sure you understood it before you headed off into the wilderness. If I happened to bump into you. Which I have now done.'

'That's not what he said when he offered me the work. He said that was all over. The referendum was history and he wasn't interested in whether someone had voted Yes or No.'

'Well, don't shoot the message-boy. That was Thursday. Things move fast in the media world, you know.'

'I'll need to check with him.'

'Don't you believe me?'

'It's not that. For a start, Mrs Munlochy might not be willing to tell me.'

'Why wouldn't she?'

'Sanctity of the secret ballot?'

'Your arse. What's she got to lose? She's ninety-nine, isn't she? It's hardly going to damage her reputation if she lets the cat out of the bag now, since she doesn't appear to have one. A reputation, I mean, not a cat. She might have a cat.'

'Do you reckon in today's Scotland the way you voted in the referendum can do you reputational damage?'

'Good question. Let's examine it. Being pro-independence used to be fruitcake territory, but now it's mainstream. It's about public perception, isn't it? How will Rosalind Munlochy want people to *think* she voted? Suppose she voted Yes. That makes her a gallant loser, a proud Scot dignified in defeat. Then again, suppose she voted No. She's on the winning side. No harm in that. Hanoverian pragmatism wins out over Jacobite romanticism. On the other hand, it's a bit shameful, isn't it, voting against your own country's freedom. It's like being a Scottish soldier on the government side at Culloden: you've come through the battle alive and intact, for which you are mightily grateful, but then you're ordered to bayonet the wounded. Leaves a bad taste in the mouth, quite apart from blood on the bayonet. So why would she admit to voting No at her age, and with her political past? She wouldn't. Even if she did vote No, she'll tell you she voted Yes. That way she gets the right pragmatic result but can still bask in the glory of her own romantic sunset. The only scenario I can't envisage is if she voted Yes but lies to you that she voted No. Nothing to be gained there, as far as I can see. On balance, then, it's almost a certainty she'll say she voted Yes. So, since we already know the answer, where's the difficulty in asking her?'

'It's not what I was asked to do.'

'You're a journalist. You have to seize the opportunity. It's not as if anybody's being coy about how they voted. I voted Yes, but then where I come from we don't have any of your Caledonian hang-ups about separation from England.'

'You're from Ireland, for God's sake.'

'Yes, but there's Ireland and then there's Ireland. Anyway, I'm from Dublin, which is different again. My point is, Grant voted Yes. Roy voted No. We're all still the best of chums. How did you vote?'

'That's my business.'

'What?' Ollie looks genuinely surprised. 'You're not going to tell me?'

'Maybe I'm coy.'

'Dougie, this is Ollie, your old mucker.'

'Like you said, I'm a journalist, after a fashion. I'll certainly be a journalist when I do the Munlochy interview. It's not appropriate to say how I voted.'

'Not appropriate? Bollocks. You don't have to tell her, but you can tell me.'

'Why? Maybe I want to keep my opinion to myself. Maybe, being the writer, I'm the best judge of how to write this thing.'

This is not meant to be a dig at Ollie's critique of my novel, but it sounds like one, even to me. Our stares meet and grapple for a few seconds, then he drops his.

'Can't force it out of you,' he says. He looks hurt, and falls into silence, reaching for the last of the biscuits to ease his troubled soul. That's the whole packet he's gone through. I don't think he even realises it. Yet I'm the one who feels guilty.

The thing about Ollie is, you can't keep him down for long. His vision drifts around the kitchen and settles on the bowel-screening kit and accompanying literature on the worktop. He stretches for it with glee.

'Ah, you've joined the dreaded catch-your-own-crap club.' He sifts through the instructions and finds the sheet of six cardboard sticks. 'But I see you've not started the test yet.'

'No, I thought I'd wait till I get back from Argyll. Looks like it might be easier in the sanctity of your own bathroom.'

'No question. My second test came round just a few weeks ago. They ask you to do one every two years, did you know that? I tell you what, it doesn't get any easier. The whole concept is totally counter-intuitive. All those years of potty-training and toilet-flushing and then in your fifties they say, forget all that, put your hand under your arsehole and shite in it. I know they also tell you to fold up some toilet paper and catch it with that but it's the principle of the thing. Then you've got to dabble about in it with a stick. It's unnatural.'

'You're not making it sound easy.'

'It isn't easy.'

'The leaflet says it is. "Quick and easy," it says.'

'Well, it would, wouldn't it? Tell me what animal in its normal habitat behaves like that? The only time I ever saw that trick was when I took the kids to the zoo once, and the chimps were at it, but they had a purpose, which was to chuck their doings at us to show what they thought about being locked up and gawped at. A kind of dirty protest.'

Sounding a bit like a public-information announcement on the telly, I remind him that the purpose of the bowel-screening test is to detect early-stage cancer.

'Yeah, well. You can line up all the rational arguments you like but none of them trumps basic human instinct. I just couldn't do it the first time, especially with the size of my arse. I find it hard to get round to physically. Even when I thought everything was in place and I was ready to release, my sphincter muscles went into protest and clammed up. Not natural, you see? I would have given up but Mhairi kept on at me. "You have to do it," she says, like it was a civic responsibility. I must have been on holiday at the time because I was in the house a lot and she was out at work. One morning I look out and here's this giant Alsatian dog having a steaming crap on our garden path. I bang on the window and he gives me this challenging look back and carries on, coils and coils of it, so I go out to the doorstep and ask him to take his business elsewhere, in fact I don't ask him, I tell him in no uncertain terms and what does the bastard do? He growls at me. So I says, "Don't you fucking growl at me," and the dog says, as he squeezes out a final question mark, "Right, so what the fuck are you going to do about it?" and I think to myself –'

'The dog said that?'

'In a manner of speaking. That was when I had my idea. I waited till he'd buggered off, then went and got the testing kit and took a couple of samples before I cleared his mess away.'

'You put dog crap on your bowel-testing kit?'

'Well, I was desperate, and Mhairi was nagging me, and it was such a relief to have Day One ticked off. The next morning when I go outside there's another enormous load sitting on the path, which had the same features and which I therefore concluded had come from the same Alsatian. I don't know what he was eating but he wasn't going hungry, that's for sure. So I go back for the gear and collect Day Two's samples. On the third morning I'm waiting for him, and sure enough the Alsatian turns up and leaves me my third lot of samples. He thinks he's insulting me but in fact he's saving my life. So I date and seal the kit and stick it in the envelope and post it, and that's me done. Funny thing is, I've never seen that dog again from that day to this. Sometimes I think he must have been an apparition or a miracle or something.'

'Jesus, Ollie, that was totally irresponsible.'

'You're telling me,' Ollie says. 'No lead, no muzzle, and he looked like he could tear your leg off in a moment. The owner should have got a hefty fine at least.'

I give him a look. He gives me a sheepish one back.

'Yeah, yeah,' he says. 'So ask me what happened when the test results came back.'

'What happened when the test results came back, Ollie?'

'Well, two envelopes arrived on the same day about a week later. One was a letter and the other was a little Jiffy bag. The letter said there seemed to be some problem with my samples and they'd like me to do the test again. I put that in the bin. The letter, I mean. In fact I burned it so Mhairi wouldn't find it.'

'And what was in the Jiffy bag?'

'A bottle of de-worming tablets.'

'What did you do with them?'

'I flushed them down the toilet. What the fuck was I supposed to do with them? We don't have a dog,' Ollie says, and he starts laughing, and I can't help joining in. I really haven't a clue whether he's been telling me the truth or not – anything is possible in the world of Oliver Brendan Buckthorn.

'The thing is, though,' he says, getting serious again, 'Mhairi thought I'd done the test, so when it came round again this year I couldn't get out of it. I just had to knuckle down and do it properly. That was about a month ago, and would you believe it, they sent me a repeat test. Nothing to worry about at this stage, they said, but they'd found blood traces, so could I do it again? It was like I was getting punished for fucking them about the first time. So I did it, and now I'm waiting, and what I'm saying to you, Douglas, is – do the shite and do it right. Because you never know.'

From having been irritated five minutes earlier, suddenly I am concerned for him. 'Are you okay? Do you feel well?'

'I don't feel any different than usual, but that's the point, isn't it? How would you know? This way, if there's anything wrong, they find out early. Do the test, my man, that's what I'm telling you.'

He scrabbles about in the packaging for another biscuit, without success. Then he stands up, towering over me, and adopts a quavery, Mr Chips kind of voice.

'Well, Elder, I'm glad we had this little chat. I hope you'll bear in mind everything I've said. Now I must be getting on – Third Form Latin beckons. And remember' – he wags a fat finger at me – 'the three rules of good literature: write about something of which you are utterly ignorant, don't split your infinitives and, most importantly, no self-abuse after lights out!'

I thank him for being such a stout fellow, and he tells me not to be so fucking sizeist, and by the time I have convoyed him to his parked bicycle we are brothers once more. He pulls something from a pocket of his tracksuit bottoms and hands it to me: a little pack of cards, about three inches by two in size.

'Almost forgot,' he says. 'I ran these off on the office printer for you. Don't tell Liffield, but I thought they'd come in handy. The paper's name might still carry a bit of weight and influence until yours rises to the giddy heights of fame. Good luck, old wanker!'

He wheels the machine down the garden path and mounts it, and I fancy I hear the tyres groaning in pain. I read the topmost card. DOUGLAS F. ELDER, FREELANCE WRITER, it says, and in the lower-right-hand corner is the logo of the *Spear*. No email address, no website, but there is a mobile phone number which isn't mine.

'In case you're wondering,' Ollie says, 'the number is mine. I couldn't risk putting the office number on it in case one of the interns answered and denied all knowledge of you. But I thought if anyone did call, wanting to check if you were bona fide, I'd be able to vouch for you. Smart, eh?'

The card wouldn't pass muster with the Trades Descriptions Act, but it may open a door or two if the doorperson doesn't inspect it too closely, and it is good to have Ollie as backup. Probably. He's printed about a dozen of them.

'Thanks, Ollie!'

'Remember to take the ball of wool!' he shouts as he wobbles off down the street.

'I will!' I shout back. But I am lying. Somewhere in the course of our discussion I have reached a decision: I am going to be the hero of my own story. I am going to be bold, or at least bolder than I have been for most of my life. Fifty is the new twenty! No checking the terms of the mission with John Liffield! To hell with that – *I* will decide which questions to ask the Munlochy woman! And no ball of wool, actual or metaphorical, to guide me home! What could be less adventurous than to be certain, even before setting off, of finding my way back again? For that is what I am doing – going on an adventure, to the back of beyond! Do I know where I'm going? No! Do I care? Not much! The only certainty is that the back of beyond is further than Douglas Findhorn Elder has ever been before!

2

CONVERSATIONS WITH A TOAD:
CONVERSATION #4

Douglas Findhorn Elder felt movement in the left-hand pocket of his tweed jacket. He had been expecting it for some time, and was only surprised that he had had to wait so long for the sensation. It told him that Mungo Forth Mungo, who had been as inanimate as a stone since leaving Glasgow more than two hours earlier, was awake and likely to want to talk.

The train was making steady progress between hills still wearing their rich autumnal robes. Above the rising moorland, grey clouds and patches of blue sky jostled for predominance. Flecks of rain struck the window occasionally but the weather did not seem too unpleasant. So far, Douglas thought, so good.

The carriage was almost empty. Several people dressed for outdoor exercise, equipped with rucksacks and walking poles, had left the train at Crianlarich, a few more at Tyndrum, and now only five human passengers remained: two Chinese women wielding guidebooks and cameras, presumably on holiday; a girl of about sixteen wearing headphones and reading a book; an elderly, ruddy-faced man who, Douglas mused, could have been a farmer or retired policeman, or perhaps a clergyman returning from a weekend of sin in the big city; and Douglas himself. The others were all seated towards the far end of the carriage. Douglas had chosen a seat that was protected from observation unless you happened to be walking past it, and nobody was. The refreshments trolley was long gone; the ticket inspector had done his duty between Glasgow and Dumbarton and not been seen since; all was peaceful. Douglas's raincoat and small suitcase with wheels and extendable handle were stowed above his head in the luggage rack, and a copy of the *Spear* was folded on the seat next to him, comprehensively read. He had a book in his suitcase but for the time being had had enough of reading. If Mungo was up for conversation, so was he. They could talk quietly without anyone noticing, and anyone who did overhear them would most likely conclude that Douglas was either on his phone or talking to himself, a harmless eccentric.

Mungo emerged, crawling up Douglas's jacket until he was at chest height. Douglas lowered the foldaway table attached to the seat in front, and the toad reached out with one hand and swung himself onto it. He settled himself in the circle designed for the placement of a cup, glass or bottle.

'Where are we?' he asked.

'Rannoch Moor,' Douglas said. 'At least I think we are. I've never been quite sure where it starts and where it ends.'

'Where what ends?'

'The moor. It's a very large expanse of . . . well, moor. Miles and miles of heather, grass and bog.'

Mungo peered out through the glass. 'Looks fine to me.'

'Aye, well, it's right up your street. Wet, and full of insects. How is your new coat?'

'Wearing in nicely, thank you. Remind me of our plan again?'

'*My* plan, Mungo. We should be arriving in Fort William in about an hour and a half. I'll find a guesthouse or hotel for the night, check where we catch the minibus to Glen Araich in the morning, and then we can take a walk round the town. I haven't been in Fort William for years. There used to be a good Indian restaurant. I quite fancy a curry this evening.'

'Do I have a say in where we go?'

'No. It's probably not a good idea taking you into a restaurant. Perhaps you could forage about outside while I'm eating.'

'Thanks a lot. Do you remember that discussion we had about waste disposal?'

'I remember you saying something about it.'

'Well, you're going to have to put me down on the floor. I'll be as discreet as I can, but my bladder is full.'

'For God's sake, Mungo. Let me go and get a paper cup or something.'

'Can't wait. It looks like somebody's spilt something under the next table. I'll go there and no one will notice.'

Douglas put out his palm and Mungo climbed in. He felt very heavy and very full.

'You must be about to burst!'

'That's why I thought I should get out of your pocket. Thanks.'

'Thank *you*.'

A minute later Douglas noticed a long thin stream tracking down the aisle in a steady and quite powerful flow. He felt guiltily responsible, as if he had allowed a child or pet to urinate on the floor. No doubt he *was* responsible: there was probably some regulation against carrying wild animals on board trains. Yet nobody who knew Mungo Forth Mungo, Douglas thought, could describe him as 'wild'. He was one of the most urbane, sophisticated toads one could hope to meet, and he was an adult, well able to take responsibility for his own actions. And was toad urine any more offensive than spilt coffee or juice?

Douglas felt a tug at the hem of his left trouser leg. He reached down and brought Mungo back to the foldaway table.

'Feeling better?'

'Much.'

'I should think you would be.'

'Now I'm hungry.'

'You'll have to wait.'

'Could we not go and find that woman with the sandwiches?'

'And what filling would you fancy? Coronation beetle? Ant salad?'

'Very amusing. I'd eat anything right now. I'm ravenous.'

'If she comes back I'll buy something and we can share it. Look at the view. That might take your mind off food.'

The clouds were winning their contest with the sky. Far to the west big mountains rose from the moor, but their tops were lost in a grey blanket. This landscape was alien to Douglas, who had never had much desire to venture far from the city, let alone go camping or hike up steep hills.

He became conscious that Mungo was not admiring the view but staring intently at him.

'What is it now?'

'Tell me more about Sonya,' Mungo said. 'Why don't you like her?'

'I do like her. What makes you think I don't like her?'

'When you speak of her it is not with any warmth. And you're not in a "relationship" with her any more, that's what you said. So I assume you don't like her.'

'Well, a relationship's a two-way thing, isn't it? It doesn't follow that you live with someone just because you like them. As it happens, I do like her. I find her very attractive, and she can be charming, but she's not easy to live with. Neither am I, though, or so Sonya would tell you – not that you and she are ever likely to have a conversation. That's really why the bidie-in relationship ended – mutual domestic incompatibility. It was her decision.'

'She requested you to leave?'

'She kind of persuaded me, with looks and glances and a running commentary on my shortcomings. When I suggested that she might prefer me to go she agreed like a shot. So: my suggestion, her decision. Does that make sense?'

'Not really. Why are you difficult to live with?'

Douglas sighed. 'Sonya used to get frustrated because I wasn't ambitious enough, assertive enough or passionate enough for her liking. She finds me altogether quite irritating.'

'Passionate enough for what?'

'To satisfy her idea of what an ideal relationship should be like.'

'It sounds so complicated. Can't you just have sex with one another and forget the other stuff? That's what *we* do, every spring.' Mungo sighed. It was a very different sigh from Douglas's.

'We're not toads, Mungo, that's the thing. We're human. We aspire to certain dreams and lifestyles, and the problem is, the reality never matches the dream. Or the lifestyle.'

'Never?'

'Some people say it does, but I think they're deluding themselves.'

'You would think that, I suppose,' Mungo said. And then he added quickly, 'I'm not judging you. As a matter of fact, I find you very easy to live with – so far!'

'Thanks.'

'Nae bother,' Mungo said, in a joco tone and with a little Chic-like swagger. At that exact moment the train shuddered and lurched sideways, nearly dislodging him from his perch. One of the toad's hands went to his head and he gave it a couple of taps, a hot and a cold.

'Almost lost my bunnet,' he said wryly. 'What happened there?'

'I'm not sure,' Douglas said. 'A dip in the track or something. We seem to be still moving, though.'

'It's made me feel rather queasy. If it happens again, I'm going back in your pocket. What were we saying?'

'You were asking about Sonya.'

'Ah, yes. How did you two get together in the first place?'

Douglas could hardly remember. It seemed to him, sitting in that railway carriage, that he had known Sonya for ever and that their relationship had never been relaxed or simple. Of course that wasn't the case. Years before, in the glory days of print media, or at least when the sunset still looked glorious, there had been a staffer at the *Spear* – Chloe or Claire or Claudia, he couldn't even remember her name – whose sole job had been to review exhibitions and write stories about art and artists, and this Clarice or Clemmy or Clodagh had persuaded Douglas to accompany her to some opening at a gallery, and a friend of hers was there, and that friend was Sonya, and Douglas found her, as he had told Mungo, very attractive, and they began to talk, and Sonya responded positively to his friendly attention – his singular and unthreatening attention – and perhaps (he thought later) this was because it was only a year or so since her partner Ben, the father of her children, Magnus and Paula, then aged twelve and seven, had walked out of the relationship and gone to Australia where he took up with another woman who had no children. And perhaps another reason why Sonya responded positively to Douglas was that Ben was a bully and Douglas wasn't a bully, she could see that, and furthermore he didn't baulk when she mentioned her children, he didn't shy away as if a relationship – if there was going to be one – with a woman with two children would be too complicated. On the contrary, he seemed very open to the idea that she came with two other small human beings, as it were, attached (although on that particular evening, a rare occasion out for Sonya because she did not have much money, they were being looked after by a babysitter), and this was because Douglas, in his late thirties, *was* open to being in a relationship with a woman in her mid-thirties with two children, since he quite liked the idea of parenthood but had never wanted to go through all the hassle of being in a relationship that changed from being sexual but non-procreative to one in which the procreation of other human beings became the prime purpose of the sexual element. He had had a few sexual but non-procreative relationships before and had enjoyed them, but they were usually brief and often ended because the other (always female) person involved wanted to change the purpose of the sexual element of the relationship from mere pleasure to procreation and he didn't, whereas now – or rather then, all those years ago – if he and Sonya became an item (as seemed likely because after two hours in each other's company they agreed to meet again, and they did, and then again, and then again with Magnus and Paula in tow, so that they *did* become an item) he could have a sexual relationship without the worry or risk of it becoming a procreative one because the procreation had already been done and Sonya was adamant that whatever else she might want out of a relationship the one thing she did not want was *any more children.* Which suited, or seemed to suit, Douglas Findhorn Elder perfectly. Although, as was now evident, it hadn't.

'All these relationships!' Mungo said, when Douglas had explained everything. 'I couldn't bear it. And so hedged around with ifs and buts and whereases. I'm amazed you humans ever get anything done at all.'

'We're not typical,' Douglas said. 'At least I'm not. But the achievers are often not very nice people. Not considerate people.'

'It seems to me you are both well out of the whole thing.'

'I'm not sure that I am out of it.'

'Oh yes you are,' Mungo said.

And that was strange, because only after Mungo had spoken did Douglas wonder if he really *had* explained everything. He had no recollection of having spoken aloud and yet he must have done, or how could Mungo have said what he said, and he have replied as he had? Unless Mungo were a figment of his imagination (could a figment be of anything else?), which his presence right there on the foldaway table belied, to say nothing of the dark stain of his excretion on the floor of the carriage. Mungo was as real as he was – or Douglas himself was not real! Could he be the figment of a toad's imagination? And be conscious of it? Surely not! Then he thought again of what had happened the other night, when Mungo's eyes had glazed over and Douglas had seemed to waken from an involuntary sleep. Did Mungo have some power over him? There was something legendary and mysterious about toads. If a toad came to your door, did this portend good or evil? If he entered your house, what came in with him? And then you put him in your pocket, carried him like a talisman. And then . . . and then . . .

It was happening again! He shook his head in an effort to waken himself fully. He realised that the train was at a standstill. For how long had it been stationary? Mungo was watching him with his black-and-orange eyes. You could see how a credulous person might detect something malicious in that look. Through the window Douglas saw a path beside the railway line, and not far away – a couple of hundred yards or so – a single white two-storey building with a sign over the door which he could not read. A narrow road ran past this building, which had space for parking in front of it, and then turned west towards the distant hills.

At the far end of the carriage the door slid open and the man who had earlier checked the tickets entered. He spoke in turn to the Chinese tourists, the girl and the red-faced farmer-cleric. He began to move down the aisle, towards Douglas.

'Time to retire, Mungo,' Douglas said, and gently he lifted him and slid him back into the jacket pocket.

[To be continued]

A WELCOME IN THE GLEN

'Is something wrong?'

'Nothing at all, sir.'

'The train gave a wee lurch back there, and now I can't help noticing that we have stopped.'

'Aye. Don't worry about the wee lurch. Wee lurches are normal on this stretch. Would you by any chance be Mr Douglas Elder, sir?'

'I would. That is, I am.'

'Och, that's a relief. I've been right through this train and here you are, the last person I ask. This is your stop, sir.'

'What do you mean?'

'This is your stop. You've to leave the train here.'

'But there isn't a station.'

'It's a request stop, sir. Not much used these days except in August for the shooting, but we've had a request in your name, so here we are. You're to alight here.'

'But I didn't request anything. I'm going to Fort William.'

'You are Mr Douglas Elder, aren't you?'

'I am.'

'Your name reminds me of something, but I can't put my finger on it. Doesn't matter. The request was made on your behalf. Somebody's to meet you and take you on to your destination.'

'Who is to meet me?'

'That I couldn't say, sir. The request came over the radio and it was indistinct. *Your* name was distinct, but not the name of the party who is to meet you.'

'Would it be Corryvreckan?'

'Aye, that could have been it. It sounds about the right length. Now, sir, we don't have much time as we need to keep to our schedule. This is quite a favour we're doing you, but our job is to provide customer satisfaction. *My* job,' he adds. 'I'm a CEO. Do you have any idea what that stands for?'

He is a very mournful-looking man, with a drooping moustache and matching eyes, like a walrus thinking about global warming. In fact, as he poses his question he slumps down in the seat across the aisle from me and pushes his cap back from his brow.

'I've no idea. You're the guard or something, is that it?'

'The guard!' he says. 'Oh, if I was the guard! Where have you been all this time, sir? I'm no more a guard than you're a passenger. You're a *customer*, and as for me, I'm a Customer Experience Operative. A CEO – that's somebody's idea of a joke, eh?' He stretches over, puts a hand on my arm, then withdraws it as if recognising the impropriety. 'I'm sorry. I get very upset thinking about my job title. It's shaming, really it is.'

'It isn't your fault.'

'*I* know that,' he says. 'That makes it worse, in a way. It's never anybody's fault. Not mine, not yours, not the bastards running the show. Oh no, it's never *their* fault. But that's not what gets to me. Will I tell you what gets to me?'

'I expect you will.'

'It's the effort, the blood, sweat and tears – all for nothing. Sometimes I could weep. I *do* weep. And other times I could laugh. I don't, though. I just keep a straight face and carry on.' He pulls himself upright, then onto his feet. 'I'll probably resign one of these days, but that's my business, and I shouldn't be troubling you with it. Now, sir, if you just slip off the train now, and walk down that path – do you see that place over there?'

'The building?'

'Aye. That's not just any building. That's a pub, a braw wee howff called the Shira Inn. There'll be an open fire there, and hot food, and a bar with draught ales and a gantry full of whiskies. There'll be a welcome in the glen, even if it's not really a glen. You'll like it there.'

'The Shira Inn?'

'Aye. If I could, I'd slip off the train and come with you, but I can't. Why? Because I'm the Customer Experience Operative. I can't leave my post. But what I am offering you, one of my Customers, is an Experience. That's my job. Go, make yourself at home, and the other party will meet you there this afternoon and take you on to wherever it is you're going.'

I am far from convinced that this is the best course of action. The man has my name and the message he has conveyed seems clear enough, but I paid for a ticket to Fort William and have a plan all worked out, requiring strict adherence to a timetable of connecting minibuses and so on. To make this unexpected change goes against the grain of how I conduct my life.

Correction: that is how I *used* to conduct my life. I recall what I told myself before leaving Edinburgh: I am going on an adventure. Am I, like a cowering, timorous horse, to refuse at the first hurdle?

'You're sure it's genuine, this request?'

'Looks like it, sir. It's in your name, after all. Stands to reason, doesn't it? Otherwise you wouldn't be sitting there and I wouldn't have found you.'

I swither, then make up my mind. Actually, what happens is that I hear a voice from the not so distant past: 'Ye cannae just breenge in.' Oh? And who says that the new Douglas Findhorn Elder can't breenge, or at least slip, *out*?

'You'll let me off, then?'

'You'll let *yourself* off,' the CEO says. 'I don't want to alarm the other passengers. If they see you go they'll all want to follow.' This strikes me as very faulty logic. 'That door through there, behind you – I've released the master lock, so it'll open if you just push the button. Wait until the door into the carriage is shut and nobody will see or hear a thing. It'll be like *The Thirty-Nine Steps*.'

'It will?'

'Aye, when the fellow gets out on the Forth Bridge and then takes off, with the police after him – it'll be like that!' He grins conspiratorially. 'You're an innocent man – wanted for murder, but *I* believe you!'

I feel a growing disquiet. Is the man deranged? And yet the message must surely be correct: somebody has worked out that it will save a lot of time and trouble to get me off the train here and take me to Glentaragar from the Shira Inn.

'Right,' I say. 'Thank you for your help. I'll do what you say.'

'Very good, sir. Glad to have been of assistance. Just give me a minute to get up to the other end of the carriage.'

He goes off with a final theatrical wink, and I wait as instructed. Then I reach up for my raincoat and suitcase – it is only a small case, with wheels and an extendable handle – and, as discreetly as I can, I exit the carriage. Once the sliding door has closed behind me I open the door onto the outside world. It feels odd, and, yes, somehow adventurous, that there is no platform and that I have to lower the suitcase and then step down onto the ballast. I hurry away from the train. The path is too uneven and stony for the wheels of the case, so I carry it.

A minute later I am in front of the Shira Inn. The car park is empty. There are black cartwheels propped against the whitewashed wall, and a set of antlers mounted over the entrance. I glance back at the train, motionless as a dead caterpillar in the vast green-brown landscape, and then I push through the door.

The bar is small but pleasant enough. A few round tables and stools are set out across the floor, and upholstered benches line the walls around larger rectangular tables. Everything is as my friend the CEO described it. There is indeed an open fireplace, and a peat fire is burning in the grate. There appears to be beer on tap. There is a well-stocked gantry. A sign marked TOILETS on a door at the rear of the bar reminds me that I have not emptied my bladder since Glasgow.

There are no customers. In fact the place seems completely deserted.

'Hello?'

No reply.

I take my chance and head through to the toilets.

When I return a man is leaning on the frame of the front door with a tea towel over his shoulder and his arms folded.

'Feel free, why don't you?' he says.

'What's that?'

'The toilets are only for the use of customers,' he says.

'For the use of customers only.'

'That's what I said.'

I decide not to pursue this one.

'There was nobody to ask. Anyway, I *am* a customer.'

His mood brightens at once. 'Oh, that's all right, then.' He walks briskly over and steps behind the bar. 'What can I get you?'

'Are you serving food?'

'Food?' His face falls again. 'What kind of food?'

'Hot food?'

'Soup and a roll, pie and chips, that kind of thing?'

'Exactly.'

'No. We've nothing like that.'

'So if folk come in from a long hike through the mountains, cold and wet and weary, you can't provide them with a warming, restorative bowl of Scotch broth?'

'No. Not today.'

'Do you have any food at all?'

He looks around, and finally his gaze settles on a space under the bar. 'We've got crisps.'

'What flavour?'

'Just the usual flavours.'

After a pause, during which I raise my eyebrows to suggest that a little more detail wouldn't go amiss, he elaborates – becomes almost garrulous, in fact.

'Plain, salt and vinegar, cheese and onion. Oh and haggis, neeps and tatties. That's all one flavour by the way, not three. You couldn't have just tattie-flavoured crisps, could you? That would be like apple-flavoured apple juice. And neep crisps! Imagine them, eh? Jesus!'

'Give me a couple of packets of the haggis, neeps and tatties. I'm starving.'

'Coming up,' he says, dipping down. 'And something to drink?'

'A whisky, I think. It's a bit chilly out there.'

He gestures with an open hand towards the gantry. 'Take your pick.'

I begin to run my eye along the rows of bottles, recognising familiar shapes and labels. One image in particular catches my attention – a roaring stag proud against the skyline.

'Is that Glen Gloming you have there?'

'Where?'

'The one with the stag on it.'

He fetches it down. It is nearly full – just one or two nips out of it.

'Glen Gloming 12-Year-Old,' he says. He turns the bottle this way and that. 'Aye, you're right enough. Good spot.'

'I had it for the first time the other day. Very nice it was too. I'd never heard of it before.'

'You learn something every day,' he says. I don't know if he is referring to me or to himself.

'I'll have one of those, then. No, make it a double.'

'Coming up,' he repeats, reaching for a stainless-steel measure.

'Where does it come from?'

He stops after pouring the contents of the measure into a glass. 'I never ask,' he says, tapping his nose. 'I just work here. Some things come in at the front door, some come in at the back, know what I mean?'

'I do.'

He tips in the second measure and fills a little brown jug with water. 'There you go.'

'What do I owe you?'

He appears to do a sum in his head. 'Well now.'

I incline my head in such a way as to indicate that he has my attention.

'Tell you what,' he says. 'Would you do me a favour?'

'A favour?'

'Aye. I need to slip out for a wee while. Would you mind the shop for me?'

'What, me?'

'No, him over there.'

'You want me to look after the bar? Where are you going?'

'Just out. Down the road a bit.' He pauses, looks at the clock behind the bar. 'Got to put a bet on.'

'A bet? But there's not a bookie's anywhere near here, surely?'

'That's true. But there's a man I know. He'll place the bet for me. A dead cert, so he says. I just need to get the money to him.'

'Why can't you just phone your bet in?'

'It's not that kind of bet. Unofficial, know what I mean? Anyway, there's no landline here and the mobile reception is non-existent.'

'So you've no contact with the outside world, even though you're right next to the railway?'

'We can commune with nature and wave at the trains, but that's about it. So, will you mind the shop while I'm away?'

'No.'

'I'll not charge you for the drink?'

'No.'

'Oh, come on, pal. Gie's a break, will you? You can have the crisps for free too.'

'But how long would you be? I'm only here till somebody comes to collect me.'

'Oh, you're expected, are you?'

'Yes. I'm just off the train and I'm waiting for a car.'

'Off the train? Is there a train broken down or something?'

'No. It just stopped to let me off.'

'Did it really? That hardly ever happens, you know, except at the start of the grouse season. Are you the only passenger that got off?'

'I am, and I'll be away from here as soon as my lift arrives.'

'When will that be?'

'I'm not sure. This afternoon, I believe.'

'Oh, well, that'll be fine, then. The roads are very slow around here. I'll only be twenty minutes. Half an hour at most. I just need to make this bet. It's very important.'

'You don't even know me.'

'You've an honest face. And, anyway, I'm locking the till.'

'Not that honest, then. What if I want another drink?'

'Help yourself. I'll not notice. Have all the crisps you can eat.'

'Suppose someone else comes in?'

He looks at the clock again. 'At this time of day? Nobody will come in.'

'So this place never gets any customers? How does it manage to stay open?'

He shrugs. 'You wonder, don't you? I just work here.'

'So, what if any customers turn up?'

'They won't, but if they do, serve them. Keep a tab. They can settle up when I'm back. Or not, if they're away before that.'

'You said twenty minutes.'

'Half an hour.'

'So they'll still be here.'

'Right enough. But they won't come anyway. I'm surprised *you're* here.'

'I wouldn't be if I hadn't got off the train.'

'Well, you did, so how about it?'

'If I wasn't here, would you go anyway?'

'And lose my job? No chance. Somebody needs to watch the fire. Oh, would you watch the fire as well? Chuck a peat on it every so often?'

'All right, but only till the car comes for me. When that happens, I'm leaving. You need to know that.'

'I'll be back before you know I've gone. Forty minutes max.'

I am thinking that I have nothing to lose. I can just walk out, whether he has returned or not. It will be as if I were never here.

'I won't be held responsible if anything goes wrong.'

'Nothing will go wrong. What could go wrong?'

'Well, you just said yourself, there could be a fire.'

'No, I said somebody needs to watch the fire. That's different. Thanks a lot, pal. I really appreciate this.'

Something occurs to me. 'Hold on a minute. How are you going to get to wherever you're going? There are no cars out there.'

'Aha!' He comes out from the bar and disappears through the back. A minute later he is wheeling a bicycle – an old-fashioned model with a saddlebag and three-speed gears – through to the front door. A helmet dangles from the handlebars by its strap, and he pauses to put it on.

'Better safe than sorry,' he says. 'Like I said, help yourself to anything. I'll be back by one, at the latest.' And with that reassuring last comment, he departs.

The clock says 11.51.

I sit and munch crisps, sip my Glen Gloming – which is as good as I remember it from the previous tasting – and watch the fire glowing in the grate. A basket full of peats is nearby. Everything is quiet. I could be alone on the planet. I will certainly hear a car's engine should a car arrive. And a car will arrive. It has been arranged. So I can relax.

At one minute after midday the first of the customers who weren't going to turn up, turns up.

THE OLD WAYS

He seems at first glance to be an ancient, tottering kind of fellow, a retired shepherd or gillie perhaps. He has a long, tangled beard, mainly grey though with darker patches on the cheeks, and a long, weather-beaten face topped by a scarcity of fine grey hair swept back from the forehead. He wears a predominantly green suit of Harris tweed, a once-white shirt and a knitted tie the colour of dead bracken. As I heard no engine I cannot imagine where he has come from unless he escaped from another carriage of the train on the recommendation of the CEO. He heads straight to the bar, leans on it for a few seconds, raps it with his knuckles, then turns and fixes me with an expectant eye.

'Where's Malcolm?'

'You mean the barman?'

'Of course I mean the barman. Who else would I mean? Where the devil is he?'

'He had to go out for a while.'

'Out? But I want a drink. Who's going to get me a drink?'

I walk briskly over, much as Malcolm might do if he were not off on his bicycle to see a man about a dog, or a horse, or whatever it is he wishes to wager his money on.

'I am.'

'You?'

'Aye. He left me in charge. What'll it be?'

'A pint of IPA. Where's he gone?'

I decide to be discreet. 'I don't know. He said he wouldn't be long.'

'Hmm.'

He sounds discontented even when saying 'Hmm'. I pick up a glass and start pouring. The beer splutters reluctantly from the tap, and I fill a

148

couple of glasses with froth before the flow improves and I manage to produce most of a pint for him.

'Better let that settle,' I say. 'I'll top it up in a minute.'

He assesses me with a jaded eye. When I return his stare I see that he is not as old as I presumed, perhaps no more than about sixty.

'Ever worked behind a bar before?'

'No.'

'Thought as much. How come you're standing in for Malcolm?'

'I happened to be passing.'

'Passing?'

'On a train, which stopped to let me off. How about you?'

'How about me what?'

'How did you get here?'

'In the usual manner.'

'Which is?'

'By car.'

'I didn't hear a car.'

'Are you calling me a liar?'

'Not yet.'

'As a matter of fact, I cut the engine early and freewheeled in, so as not to disturb the peace.'

I swallow an unfriendly riposte to this. 'And what brings you here? Other than the car, I mean.'

'I play here. Every Monday night.'

'Play what?' I look around in case I have somehow failed to notice a darts board or a pool table. When I look back at him I revise my estimate of his age downwards, to fifty or less. The face is just well lived in. It reminds me, vaguely, of someone else's.

'Guitar,' he says. 'Did Malcolm not tell you about me?'

'He didn't, but then it's a long time before tonight. He probably thought it wasn't necessary.'

'So the name Stuart Crathes MacCrimmon means nothing to you?'

I shake my head. 'Nothing.'

He shakes *his* head. 'Dear, dear. Is that pint not ready yet? I'll bring in the gear while I'm waiting.'

He exits. Curiosity leads me to the door to watch. Some distance away, a rusty, yellow, box-shaped, lopsided car has been abandoned against a rusty, lopsided fence, and to this vehicle the man MacCrimmon walks. 'The gear', which he removes from the back seat, consists solely of a battered guitar case. I glance in the other direction. To my surprise I see that the train is still where I left it. Half an hour must have passed – I assumed it was long gone. I wonder if perhaps I should forget about the new arrangement, and stick to my original plan.

Curiosity and I nip back inside before the bearded fellow sees us. When he enters he places the battered guitar case in a corner of the room furthest from the fire, opening the lid to reveal a battered guitar. He comes for his drink.

'The strings are sensitive to temperature change, you see,' he says, speaking as if to an ignorant child. 'They have to adjust to the atmosphere before they can be played. The instrument has to breathe.'

I do not like him or his attitude. He is a haggard, nasty old man (I revise my estimate of his age back up to seventy, and decide I must have been mistaken in seeing a resemblance to anyone I know), imperious and self-satisfied, yet with no apparent reason for being either. I am conscious of an overwhelming desire to burst his balloon. It grows and grows, this desire, until I can contain it no longer and like cartoon ectoplasm it issues from me and forms itself briefly and enormously into a likeness of Ollie Buckthorn before dispersing into the air.

'When do you start?'

'Later,' he says. 'About six. Or seven.'

'That's a lot of breathing for one guitar. What will you do in the meantime? I mean, apart from pace yourself?'

He glares at me. 'Are you so ignorant of the old ways?'

'Enlighten me.'

'The old ways are not learned in a day,' he says, 'nor in a year, no, nor in ten years. They are learned in a lifetime, and carried from one life to another in the carrying stream of life. In the intervening period between now and my playing I will think on these matters, that is what I will do.'

'Feel free, why don't you?' I say, adopting the tone of Malcolm the barman. I can be everyone and anyone today, and no one will know I am not.

'You might learn something if you did the same,' MacCrimmon says. 'Before the song was the word, and before the word was the thought. Song is story, and story is song, and thought precedes all. I am a bard. This is my craft, and this my occupation.'

'Terrific,' I say, placing the pint on a cardboard mat in front of him and consulting a price list that lies beside the locked till. 'That'll be three pounds and forty pence.'

There is also a notebook and pen which may come in handy. When I open the notebook I see that the first few pages are full of handwritten details of drinks purchased on previous dates. Most of these entries have been scored off but a few have not.

'Malcolm has the key to the till so I've no change. If you don't have the exact money I'll just write it down in this wee book and you can settle up with him later.'

'That will not be necessary,' says Stuart Crathes MacCrimmon. 'Here, they understand the old ways. I am paid in kind for my music, my songs and my stories. In the old tradition, food, drink and hospitality are proper tributes to the bard.'

'Well, Malcolm didn't say anything about that. He just said I was to keep a tab if anybody came in. So I'll write it down anyway.'

MacCrimmon pulls at a strand of his beard, which has the effect of making him jut his jaw at me. For a second I think the beard will detach. 'You know not of what you speak. Am I not descended from the great MacCrimmons, hereditary pipers for untold generations to the chiefs of Clan MacLeod?'

'I have no idea, but if you are, isn't playing a guitar a bit of a comedown?'

'When you insult me you insult my fathers, and my father's fathers before them.'

'Fuck off the lot of you, then,' I say, for he is beginning to annoy me.

I think the feeling is mutual.

'Make your mark in your wee book, and see what good it does you,' he says.

After this exchange we don't have anything left to say to each other. He takes his pint over to a seat next to the guitar case, and sits glowering into the mists of departed time.

I write the date in the notebook, and then the following:

Stuart Crathes MacCrimmon, 'bard': 1 pint IPA, £3.40

Then I add another measure of Glen Gloming to my glass and return to my seat by the fire.

A few minutes later I hear voices outside, and the sound of boots being scraped and thumped, presumably to relieve them of mud and similar debris. The door opens and two men and two women in brightly coloured jackets enter, in a kind of clump. They have rucksacks and poles, which they pile up beside one of the larger tables before removing their jackets to reveal brightly coloured fleeces. They are all about the same age, although it is difficult to say what that age is – somewhere between forty and sixty, I reckon. About my age, in other words. I take an instant dislike to them and their hearty outdoor energy. The two women sit at the table while the men, a red-bearded one and a black-bearded one, approach the bar. Their beards are neatly trimmed, and make the beard of the bard MacCrimmon look even more bedraggled than it is.

I take up my position and ask what I can get them.

'A pint of IPA, a pint of Guinness, a gin and tonic and a dry white wine,' says the red-bearded man. 'And can we see your food menu?'

'No, because there isn't one,' I say, as I begin to assemble the drinks. I start with the Guinness, remembering from years of observation from the other side of bars that it takes longer and that the done thing is to pour about two-thirds of it, leaving that to settle before topping it off.

'You don't have any food?'

'No, nothing.'

'No filled rolls or pies or anything?'

'Not a sausage.' What a joy it is to be a miserable bastard.

'He's new,' Stuart Crathes MacCrimmon calls out. 'He's just off the train, so he says, though I doubt it, because there isn't a station here.'

'It's a request stop,' I say.

'He is an upstart with no knowledge of the old ways or indeed of anything.'

'You be quiet,' I say, 'or I'll put you out.'

'He can't even pull a pint.'

'Ignore him,' I tell the red-bearded man. 'I'm standing in for the usual barman. The food situation, I concede, is not ideal, but that's how it is and I can't do anything about it.'

'No sausages, you say?'

'None. There's crisps, that's all.'

'What flavour?'

'Just the usual flavours. Plain, salt and vinegar, cheese and onion. And haggis, neeps and tatties. That's all one flavour by the way, not three.'

'There's only crisps!' the red-bearded man shouts to the women.

'For God's sake. Well, just get a selection.'

'Eight packets of assorted crisps,' the man says.

'Coming up,' I say. 'There is only this white wine, a Chardonnay. It's cold but I doubt it's dry. That all right?'

'It'll have to be, won't it?'

'I've no access to the till, by the way, so I'll just write down what you owe and you can pay when the real barman comes back.'

'When will that be?'

'Soon, I hope.' I pass the drinks and crisps over and consult the price list before entering the details in the notebook.

'Some place, this,' I hear the other man say to his companion as they carry the drinks to their table.

I resent his comment. I go to the fire and put some more peats on it.

'At least it's warm,' I say.

'Too hot, if you ask me,' one of the women says, divesting herself of her offensively bright fleece. 'Could you not put anything more on the fire, please?'

I am not happy with Malcolm. I said I wouldn't be held responsible and here I am being held responsible for all kinds of things. I add another Glen Gloming to the quantity remaining in my glass. I am generous with the measure. In fact, I don't bother to measure it.

I hear a vehicle pulling up outside and its engine being switched off. Quickly I go to the door to see if it is my car – the one that is going to take me away from all this. It is not. It is *a* car, from which five young people are emerging, full of laughter and chatter. They will double the number of people enjoying the hospitality of the Shira Inn. I hate them.

Enough of this, I think to myself. I will take my whisky, my coat and my suitcase and get back on the train.

No I won't. Because the train is no longer there. The train has gone.

The car party is approaching. Where do all these people come from?

'You open, mate?' one of them says, hardly checking his pace. His accent reveals him to be a Friend from the South. His companions – two females and two males, I note without interest – continue on into the Shira Inn.

'Mate?' He has stopped at the door and is waiting for my response.

'Yes, we're open,' I say. 'I'll be with you in a moment.'

And in a moment, because there doesn't seem to be anything else to do, I am.

A WOMAN IN DARK CLOTHING

It's a Monday afternoon but the Shira Inn does the kind of business that might please a city-centre publican – Barry, of the Lounger, for example – on a weekend night. By three o'clock I have been behind the bar more or less constantly for three hours, only stepping out to retrieve empty glasses and – when I remember – to pitch another peat from the basket into the grate, in defiance of the general view that the place is melting. As far as I am concerned if the conditions inside drive them all outside, so much the better. Earlier, as the inn filled up, I retrieved my belongings, hung up my coat and stashed the suitcase behind the bar, where it frequently obstructs my movements. I have little opportunity to wonder if the Customer Experience Officer has deceived me, and why on earth he would do such a thing. One thing is certain: there is no chance of my catching the next train, as I am miles from an official stop. And one thing is uncertain: whether the lift that I was told is on its way will materialise. I appear to be stuck where I am – unless I can escape by some other means.

As more and more customers arrive, order drinks and are disappointed by the limited choice of food (after a while, only haggis, neeps and tattie crisps remain), I repeatedly ask if anybody can give me a lift, north or south, when they depart. But either they are hikers without transport, or their vehicles are fully occupied, or they think I am joking, since surely, being the only person on bar duty, I cannot desert my post? And in any case nobody is ever ready to leave when I am, or they go when I am distracted by the demands of somebody else, and so the minutes and hours creep on. It occurs to me that I may have fallen for a trick such as the one Heracles played on Atlas, when he persuaded him to hold up the sky for a moment and then buggered off with the golden apples. I don't know what Atlas did to assuage the bitter memory, but I take refuge in the solace of Glen Gloming whenever I can.

The early entries I made in the notebook look like this:

Stuart Crathes MacCrimmon, 'bard': ~~1~~ ~~2~~ 3 pint^s IPA, £3.40 ea.
4 walkers: 1 pt IPA, 1 Guinn, 1 w. wine, 1 G&T: £12.20 × 2 = £24.40 +
  8 crisps £6.40 = £30.80✓
5 folk out of car: 1 ginger beer, 1 lager, 1 IPA, ½ lager, 1 r. wine, 5 crisps,
  £17.00✓

But when a number of cyclists, a carload of thirsty Norwegians, a plumber and his apprentice and a team of birdwatchers arrive in quick succession, I give up the recording process, begin to round the bills down to the nearest five pounds and take whatever money people are prepared to hand over. Some challenge my arithmetic, demanding to see the price list and suggesting lower totals for what they have bought. A few refuse to make payment unless I can supply them with a receipt, which I can't. Most gladly accept my bargain deals. I stuff the proffered notes into a back pocket. The twitchers, becoming wise to the fact that the plumber is holding out against paying anything, try to haggle retrospectively for a rebate. The cyclists sneak out without settling up while I am disputing with a woman and her daughter, both dressed in black, their assertion that the fact that they have been at a funeral entitles them to a discount on their rum and Cokes. Stuart Crathes MacCrimmon, of course, steadfastly refuses to part with any money, but I continue to pour him pints even after I have stopped keeping a tab for him. Malcolm can sort it all out, and if he can't then that is his problem, not mine.

Around four o'clock, by which time I am feeling more and more like Atlas and less and less like Douglas Findhorn Elder, let alone Heracles, there is a renewed surge of business. The twitchers – who are present in such flocks that I find it hard to count them, especially as, to my untrained eye, they all look remarkably similar – decide to have one last round. This requires me to pour a seemingly endless number of pints, some of lager, some of heavy. As fast as I place these on the counter, they are taken away for consumption. I suspect that a scam is in operation, but I no longer care. I run out of pint glasses and move on to half-pint ones. Then the demand eases a little, and I become aware of the reason: somebody has come to assist me. A woman in dark clothing, slight of build and adept at avoiding collisions – these are the only observations about her I am able to make – is passing out the full glasses and going on excursions to the outskirts to bring back empty ones. She does not speak to me, but she begins to impose some order on the throng of drinkers, repelling their loud demands and shooing them away with a firm but not unfriendly resolve. In the same way that MacCrimmon's face stirred a hazy memory, I keep thinking that her voice reminds me of somebody else, but can't think who it might be.

Outside the light is fading. People are drinking up and going. I am delighted, and take an almost proprietorial pleasure in seeing the Shira Inn return to quietness. At last the only people remaining are the Norwegian party – who, I have learned, are attempting to retrace the footsteps of their Viking ancestors and who, ironically, have been the most patient and well-behaved of all my clientele – the bard MacCrimmon, my blessed helper and myself. I sit down on a bench recently vacated by several birdwatchers, put my back against the wall and close my eyes, while the woman quietly works her way round the tables collecting dead glasses and empty crisp packets. On one of her journeys, gently and without a word, she sets something down on the table at which I am sitting. I sense the movement and open my eyes. In front of me is a small tumbler of whisky and a packet of haggis, neeps and tatties crisps. I gratefully raise the whisky to my lips – it is Glen Gloming – and speak to her for the first time.

'You are very kind, whoever you are. Give me a minute and I'll come and help you.'

'You're fine,' she says. 'Stay where you are.'

Oddly enough, she is right. I *am* fine. The fire's soft hiss, the Norwegians' collective murmuring, the soft clink of glasses being washed and left to drain – these are the relaxing background sounds of the next few minutes. I think vaguely of Malcolm and whether he will ever come back, and what I will do with the money in my back pocket if he doesn't, but these too are relaxing thoughts. It is as if the world has ceased to spin and all will remain as it is, calm and serene, for eternity.

And then Stuart Crathes MacCrimmon takes up his guitar and starts to sing.

CONVERSATIONS WITH A TOAD: CONVERSATION #5

Douglas Findhorn Elder felt movement in the left-hand pocket of his tweed jacket. Earlier he had taken the jacket off and hung it on a hook while he was busy serving customers, but now that the Shira Inn was less crowded he had put it back on. The movement startled him: he had completely forgotten about Mungo Forth Mungo, who presently emerged and settled himself discreetly on the bench beside Douglas.

'What is that infernal racket?' the toad asked.

'It's a bard,' Douglas said. 'How are you?'

'Quite well, thank you. I've been asleep. Have I missed anything? Where are we? Have we arrived yet? What's a bard?'

'So many questions,' Douglas said. 'You have missed plenty but nothing of importance; we're in a pub called the Shira Inn, we are miles from where we should be so no, we have not arrived yet; and as for what a bard is – well, it would take a long time to explain, but *that* is not a bard.'

'You just said it was.'

'I was paraphrasing. Not a true bard. Are you still hungry?'

'I am, now that you mention it.'

'Try some of these. The flavour is haggis, neeps and tatties. Don't even ask. You might find them a bit salty.'

'I like salty. Snails are salty, or can be.'

'These are drier than snails.'

Mungo started sucking in and gulping down the crisps. 'Very nice, if a little sharp round the edges. Will those other people think you are talking to yourself?'

'Possibly. I have my hand over my mouth just in case, but actually I don't much care. Can you hear me all right?'

'Not badly, considering the competition. What exactly is he doing?'

'He appears to be singing a ballad. That irregular strumming sound is him accompanying himself on the guitar. Unfortunately the chords are completely at odds with the melody, in terms of both harmony and tempo. I'm not even sure that there is a melody. I keep thinking if I listen long enough I'll pick it up, but it seems to change with each verse.'

'What's it about, this ballad?'

'A good question. If I knew, I would happily bring you up to speed on the plot. Ballads often have excellent plots, but I can't make head or tail of this one.'

'A ballad is fiction then, like a novel?'

'Yes, only in the form of a song. But not all ballads are fiction. Some are based on real historical events. But then, a lot of novels are too.'

'We discussed this before. Thinly disguised autobiography. The ordinary life made extraordinary. The gauzy border between reality and imagination.'

'Did we put it like that?'

'I think so. We weren't quite agreed. Is that him finished now?'

'Aye, thank God. Ah no, he was just taking a drink. Shame.'

'Those other people seem to be enjoying it. What's wrong with them?'

'They're Norwegian. I'm not sure that they are enjoying it. They're just very polite. Or possibly stunned.'

Mungo continued to occupy himself with the triple-flavoured crisps, while Douglas took occasional sips of whisky and considered what to do next. Perhaps the Norwegians might be able to squeeze him (and Mungo) into whatever transport they had, whenever they finally left. Perhaps the woman who was still clearing away glasses had a car. Perhaps, if Malcolm the barman should ever reappear, he could summon a taxi. This idea prompted Douglas to retrieve his mobile phone from the inside pocket of his jacket, and check for a signal. Just as Malcolm had told him earlier, there was none.

The woman was behind the bar again. She had done a wonderful job: the place was almost back to normal. Douglas watched her wiping down the surfaces with quick, neat efficiency. He could not help noting her quick, neat shape, the way her fair, slightly wavy hair fell across her face as she worked, the strip of white skin that appeared above the waist-band of her trousers when she stretched for something.

Douglas chided himself. Here he was, spying on her exposed flesh, and he did not even know her name. Dear, dear, dear, he thought. You are out of order, Dougie.

She came over. 'That's better,' she said. 'How are you now?'

'Recovering gradually. I'm Douglas,' he said, half-rising from his seat. 'I haven't thanked you properly. I was just about to throw in the towel when you arrived. You saved the day.'

'Not a problem,' she said. Their hands clasped briefly. 'I'm Xanthe.'

'That's an uncommon name.'

'It's Greek.'

So also was her nose, he thought. To some it might be disproportion-ately long for her face, its bridge too prominent, but to Douglas it was of classical size and form.

'It's a fine nose,' he said. 'I mean name. It suits you.'

She gave him a quizzical look. 'It should. I chose it myself. I'm just going to freshen up a bit. Then I'll heat up some of the soup that's through in the kitchen. Would you like some?'

'Malcolm said there wasn't any soup. He said there was no food at all. Malcolm's the barman, by the way. I was just standing in for him.'

'I guessed that. Malcolm's a lazy sod. There's always soup.'

'You know him, then?'

'I know him. I haven't checked what kind of soup.'

'I'd eat almost anything that wasn't a crisp. How long does this bloody ballad go on?'

'There's no way of telling. He's improvising. It's the MacCrimmon way.'

'You know him, too?'

'I do. If you don't like the song, ignore it.'

'Believe me, I'm trying. And does he know you?'

This question seemed to puzzle her momentarily. 'No,' she said after a few seconds. 'No, MacCrimmon doesn't know me.'

Look,' Douglas said, 'I don't suppose you're leaving later, are you? I really need to get a lift to Fort William. Tonight.'

'No, I'm not leaving. I don't have a car anyway. And that's a little exploitative, don't you think?'

'Yes, it is. And graceless, too. I'm sorry.'

'Okay.'

He was sorry, too, for thinking of her in bits – her hair, her backside, her nose – instead of as a whole person, but he didn't apologise aloud for this. And in fact he *was* thinking of her as a whole person: her whole person overwhelmed his sensibilities. He couldn't analyse why and didn't want to try. She just did, and he liked it. Xanthe: what a charming name!

She hurried off before he could ask more questions. She seemed to know her way around, and suddenly it became clear to Douglas why. She must work there. Obviously she must be Malcolm's wife or girlfriend. She probably habitually covered his absences and cleared up after him. And this was her on duty for the rest of the evening.

He was disappointed. More than anything he was disappointed in himself, for not seeing it at once, and for allowing his mind to run away with a little fantasy.

'What little fantasy is your mind running away with?' Mungo was tugging at the hem of his jacket and peering up at him with mischief in his eyes.

'How do you know what I'm thinking?'

'I don't. I know nothing. You were away somewhere, that's all. What *were* you thinking?'

'Mind your own business.'

'Aha. Well, *I'm* impressed anyway.'

'With what?'

'Nothing, nothing.'

Douglas did not quite believe in the innocence of toads.

'I can understand,' he said, 'why your kind had a bad reputation in the old days. I see why people would have ascribed evil intent to you. You have a look about you.'

'The old days? You're sounding like him over there. If I may quote the poet Henryson, "Thou should not judge a man after his face." I believe the speaker of that line was a toad.'

'You're at it again. How is it possible for you to quote Robert Henryson? He's been dead five hundred years. How have you even heard of him?'

'Let's not go over this again. Longevity. Knowledge transference. Memory. Remember?'

'Well, if you know about Henryson, you must surely know what a ballad is. And a bard, too. So either your system doesn't work too well or you were being deceitful.'

'Ah, you have found me out. See how the guilt is written all over my face.'

'Why are you being such a smart-arse?'

'I just like to keep us both on our metaphorical toes.'

'You're not real, Mungo. You're a wee shite, in fact.'

'Can't help it. It's in my nature. You'll be wanting to cast me into the fire next.'

'I assure you, however much you might try to provoke me, you're in no danger from me.'

'I'd better not be. My vengeance would be awful. I'm joking, by the way. Or am I?'

'Oh stop it.'

'What does the phrase "freshen up a bit" mean?'

'Give it a rest, will you?'

'I was only asking. It sounded promising, but perhaps your mind *was* as blank as your face. I take back the poet Henryson's words and eat them.'

Across the room, Stuart Crathes MacCrimmon finally drew his performance to a close. The Norwegians, who had been listening to him in what was either respectful or dumbstruck silence, broke into wild applause, thumping the table and cheering and whooping.

'Oh God, don't encourage him,' Douglas muttered, but then thought that they might just be expressing relief. The bard, anyway, had the sense to quit while he was ahead. Offers of drinks were made: MacCrimmon accepted as many of them as he reasonably could, and put his guitar down. A couple of the men made their way to the bar. Xanthe was still absent, and they looked expectantly towards Douglas.

Before he could decide whether or not to serve them, the front door clattered open and Malcolm rode in on his bicycle.

'About bloody time,' said Douglas.

'Hail to the chief who on a Triumph advances,' said the bard.

Malcolm dismounted, waved cheerily at them each in turn, parked his bike through the back, and returned to serve the Norwegians. Only after that did he come over to Douglas's table.

160

'What the hell happened to you?' Douglas demanded.

'Everything! You wouldn't believe it if I told you!'

'Try me.'

'Flock of sheep on the road, followed by a puncture, followed by the man I was looking for not being where he should have been. Had to hunt across half the county for him. All been fine here?'

'No,' Douglas said.

Malcolm pulled up a stool and sat on it.

'Sorry to hear that. What's been the problem? Is that a packet of crisps on the bench? They're terrible for getting grease on the fabric. Could you put them on the table?'

Douglas slid a hand, palm up, behind him, and felt Mungo crawl into it. He dipped him gently back into his jacket pocket, then retrieved the crisps.

'The problem,' he said, 'is that it's been going like a fair ever since you left. I've never sat down.'

'Aye you have.'

'Ten minutes ago. Is it like that every day?'

'No, never. I sometimes wonder how the place survives. Quite a bit of passing trade, then?'

'As soon as you left they started arriving. He was the first.' Douglas jerked a thumb at MacCrimmon. 'He hasn't paid for anything all afternoon. You were away for hours.'

'Like I said, I was held up. One damn thing after another. You'll not have had time to write everything down in the book, I suppose?'

'No, I have not.'

'Good man! Well, if you just hand over whatever you took, I'll ring a few sales through the till later. Got to keep the taxman satisfied, eh?'

'*That's* how the place survives,' Douglas said. 'Dodgy whisky through the back door, cash in hand out the front.'

Malcolm sucked air through his teeth. 'That's not a nice word, "dodgy",' he said. 'I thought you liked the Glen Gloming.'

'Bugger the Glen Gloming. I bet the Shira Inn never makes a trading profit.'

'Well, it's tough doing business in an off-the-beaten-track place like this.' Malcolm's hand was outstretched. 'If you give me the takings, I'll get you another dram.'

'Off the beaten track?' Douglas gave a bitter laugh. 'I'm surprised the track hasn't collapsed under the weight of traffic.'

He had a wad of notes in one back pocket, and a smaller wad in the other. He drew out the fatter of the two, and Malcolm whistled.

'Whoah! You're right, you *have* been busy! I'll make that a double. Is that the lot?'

There was more than three hundred pounds on the table.

'It is,' Douglas said, feeling the folds of another sixty quid being moulded by the curve of his left buttock.

'Well, make yourself at home and I'll get you that drink. Surprised you're still here, to be honest. I thought your lift must have come hours ago. But that's the magical lure of the Shira Inn for you. Couldn't bear to leave us, could you? We close at eleven.'

'Did you win?' Douglas asked, as Malcolm stood up to go.

'Did I what?'

'Win. You went to place a bet. So you said.'

'Oh, that! No. Didn't lose either, mind. My man talked me out of it. He'd had another look and it wasn't such a dead cert after all. Said we'd be better to wait until next week.'

'Hello, Malcolm.'

Xanthe had reappeared. She had freshened up very well, in Douglas's opinion, although it was also his opinion that she hadn't needed to. She had changed out of the dark top and trousers and was now wearing a pair of faded jeans and a white smock with a neckline embroidered with a design of blue and yellow flowers.

'Oh, hello, Xanthe,' Malcolm said, without surprise. 'You here again?'

'I am. I just put myself in the usual room. Is that okay?'

'You know the ropes, girl. This is Xanthe, one of our regular irregulars. She comes here to commune with nature, don't you, Xanthe? This gentleman has very kindly been helping out behind the bar. I'm sorry, I don't even know your name, pal.'

Gentleman? Pal? Douglas realised he disliked Malcolm as much as he disliked MacCrimmon.

'It's Douglas,' Douglas said. 'Douglas Elder.'

'Hello, Douglas,' Xanthe said, and she flashed him a lovely smile and opened her eyes very wide.

'Not Douglas Fir, eh?' Malcolm said with a guffaw.

'No.'

'I'm heating up some soup,' Xanthe said. 'Do you want some, both of you?'

'Soup? Is there any?'

'Yes, Malcolm. Scotch broth.'

'Lovely. Don't tell everybody.'

'There's plenty.'

But the Norwegians were leaving. They waved friendly waves at Douglas and took a few phone-snaps of Stuart Crathes MacCrimmon, who was flushed of face and barely able to speak. He sat behind a collection of drinks that included two pints of IPA, three drams and what looked suspiciously like a specimen of that dangerous brew, a 'wee heavy'. On the positive side, Douglas assessed, MacCrimmon was well past the point of either soup or song. On the negative side, at least as far as the bard himself was concerned, if he managed to drink what was in front of him he would probably be dead before closing time.

'Does he often get into that condition?' Douglas asked Malcolm, who by now had his feet up by the fire and was reading a copy of the *Racing Post*.

'MacCrimmon? Aye. Every time he's in, in fact.'

'That's terrible. He's killing himself.'

'We've all got to go some time, pal.'

'Can we get one thing straight? I'm not your pal.'

'Suit yourself.'

'You shouldn't be feeding him all that booze for free.'

'You want me to charge him for killing himself?'

'It might slow him down a bit.'

'Well, maybe, but it's not that simple. You see, we respect the old ways here.'

'That's bollocks.'

'It may be bollocks to you, but it's sacred to him. Live and let live, that's what I say. Pal.'

'Douglas!' The plaintive cry sounded from Douglas's jacket.

Douglas put his hand in his pocket and felt Mungo's fingers urgently gripping one of his own.

'Wait a minute,' Douglas hissed.

'I can't.'

'What do you mean, wait a minute?' Malcolm demanded.

'I wasn't talking to you.'

'Aye you were.' Malcolm put his paper down.

'I need to go outside. Now,' Mungo croaked.

'Be quiet,' Douglas said.

'Don't you tell me to be quiet,' Malcolm said, half-rising.

'I wasn't,' Douglas said. 'I was telling myself. I often do, it stops me getting overexcited. I think I'll go outside and get some fresh air.'

'Good idea,' Malcolm said, relaxing again. 'Go and cool off a bit.'

'I will,' Douglas said as he left. 'Patronising bastard,' he added as the door swung shut behind him.

The moon was rising. In its light, the moor was vast. The mountains were lost in the distance and the railway line was a feeble admission that humans were simply passing through, and would be gone shortly.

Mungo sent a stream of urine across the parking area, now empty of vehicles apart from the bard's heap, which had taken on the appearance of a bloated yellow cow, expired against the fence. If the toad noticed the moon, he made no mention of its beauty tonight. Instead he began to do stretches and bends.

'You almost got me into a fight,' Douglas said.

'Nonsense. I was saving your jacket. I had to get out anyway. I was too hot and I need some proper sustenance and a bit of exercise.' He punched the air a few times. 'Am *I* no a bonnie fighter, by the way?'

'No,' Douglas said.

'Och well. I'm away to do some exploring. There's a wonderful sense of decadence in the atmosphere.'

'That'll be the peat.'

'I take it we're not going anywhere else tonight?'

'Doesn't look like it. There seem to be rooms. Xanthe's got one. Malcolm will have to let me stay.'

'Fine. Then I'll see you in the morning. Or later tonight. I'll find you, anyway.'

'Will you be all right?'

'Don't worry about me. What about you?'

'I'll just have to make the best of it.'

'You will,' Mungo said. 'I don't think you'll have a problem finding a bed for the night. And I'll tell you something for nothing about that.'

'What?'

'You won't be sharing it with Malcolm. Or with the bard creature, come to that.'

Before Douglas could reply, the toad had gone, off to explore the decadent delights of the moor.

The man turned back, drawn by the irresistible aroma of Scotch broth.

[To be continued]

SMALL TALK

Where all those people came from or went to I do not know, but the arrival of darkness brings no more custom to the Shira Inn. The four of us – Malcolm, Xanthe, Stuart Crathes MacCrimmon and I – have the place to ourselves. The bard does not partake of the soup: he remains slumped in his far corner, occasionally surfacing to sample one of his drinks, then falling asleep again. Malcolm and Xanthe ignore him, and after a while, as my concern that his demise is imminent diminishes, I ignore him as well.

Malcolm too, full of broth, is soon slumbering by the fireside. Xanthe and I clear away the plates and she joins me at my table, after first pouring herself a large red wine and refilling my tumbler with Glen Gloming.

'Are you trying to get me drunk?' I ask. Close up, I notice lines about her mouth and eyes – vestiges of laughter or struggle or perhaps just life. I like those lines.

'I think you already are, somewhat.'

'Somewhat. Aye, probably.'

'Why would I be trying to get you drunk?'

There is definitely something familiar about her. Whenever I look at her I look away in case she thinks I am looking at her.

I shrug. 'To help me drown my sorrows? The thing is, Xanthe,' I continue, fixing my gaze on my whisky, 'I am trying to get to somewhere and this is not it. I am on a mission.'

'What kind of mission?'

'I'm a journalist. No, I can't honestly claim that. I used to work in newspapers – a newspaper, the Spear, in Edinburgh. I don't any more, but I've been given this mission to accomplish – a job, an assignment – and that's why I've ended up here. Tomorrow I'm supposed to be somewhere else to interview somebody, and my plan was to be in Fort William tonight and go to this other location in the morning, but then the train stopped here and I got off it – I shouldn't have, but I was badly advised – and then it left without me and now I'm stuck here with no idea how I'm going to get away. So, getting drunk seems a reasonable thing to do in the circumstances, and if you are assisting me in that project then I am grateful to you.'

'Where are you trying to go?'

'Somewhere called Glentaragar. Somebody was supposed to meet me here and take me there. As far as I can ascertain, it's about the most inaccessible place on the Scottish mainland.'

'You're exaggerating. There's a minibus from Fort William that takes you close. I suppose that was how you were hoping to get there?'

'That's exactly what I intended. You know of Glentaragar?'

Her response is to break briefly into the tune of 'The Road to the Isles', a lively little number made popular by Harry Lauder, Kenneth McKellar and others. 'By Loch Glass and Glen Araich and Glen Orach I will go,' she sings, and those few notes are sweeter by far than anything MacCrimmon has produced in the previous two hours. 'Yes, I know of it. There's absolutely no point in trying to get to Fort William tomorrow – you'd never make it in time to catch that bus – but you must have worked that out for yourself, hence the drowning of sorrows. Your best bet is to start walking.'

Something has happened to her voice, or to my hearing. Her words come and go as if spoken by an announcer on a distant radio station – distant perhaps in time as well as space. Her voice is like MacCrimmon's face – vaguely reminiscent.

'But it must be miles away,' I say. Weirdly, my own voice also sounds remote to me. I used to know it so well.

'About thirty,' she says, 'taking all the bends into account. The road from here goes to Oban eventually, and there's a junction with another road off to the right that's quite easy to miss, and that goes to Glen Orach, and from there it's not far to Glen Araich, and then you're almost there. If you put out your thumb you might be lucky. There's so little traffic on these roads that if somebody does come along they usually take pity on you.' Now she sounds like an actress on the not very clear soundtrack of a 1940s movie. I blame the Glen Gloming, and take some more in order to concentrate.

'And if they don't?'

'You just keep walking. That's how *I* get around. I find it liberating not knowing how long it might take or how far I might have to walk. And walking isn't *that* much slower than driving in second and third gear, which is what that road requires.'

'Is that how you got here today, by walking?'

'Yes. And two women coming away from a funeral in Oban stopped for me.'

'Those tight-fisted crows. Sorry. So you don't work here?'

'Oh no. Not officially. I just come for a break now and again.'

'To commune with nature, Malcolm said.'

'If there's any about. Don't let Malcolm bother you. He thinks he's smart and he isn't, but he's all right.'

'Hmm. I thought maybe you and he were . . .'

She laughs uproariously. 'God, I'd have to be desperate.' Then, more quietly. 'Sometimes I have been. That's why he lets me have the room for almost nothing.'

This is – or seems to be – such a frank admission that I don't want to think about the implications.

'I know this is a silly question,' I say, 'but have we met before?'

'Before today? No.'

'You seem familiar. From Edinburgh, perhaps?'

'I haven't been in Edinburgh for years.' She glances over at the sleeping barman. 'I pretended you and I hadn't met when he came in. If he knew I'd been helping behind the bar he'd have tried to get more money out of us. I hope you took a cut for yourself. Did you?'

I hesitate, which is enough for Xanthe.

'I'm so glad. It was a rotten trick he played on you. He probably went home to watch TV. He's a lazy sod.'

'What about you? Did you take a cut?'

'Bed and board, that's my reward. Oh, that rhymes.' She has been drinking her wine fast and now she knocks back the last of it and says, 'I *am* trying to get *me* drunk, incidentally.'

'Why?'

'Why not? Would you like a refill?'

'One more for the road,' I say. 'Although in fact I'm probably going to have to spend the night stretched out on this bench.'

'I have an idea about that,' Xanthe says. She goes to fetch us more drink. The bard does not stir, nor the barman. The fire glows. Xanthe returns.

'You can share my room,' she says. 'It'll be much more comfortable for both of us. We'll finish these and sneak you up there while Malcolm's snoozing. Or we can take them with us now, if you prefer?'

'Let's drink them here,' I say, hearing myself slurring in the distance. 'In case of spillage.'

I have a sudden image of the woman I once loved in Edinburgh, or the woman I thought I loved, or the woman I never loved. I forget her name for a moment, then I remember. Sonya. Sonya Strachan and her son and daughter. My happy ex-family. Then I look at Xanthe, just inches from me.

Have I come to Argyll to interview Rosalind Munlochy? I think not! Surely *this* is the adventure I came for! But is it really happening?

'Curly-haired men always make me go weak at the knees,' Xanthe says. Her hand, somehow, is resting on my thigh. 'Even when I'm sitting down.'

'I don't have curly hair,' I say.

'I bet you do,' she says. 'But I was just making small talk. Shall we go to bed?'

'Is that small talk too?'

'We can stretch it out if you want, but why would we do that?'

I put my hand on top of hers. 'To see if it was just a dream and then wake up from it?'

'That would be disappointing. Do you have any small talk yourself?'

I ponder this for a minute.

'Dogs or cats?' I say. 'Which are cleverer?'

'Dogs. Anything else?'

I have another ponder. 'No. Nothing else.'

'Come on, then.'

The room upstairs has a coombed ceiling and a dormer window. You can stand up straight in front of the window, pull back the flowery curtains and look out at the stars, but you can't stand up straight anywhere else because most of the rest of the available space is taken up by a double bed. It has white sheets, and blankets and an eiderdown, and there is a lamp on a table to one side of it. From bedclothes to patterned wallpaper it is all about thirty years out of date. I love it.

Xanthe sits on the edge of the bed and bends to take off her shoes.

To give myself something to do other than watch, I open a cupboard and find that it isn't a cupboard, though it probably once was. Inside is a tiny handbasin and a toilet. You can't stand up straight in there to do anything, so I sit down.

When I come back out Xanthe's clothes are folded on a chair and she is under the covers.

I say, 'Is this really happening?'

'I would say so,' she replies.

'Well,' I say, 'I hope this scene ends before we get to the end of it.'

She looks puzzled. 'Explain that?'

'Don't you have a dread of being caught in flagrante delicto? Or even just in your socks with a relative stranger? You just want to bypass the embarrassing bit.'

'That's why I'm in here,' she says, 'but I'm not embarrassed. And I'm not wearing any socks. Do you want me to turn out the light?'

'Yes. No. I like looking at you. Maybe if you could dim it a bit?'

'I don't think the electrics here can manage that level of sophistication.'

'Dim your eyes for ten seconds, then.'

By the time she undims them I am in beside her.

We don't indulge in small talk for a while after that. Then the question of putting out the light arises again. This time Xanthe asks me if I'll do it. She says she has a sense that somebody or something is in the room watching us. I assure her that we are alone and not to worry about it. She says she'll be more relaxed in the dark. She seems pretty relaxed already, but she insists.

'Can you reach the switch?'

'I'm trying to. I can't find it.'

'Yes you can. It's down there. Oh.'

'Sorry.'

'Don't apologise. Just a bit further over. Ah.'

'Oh. Nearly. Hang on.'

'Ooh. Not sure if I can.'

'I'm just . . .'

'Ah.'

'Got it.'

'Ah. Yes.'

'Better?'

'Yes.'

'Sure?'

'Yes, yes.'

We race the scene to its end. It is a close thing, but the scene finishes just ahead of us.

CONVERSATIONS WITH A TOAD: CONVERSATION #6

Douglas Findhorn Elder woke to the sound of small birds chattering outside his window. It took a few moments for him to realise that it was not, in fact, *his* window. The flowery curtains were unfamiliar. They were still closed but they were faded and thin, and morning light was doing its best to enter the room through them. City sounds were absent. As memory returned, Douglas reached out a hand for Xanthe.

He sat up. She was not there.

He got up and checked in the toilet that had once been a cupboard but she wasn't there either. Her clothes were absent. Every trace of her, in fact, was gone, apart from the smell of her body and her perfume in the bed, to which he now returned. Pressing his nose to the sheets and inhaling deeply triggered in Douglas a rush of satisfaction and simultaneously a confused sense of loss. He repeated the exercise several times, like an anteater grubbing around for breakfast, until he felt light-headed. This only partially helped to relieve what was shaping up to be a terrible hangover. He went and splashed cold water on his face, gave himself a cursory wash, and got dressed.

When he pulled back the curtains he found that the window looked down onto the parking area in front of the inn. It was empty. Even the rusty yellow car in which Stuart Crathes MacCrimmon had arrived was away. Douglas wondered if the bard and Xanthe might have left together.

Why had she gone? Where had she gone? Why had she not even woken him to say goodbye?

Bereft. That was how he felt. And a bit sick.

The sky was bright and blue overhead, but to the west and north it was dark and grey. It was in that direction that he needed to go.

He checked his watch. It was ten o'clock. He was late. Not late as in dead: *the late Douglas Elder.* (He felt at his wrist for a pulse, and found he still had one.) Late as in late. He was stuck miles from where he should be, beside a railway line but far from a station, beside a road but with no transport, equipped with a mobile phone but without a signal, and he was going to be late for an interview.

Both inwardly and outwardly he cursed the bard, the fickleness of woman, and the fates, which seemed to be conspiring against him at every opportunity.

He contemplated abandoning the attempt to reach Rosalind Munlochy, but as this would also mean abandoning his future in freelance journalism and would not solve the problem of his being stranded, he rejected the idea.

Downstairs all was silent, clean and still. The fireplace had been cleared out and reset with paper and kindling, the peat basket had been refilled, the chairs and tables were in place. There was no sign of Malcolm – a small mercy – nor of his bicycle, which would have been a severe temptation. Actually, not a temptation at all: Douglas would have commandeered it in seconds. He went through to the kitchen, rooted about in cupboards and the fridge for the makings of breakfast, and made some. Eating food, he knew, was likely to improve the way he felt, and indeed the worst effects of the night before's alcohol intake diminished after a mug of coffee, a couple of boiled eggs and some toast.

After that, there didn't seem much point in lingering. He found his suitcase behind the bar where he had stowed it, and his raincoat on the peg where he had hung it. Then he stepped out of the Shira Inn, as if out of some strange dwelling in a fairy tale where impossible things were possible.

'Ah, there you are at last,' Mungo Forth Mungo said.

'Jesus!' Douglas said, clutching at his heart. Then, hoping to disguise the fact that, once again, he had quite forgotten about his travelling companion, he added quickly, 'Good morning, Mungo. How are you?'

'I'm well, thank you. The quality of insect hereabouts is generally very high. And plenty of them, too. I've had an excellent night. How was yours?'

'Good, thanks.'

'Sleep well?'

'Yes, Mungo, very. Did you happen to, er, see Xanthe this morning?'

'The uncommon woman? No. Missing her already? Or has she just *gone* missing?'

'Not missing. Just gone. In fact, everybody's disappeared.'

'Well, I haven't seen a soul.'

'What about the bard. Did you see him leave?'

'No. Mind you, I've been dozing quite a bit, waiting for you, so he could easily have slipped by me. What's the plan? Is there a train due?'

'There may be, but it won't stop for us. The plan, such as it is, is to start walking and hope for a lift – and a phone signal, so I can let the people at Glentaragar House know I've been delayed.'

'*We've* been delayed.'

'They don't know you're coming.'

'I'm not happy about getting in a car, you know.'

'Tough. If you get in my pocket just now, we'll make a start.'

'I'd rather stay out if it's all the same to you. It's going to rain and I don't want to miss it.'

'I can't go at your pace.'

'What if I sit on your suitcase as you pull it along?'

'It could be a bumpy ride.'

171

'I'm good at gripping and clinging on. It's something I do every spring. Do you know what amplexus is?'

'No.'

'Look it up in one of your books. Your suitcase shall be to me as a very stout and fertile female toad in the season of spawning. Nothing will shift me.'

'Well, don't make a mess.'

'Don't be crude. It's the wrong time of year, and anyway your suitcase is going to get a thorough rinse.'

This was true. The sky was rapidly darkening and even as Mungo climbed aboard the case a few drops fell. At the same time something landed on Douglas's neck and bit it. He turned up the collar of his raincoat. Mungo turned his face to the sky. They set off down the single-track road.

'This is the life,' Mungo said.

'It's not much of one,' Douglas said.

'Don't be so negative. What's the alternative?'

The rain thickened and hardened. Douglas trudged on. He said, 'I don't suppose you have any sense at all of what an afterlife might be, do you?'

'What, after life? Decomposition? Being eaten by something?'

'No. More life. Life after death. Immortality.'

'I sort of understand the concept. It's like one of your myths or legends, isn't it? Good for illustrating what life's about to young or simple minds, but unhelpful beyond that. Nobody takes it seriously, surely?'

'Some people take it very seriously. They're prepared to die in defence of their own particular version of it – or kill for it, which is worse. Anyway, I had this idea the other day – it popped into my head unbidden, on my fiftieth birthday in fact – that my immortality warranty had run out, or was about to.'

'Your what?'

'That was my reaction as well. It wasn't a phrase I was familiar with, but there it was, in my head. And although I still don't know what it means, I'm thinking now, suppose something has happened to us. Suppose when we left the train we were actually moving from one life to the next, and that Customer Experience Officer character was some sort of angel or usher, directing us on, and the Shira Inn was a waiting room between lives, and now this is us starting out into eternity. Are you with me?'

'Physically, yes. Conceptually, only just.'

'And for me it's a kind of hell, with constant rain and aching feet and biting insects and a road that goes on and on for ever, whereas for you it's a kind of paradise, with constant rain and insects and the same never-ending road. And yet we're going down that road together. Does that make any kind of sense?'

'None. You are drivelling. It's a tendency I've had occasion to remark on before. You should give your imagination less slack. Anyway, where does this immortality-warranty thing fit in? If it's run out, then you can't be immortal. You must be dead. But you're still conscious, still able to imagine things and talk drivel, ergo you must be alive. *Toad erat demonstrandum*, if you'll excuse the pun.'

'Ah well, Mungo,' Douglas said – the rain was now a steady downpour, and he was growing soggier by the second – 'I surely couldn't be having this conversation with you in hell, and I'm damn sure I'm not in heaven, so thank you. I just needed a little reassurance. It's so bloody wet. I hope a car comes along soon.'

'I hope it doesn't,' Mungo said. 'We have hope in common, at least. And as somebody once said, to travel hopefully is a better thing than to arrive.'

'Did they?' Douglas said. 'Well, whoever said that was a fool.'

[To be continued]

AN ECSTATIC SCARECROW

The rain falls relentlessly. Mostly it falls vertically but sometimes, if the breeze picks up from the west, it falls horizontally, slapping me about the cheeks and sneaking its way between the buttons of my coat as if it has some kind of slippery, interfering authority to check that the layers of my clothing are comprehensively soaked through. Once or twice it even contrives to fall upwards, by bouncing off the road with such force that it penetrates to my skin from below. Whenever I glance at the sky to see if there is the possibility of a let-up, all I see is a darker shade of black. The road stretches on, twisting occasionally to trick me into thinking that if only I go round the next bend I will come across some habitation, some meagre shelter, or even a sign telling me how many more miles lie between me and Oban or Glen Araich or Glen Orach or anywhere. To discover that it is only a hundred miles to Inverness would be something. It would prove that I am still in Scotland and/or the land of the living. But there is neither sign nor shelter. There is nothing but the road and the rain and

Douglas Findhorn Elder marching towards his fate and the trundling rumble of his suitcase behind him.

And then, suddenly and miraculously, there *is* something else. I mishear it at first as the sound of water hurrying along the road at my heels, a swishing sound, and as my shoes are already drenched I do not bother to turn to inspect the latest torrent that I assume is about to engulf them. But I detect another noise, that of an engine, and with it the *thwack-thwack* of windscreen wipers working at the double. Oh joy! A car! I stop, turn, let go of the suitcase and stick out both arms, thumbs aloft, like an ecstatic scarecrow. The black car bearing down on me has its headlights on, and I hope the driver sees me in time because if he or she doesn't I will be flattened. Nothing is going to make me step aside. If the car crushes me, so be it. This, then, is and will be the fate towards which I have been marching – to die an ignominious death under its wheels on an unclassified road in the West Highlands.

Conveniently, the car is a hearse. That will save the bother of calling an ambulance. Thwarting the gods, however, the hearse comes to a halt some yards from me. The driver's window is wound down. A head pokes out and a voice – a voice I know! – shouts at me as I stand there with my arms still outstretched.

'Hih! Come doon aff your cross a minute! Are you a local? Gonnae tell me where the fuck I am?'

I lower the arms and advance.

'Hello, Gerry,' I call out.

The last thing Gerry can be expecting is that the bedraggled stranger blocking his further progress will address him by his own name. He handles it pretty well. A lesser man might panic, believing himself caught up in one of those paranormal nightmares that are reputed to occur regularly on lonely country roads in inclement weather. Gerry merely sticks his head further out into the deluge and stares at me for several seconds, during which time a considerable quantity of rainwater must enter his open mouth. Finally he speaks.

'Who the fuck are you?'

'Let me in and I'll tell you. And somehow, I swear, I'll guide you out of here.'

This is the clincher. Gerry does a quick assessment of the situation and reaches the correct conclusion. 'Right,' he says. 'Sling that in the back and hop in, whoever you are.'

I sling and hop. Never have I slung and hopped more swiftly nor indeed more gratefully. The back of the hearse is empty: in it, my suitcase assumes the appearance of a coffin for a smallish dog or other pet. I plant myself at the passenger end of the bench seat occupied at the steering-wheel end by Gerry the apprentice undertaker. He is wearing a white shirt, black tie and striped trousers, and his long-tailed coat is folded on the seat between us.

'Last time we met was in Morningside,' I explain, and there is something glorious and *meant* about the way that comes out. *Well Met in Morningside*: it has a ring to it, like *Ice Cold in Alex* or *Last Exit to Brooklyn*. 'At a funeral, a week ago. Douglas Elder,' I add, and I reach out a hand and he grasps it.

'No Douglas Fir, eh?' Gerry says, laughing, and I laugh with him, because right then it is one of the wittiest remarks I've ever heard. Not that you would think so from Gerry's laugh, which sounds as if he is experiencing the kind of pain that might be caused by walking on hot coals.

'Aahaaha! I'm Gerry by the way. But ye ken that already. Ye're totally drookit, man. I'll gie the heating a blast, dry ye oot a bit. Whose funeral?'

'Ronald Grigson's. A former colleague of mine. You and I had a blether outside the church.'

'Oh, right! I mind ye noo!' Gerry says. 'You're the one that was late. Good tae see ye, man. Whit the fuck are ye daein oot here?'

'I could ask you the same question, but I suppose with you the answer is obvious. You're here to . . . make a collection?'

I don't know why I use that phrase, but it has an odd effect on Gerry. 'Aye!' he says, tapping his nose and shaking his head in a marvelling way. 'How did ye ken? But I'm lost. There's nae signs or nothing. So when I seen ye up ahead, I thought, thank fuck, I'm saved!'

'Gerry,' I say, 'when I saw you, I thought exactly the same.'

'I could've been wandering roond here for the rest of my fucking life.'

'Me too. So let's not waste any more time. Drive on, MacDuff!'

'Whit?'

'Just drive. Where are you trying to get to?'

'Some hotel,' Gerry says. The transmission is automatic – ideal for funereal smoothness and sedateness, I suppose. Gerry shifts the control to DRIVE and we ease forward. 'That's the pick-up point. I passed a pub back up the road twenty minutes ago and I thought that was it but it wasnae, and there was naebody aboot tae get directions either. It was like the *Mary* fucking *Celeste* in fact. The place I'm looking for is called the

Glen Lodge or something. I've got it written doon here.' He starts to scrabble around in the door pocket.

'The Glen Araich Lodge Hotel?'

Gerry slaps the dashboard. 'Aye, that's it! Talk aboot luck, eh? Thank fuck I stopped for ye. I'm no supposed tae pick up passengers, ken, no live ones anyway, but I'm no really sticking tae the company rules on this jaunt. Ye never shopped me for having a fly fag that day, did ye? Ye're solid, man. D'ye ken where this lodge place is, then?'

'No, but it's where I'm heading as well. Between us, we'll find it.'

Like Gerry I am momentarily elated, but then a sobering thought strikes me. It will be *my* luck if I reach Glentaragar House only to find that the whole trip is in vain.

'Who's your customer?' I ask. 'You're not going to Glen Araich to collect an old lady from a big house near there, are you?'

Gerry is peering intently through the windscreen so as to keep us out of the ditches, but he manages a glance across at me, and laughs his high, painful laugh.

'Aahaaha! Aye, that'll be right! Dinnae be daft, man. Do you think I'd be on my ain if I was coming for a body? And what the hell would an Edinburgh undertaker be daein aw the way oot here?'

'That did occur to me. I'm relieved, Gerry. The reason *I'm* out here, to answer your earlier question, is I'm on my way to interview the old lady in question, and it would have broken my heart to find her dead on arrival. My arrival, that is.'

Gerry, until now so friendly, looks suddenly suspicious.

'What are ye gonnae question her for? What's she done?'

'Plenty.'

Gerry's complexion couldn't be much paler, but he blanches like a cauliflower. 'Like what?'

'Loads of things. Written books, been an MP, travelled in the wilds of Canada. She's about to be a hundred and she's had a life. She's famous, or she once was. I'm going to ask her about some of the things she's seen.'

'Ye mean, like a witness?'

'A witness to history.'

'Oh, right. Ye had me gaun there. Ye're no the polis, are ye?'

'No, of course not. Whatever gives you that idea?'

'When I hear aboot folk getting questioned it's usually the polis that are daein the questioning.'

'Relax, Gerry. I'm on a job for a newspaper.'

'Aye, well, ye would say that, wouldn't ye?'

'Here.' I pull my sodden wallet from my trouser pocket. The sixty pounds are there, damp but entire. So too are half a dozen of the cards Ollie prepared for me. I peel one away from the leather and hand it over. 'Satisfied?'

Gerry inspects it briefly and drops it on top of his coat. 'Fair enough. But anything I say to you is aff the record, aw right?'

'Absolutely. It's not your story I'm after. But still, if you're not collecting the dead, what are you collecting? What's going on?'

'Haud on a minute. What's this?' Gerry says.

We have reached a junction of some sort, where our road meets two others in an informal kind of way, as if they've got together by chance and might very well not see each other again for a while. With there being no signposts or road markings, we are faced less with a choice than with a gamble. Left looks slightly wider than right, and doesn't have grass growing up the middle. I remember what Xanthe told me last night, although it is quite hard to convince myself that last night wasn't a dream.

'That must be the road to Oban, Gerry,' I say, pointing left. 'We go right.'

'I trust you, Douglas,' Gerry says, and guides the big car round. It just about fits, and we continue on our way. I am beginning to steam nicely.

'I think maybe it's lifting a bit,' Gerry says, cracking open his window to let some fresh air in.

'If you're not fetching a body, what are you doing?' I ask again.

'Ah well.' He drums the wheel with his fingers. There is a hunted expression on his thin white face. 'Can I trust you, Douglas?'

'You just said you did.'

'So I did. Thing is, I've kind of borrowed the motor for the day.'

'Borrowed it?'

'Aye. It'll no be missed, because it's the reserve car, and they only ever use it if there's a sudden surge in business, like a plague or something. I've been there a month and it's never been oot once. They don't even keep it on the premises, it's in a lock-up and naebody will ken it's no there if it isnae needed, which it isnae, I checked the diary. And they'll no miss me cos it's my day aff. So I borrowed it. Borrowed the key, borrowed the key tae the lock-up, and as long as I get back tae Edinburgh the night, replace the fuel, gie it a wee wash and put it back where I found it, naebody'll ken. It'll be just like that fly fag I had last week.'

'Maybe not quite,' I say. 'But you've not done all that just so you can have a nice wee run in the Highlands. So why?'

'I'm daein somebody a favour. He's a pal, kind of. It's a wee job, ken, a wee collect-and-deliver job. Like stand-and-deliver only nae guns. At least I hope no, aahaaha! Some goods that he's needing shifted.'

'Wouldn't it have been easier to use a van?'

'Eh, no. Because I dinnae hae a van, and he didnae want tae pay tae hire one, the guy I'm daein the job for, the favour I mean, and I couldnae afford tae hire one and I dinnae hae a driving licence anyway. No a valid one.'

'So you've taken a vehicle from your employer without permission, and you're driving it without insurance or a licence in order to shift unspecified goods for a pal. No wonder you're worried.'

'I'm no worried. My pal just needs the job done this week, that's all. Like today. Like now.'

'And if it isn't?'

'He'll probably break my legs.'

'Fucking hell, Gerry. What kind of pal would do that?'

'An angry one. Naw, dinnae look at me like that, man, it's nae sweat. It'll all go like clockwork, specially now you're with me. We'll find this lodge hotel place, load up and be on our way and be hame in nae time. It'll aw be done and dusted by midnight.'

I don't like the assumptions Gerry seems to be making and feel a need to put him right.

'Hold it there, Gerry. I appreciate the lift and all that, but there's no way I'm getting involved in any scheme that involves some pal of yours breaking my legs if something goes wrong. Which, from what you've told me, is what a man I met yesterday would call a dead cert.'

'Naw, it'll be fine. Naebody's gonnae break *your* legs. If anybody's legs are gonnae get broke it'll be mine, but that's no gonnae happen either because I'll deliver the merchandise, my debt'll be paid aff and everybody'll be happy.'

'What debt? You said you were doing this so-called pal a favour. And what is the merchandise, Gerry? Is it drugs? Because if it's drugs you can stop the car right here and I'll start walking again.'

'Naw, it's no drugs. Calm doon, man. Ye dinnae have tae be involved if ye dinnae want tae be. Just help us oot wi the directions and gie us a hand wi loading the stuff and we'll be quits.'

'What stuff?'

Gerry taps his nose again in that meaningful way that means very little to me, other than to remind me of Malcolm the barman. 'Show ye when we get there. Some road this, eh? Hope we don't meet anything coming the other way.'

We drive round a tight right-hand bend, over a humpbacked bridge followed by a tight left-hand bend, and meet something coming the other way: a minibus. Beside the bridge is a muddy patch of grass just wide and long enough to accommodate a hearse, so Gerry slides us into it, and the driver of the bus, which appears not to have any passengers on board, honks his horn and goes on his merry way.

'That must be the bus I would have been on if my plans hadn't got screwed up,' I say. 'We're on the right track.'

Shortly after this the road does become more or less a track. And a mile or so later we pass a handful of cottages huddling like dirty sheep beside a river, and that, I guess, is Glen Orach.

'What time is it?'

'Two-thirty,' Gerry says. 'Soon be there, eh? And it's definitely lifting.'

Half an hour later we come over the brow of another hill and coast down to a white harled building of three storeys with a round tower at one end. From a pole on the tower a saltire hangs limply. Lettering in black paint on one wall proclaims that this is the Glen Araich Lodge Hotel. Gerry swings the hearse in below an archway and brings it to rest outside an oak door covered in iron studs. Behind us is a collection of outbuildings, and beside the hotel is a spongy-looking nine-hole putting green.

'D'ye play golf?' Gerry asks as we get out and stretch our limbs. 'We might get a wee round in. I think the sun's gonnae come oot.'

There is one other vehicle parked outside the hotel: a rusty yellow model with a distinctive leaning posture suggesting less than perfect suspension.

'I wouldn't bet on it,' I reply.

A MARKETING THING

It appears that the hostelries in this part of the country favour a laissez-faire approach when it comes to welcoming would-be patrons. Whereas at the Shira Inn the barman takes the arrival of a customer as an opportunity to disappear for the afternoon, the Glen Araich Lodge Hotel's policy seems to be to have no staff at all and leave anybody who turns up to fend for themselves. That is what Gerry and I now do. We use the toilets, we help ourselves to coffee from a drinks machine in the main lobby, and while Gerry goes exploring I take some dryish – or dampish – clothes from my suitcase, change into them and spread the things I have been wearing over a few chairs in the bar. I expect to find Stuart Crathes MacCrimmon in there making the most of the hospitality but there is no sign of him. Back at the reception desk I ping the service bell a few times. Nobody answers.

Gerry reappears. 'Nae need for that,' he says. 'I've found what I've come for.'

'There's a phone here,' I say. 'I'm going to make a call.'

'Leave it the now. Why tell folk we're here if we dinnae have tae? I'll get loaded up and on my way, and ye'll never see me again in your puff. That's what ye're wanting, isn't it?'

'Gerry,' I say, 'I've nothing against you, and I won't forget that you rescued me in my hour of need, but you're right. As far as any future relationship with you, let alone your merchandising pal, is concerned, I'd rather not have one.'

'That's what I just said, only in aboot hauf the words. Stop wasting your breath and gie us a hand then, and I'll get oot your road.'

He leads me to the outbuildings and we enter the nearest one through a doorway that requires the lowering of our heads. Inside is a storeroom piled with packing cases, bits of furniture, rolled-up rugs and old appliances, but a narrow path across the stone floor has been left clear, and this brings us to a second low doorway. Gerry pushes open the door. The afternoon light, which barely reaches this far, nevertheless reveals bales of straw stacked high, with a few lying in a heap to one side – Gerry's handiwork. He pulls another bale down and adds it to the heap. He makes a fanfare noise – 'Ta-ra!' – and follows this with a burst of agonised laughter.

The space behind the straw is crammed to the roof with cardboard boxes. Gerry rips the lid of one open, reaches in and hands something to me. It is a bottle, and although I cannot make out the writing on the label I recognise the familiar image of the howling stag. We appear to be in the presence of the bulk of the world's supply of Glen Gloming 12-Year-Old Single Malt Scotch Whisky.

'What's all this doing here?'

'Waiting for me,' Gerry says. 'I'm gonnae back the motor over. You start bringing the boxes oot.'

As it says somewhere in the Book of Ecclesiastes, there is a time to argue and a time to cooperate, a time to speak and a time to shut the fuck up. I like Gerry but I do not want to prolong our association. The simplest and quickest way to bring it to a close, it seems to me, is to load up the hearse and see him off, preferably without being spotted in his company. My phone call to Glentaragar House can wait.

I start shifting boxes from behind the bales, carrying them one at a time to the first outer door. As Gerry predicted, watery sunlight is now putting on a show. He has the back of the hearse open and has pulled all the wee curtains shut, and as fast as I bring the boxes to him he stacks them in the space usually reserved for the dead. We speak not a word for the best part of forty minutes. He, like me, seems seized by a strong desire not to be disturbed or distracted from his labour.

About halfway through the process, one of the boxes slips as it passes between me and Gerry. It lands with quite a thump on the ground, and we decide we'd better inspect the contents for damage. All is intact, and we are about to resume when, as I fit the last bottle back into position, something makes me stop and pull it out again.

'Look, Gerry.'

The bottle has the same, familiar square shape, but the stag that usually graces the label is gone. In its place is a silhouetted angler up to his thighs in a rushing river, and the name on the bottle is 'Salmon's Leap – Single Malt Scotch Whisky, Matured for 10 Years'. We check the other bottles in the case: they are all the same. We open a couple of cases already in the hearse: they contain bottles of Glen Gloming. The cases waiting by the doorway are full of Salmon's Leap. But when I hold a bottle of Glen Gloming and one of Salmon's Leap up to the light together, there is no visible difference between their contents.

'I think that's what in the film industry they call a continuity error,' I say.

'Aye,' Gerry says. 'Or maybe no. Don't suppose it matters what name's on the stuff. My pal never said nothing aboot the name. He just tellt me where it was.' He turns the bottle of Salmon's Leap and studies the label. 'See that? Why would ye dae that? It must be fucking freezing. I never fancied fishing, but then I don't like whisky either. Maybe it's a marketing thing, eh?'

'That's exactly what it is, a marketing thing. Whisky's not your spirit of choice, then?'

'Naw, I hate the stuff. I dinnae drink alcohol or I might think aboot pauchlin a few, but this is like shifting Bibles tae me – nae temptation.'

'I think they're already pauchled, Gerry.'

'Aye, right enough. You keep a couple of bottles for yersel, then. Naebody'll notice.'

'I'll take one of each,' I say. 'See if I can tell the difference.'

'Good luck wi that. Makes me want tae boak, whisky. Glen Boak, that would be a good name for it. Aahaaha! Right. Let's get this job finished.'

It's amazing how many cases of whisky you can get in a hearse. No human corpse, however large, ever weighed down that vehicle as it is weighed down by the time we finish. I have a momentary vision of Ollie Buckthorn squashing the air from his bicycle tyres, and I suggest to Gerry that he will need to go carefully with such a load. He agrees. We close the back of the hearse and walk round it to make sure that the curtains block any view in from the outside. Then we replace the straw bales in front of a much-diminished stock of whisky in the outbuildings, and come back into the daylight.

'Right,' Gerry says. 'Let's see if we can find a couple of putters and golf balls. We'll hae a quick round and then I'll be aff.' He watches my face for a moment, then cracks. 'Aahaaha! Had ye gaun there, man! Relax! That grass is far too wet tae play on. I'm just gonnae head. Sure you don't want a lift back tae Edinburgh?'

'Quite sure, Gerry,' I say. 'I've a job to do, remember?'

'Me tae,' Gerry says. 'Got tae keep the customers satisfied, eh?'

'That's very true.'

'Or they'll break your legs. That's a joke, man.'

'Is it?'

'It better be. Well, cheerio, then.'

'Cheerio, Gerry.'

He gets behind the wheel, starts the engine and gives me the thumbs-up. What an optimist! I give him the thumbs-up back. Then, with a creaking, low-slung, ponderous dignity, Gerry in his borrowed hearse rolls out of my life, never, I sincerely hope, to enter it again.

CONVERSATIONS WITH A TOAD:
CONVERSATION #7

Douglas Findhorn Elder took two small glasses from behind the bar of the Glen Araich Lodge Hotel and placed them on a table already occupied by – if their labels were to be believed – a bottle of Glen Gloming 12-Year-Old and a bottle of Salmon's Leap 10-Year-Old Single Malt

Scotch Whisky. He opened the bottles – they had corks surmounted by plastic tops in their necks, but no foil seal to prevent them being tampered with – and poured an equal measure from each. He filled a jug with water from a tap behind the bar and added a small quantity to each glass. He raised the glasses together to the light. He sniffed them mightily in turn. Closing his eyes he moved the glasses round on the tabletop, stood and walked to the bar and back, then swapped the glasses again several times, until he was completely certain that he was completely uncertain as to which bottle he had poured whisky from into which glass. Only then did he allow himself to sip, first one, then the other, then the other, then the first.

They were identical.

He sat and pondered this not unanticipated discovery. The bar was silent but for the ticking of a clock on one wall. The time was ten-past five. Through a grimy window he saw that clouds were gathering again. If he listened really hard, he fancied he could make out the faint hiss of his clothes as they dried on the chairs around him. He found his mobile phone and checked for a signal. Nothing. On the screen were the words EMERGENCY CALLS ONLY and he contemplated making one of those but it wasn't really an emergency and anyway he didn't expect anyone would come. Any real emergency would be over long before they – whoever they might be – arrived.

Mungo Forth Mungo entered. He took a turn round the room. He looked disgruntled but that was his default expression. He had every right to be disgruntled, Douglas thought. The hotel was in a dilapidated condition. Everything looked, felt and smelt damp, dirty and cheap. Of course, dampness would not disappoint Mungo but Douglas reckoned that in other respects the toad was quite fastidious, and that he knew poor quality and bad taste when he saw it. The hotel was full of both, from chipboard panelling to plastic lampshades and garish flock wallpaper. Who knew what the bedrooms would be like?

'Are we there yet?' Mungo asked.

'No. We are one stop short of our final destination. I'm going to make a call and ask if someone can come to collect us. The weather's closing in again, it's a five-mile walk and I'm not up for that. I'm pinning my hopes on the Corryvreckan lunatic. Did I really say that?'

'You did.'

'I thought so. I just don't want to have to spend the night here.'

'Perhaps you could borrow that car outside?'

'The bard's? That's not a bad idea, but I have a strong objection to borrowing a vehicle without the owner's permission.'

'Would that be a moral objection?'

'More a fatalistic one. The sense that, if I do something like that, fate will bite me in the bum in due course.'

'That sounds like the same kind of objection to me. What if the owner has been generous enough to leave the key in the ignition? Which he has, incidentally. I climbed up and had a look.'

'That's a warning sign. It makes it even more likely that there would be payback later. Mungo, I've just been aiding and abetting someone in the crime of bootlegging, so I've already tempted fate once today. Whether I've got away with it or not I don't know, but the key in the car is fate's way of tempting me to have another shot. I wonder where MacCrimmon is. He can't be far. If he's in a good mood and sober he could drive us there himself. I'll have a hunt for him if my phone call is unsuccessful.'

Douglas left Mungo gathering spiders, of which there were a considerable number resident in the hotel, and went to the reception desk to use the telephone. It rang for a long time and while it rang he opened the register and noted that nobody was recorded as having stayed in the past month. Just when he was about to give up, the receiver was lifted and the familiar though still distant voice of Miss Coppélia Munlochy sounded from the Striven family pile. Douglas pictured her at the other end of the line as a straight-backed, unsmiling frump in a draughty hallway, but also, for no obvious reason, as a curvaceous, welcoming beauty reclining in a wicker chair in a white muslin dress in a bright, airy conservatory surrounded by thriving tropical plants.

'Glentaragar House.'

'Miss Munlochy? This is Douglas Elder speaking.'

'Mr Elder. We expected you this afternoon.'

'Did you? Well, I'm sorry, but I expected you, or your Mr Corryvreckan, at the Shira Inn yesterday.'

'The Shira Inn?'

'Yes. The message I received on the train was that I would be met there and driven to Glentaragar.'

'What message?'

'You didn't send a message to the train?'

'Does that sound likely? One can't ask trains to stop just anywhere. There isn't even a station at the Shira Inn.'

'The guard told me it's a request stop.'

'Really? So you got out?'

'I did.'

'And where are you now?'

'I'm at the Glen Araich Lodge Hotel.'

'I see. Are you being looked after?'

'No. There's not a soul about. I was wondering, would there be any chance of somebody coming to collect me?'

'From the Glen Araich? No, I'm afraid not.' There was a slight pause. 'Corryvreckan isn't here at the moment.'

'I'd walk but it's getting late and the rain is on again. I'm not sure of the way. All in all, it's been a bit of a nightmare journey and I'm very tired.'

'Well, you would be, after a nightmare journey.' Douglas could not determine from her tone whether she was making a friendly or an unfriendly joke. Perhaps she wasn't making a joke at all.

'Did you come by minibus?'

'No, I came by hearse.'

'Oh, that's novel.' Did he hear a smothered laugh?

'Yes, well, there wasn't anything else available. Look, it's such a shame to be so close and yet not manage the final leg tonight. I don't know how that message reached me if it didn't come from somebody at your end, but I'm prepared to accept that an honest mistake was made. Couldn't we start afresh? I don't suppose *you* could come for me, if Mr Corryvreckan can't?'

'No, I couldn't, Mr Elder. I don't drive. I agree with you, a mistake has been made, but not by us. Perhaps it would be better, after all, if you stayed at the hotel, and Corryvreckan came for you in the morning. Shall we say about ten? You wouldn't have interviewed my grandmother today anyway, so you'll not have fallen far behind your schedule.'

Where had he heard that voice before, Douglas wondered. *Had* he heard it before? (Other than on the telephone, obviously.) Was it three days or four since they had last spoken? He felt as if he had been away from Edinburgh for years.

'That's true,' he said, 'but is that really the best you can suggest?'

'I'm afraid so.'

'Well, it's very disappointing, but if that's the way it is, I'll look out for Mr Corryvreckan in the morning. And meanwhile I'll just have to hope someone shows up who can give me a bed for the night here.'

'If they don't, I suggest you help yourself. Go upstairs and take the first unoccupied room you find.'

'That shouldn't be difficult. Nobody else is staying here.'

'The beds are usually made up. Make yourself at home. Look in the kitchen for food. You can settle the bill in the morning before you leave.'

'You seem to know your way round the place?'

'I know something about it. And after all, you mustn't go hungry.'

'It's very odd, isn't it, that there shouldn't be anybody here at all?'

'Not especially. The tourist season is over. Things are more informal at this time of year. More relaxed.'

'*Is* there a tourist season?'

'Not much of one.'

'Well, I don't find the place relaxing. Actually it's quite unnerving.'

'There is no need to be nervous, Mr Elder. You're not a character in a gothic melodrama, you know.'

Again, Douglas couldn't detect if she found his predicament amusing. She certainly wasn't showing much sympathy.

'Oh, am I not?' he said. 'Are you positive Mr Corryvreckan can't collect me?'

'Quite positive. And by the way, it's not *Mr* Corryvreckan, it's just Corryvreckan. He is quite particular about that.'

'I'll do my best not to upset him,' Douglas said, attempting sarcasm.

'That would be appreciated. Until tomorrow, then. Good night, Mr Elder. I do hope you sleep well after all your adventures.'

She hung up and Douglas was obliged to do the same. Whether or not she had immediately dissolved into a fit of laughter he had no idea, but he for one was not amused by his predicament. In fact, he felt as disgruntled as Mungo habitually looked.

Coming out from behind the desk his arm knocked the register off the shelf and onto the floor. When he retrieved it a sheet of paper fell from it, a handwritten list on which was written:

Highland Gold
Highland Heart
Queen of the Glens
Islay Dew
Salmon's Leap ✓
Stag's Breath (already taken)
Stalker's Joy
Fingal's Cave
Glen Gloming ✓
Mountain Tarn

Frowning, Douglas returned to the bar. He wanted another drink, and he was beginning to feel faint with hunger. He would have to hunt down a bed *and* some food – *and* of course Stuart Crathes MacCrimmon. He had forgotten to mention the possibility of a lift from the bard. If that proved to be an option, he would have to call Miss Munlochy back and say he was on his way.

'Well?' Mungo asked.

'Looks like we're stuck here for the night. Do you want a drink?'

'Some red wine would be good, if there is any.'

Douglas found a bottle and opened it, splashed some wine into a tin ashtray and placed it on the floor. Mungo took up position with a small exhalation of pleasure.

'Crisps?' Douglas said.

'Not haggis, neeps and tatties again?'

'That seems to be all there is.'

'I'll pass, thank you. There is a sufficiency of indoor wildlife.'

'I'll go and locate the kitchen in a minute and see what else there is. I'm famished. But first . . .' He knocked back what whisky was left in the two glasses on the table, and refilled one of them with Salmon's Leap, or Glen Gloming by another name.

'I mentioned bootlegging earlier,' he said. 'Do you know what bootlegging is?'

Mungo gave him a look.

'Sorry, silly of me to ask. Well, it seems to me that whoever runs this place must be up to their eyes in it too. They can't *not* know about all that whisky stashed outside.'

'And what are you going to do? Tell the police?'

'No, but –'

'Ah, this is another of those fate-versus-morality things, is it?'

'Kind of. It makes me feel uncomfortable.'

'But not so uncomfortable that it stops you drinking the whisky?'

'Don't judge me, Mungo.'

'I'm not judging you. You're doing a fine job of that yourself. What do I care?'

'What a weird day this has been,' Douglas said.

It was about to get weirder. The front door of the hotel banged open and shut, and Douglas heard somebody moving about at the reception desk. The bell was pinged. 'Hello? Hello?' a voice called.

'There's no one there!' Douglas shouted.

'Oh, but there is,' the voice said, coming closer to the bar. '*You* are! That's why I rang the bell, to see where you were. I knew you must be somewhere. And you are in there!'

'I'll be discreet,' Mungo said discreetly, leaving his wine bath and heading for the shadows, where no doubt a selection of food awaited him.

The owner of the voice entered, opened his arms wide and said, 'Well, well, this is all very fine. Good evening and welcome to the Glen Araich Lodge Hotel. I hope your stay here will be a thorough pleasure to us all, yes indeed. I'm sorry I was not able to welcome you earlier. I was unavoidably detained.'

He seemed at first glance to be an ancient, tottering kind of fellow, a retired shepherd or gillie perhaps. He had a long, tangled beard, mainly grey though with darker patches on the cheeks, and a long, weather-beaten face topped by a scarcity of fine grey hair swept back from the forehead. He wore a predominantly green suit of Harris tweed, a once-white shirt and a knitted tie the colour of dead bracken. In every respect except for his cheerful demeanour he was the living image of the bard MacCrimmon, whom Douglas had last seen in an alcohol-induced coma at the Shira Inn, and whose rust-bucket of a car was parked outside.

'MacCrimmon!' Douglas cried, almost joyfully.

'What, what, what? My name is MacLagan, Ruaridh MacLagan. Well, well, here we are. I see you have already begun the celebrations. I will join you for a small libation before you sign the register, and then I will show you to your room. Will you be wanting a little supper this evening?'

'Yes. No. I mean, wait! Can't you take me to Glentaragar House? I'm expected there. You could run me up in your car.'

'My car?'

'Aye, it's sitting outside. Please, I know we got off on the wrong foot yesterday, but you'd be doing me a huge favour. It wouldn't take more than twenty minutes of your time, would it?'

'To go to Glentaragar House and back? It would take double that. A poor road it is to Glentaragar, a poor road indeed. And what is this you say about yesterday? You are mistaking me for someone else, my friend, but if ever we had been on the wrong foot, as you put it, it would be my dearest wish to be on the right one now. As for driving you to Glentaragar, I cannot do it. You refer to a car outside. That is not my car. I do not have a car.'

'But I saw you take your guitar out of it yesterday at the Shira Inn. You are MacCrimmon, Stuart Crathes MacCrimmon.'

'The popular entertainer? Well now, that would explain your confusion. I am the manager of *this* establishment. The Shira Inn is a place I have never seen, nor have I ever met the gentleman to whom you refer, but I have heard that there is a strong though purely coincidental resemblance between us. I see you have two bottles of whisky before you. May I ask, did you take these from the bar or are they your own personal bottles? If the latter, I regret to inform you that only beverages purchased on the premises are permitted to be consumed in the public areas of the hotel.'

'You deny that you are MacCrimmon?'

'I do. I am MacLagan. I will not tell you a third time.'

'Then what is his car doing outside?'

'I have no idea, but if he does not remove it by tomorrow there will be trouble, I tell you. And a parking fine. Now, I must ask you again, do these bottles belong to you – or to me?'

A new sharpness was in his voice, portending menace or even violence. And this was striking because up until that point he had spoken in a light, gentle manner quite unlike the surly tones of MacCrimmon, and in an accent that Douglas took to be local. He was also staring at Douglas with a great intensity, and Douglas understood this stare to mean that MacLagan knew of the store of illicit whisky, that he knew that Douglas knew of it, and that claiming ownership of the bottles would be an admission of that knowledge. And that it might not be wise to make that admission.

'I – I did take them from the bar. There was nobody about and I needed a drink.'

MacLagan was all geniality again in an instant. 'Well, and what would any sane man do in the circumstances but help himself to his favourite tipple. Or, indeed, tipples. We will say no more about it. On the house, on the house. I see you have two glasses also. I will avail myself of one of these, and let us raise a toast to the hospitality of the glens, for which indeed they are famous. Which of these two fine whiskies is in fact your favourite? Myself, I cannot make up my mind. Sometimes I incline towards Glen Gloming, sometimes I am all for the Salmon's Leap. Ach well, the night is yet young. We can test them to destruction if we so choose. To the hospitality of the glens, Mr –?'

'Elder. Douglas Elder.'

'Elder as in the Kirk? Kirk as in Douglas? Douglas as in Fir? *Slàinte mhath!*'

'*Slàinte mhath*,' Douglas said weakly.

'Now, did you say you would be wanting some supper?'

Any minute now, Douglas thought, he would wake from a terrible dream. But for the moment he was defeated by physical and mental exhaustion. It was all he could do to sink back in his chair and feebly mutter, 'Yes.'

'Very good,' said Ruaridh MacLagan. 'I will go and see what the food options are. I think there may be some soup.'

As soon as he had gone, Douglas hissed in the general direction of the windows, 'Mungo, where are you? Show yourself.'

'That's what I thought you would *not* want me to do,' Mungo said, emerging from behind a curtain of garish design, like a comedian coming on stage.

'Were you a witness to that?'

'I was. As you surmised, up to his eyes in the smuggling business!'

'Never mind that. Reassure me that I am not mad. That was the bard, wasn't it? Stuart Crathes MacCrimmon?'

'There was some doubt, as I recall, as to whether "bard" was the right term, but yes, it was the same individual.'

'He denied it.'

'Wouldn't you?'

'Either he thinks I am stupid, or he believes himself to be a different person. Mad, in other words.'

'So it would seem. Unless of course *you* are mad, in which case the confusion would be yours, not his.'

'But you also think it's MacCrimmon.'

'Yes, but you have previously expressed incredulity that you and I have a speaking relationship at all. I am a toad, remember. I don't think my agreeing with you proves much. Some would say that if proof of your insanity were needed, citing me as a character witness would provide it.'

'I'll have to think about that. Watch out, he's coming back.'

'Enjoy your evening,' Mungo said. Halfway behind the curtain, he added, 'Oh, and leave your jacket somewhere handy, would you? I could do with a wee nap.'

'I have brought the register for you to sign,' MacLagan said, beamishly. There was a clatter as his toe connected with the ashtray on the floor. 'Well, well! How on earth did that get there?' He picked it up, shook his head at the dregs of wine in it, and placed it on the bar. 'Never mind, this carpet has seen a lot worse than that in its time, I can tell you! Now, we have a nice room available for you at a very reasonable rate. And the soup of the day is Scotch broth. I have put it on to heat.'

[To be continued]

THIRD AND FINAL EXTRACT FROM NOTES FOR AN AS YET UNWRITTEN BIOGRAPHY OF ROSALIND MUNLOCHY BY DOUGLAS FINDHORN ELDER, AUTHOR; COMPOSED FROM PREVIOUSLY CITED SOURCES. NO PART OF THIS WORK MAY BE REPRODUCED, STORED OR TRANSMITTED IN ANY FORM OR BY ANY MEANS, ELECTRONIC, MECHANICAL, INCLUDING PHOTOCOPYING, RECORDING OR ANY INFORMATION STORAGE OR RETRIEVAL SYSTEM, WITHOUT THE EXPRESS WRITTEN PRIOR PERMISSION OF THE AS YET UNIDENTIFIED PUBLISHER

After leaving the House of Commons, Rosalind had more time to devote to her family, to the estate, to local politics, and to her writing. Between 1952 and 1966 she published a second collection of verse, a volume of anecdotes and folklore connected with the Striven family history, a number of polemical pamphlets on various subjects, six novels and a memoir, *Some Life* (1966). The novels are *A Hairst Moon* (1952), *The Weathervane* (1955), *McCaig's Folly* (1959), *To Shun the Devil* (1960), *Indifference* (1962) and *All and Nothing* (1965). The first two of these sold moderately well, but thereafter her fiction became less and less noticed, and there was a prophetic knowingness in the title of her final novel, *Is This Where It Ends?*, published by the soon to be defunct Winstanley Press of Wigan in 1969. But she never resented her relative lack of literary success. 'To have an imagination is commonplace,' she once said, 'but to have one's imaginings printed is a privilege and a rare delight, like seeing one's dreams projected on a cinema screen.'

In 1964 Rosalind and Ralph separated. He was sixty-one, she forty-nine. The split, brought about partly by Ralph's increasing desire to live in a warmer climate and Rosalind's determination not to abandon

Glentaragar (by now reduced to the big house and garden and a few acres of rough pasture), was amicable. (Ralph eventually settled in Biarritz, and he and Rosalind continued to correspond until his death in 1978.) The children had meanwhile all left home, at least for the time being. Each had inherited the Striven genetic disposition towards making an effort. Gabriella was striving to make a breakthrough as a scriptwriter in Hollywood, Gregory was striving to be a lawyer in Edinburgh, and Georgina was striving to have fun in London, going from party to party and, almost as rapidly, from boyfriend to boyfriend. Rosalind, left alone in Argyll, was restless and frustrated. She decided, in the year of her fiftieth birthday, to go on an adventure.

A Striven ancestor had been a trapper and fur trader with the Hudson's Bay Company in the nineteenth century, and Rosalind had had, from childhood, an interest in the vast, empty territories over which this character had wandered. That summer she took a flight to Toronto, then went by train to Calgary, Edmonton and on to the end of the line at Waterways, thence by road to Fort McMurray. From there, by barge and boat, and in the varied company of government officials, geologists, ecologists, missionaries, Indians, Métis and other travellers, she followed the Athabasca River to Lake Athabasca, the Slave River to Great Slave Lake, and the great Mackenzie River as far as Fort Norman. A pontoon plane took a small party to Great Bear Lake, part of which they explored by canoe. Rosalind returned to Fort McMurray by a series of plane hops, and retraced her journey to Toronto before coming home. The trip took three months and, according to the journal she kept, cost 'an inordinate amount of money, which I somehow scraped together despite not having it'. Back in Glentaragar, she felt she had been in some magical land very like the West Highlands, only magnified a thousand times. The experiences of that summer are recounted in *Some Life* and many of them found their way into her novel *All and Nothing*.

Rosalind became a grandmother for the first time the following year, when Gabriella, who had married and settled in California, had a son, David. Gabriella had two more children, both boys, in 1967 and 1969. Rosalind visited them in the early 1970s, but the trip was not a success and was not repeated. At the time of writing she has five great-grandchildren in different parts of the United States. Gregory, who declared his homosexuality in the mid-1970s, had a successful career in commercial law, retired to Provence and died in his sleep in 2010. Georgina eventually tired of London, moved to Glasgow, gave birth in 1976 to a daughter whom she called Coppélia while refusing to name or acknowledge the child's father, and in due course came to live with Rosalind at Glentaragar. In 1990, at the age of forty-eight, Georgina drowned in a swimming accident near Oban, at almost the same spot where her grandfather had perished many years before. When this tragedy occurred Coppélia was fourteen years old. Coppélia has remained with her grandmother ever since, and has taken over most of the responsibility for running Glentaragar House. The building, which stands on the site of an older fortified house, dates from the 1820s and is the only surviving example of the Ossianic-Palladian style championed and developed by the Nairn-born architect William Garrison Buchanan (1789–1830). It is in need of considerable renovation.

OUT OF ORDER

My host, whom I strongly suspect of deceit, delusion or doppelgangsterism, has me enter my details in the register before taking me upstairs. While I am writing he expresses the hope that I will be paying in cash as regrettably the card-processing facilities are out of order owing to a technical issue. I ask what the rate is for a single night's stay. 'How much do you have on you?' is his response. Were he not so obviously in financially straitened circumstances, I would refuse to enter into these sordid negotiations. I pull first one, then a second £20 note from my wallet, then a £10 note, pausing significantly after each presentation as if about to withdraw the increase. At the third stroke, as the Speaking Clock used to say, he can bear the tension no more, seizes the £50 from me and says that that will be adequate unless I require breakfast. I suggest that we discuss that in the morning. He says he will go and see to my supper, and wishes me a pleasant stay.

The room is not pleasant at all. It is cramped, cold and hideously decorated, but it will have to do. The contrast between it and the warm, nest-like cosiness of the room I shared with Xanthe last night – was it only last night? – is stark. Oh for Xanthe to appear at this moment! But, once again, it seems more than likely that our encounter was nothing but a blissful dream.

I have very low expectations of the meal, but to be fair to MacLagan he produces not only a tasty bowl of Scotch broth and some crusty bread to go with it, but an individual chicken pie, peas and oven chips. He has switched on a fan heater, which has warmed the room up – so much so that I remove my jacket – and he hovers anxiously around while I eat, asking repeatedly if everything is to my satisfaction. Would I not like a wee something to go with my meal? Convinced as I am that Ruaridh MacLagan is Stuart Crathes MacCrimmon, I decline, and consume only tap water. If his behaviour at the Shira Inn is any gauge, it is only a matter of time before he himself has a wee something, and that wee something is likely to lead to a larger something. I do not wish to encourage him. If strong drink is to be taken at all, let it not be taken early. I will need a clear head for the morning.

No sooner have I eaten the last pea than MacLagan sweeps my plate and cutlery away to the kitchen, and no sooner has he returned than he is pressing a dram on me – 'On the house, on the house!' – and pouring himself a pint of beer and a dram, too. I accept but say I am tired and will soon be retiring to bed.

'I quite understand. You will have come a long way today?'

'From the Shira Inn.'

'Yes, you mentioned that before. And how far would that be roughly?'

'You should know. You made the journey yourself in your wee yellow car.'

'Ah now, Mr Elder,' he says, wagging a finger at me.

'What?'

'You are doing what you did before, confusing me with somebody else.'

'Oh come on, MacCrimmon! There's only the two of us here. You can drop this silly pretence.'

'There is no pretence on my part, I assure you. This MacCrimmon, I understand, is a poet, a teller of tales, a singer of songs, a tradition-bearer. Is that correct?'

'You know it is. "Bard" is the word you use to describe yourself.'

'I will disregard that. I have heard – I cannot quite remember from whom – of the likeness between us. It is remarkable that I have never laid eyes on the man. Well, well, if the car outside really is his, perhaps we are destined to meet at last.'

'The easiest thing would be to look in a mirror.'

He tuts at me and refuses to come clean, yet when he looks from under his wild brows it is in such a way as to imply a secret shared between us. Prolonged isolation, I decide, must be the cause of his derangement. I am tempted to keep drinking with him, to see if his mask slips once he is well and truly ablaze, but on the other hand I really cannot be, as my Erst-while Colleague Grant McKinley would put it, ersed.

'I'm away to my bed,' I say. 'I will be leaving at ten o'clock.'

'Ten o'clock, is it? So early? And how, exactly, will you be leaving?'

'Someone from Glentaragar House called Corryvreckan is coming for me. Do you know him?'

'Corryvreckan is well known in these parts,' he says, moving to the bar. 'You will be in good hands, all being well.'

'All being well?'

'*If* he turns up.'

'It's been arranged by Miss Munlochy.'

'Has it? And how did that happen?'

'I spoke to her on the hotel phone earlier – before you appeared.'

'Well, that would be miraculous if it were true, since the telephone line has been out of order all day.'

'I can assure you it wasn't at about five o'clock.'

Behind the bar there is a phone that I haven't previously noticed. MacLagan lifts the receiver to his ear, rattles the connection, holds the receiver out to me and says, 'You were fortunate then. Quite dead. Are you sure you spoke to Miss Munlochy?'

'Of course I'm sure. Do you think I imagined it?'

'I could not say. Well, we will see in the morning. Can I not persuade you to take a nightcap?' He holds one of the whisky bottles up.

'Absolutely not.'

'Very well. I will just have a wee one myself.'

'Good night, Mr MacLagan.'

'Call me Ruaridh,' he replies, but his eye is fixed on the golden flow of whisky from bottle to tumbler. 'Good night.'

I am exhausted. Upstairs in my room I have left my mobile phone to charge, and I check it now in the vain hope that there might be a signal. There is none. I crawl between damp sheets, shiver, think fondly and bit-terly of last night, and close my eyes. My last thought is that I have left my jacket in the bar, and that MacLagan will probably be rifling it in search of money. Fortunately I keep my wallet in my trousers, and they are folded on a chair at the foot of the bed.

A VISITATION

An irregular but repeated tapping worms its way into my sleep and finally shakes me out of it. It is still dark. I switch on the bedside lamp. The knocking at the door continues.

'Who is there?'

'It is I, Ruaridh MacLagan. May I come in?'

'What time is it?'

'It is six o'clock. I am sorry to disturb you, Mr Elder, but I must speak with you.'

'Can't it wait for an hour or two?'

'No. It is a matter of life and death.'

'Is the hotel on fire?'

'No. *My* life and *my* death. Please may I enter?'

I sit up and put my back against the headboard. 'Come in, then.'

In he comes, as white as a sheep, and as sheepish, too. I was expecting, when I went downstairs in the morning, to find him dead-drunk, but if he is drunk now he disguises it well. He looks as if he has had a severe shock.

'In case you are missing it,' he says, 'you left your jacket in the bar.' He sits heavily on the chair at the end of the bed, and consequently on my trousers. He clutches his head with his hands.

'You woke me at this hour to tell me that?'

'No, no, that is incidental. A great and terrible thing has happened. Are you a religious man?'

'No.'

'Do you believe in ghosts, spirits, apparitions?'

'No.'

'Nor I, until tonight. Mr Elder – I have had a visitation.'

'So have I,' I say unkindly.

'A miraculous though at the time terrifying visitation,' he says. 'After you left me, I sat for a while, musing on the things we had discussed. And I confess and admit that I aided my cogitations with another glass or two of *uisge beatha* – the water of *death* I should call it after tonight's experience! I suppose I was puzzled – needled – by your repeated assertions that I was this other fellow, the bard. We must really look identical, I thought to myself, or such a gentleman as Mr Elder would not have been so insistent. Could it be that this bard was my long-lost brother?'

'You have a long-lost brother?'

'Not to my knowledge, but I could think of no other explanation. And then I wondered – if that really was his car outside – where was he? Perhaps he was asleep in the car! Perhaps he was dead! So I took a torch and I went to have a look.'

'Did you find him?'

'No.'

'I'm not surprised.'

'I opened one of the doors but there was nothing there except a guitar case, just as you had mentioned. And so I came inside again.'

He puts his head in his hands once more, for such a long time that I wonder if he has gone to sleep. I almost nod off myself.

'I must have nodded off,' MacLagan says, his hair sticking out crazily above his ears, 'but something made me come to with a start. It was about midnight. I felt that I was not alone – that there was a presence in the room. I looked at the chair on which you had hung your jacket and there it was!'

'My jacket?'

'The most enormous, ugly brute of a toad I have ever seen.'

'A toad? On the chair?'

'Precisely.'

'Come now, MacLagan! It's not the season for toads, even indoors. You'd had too much whisky, you said it yourself. You fell asleep and woke from a nightmare.'

'I woke *to* a nightmare, Mr Elder! I will not deny that I was somewhat the worse for wear, but that creature was no more than three feet away from me, and it was real. I could smell its foul smell, I could have reached out and touched its revolting, wart-covered skin and, worst of all, I could see it watching me with its evil eyes.'

'How big, did you say?'

'Enormous! Like gobstoppers.'

'I meant the whole toad.'

'It was the size of these two fists of mine clasped together, doubled and doubled again!'

'Och, away. That would be a cane toad. You don't get them here.'

'I'm telling you the truth. I was rigid with fear. I could not move. I sat, and it sat, and I could not break the hold of that wicked stare, and then, Mr Elder – it spoke!'

'Right, that's enough,' I tell him. 'Either go and get some sleep or phone for a doctor. You are clearly not well.'

197

He is on a roll now, however. 'There is no telephone, and no doctor. The toad spoke in a clear, deep voice such as I never wish to hear again. It spoke of the sins of the past and the sins of the present. It spoke of the error of my ways. It spoke of my destiny.'

'And what is your destiny?'

'To repent. To put aside sin and to serve. You see, Mr Elder, you are blessed by the simple ignorance of modernity. Here in Glen Araich we still carry the burden of the old ways.'

I groan. 'Don't start on about them again, please.' But he is unstoppable.

'Years ago, these heather hills were home to many illicit stills, and the local men who made the whisky were at war with the excisemen who came among them, in the name of a hated government, to destroy their livelihood. Often by night the spirit they made would be brought by packhorse from further up the glens, down the whisky roads to this very building, which used to be the manse, for it was the trysting-place with the smugglers who would take the casks to the towns and cities of the south. Oh, the minister was in on the secret, be assured of that, and he and the people of the glens made a tidy living for themselves. But then the people left the glens, and without the people the old ways withered, and the Kirk too, and the manse became the hotel you see today. But it is as hard to make a living in Glen Araich now as it was two hundred years ago. So I revived the old ways, though there are no illicit stills now. It is not from these hills that today's spirit comes. Today's spirit comes –'

'Stop!' I cry. 'I don't want to hear about this. It is a very dangerous subject.'

'You are right,' MacLagan says, 'and that is what the giant toad told me. "You are deep in iniquity," it said, "and if you do not desist you will be found out and cast into the outer darkness. You will go to prison or you will have terrible things done to your body." And the monster spoke of a man who would skewer me and hack off my legs and arms with a sharp blade, and of the writhing agony of my death, and it altogether scared the wits out of me. "What must I do," I asked, "to be spared such a fate?" "Avoid strong drink of all kinds," it said, "except a little red wine for bathing, and have no more dealings with the chariot of death!" And though it spoke in riddles I knew of what it spoke, and I am resolved. Whisky no more, whisky-smuggling no more. For me, those days – those old days and old ways – are over.'

'Pass me my trousers, MacLagan. I'm wide awake now so I may as well get up. Did the toad tell you what you should do instead?'

'Yes. "Get thee to Oban," it said, "or to Fort William or Glasgow, and become a servant of the iron horse." By which, I deduced, he meant the railway. Your trousers, Mr Elder. "Relinquish the wages of sin for they are death. Seek out the vacancy that shall shortly appear for the post of Customer Experience Operative, and apply for it." I had to ask the beast to repeat the message, so I could write it down. And then those terrible eyes seemed to glaze over, and it spoke no more. And I felt myself becoming drowsy, and I think that it cast a spell on me, for I went into a kind of trance, and when I came out of it about half an hour ago the thing was gone, and only your jacket was there, and I had to come to you at once. I am sorry to have disturbed you, but I had to tell you what has happened.'

I am up and about now, and more or less dressed.

'MacLagan, it's clear that you've had a nasty shock, and you need to go to bed. I believe when you've had a sound sleep you will realise that you have suffered an attack of nerves, brought on by financial worry and too much drink. I cannot say if there is a future for you here, but I doubt there is one on the railway as a CEO. You only imagined that advice. Do nothing hasty or drastic. There is no such thing as a speaking toad.'

'On that we must agree to differ,' MacLagan replies. 'I know what I saw and heard. However, you are right, I do feel somewhat discombobulated, and will retire for an hour or two. Thank you for your advice, Mr Elder. It is a great relief to have talked to you. As you will not be leaving until ten o'clock, I invite you to fill the intervening hours by helping yourself to breakfast at no extra charge. You will find porridge oats and bread in the kitchen cupboard, milk, butter, eggs and bacon in the fridge. Now, if you will excuse me, I will depart, and if I am not there to wave you goodbye when Corryvreckan comes for you, please do not take it personally.'

'I won't,' I say, and Ruaridh MacLagan leaves my room and my life, never, I sincerely hope, to enter it again.

THIS PRESENT MADNESS

Having made myself a full breakfast from the aforesaid ingredients, I repack my case and bring it downstairs. As I am passing the reception desk I go to test the telephone: there is no dialling tone, which is somewhat disconcerting. However, I do not allow myself to doubt that I spoke to Miss Munlochy yesterday evening, and settle myself in the bar with a cup of coffee, to fill the hours until ten o'clock.

In one corner of the room is a little library of books, composed mainly of volumes of local interest, including some fiction. Among the latter is a copy of that perennial favourite *Whisky Galore* by Compton Mackenzie. It is many years since I have read this, but on a whim I open it and find the famous passage that lists all the whisky brands salvaged from the SS *Cabinet Minister*. In amongst them, as I anticipate, are the names 'Glen Gloming' and 'Salmon's Leap'. Wherever the whisky in the outbuildings originated, it has evidently been relabelled with these and other names: perhaps as each new batch arrives, a new title is selected for it. Where else to go for inspiration than to that glorious list? 'It may be doubted if such a representative collection of various whiskies has ever been assembled,' Mackenzie wrote. Quite right!

I feel I have narrowly escaped being caught up in a very murky affair. It was with considerable anxiety that I helped Gerry load contraband liquor into the hearse, and with considerable relief that I saw him drive away with it. Now Gerry is long gone and very soon I too will be on my way. Our paths will not cross again. The Corryvreckan character will appear, and I will make the final part of my journey without, I hope, further diversions or distractions. Later in the day – and it looks like being a fine day – I will do what I have come to do: interview Rosalind Munlochy. According to her granddaughter she is in good health, but what does that mean when you are nearly a hundred? How long will she last without a break? How long will I last? With all the complications of the last few days, I have not prepared properly for the interview. I should have a sheet of questions ready but I have nothing except the information I was given by John Liffield and a little more gleaned from the internet. Well, I will just have to wing it, but that will be all right. I am on an adventure. Winging it is exactly what I *should* do.

'So long as your middle name isn't Icarus.'

Where did that come from? I stare wildly around. I am alone. It must have come from within my head, but why, then, did it sound as if from somewhere else? Is someone hiding behind the bar? I stand up.

'My middle name is Findhorn,' I say loudly, approaching the chip-board facade.

Silence.

I peer over the bar. There is nobody and nothing there – except a guitar case. The guitar case of Stuart Crathes MacCrimmon.

I go round the bar to open it. The guitar is inside, but also, stuffed behind the neck of the instrument, are what appear to be the remains of a deceased animal.

Gingerly, I ease them out. They come apart in my hands and, revolted, I drop them.

Two deceased animals lie on the floor.

No they don't. I bend, and pick up – a thin grey wig and a long false beard.

I return to my seat and swallow a mouthful of cold coffee. I check that I am alone. I check the clock. It will be another hour before Corryvreckan – Corryvreckan! – comes to rescue me from this present madness. I close my eyes and wait.

CORRYVRECKAN

At ten o'clock precisely the front door of the hotel bangs open and shut, and I hear somebody moving about at the reception desk. The bell is pinged. 'Hello? Hello?' a voice calls.

'I'm in here!' I shout, standing up in readiness.

The owner of the voice enters. He is clean-shaven but the presence or absence of hair on top of his head cannot be determined owing to a deer-stalker, which is crammed down upon the ears. He wears a predominantly green suit of Harris tweed, a once-white shirt and a knitted tie the colour of dead bracken. Except for the deerstalker and the lack of beard he is the living image of the hotelier MacLagan, whom I last saw in a state of shock in my bedroom, and of the bard MacCrimmon, whom I last saw in a state of unconsciousness at the Shira Inn. But when the new arrival speaks it is in a slow, soft, West Highland voice that I have heard on the telephone, and that I associate with the name Corryvreckan.

'Good morning. And it is a good morning, compared with what we have been enduring these last two or three days. Mr Elder? My name is Corryvreckan. I have come to convey you to Glentaragar House. Is that your suitcase? Allow me.'

'MacLagan!'

'No, I have not seen Ruaridh MacLagan this morning. Have you set-tled your account with him?'

'Yes, but –'

'Very well. Then there will be no need to disturb him. The car is outside. Please follow me.' He extends the handle of my suitcase and sets off at some speed, wheeling the case behind him.

I pick up my raincoat and go in pursuit. The rusty yellow car is parked at the front door and Corryvreckan is putting my case in the boot.

'That's MacCrimmon's car,' I say.

He closes the boot. 'Would that be Stuart Crathes MacCrimmon the folksinger?'

'Who else?'

'Does he have one of these too? I have never met him. It was made in Russia. It is very economical and not too precious about the potholes.'

He holds the passenger door open for me.

'He also has a guitar and a beard,' I say pointedly. 'As does Ruaridh MacLagan.'

'No, no, Ruaridh MacLagan does not have a guitar. Please get in, Mr Elder. You are expected at the big house.'

I consider my options. I do not appear to have any. I get in.

'Drive on, MacDuff,' I say to myself, as Corryvreckan slams the door shut and walks round to the driver's side.

CONVERSATIONS WITH A TOAD: CONVERSATION #8

Douglas Findhorn Elder opened his suitcase and contemplated whether or not to unpack it. The case contained some changes of underwear, two shirts, a spare pair of trousers, a woollen jumper, socks, handkerchiefs, pyjamas and a sponge-bag. There were also sundry papers bearing information on Mrs Rosalind Munlochy, a notebook in which, among other things, he had recorded details of minibus travel to and from Glen Araich, and a small tape-recording device, old-fashioned but reliable. He decided not to unpack. It didn't seem worth the trouble. If he interviewed Mrs Munlochy that afternoon, and if Corryvreckan returned him to the hotel next morning, he could catch the bus to Oban and from there a train south. This was Wednesday. By Thursday evening he could be home.

Douglas felt a little shaken. The road up Glentaragar had been ferocious. A barely legible sign at the foot had declared it unsuitable for caravans: this was an understatement, akin to saying that the Sahara Desert was unsuitable for penguins. There were collapsed embankments, perilously angled trees, many broken branches, gravel and mud being scattered across what remained of the tarmac by brown rivulets, alarming cambers and gradients – and that was just for the first two miles. When they came to a crumbling stone bridge, where the road divided, Corryvreckan took the left fork.

'That was the Fairy Bridge,' he said when they were safely across it, 'so-called on account of an ancient legend that fairies once lived beneath it.'

'Folk believed anything in those days,' Douglas remarked.

'They were not as gullible as you might think.'

'Nor, it may surprise you to learn, am I.'

Corryvreckan ignored this. 'The fairies have great powers and are not to be mocked,' he said.

'If you say so,' Douglas said, not without a sneer in his voice.

'I do say it. One never knows when one may fall under their spell.'

He halted the car and pointed to his right. 'You will notice on the far side of the burn some old houses with their roofs off. Only thirty years ago there were people living in them.'

'Where does that other road go?'

'Nowhere. It ends just beyond the last house. Further up the road we are on you will see other habitations – just rickles of stone now, where the deer take shelter from the wind. But in the old days there was a whole community of folk in the glen. Sad it is today to see it so empty.'

He sighed – a rather practised sigh, Douglas thought, that went with the inverted syntax and high pitch of his lament.

'Ah, the good old, bad old days,' Douglas said.

Corryvreckan did not rise to the bait. 'I will not be able to speak for the next while,' he said, releasing the handbrake. 'The road becomes difficult from now on, and I must concentrate.'

In addition to all the former hazards, the way then became dotted with potholes, many so full of water that Douglas had no idea how deep they were. Corryvreckan drove slowly but steadily, mostly in second gear, and knew which holes to go round, which to navigate gently, and which required a burst of speed to get through with the least impact. Reduced to silence and a slight nausea, Douglas took in what he could of the surrounding scenery: it was composed entirely of rocks, trees, heather, grass and water. Although the sun was shining in an almost cloudless sky he did not have the impression that the glen could ever really dry out. It seemed a hard country to care about much, and yet, he thought, it possessed a ragged, wild beauty that, if it were home, one might not wish to leave and never see again. On the other hand, perhaps people couldn't get away fast enough when the opportunity arose. Corryvreckan had spoken of a good number of glen dwellers, but nobody, surely, could make a living off this land today?

The road became little more than a muddy track between boulders. The head of the glen was reached, the track levelled out, and suddenly Corryvreckan was swinging in between two stone pillars from which hung rusting iron gates, fixed permanently open against ranks of rhododendrons. The approach to Glentaragar House was short and straight. It passed through mixed stands of larch, pine and birch, and finished in a courtyard at what was apparently the rear of the building. This was disconcerting to Douglas: after such a journey, he had expected to be met with an imposing frontage in the baronial tradition. It was almost indecent to sneak up on the house from behind, especially as it was quite modest in size and style.

However, when they got out and entered through a cold basement corridor punctuated by a number of doors, and then went up a stone spiral staircase and through a heavy door into a hallway, it made sense: they had come via the old servants' quarters. There was a doorless booth of dark varnished wood beside the door, in which Douglas noted a telephone, a model with a circular dial, set on a little shelf next to two or three ancient-looking directories. At the other end of the hall was an enclosed lobby of ornately carved oak, inset with coloured glass. This lobby had doors on each side, and beyond them was a further great door, also of oak. Corryvreckan led Douglas into the lobby, in which were stands containing walking sticks, crooks and umbrellas and, under a bench, assorted items of outdoor footwear. He opened the massive front door. Half a dozen wide steps led down to a broad stone avenue, which bisected a long, mossy lawn enclosed by a low drystone dyke on the left side and a much higher, mortared wall on the right. At the lawn's far end were gates and a row of impressive oaks.

'You will understand,' Corryvreckan said, 'that in the old days everything and everyone came up the loch, which you cannot see from this level but which is beyond those trees. The house looks south and west. It has the sun upon it all afternoon and all evening.'

Douglas saw the truth of this statement. The sun was behind them now, but very soon it would come over their left shoulders and its warmth would be upon their faces. He glanced up at the front of the house. The stonework was simple, the windows large but unpretentious. The house, he thought, was plain and sturdy, and sat like a creature used to bracing itself against westerly winds.

Then Corryvreckan took him up the main staircase and he noticed signs of fragility: stains down one wall where the rain had got in; woodwork badly in need of repainting; a cracked windowpane; loose boards at the top of the stairs. They turned right, along a short corridor hung with oil paintings of historic Strivens, and Corryvreckan – having shown him the bathroom he was to use, which was at the far end of the corridor – left him in his room. 'I will give you a little time to settle in,' he said, 'before taking you to Mrs Munlochy.'

It was an enormous room. Most of the Elder residence back in Edinburgh could have fitted into it. It had one vast window stretching from ceiling to floor, from which Douglas saw a long stretch of water – the loch, presumably, that Corryvreckan had mentioned. It was odd – he had not thought of there being a loch anywhere near the house. He would need to consult a map to get his bearings.

The window had no curtains but it did have working wooden shutters, which might counter the draughts. A ladder would have been handy to scale the formidable double bed. There was a wardrobe of some dark wood, empty but for a couple of spare blankets and a few wire hangers, and a matching chest of drawers. The fireplace, of stone and slate, was also empty. There was a cast-iron radiator, stone-cold, against one wall. A chandelier, which had been elaborately decorated by a spider, boasted half a dozen bulbs, but when he flicked the switch beside the door he could see that the light it would throw out would, come evening, be feeble. He noted also that the switch and electrical sockets were of brown Bakelite, and that the plug of the bedside lamp had two round pins. Glentaragar House, or at least this bit of it, was seriously electrically challenged. This made him check his mobile phone. Previously the screen had displayed the words EMERGENCY CALLS ONLY. Now, beneath that, was a legend he had never seen before: NO EMERGENCY CALLS EITHER. Hopeless. He dropped the phone into his jacket pocket. Then, feeling a little cold, he took the jacket off and replaced it with his jumper.

Three threadbare rugs were placed in such a way across the floorboards that one could walk from door to bed without treading, if barefoot, on cold wood. Everything about the room was grand, austere, dignified and faded. In the winter it would be an icebox. Now, at the end of October, Douglas rather liked it, even its musty aroma – a combination, he thought, of mouse and very old wood.

Mungo Forth Mungo, whom he had extracted from his pocket once Corryvreckan had gone, had also been taking in the surroundings, poking his snout into corners and lashing out with his considerable tongue along the skirting boards.

'I take it we have finally arrived?' he asked.

'Yes, this is Glentaragar House,' Douglas said. 'What do you think?'

'It's an improvement on the hotel,' the toad replied. 'I prefer this more Spartan style – not that I saw your bedroom last night. I remained in the bar when I wasn't outside.'

'I wanted to ask you about that. Did you have some kind of conversation with MacLagan? He came to see me at six o'clock claiming to have met a giant toad who told him he was up to his neck in sin.'

'Giant?'

'About the size of a cat, from his description.'

'I did puff myself up a bit, but he's exaggerating. I wanted to teach him a lesson. He went through your jacket pockets, you know.'

'I thought he might.'

'I saw him at it when I came in from dinner.'

'Do you never stop eating?'

'Seldom. One has to guard against the possibility of privation. I waited till he'd dropped off and then I positioned myself to give him a fright.'

'Well, you managed that fine. But what were you hoping to achieve by advising him to get a job on the railway?'

'A resolution to your ethical dilemma. Since you seemed to want to knock this bootlegging business on the head without getting involved, I thought I could shift the dilemma on to MacLagan.'

'Is that why you put him in a trance?'

'I didn't put him in a trance.'

'He thinks you did.'

'Rubbish. He was drunk. After our little exchange he fell asleep, and so I crawled into your jacket and did the same. I woke up briefly once and he'd gone. He must have been seeing you. Was he suitably chastened?'

'At the time, yes. I sent him to his bed and told him to consider his options when he woke up. The trouble is, the man who goes to bed as MacLagan doesn't necessarily wake up as MacLagan, so he might have forgotten.'

'The toad who goes to bed as Mungo always wakes up as Mungo. Sometimes he wishes he hadn't. The journey from there to here was extremely unpleasant. I was nearly sick in your pocket.'

'Thank you for not being. You'll not have seen Corryvreckan then?'

'No, not yet.'

'Take a good look at him when you do. It's MacCrimmon, or Mac-Lagan if you prefer, without a beard.'

'I see. Has he shed it?'

'It's more complicated than that. It was a false beard.'

'A disguise?'

'Yes, but there doesn't seem any point in making an issue of it.'

'Why not?'

'Because I don't think he's aware it's a disguise. I think he suffers from a three-way split personality.' There was a knock at the door. 'That'll be him now. I'm about to meet Rosalind Munlochy. Want to come?'

'Absolutely.'

'Hop in then.'

Douglas went to the door. It took him twelve paces to get there. Corryvreckan, still wearing his deerstalker, stood outside. 'If you would care to follow me, please,' he said.

They retraced their steps to the head of the stairs, then proceeded to the left wing, down a corridor hung with oil paintings of Highland scenes. Corryvreckan knocked at the third door along.

'Come in, Corryvreckan,' a thin, clear voice called, and some deep memory was stirred in Douglas, of a vintage film in which a Highland postmistress makes contact with an island by radio. This voice was rather more aristocratic, but it had the same black-and-white precision, the same sense of belonging to a bygone age. Corryvreckan turned the brass handle, and in they went.

Douglas expected to find himself in a room as large and barren as the bedroom, but the reality was very different. This room was smaller but packed with furniture – armchairs and a sofa, a writing desk, a standard lamp, and bookcases ranked and double-ranked with books. Other shelves and surfaces were covered with knick-knackery, lamps, small plants and arrangements of dried flowers. On the wall hung paintings and prints – bright, modernist and abstract – and on the floor was a red cord carpet overlaid with thick Persian rugs, so that the room was riotous with colour. The centrepiece was an open fire heaped with logs, which filled the place with a friendly, welcoming heat. There was a window with a built-in seat, and even from where he was standing Douglas could see the shimmering loch through the glass. It was the kind of room from which, on wet, cold or windy days, one would never wish to shift. And in the armchair nearest to the fire sat someone who looked as though she had not shifted for some time.

'Mr Elder,' Corryvreckan said.

'Thank you, Corryvreckan,' said Rosalind Munlochy. 'Would you tell Poppy that Mr Elder is here? And you may bring the coffee directly.'

'I will do that,' Corryvreckan said, and he touched the peak of his deerstalker and withdrew.

[To be continued]

FIRST-NAME TERMS

Rosalind Munlochy is small and neat, her skin as brown and lined as the shell of a Brazil nut. She is in an armchair next to the fire, with several cushions and a rug packed around her as if to hold her in place: she is like an unhatched egg in a nest or, rather, like a chick – a very young one, and consequently prehistoric-looking. Her white hair is so fine and light that it seems to sit above her skull in a cloud. She wears pink-framed glasses on her sharp, straight nose, and behind the round lenses her eyes are blue and bright. There is a downward turn to her mouth that nevertheless is a kind of smile, or holds the promise of one.

'Good morning, Mr Elder.'

'Good morning, Mrs Munlochy.'

'Won't you sit down? Not in that chair or you will squash the cat. I won't get up. I'm a little stiff in the mornings. If the weather holds we might get out later.'

'Really?' I take a seat opposite her. The cat referred to, a tabby well camouflaged against the upholstery of the chair next to hers, sleeps on.

'If it stays dry and the wind has dropped. If there is one thing I can't cope with it is the wind. It blows me about like a leaf. I'd like to show you what's left of Glentaragar's policies. What is your first name? I think they told me, but I have forgotten.'

'It's Douglas.'

'Douglas Elder.' The downward smile briefly becomes an upward one, as if a joke has passed over her face. 'The cat's name is Sitka but she doesn't answer to it. She doesn't answer to anything, she just sleeps all day. You've come for the interview. Now, how shall we play this?'

'Play what, Mrs Munlochy?'

'That, precisely. Formality. I can't be doing with it, can you? Shall we be on first-name terms until some reason arises for us not to be?'

'That's fine by me.'

'Let us practise then. Douglas. Your turn.'

'I'm sorry?'

'You have to call me Rosalind.'

'Rosalind.'

'Douglas.'

'Rosalind.'

'Excellent. We shall get along very well – until we don't.'

Had Corryvreckan frisked me in the corridor he couldn't have disarmed me more efficiently.

'Remind me,' she goes on, 'what exactly am I supposed to be interviewing you about?'

'Actually, I'm supposed to be interviewing you.'

'You're not here about a job?'

'No.'

'Oh. Well, that's good, because there isn't one.' A musical chuckle follows. 'What do you want to interview me about?'

'Your life. Your thoughts on Scotland, past, present and future.'

'Oh dear. Yes, Poppy did say something about it. Are you from a newspaper?'

'Yes, the *Spear*. I have a card here.'

'Never mind that. You have tracked me to my den whether you have a card or not. I don't read the papers now. There is nothing in them I haven't read before. The *Spear* used to be rather a good newspaper, but that was a long time ago. Have you been there a long time?'

'More than twenty years.'

'Not long then.'

'Actually' – I find I cannot lie to her – 'I don't work there any more. This is a one-off job the editor asked me to do.'

'Oh? Should one of us be flattered by that?'

'Probably not.'

The smile passes over her features again. 'You know why the *Spear* is called the *Spear*, don't you? Apart from it being a sharp weapon?'

'I thought that was the reason.'

'One of the reasons. But "spier" is also a Scots word meaning to inquire or interrogate. That was a pun that was understood when the paper was founded in the nineteenth century. It was understood when I was a young woman, too. I'm surprised you didn't know that.'

'Well, now that you've reminded me, I think I did. I'd forgotten. Someone told me when I first started. A man called Ronald Grigson. He had that sense of tradition. The paper has a very different ethos now.'

'Well, perhaps that's inevitable. Even the best traditions have to end some time. Some aren't even traditions.'

Behind me the door opens and Corryvreckan enters with a tray of coffee things, which he places on the desk.

'We always have coffee about now,' Rosalind says, 'with Abernethy biscuits. The origins of which have almost nothing to do with Scotland, which proves the point I was making. Thank you, Corryvreckan. Just leave it there.' When he has gone, she says, 'He's a wonder, that man. I don't know what we'd do without him.'

'Yes, he is a wonder. I've been wondering quite a bit about him,' I say.

She gives me a quick look, but only asks, 'How was the drive up the glen?'

'Challenging.'

'It always was. It is some time since I last did it. It was a battle to have the road metalled in the Fifties and it's been a battle having it repaired ever since. The Council say they can't justify the cost when this is the only occupied property in the glen, but if the road had been properly maintained perhaps some of the people would have stayed. I used to say that if they couldn't afford to mend the road I couldn't afford to pay my rates, but I had to or they would have debarred me from being a councillor. I don't trouble myself with all that any more, but Poppy has taken up the cudgels, and she says they've promised to fill in the potholes next year. Well, we'll see! Ah, here's Poppy now. She can pour. Poppy, this is Douglas Elder. We are on first-name terms already. Douglas, this is my granddaughter Poppy. Her mother called her Coppélia for reasons I shall never understand. I call her Poppy for short.'

'Hello, Poppy,' I say, standing up.

'Hello, Douglas,' Poppy says. Only it isn't Poppy, although it must be because that is how Rosalind has introduced her. But when I slept with her two days ago she was Xanthe.

It is fortunate that I am not already holding a cup of coffee, because if I were, I would undoubtedly have spilt it. The way she says, 'Hello, Douglas': it is *her* voice, the one I've heard on the telephone at the weekend and again only last night, but is it also Xanthe's? Xanthe sounded less posh, more Scottish – but immediately I have to question what that means, 'more Scottish'. Perhaps Poppy doesn't sound any different – not to herself or her grandmother anyway. It is *my* problem, not theirs – if it is a problem. How can I not have recognised her voice that night at the Shira Inn? How can I not have put two and two together: she and MacCrimmon were gone in the morning. Surely, as I suspected, they left together, and now it is clear why – because they were going to the same place.

Yet they barely acknowledged one another at the Inn. I seem to remember Poppy saying that MacCrimmon didn't know her. Was that a barefaced lie? And the bard was a complete wreck by the end of the night. Was he able to drive in the morning? Perhaps Poppy took over. But she told me on the phone – at least, I think she did, but am I imagining it? – that she didn't drive.

I am all but speechless. Poppy – I can hardly think of her by that name, but have to try – asks me if I take milk in my coffee. 'Yes, please,' I say, thinking of her in bed saying she has no socks on. Do I want sugar? 'No,' I say, inhaling her perfume from the sheets of that bed. A biscuit? 'Thank you,' I murmur, trying to put other memories from my mind.

She places her own coffee on one of the wee tables, and in a single swift movement sweeps the cat up with one hand and sits down in its chair, with the creature, barely having woken, resettling itself at once on her lap.

She is dressed in a thick grey jumper speckled with other colours, and a pair of blue jeans tucked into brown boots. She appears not to be wearing any make-up, and the only jewellery I can see is a silver bracelet on one wrist. Everything about her is plain and understated and ordinary. I could weep, she looks so good.

Am I to say anything? What am I to say in the presence of Rosalind Munlochy? That her granddaughter and I are already intimately acquainted, that she comes and goes by another name and that in some way I have been tricked, deceived, misled by her? Have I been? Perhaps Poppy suffers from the same kind of personality disorder as Corryvreckan? Perhaps Poppy does not recognise me, and only Xanthe could?

Not for the first time in recent days, I question whether I am awake or dreaming.

'Well, here we are,' Poppy says.

'Yes, here we are,' I reply. 'I'm a little confused.'

'Already?' Rosalind says. 'You've only just arrived.'

Looking at me directly, Poppy says, 'You've had a difficult journey, Douglas. You're probably disorientated. But we're glad that you have come.' And her eyes seem to assure me that I am not dreaming, that she knows exactly who I am, and that her welcome is not false.

'Very glad,' Rosalind says.

'We don't get many visitors,' Poppy continues. 'My grandmother has been much looking forward to your company. Haven't you, Gran?'

'Yes, indeed,' Rosalind says, 'although I'm afraid he will find us dull.'

'I don't think I will,' I say.

Poppy smiles. 'I don't think you will either.'

'Then I am outvoted,' Rosalind says, 'and it will all be great fun.'

I glance sharply at her. Her eyes shine behind the pink, round spectacles. Are these women laughing at me? Does Rosalind already know what happened at the Shira? Did Poppy rush home to tell her?

'I think,' Poppy says, 'that you two should start your conversation right now. It's half-past eleven already. I'll make you a sandwich for lunch and you can just keep going.'

'We're going out later,' Rosalind says, 'if the weather holds.'

'That's good. Perhaps after that I could borrow Douglas to help me in the kitchen? Would you mind, Douglas?'

'It would be a pleasure, Poppy. We can get to know each other properly.'

She doesn't even blush. 'Good. We tend not to eat too late in the evening, as my grandmother gets tired.'

'I do,' Rosalind agrees. 'I'm never up beyond nine. It's like being a child again. You'll have to entertain yourselves after that.'

'Well, in that case, if you don't need anything else, I'm going to leave you together for an hour or two,' Poppy says. She slips out from under the cat, kisses her grandmother on the cheek, and makes a dash for the door.

I stand up. 'I'll just go and get my notebook from my room, Rosalind. Be back in a minute.'

I catch up with Poppy halfway along the corridor, and stay her with a hand on her shoulder. 'What's going on?'

'Nothing,' she says.

'Nothing?'

'Everything. Please don't be angry.'

'We need to talk.'

'Yes, but not now. Talk to Rosalind. It's as she said, we can entertain ourselves later.'

'I can't wait till later.'

'Neither can I, but we'll have to.'

'That's not what I meant. You have to tell me what's going on.'

She pulls away. 'I will.'

'Did I speak to you last night, on the phone?'

'I'm sorry?'

'It's a simple enough question. Did I speak to you last night?'

'Did you? Last night? I don't think so.'

'I phoned from the hotel. Surely you remember?'

'No,' she says. 'I don't.'

I feel the sickness from the car journey returning. 'You're lying,' I say.

'Douglas! I'm not lying. If you phoned I have no recollection of it. I'm sure you didn't because I tried to phone the hotel last night and I couldn't get through.'

'What?'

'Are you all right?'

'I'm not sure. Poppy?'

'Yes?'

'Who are you?'

'Poppy. I'm Poppy Munlochy. Go and do the interview.'

She has been frowning. Now she laughs, and runs down the corridor like a woman half her age, whatever her age is.

I am in a play, I think to myself. I am an actor in a play, but it's as if I've just woken up on stage with no knowledge of who wrote the script, of my lines, my part, what scene we are in, whether it's a tragedy or a farce or who all the other characters might be. And I can't walk off again. There is an audience out there waiting for me to die – in the theatrical sense – and I'm not ready to do that. I must carry on as if I know what I am doing.

So I do. I collect my notebook and tape recorder, and return to the room where Rosalind Munlochy is waiting to be interviewed.

EXTRACTS FROM TRANSCRIPT OF AN INTERVIEW
BETWEEN DOUGLAS FINDHORN ELDER AND ROSALIND
MUNLOCHY, CONDUCTED ON 29TH AND 30TH OCTOBER
2014 AT GLENTARAGAR HOUSE, GLENTARAGAR, ARGYLL

ELDER: Do you mind if I record our interview?

MUNLOCHY: I don't mind what you do, so long as you tell the truth and don't leave anything out.

ELDER: Well, I won't be able to include everything. We have a lot of ground to cover and the *Spear*'s editor will give me only so much space.

MUNLOCHY: I understand that, of course. All I ask is that you do not lie by omission.

ELDER: I will try not to do that. There is one matter that the editor was most insistent I should ask you about.

MUNLOCHY: I thought that might be the case.

ELDER: But I'm not sure I'm going to.

MUNLOCHY: Why not?

ELDER: Because there's a principle involved. The principle of privacy.

MUNLOCHY: No, no, I'm beyond that. I want to be completely open about everything.

ELDER: Well, we can come to that later.

MUNLOCHY: As you wish. What do you want to discuss first?

ELDER: Well, I've been reading your memoir, *Some Life* –

MUNLOCHY: An inconsiderable book.

ELDER: I've been enjoying it.

MUNLOCHY: I dashed it off. I omitted most of my life up to that point. Hence the title, in part.

ELDER: Why did you write it like that?

MUNLOCHY: Because I was too occupied with everyday things to dwell overlong on the past. I was on the County Council. I was running this house unaided. There were various campaigns requiring my attention. That book was a pause for breath, but only a very brief pause.

ELDER: Did you never think of expanding it, or writing another volume of autobiography?

MUNLOCHY: Certainly not. One was quite enough.

ELDER: Are you writing anything now?

MUNLOCHY: Such as?

ELDER: Poetry, fiction?

MUNLOCHY: Good Lord, no! I said everything I had to say in those departments long ago. Writing was never a compulsion with me as it is for real writers.

ELDER: You didn't regard yourself as a real writer?

MUNLOCHY: I don't.

ELDER: And you stopped writing because you had nothing more to say?

MUNLOCHY: No. Writing is only one mode of expression. I stopped writing because I had nothing more to write.

ELDER: Can we go back to *Some Life* for a moment? You wrote it half a century ago, and much of it concerns the trip you made to northern Canada the previous summer. Let's start there. Why did you make that trip?

MUNLOCHY: I explained all that in the book.

ELDER: Yes, but hardly any of the present readers of the *Spear* will have read the book.

MUNLOCHY: How fortunate for us all! Very well. I had an ancestor, a great-uncle called Gilbert, who was in the fur trade. I never knew him – he was born in 1820, the year George III died, and he went to Canada in the middle of the century and never came back.

ELDER: I was going to mention, by an amazing coincidence I too had a great-uncle called Gilbert.

MUNLOCHY: What's amazing about that? Gilbert's not so unusual a name. It would be amazing if they were one and the same, but they can't be.

ELDER: No, they can't. But it does amaze me that here am I talking to you in 2014 and if your great-uncle hadn't gone away you might have known a man born in 1820.

MUNLOCHY: Then you are easily amazed. After all, I did meet his sister Gladys, and she was born a year earlier. She died when I was three and she was ninety-eight. All I remember about her is that she dressed in black from head to toe and creaked when she moved. No doubt that was her stays.

ELDER: You go back two generations and you're almost at Waterloo.

MUNLOCHY: And actually are at Peterloo. If the Strivens aren't killed in war or by accident they tend to live long. One shouldn't make too much of this – these are only numbers after all. Gilbert was much talked about in the family. We admired him, partly because he survived being mauled by a grizzly bear and partly because he was a rogue. Perhaps that helped when he met the bear. He had a complete disdain for people in authority. He worked for the Hudson's Bay Company but he didn't like their monopoly of the trade and so he ran his own business, quite against the rules, alongside his official job. He had lots of children by different Indian women but there was no shame in that, in fact there was pride, and he looked after them all, which was another mark in his favour. He sent letters in brown ink from time to time, with little sketches and maps in the margins, and I was allowed to look at these when I was a girl and they fired my imagination. All this is in the book. Well, I decided to have a look at some of the places he'd been – to follow in the footsteps of my infamous ancestor. It's important to do that, I think, to go where your people have gone before you. Why are you looking at me like that?

ELDER: *My* Great-uncle Gilbert wasn't much talked about in our family but when he was it was with a wagging finger. He wasn't admired, and I certainly wasn't meant to follow in his footsteps.

MUNLOCHY: Why not?

ELDER: Well, I . . .

MUNLOCHY: Yes?

ELDER: Well, I was told that my great-uncle was mad. And it seems he walked into the sea and drowned himself. I'm sorry.

MUNLOCHY: Why are you sorry? It must have been a long time ago.

ELDER: I was remembering what happened to your father.

MUNLOCHY: I see. You thought you would upset me. That, too, was a very long time ago. I was only nine.

ELDER: And I was thinking of your daughter, Poppy's mother.

MUNLOCHY: Georgina? Well, we will come to her, won't we?

ELDER: Yes, if you are prepared to talk about it.

MUNLOCHY: I've been preparing for that for a long time. 'Mad' is a loose kind of word, isn't it? Convenient, but seldom helpful. It means so little, and yet it implies so much. Do you ever think that you might be mad?

ELDER: Sometimes. Do you?

MUNLOCHY: There hasn't been a day in my life when I haven't. But one has to work on the basis that one isn't, that the world really is as one perceives it to be. Otherwise everything would be impossible. That's all life is really, a matter of perception. Of course, the world itself *is* mad.

. . .

ELDER: Tell me more about your time in Canada. Why did you choose to go that year, in 1964? Did you perhaps feel you wanted an adventure?

MUNLOCHY: Why would I want an adventure?

ELDER: Because of your circumstances, the age you were?

MUNLOCHY: I'd already had plenty of adventures. I did need a change, though. Ralph and I had parted, and I decided to get away from here for a while. Everybody else had, or was going to. My children were gone. So were most of the people in the glen. I was depressed, I suppose, although I didn't think of it like that at the time. I don't like feeling sorry for myself, you see. Do you know, Douglas, that when I was born there were a hundred and fifty people living in Glentaragar? There was a school at Glen Araich, and a church, and goods of all kinds came in by puffer and cart every week. The war changed everything – the *first* war. The young men went away to fight and many didn't come back and that was when the real decline set in, though in truth folk had been leaving before the war. Even in the 1930s there were a dozen families still in the glen, with children and grandchildren, but the Depression took some away and the War took more, and Canada and Australia yet more when it was over, and by the 1960s only a handful were left – mostly the old who had no reason to go. Life would be better elsewhere, or so it was said. I'm not sure that it was, but it seemed that way, and certainly that it would be easier, so people went.

ELDER: Corryvreckan said something about the old days when he drove me up this morning. He talked about there having been a real community in the glen.

MUNLOCHY: Corryvreckan is a splendid fellow, but he doesn't know what it was like when the glen was full. He likes to *think* he remembers, but he doesn't. It was almost all lost before he came – the church, the school, the language. There was an old lady who had no English at all when I was a girl. Now only Corryvreckan has the Gaelic, and he doesn't have much of it, and nobody to speak it to but himself.

ELDER: You and Poppy don't have it?

MUNLOCHY: I have a few scraps, that's all. Childhood leftovers. It wasn't our language, it was theirs.

ELDER: So, as a child of the big house, did you feel part of the community?

MUNLOCHY: We were part of it but also apart from it. We weren't the same as the people of the glen, but nor did we fit in with our own class, who thought we were a bad lot. The Strivens were too sympathetic to the people, that's what the rest of the gentry thought – but *they* were nearly all incomers. The local children walked down the glen to school every day, and sometimes we went with them, my brothers and sister and I. We had governesses but we were so ungovernable that they were always giving notice and so then we went to the school at Glen Araich. We behaved ourselves there, it was the strap across your palm if you did not. On the whole, though, our education was *extremely* informal. One wouldn't get away with it today, but we belonged to a caste that could get away with almost anything ... Sometimes, Douglas, I think that cat is actually dead. Would you prod her for me?

ELDER: No, not dead. You were saying you could get away with things, because of who you were ...

MUNLOCHY: Yes. We will come to that. When we were older we were sent away to boarding schools, though not very *good* schools because our mother couldn't afford them. But we were talking about Canada. I went there to retrace Gilbert's footsteps, as far as I could. He died in a cabin beside the Great Bear Lake, and I wanted to see that place. There was no cabin, no grave, no marker, but paddling a canoe on the water, camping on the shoreline, I felt a connection. And *that's* why I went, to feel that connection.

ELDER: And when you came back, did you still feel a connection with Glentaragar? Or did you return to a place that was dying, or perhaps had already died?

MUNLOCHY: Well, it had, in a way. You only had to look around. The distances in Canada were simply vast, the scale of everything was so much bigger, so it was hard to think that here we were only a hundred miles from Glasgow and yet we might as well have been on the moon as far as people in Glasgow were concerned! How could we be so far away when we were so close? It's one of the things I've always argued for – not just maintaining the glen road but better communications generally between Highlands and Lowlands, better land links and better sea links. If you break those links it is not surprising that people leave.

ELDER: Because of the remoteness?

MUNLOCHY: I dislike the word 'remote' intensely. It is very pejorative, like that other phrase people use, 'the back of beyond'. When we go out later, I will show you how we used to communicate with Glasgow and everywhere else. It wasn't by land, which has always been difficult. It was by water. There's a map on the wall over there, do you see it? It looks odd, doesn't it? That's because it challenges your way of imagining the world. It's a map of Scotland and Ireland on a vertical south-west to north-east axis, and what it makes you realise is that before there were roads there was water, and the Minch and the Irish Sea were the main thoroughfares. That's how people moved around, trading goods and ideas and, yes, fighting and stealing too. And what is right in the middle of the map? Look closely. It's Iona, Columba's island. He didn't wash up there by accident, he chose it. It wasn't some remote, hard-to-get-to place. It was the centre of his world. And Glentaragar is just a couple of lochs and a short sea trip away from Iona. And this is why I have never given up on this place, my home, the home of my ancestors, because even though it looks as if we are dying we are not dying. We continue to be here. We *are* still here.

ELDER: That's a powerful opinion, but do you not think that it is, in the end, a romantic one? The modern world isn't Columba's world. Iona *is* remote, and Glentaragar too. I'm not being pejorative in saying that, it's a fact. And, forgive me, but you are about to be a hundred, and your grand-daughter and Corryvreckan are the only people who will be here after you have gone. Can there really be any hope for a place like this?

MUNLOCHY: Yes, there must be. In the far north of Canada I felt that people had hardly made an impression on the land. It was wilderness and you were lucky if it let you keep a foothold in it. But here in the Highlands it is quite different. The land and people coexisted and then the people were ejected – not by the wilderness but by other people. People of my class. You asked whether I still felt a connection with the glen on my return, and my answer is that I felt it even more strongly than before. And I still feel it and that *is* about hope for the future. If you don't have hope you don't have anything. If you don't believe there's a future then what good is the past? It's a waste of time thinking about it.

ELDER: But for you, at your great age, don't you spend a lot of time thinking about the past?

MUNLOCHY: Only when I'm asked to. Why would I?

ELDER: Because, in the nature of things, you have much more past than future to think about.

MUNLOCHY: It's true that I don't look very *far* into the future. That really would be presumptuous. Sometimes I only think half a day or half an hour ahead. But I very seldom look back. Dwelling on the past – what's the point if your conscience is clear? We will, however, as we've already discussed, come to that.

ELDER: To what?

MUNLOCHY: To the matter your editor sent you to ask about.

ELDER: I'm not sure I understand.

MUNLOCHY: Do you wish to talk about it now?

ELDER: Well, I was planning to leave it till later.

MUNLOCHY: Then let's not disrupt your plan.

ELDER: Okay. Where were we? So, if you don't dwell on the past, what do you do? You seem to be in remarkably good health, but there must be many days when you are housebound by the weather, and you yourself said that you haven't left the glen for a long time.

MUNLOCHY: I *am* in remarkably good health. I sometimes don't quite believe it, and have to pinch myself. But then again I heard on the radio the other day about a woman who abseiled down a tower in Plymouth to celebrate her hundredth birthday. Why she wanted to do such a thing I have no idea, but she did. And I've heard of others who have jumped out of aeroplanes or gone scuba-diving, so there are more of us than you might think, keeping reasonably well. The thing is not to worry about it. Worry kills everything. I just wake up and get on with things. I am warm and comfortable in this room, and if it's too wet or windy to go outside I walk up and down the corridors for exercise. For six months of the year Poppy and I work in the garden – I'll show it to you later. We grow a lot of vegetables, and there are some fruit trees, and a greenhouse, and some adorable hens which give us eggs and are themselves eventually quite good to eat. The garden is our domain. Corryvreckan does the heavier work – chopping logs and repairing the roof and so on. You'll notice we don't have a television. We tried it once, in the 1970s, but the reception was terrible and I expect it wouldn't be any better now. Not having a television is good for the health, I think. I have the radio for news if I want it, and for music. The BBC, whatever else it has come to, still makes some excellent radio programmes. And there are always books to read, or to reread. My eyes get tired in the evening so Poppy reads to me, which I like very much. So you see, there is never really a shortage of things to do.

ELDER: Your own centenary is just a few days away. How do you intend to celebrate it?

MUNLOCHY: I don't.

ELDER: Not at all?

MUNLOCHY: A hundred is only a number to which some humans have attached undue significance. Actually it means nothing more than five sets of fingers and toes.

ELDER: So receiving a telegram from the Queen will mean nothing to you?

MUNLOCHY: Less than nothing. I am a republican.

ELDER: Some people, picturing you as the lady of a big house in the Highlands, would say that that is merely a conceit.

MUNLOCHY: They can say what they like. I am not interested in their opinions. I couldn't help what I was born to any more than they could, or the Queen for that matter. That doesn't justify the continued existence of queens.

ELDER: Or of Highland estates.

MUNLOCHY: I agree. As you will have noticed, we are much reduced. However, abolishing Glentaragar House will not repopulate the glen. If it could, I would be the first to reach for a sledgehammer.

ELDER: You said you admired your great-uncle's disdain for authority. Do you share that disdain?

MUNLOCHY: Yes, but I would qualify it. I respect authority that's been earned, that knows what it's talking about and is not complacent. If someone is an authority on herons, say, or the works of W. B. Yeats, that is admirable and useful.

ELDER: As well as a republican, you've been many other things politically. You once espoused the radical socialist cause. Do you still hold those extreme views?

MUNLOCHY: In principle, yes. They weren't extreme then. They were extreme times and one's ideas were shaped by the times. In the 1930s, with fascism raging across Europe, what choice did I have but to take the opposing view?

ELDER: Do we live in less extreme times now?

MUNLOCHY: You must ask the young that question, not me.

ELDER: You were accused by Willie Ross of political promiscuity. You were a communist, a socialist, a Scottish Nationalist, an Independent with Liberal sympathies – was his accusation just?

MUNLOCHY: He said I was a butterfly. I don't think he said I was promiscuous. I advocated free love too, and practised it, but that is not promiscuity either. I was for freedom but not for freedom without responsibility. In fact there *is* no freedom without responsibility. The most important thing is to be able to change your mind, and to move with the times. That is why one must look to the future. Ask the young what they think.

ELDER: Do you miss your public life, your political life? Even after you left Parliament, you were very active in local affairs.

MUNLOCHY: No, I don't miss it. This is my life now. I was much younger then. I was probably your sort of age – how old are you?

ELDER: I'm fifty.

MUNLOCHY: I was younger than that when I lost my seat in the Commons. Much younger. I needed to be rushing about. When you are young you must rush about. When you are older you don't have to. Things stop being a blur and come into focus. You appreciate the detail of the world. That's why it is fine not to leave the glen, hardly even to step outside the garden. So long as we are here the world is here. And even when we are not . . .

ELDER: Yes?

MUNLOCHY: Something survives.

An hour goes by as if it were ten minutes. So much for the pace of life being slow in a place such as this. Corryvreckan appears, sent by Poppy with more coffee and a plateful of sandwiches. I am disappointed but not surprised that she has not brought them herself.

I switch off the recorder while we eat. Already I have plenty of good quotes: by the time I have put in the background material to contextualise Rosalind's words, I'll be breaching the four-thousand-word limit Liffield proposed. Rosalind has not written her own full autobiography and surely will not do so now. But perhaps her biography is waiting to be written, and perhaps I, Douglas Findhorn Elder, am waiting to write it. And yet there is something about her, this bird-like, ancient, ageless fairy-queen of a woman, that defies the idea. A biography from birth to death! I can hear her ridiculing the proposal even as her jaws work at a piece of sandwich.

'My editor,' I say, 'thinks we should portray you as a kind of mother-of-the-nation figure. How would you feel about that?'

'I would strongly object. That's a very foolish idea. I don't feel at all maternal towards the nation.'

'You stopped writing but you still have much to say,' I say. 'What surprises me is that you haven't had a steady stream of people coming to consult you.'

She chuckles. 'Like an oracle? Because of this silly number I'm approaching?'

'Not just because of that. For the last two or three decades you seem to have been, well, forgotten. I have to admit, a week ago I didn't know anything about you.'

'I'm not surprised. Society doesn't remember much from the day before yesterday. I mean, *really* remember. It is more interested in fashion than wisdom, and everything is disposable. Not that any guarantee of wisdom comes with longevity. I am about to start havering, Douglas. Is that thing switched off?'

'It is.'

'Good. Then I'll continue. In medieval Edinburgh they had a noxious swamp called the Nor' Loch, into which they threw all their rubbish and waste until at last it was such a danger to public health that they had to drain it. It became Princes Street Gardens. That's a metaphor for the

Enlightenment. I was lucky. When I was born the garden was still flourishing and knowledge still useful. Knowledge could free us, improve and empower us. But what we didn't notice was that knowledge was itself becoming an engulfing swamp. People wade in it now without any sense of direction or any notion of what it is they are wading in. The philosophical stepping stones and walkways are submerged. Many people can't distinguish between cleverness and wisdom. However, there speaks a woman with no experience of computers or the internet so I may be talking through my hat. Am I talking through my hat, Douglas?'

'Yes and no. It's an interesting hat. You are an interesting person, and not just because of your age. That's why I'm wondering why you have been neglected.'

'I was happy to be. There was a time when I did not want to speak or be spoken to.'

'Why not?'

'That is the matter we have not yet come to,' she says.

The happiness is gone from her face, and this, combined with her last words, puzzles me. It does not fit with the trajectory of the interview as I have envisaged it – moving through phases of her life towards her thoughts on the independence referendum. Knowing how fatal to spontaneity and frankness it can be to discuss something with the tape recorder off and then cover the same ground again, I change tack.

'I suppose what I'm thinking is that there should be another way of depicting you and your life – not your past life, but the one you are living now, with Poppy and Corryvreckan here in Glentaragar. There should be another way of capturing it.'

'Such as?'

'A film, perhaps. A documentary film, but one made so unobtrusively that you would hardly know it was going on.'

'Why?'

'Because it's very special, this life of yours. I'm not just saying that. I really feel it.' Which is true.

She dabs a spot of egg mayonnaise from the corner of her mouth, staring hard for some time at the fire. Eventually she bestows one of her warm smiles on me.

'I'm glad. You have not come here in vain, then, whatever you write in the *Spear*. What makes our life special, do you think?'

'I don't know.'

'Even better! You are learning. Perhaps you will take something of this place away with you when you go.'

'I will.'

'And perhaps you will come back again.' She finishes her coffee. 'And now it is time for a nap. Put two or three more logs on the fire, Douglas, and sit very still. I am going to have half an hour's sleep, and I advise you to do the same. When we wake up, we will go out into the garden.'

'What about the rest of the interview?'

'Oh, we have plenty of time for that. Logs, please.' She waves her tiny hand at the fireplace, pushes herself back into her cushions and closes her eyes. I put logs on the fire. 'Thank you,' she says. A minute later she is snoring gently.

I think of escape, of going in search of Poppy, but to leave Rosalind by herself would feel like an act of betrayal. I don't know why, but it would. We have plenty of time, she said. I am not so sure. I have the rest of the day and night at least, and tomorrow morning. And I do feel sleepy in the hot, crowded room.

The cat, Sitka, watches me with one lazy eye, as if she has decided to wake and keep watch while Rosalind sleeps. I close my own eyes, just for a minute.

A MATTER OF PERCEPTION

A carriage clock above the fireplace chimes twice. Simultaneously I receive a poke in the ribs from something hard, which I discover to be the business end of a walking stick.

'Wake up, Douglas,' Rosalind says. She is out of her chair, standing like a child wanting to play, except that the child has a wizened old lady's face. The stick is thin and dark with a brass ferrule at its base.

'It is two o'clock. The sun is shining. Don't you have any more sensible shoes than those? If not you can borrow some boots downstairs.'

When I stand, I tower over her. She clutches my right forearm in her left hand and steadies herself with the stick. Actually the stick seems superfluous: she feels astonishingly secure despite her fragility.

'Sitka, are you coming? No, I didn't think so. I don't know why I bother asking. Lazy beast.'

Down in the oak-lined lobby Rosalind sits on the bench while I help her into a pair of light boots, then root around for a pair of wellingtons that fit me. She points out a dark green waxy jacket and I hold it for her to put on. It comes down to her knees. 'You had better do me up,' she says, 'or Poppy will be cross. My fingers can't work the zip very easily.' The jacket is mud-streaked and smells of earth and things left for a long time in its pockets. One of these is a woolly hat, which she pulls so far down over her ears that half her face disappears. 'Help yourself to a coat,' she says, but when I open the front door there is such warmth in the sun, and the high clouds are moving so slowly, that I decide to do without. Then we descend the stone steps and along the avenue that cuts through the lawn, towards the row of oak trees.

'In my childhood there were ornamental shrubs and flowerbeds here,' Rosalind says, 'but Ralph took them all out when I was a Member of Parliament. We had no gardener by then, and Ralph said he didn't have time for that kind of gardening and I quite agreed with him. The children used this area for everything from archery to football and every so often we'd let some sheep in to keep it trim. It's mostly moss now, which at least doesn't need much looking after. Come along.'

About halfway down the avenue a path goes off to the right, leading to a wooden door set into the high wall that runs along the lawn on that side. Rosalind turns the handle in the door and pushes. Nothing happens.

'All that rain must have warped the wood,' she says. 'Could you put your shoulder to it and give it a good shove, Douglas? I want to show you our pride and joy.'

I shove, the door gives way, and through it we go. On the other side is a not insubstantial vegetable garden, fully surrounded by the wall, and laid out in tidy beds intersected by gravel paths. Most of the beds are empty, but those that aren't contain small stands of vegetables at various stages of maturity: I recognise kale, leeks, carrots, onions and turnips but there is much more. Against the south-facing wall are espaliered pear trees and some small apple trees, bare of fruit and foliage. Elsewhere there is a fruit cage, a large greenhouse with some missing panes boarded over, and big pots full of parsley, thyme and mint. Hens are scratching around near their lodgings under the west wall. The walls trap the sun with great efficiency and even though it is nearly the end of October the heat is remarkable.

'Are you a gardener?' Rosalind asks.

'After a fashion. My father used to grow a lot of vegetables, and I learned what I know from him. But I don't grow much nowadays. There doesn't seem much point, for one.'

'Your father is dead, I take it?'

'No, not quite. He's in a home.'

'So am I, but I take it his is not his own. Why?'

'The usual complications, from which you don't seem to suffer.'

'I see,' she says. I can tell that my answer does not satisfy her. 'I could take you round plant by plant if you like,' she continues, 'but I'll spare you that. However, we will go over and speak to the hens, because one always should, and that way you can see for yourself that this is not the place of desolation some might think.'

'I can see that already.'

'I don't mean the garden. I mean the house, and the glen. As we were saying earlier, it is a matter of perception.'

Despite herself, she cannot resist showing me what they are growing – 'they' being herself and Poppy, although Poppy, she admits, does all the heavy labour now. 'I can weed quite well sitting down, and I can do a lot in the greenhouse, but digging and planting are not realistic. It's hard for Poppy, but then, we grow so much less than we used to. If we could get our produce to market, we could use the whole garden again, and even employ someone.'

'As well as Corryvreckan?'

'I never really think of him as an employee, but I suppose that's what he is. We do pay him. I wouldn't like you to think we don't.'

'Corryvreckan seems a complicated person,' I say. 'Does he not also have the hotel?'

Her eyes look up at me from under the woollen rim. 'I understand that you must be curious about Corryvreckan,' she says. 'Anybody would be. I will tell you about Corryvreckan later, or Poppy will, on condition that it is not for your newspaper article. That is an omission I insist upon. You are right; he is complicated. Here are the hens coming to meet us.'

She speaks to the hens for some time, and after a while I join in. I have never been in the close presence of hens before. I have always imagined them to be very stupid, but they don't seem to hold this against me. I rather enjoy their company, and they seem to like ours. After this we return through the wooden door and walk down to the oak trees and the gates that stand beneath them. Unlike the gates at the top of the glen, these are shut, but it is easy to unbolt one and swing it wide enough for us to pass through.

'Behold, the world,' Rosalind says.

A well-made track, which appears to come round the outside of the walled garden and presumably begins at the back of the house, runs away from the gates, dropping in steepish bends through scrubby woodland towards the head of the loch I saw earlier from my window. The loch is perhaps a mile away, a few hundred feet below us – more or less at sea level, I guess – but it is what lies beyond that catches and holds the eye: hill after hill after hill ranked like cut-out models, their outlines intersecting, the light accentuating their contours and peaks one minute and softening them the next. Strips of water lie between and among them, now black, now silver, and stretched behind it all is the curve of the horizon and the western sea.

'That is Morven, and there is Mull, and over that way is Ardnamurchan, and up there is Ben Nevis with his white bonnet on,' Rosalind says, pointing in this and that direction. If I see half of what she sees I am lucky. I feel a profound geographical insecurity because she speaks with such certainty, and when finally I comment I reveal my ignorance.

'So, is that Loch Araich down there?'

'No, no, don't be silly, how can you say that? Loch Araich is behind you, at the foot of the glen. That is Loch Glaineach and its outflow goes into Loch Glas, which is a sea loch. In the old days the puffers came up Loch Glas and beached themselves on one tide and took themselves off again on the next. There was a store, owned by people called Lamont, and they would bring their goods by cart to Loch Glaineach where there was a big flat boat like a barge. Everything was loaded onto that and brought to the top of the loch where there was another store, and we sent a cart down from here to fetch whatever goods had come in, and from here they were carried all the way down the glen. That's a very good track, as you can see; it wasn't hard on the ponies to pull the cart, and there were handcarts too, a couple of strong lads could manage one of those easily. So there was a constant traffic up and down between here and the lochs, and not just on the days when the puffer came, because we had the stores to keep everything dry, and also at certain times of the year sheep and cattle were driven down the lochside to the Lamonts' store and loaded onto the boat to go to Oban or Glasgow. And that is why the house is where it is, and why it looks to the sea. Everything came in from the sea, and the glen was kept alive by that route. Now everything is back to front and no wonder it doesn't work. Do you understand?'

I nod. 'I do,' I say, even though I don't, not really. We stand in the warm afternoon sunshine, Douglas Findhorn Elder and Rosalind Isabella Munlochy (née Striven), and I try to imagine a barge on the black water and people and ponies going up and down the track and boys pushing handcarts shouting and laughing at each other in Gaelic and the glen full of families – I try to imagine all of it, and it is a struggle, it is a dream really, but when I glance at Rosalind I see that it is real enough for her. Perception, as she said, being everything.

She says, 'When I asked, this morning, if you had come about a job, and that if you had there wasn't one, I was rather wishing that there was. I was wishing there were a dozen jobs, and that you were only the first to come about one of them. That is, I know, a fantasy, but it would be good, I think, if there were just one job. Do you think you would be interested?'

'What would it be, this job?'

'Oh, I don't know. General factotum. What we used to call an orra-man. A hewer of wood and drawer of water. A spear carrier.'

'I used to be one of those. It was our nickname for ourselves on the newspaper. But that job sounds like Corryvreckan's.'

'Yes, but Corryvreckan won't be here for ever. And it would be nice if we could justify two such jobs. Would that interest you?'

'I'd need to think about it.'

'Yes. I don't suppose we could, though. Justify it. I should speak to Poppy about it if I were you.'

And a little later she says, 'What about caretaker? I like that title. One who cares. One who takes care. That's a job worth doing, isn't it?'

'It sounds like Poppy's job.'

'Yes, only Poppy doesn't have a job, poor girl.'

I feel she may be about to say more, but just then a little breeze starts up and she turns away from it in her dirty, earth-smelling jacket down to her knees, and her bird's head with the tea-cosy hat on top of it nods up at me, and she says in her not quite yet one-hundred-year-old voice, 'Give me your arm again, Douglas, and take me back to the house, before I am tipped off my feet.'

A PLAY WITHIN A DREAM

When we walk up the steps to the big front door it is opened to us by Poppy. A small thrill of pleasure runs through me on seeing her, swiftly followed by another when she smiles. Her smile is divided equally between myself and Rosalind yet I harbour not a jot of jealousy towards Rosalind.

I have to remind myself that I am very angry with Poppy/Xanthe/Coppélia. Would Delilah be a more appropriate name? I should mistrust her deeply, anyway. And I should be looking forward to my release from the frustrating situation I am in. But actually I don't feel like that at all. I feel curiously comfortable, and unhappy at the prospect of the experience that I'm having – whatever it is – coming to an end.

'Everything all right?' Poppy asks.

'We have done no work at all,' Rosalind tells her. 'I was acquainting Douglas with his surroundings. You can have him now.'

'In that case,' Poppy says – again, without a glimmer of shame – 'we can make dinner together.'

'What about the rest of the interview?' I ask.

'Tomorrow,' Rosalind says. 'I never say anything sensible after I've spoken to the hens. I'm not blaming the hens, but I'm afraid it's true. I shall go and read a reproving book for an hour. Bring me a glass of something later, will you, my dear?'

'I will,' Poppy says, helping Rosalind out of her jacket, hat and boots and restoring her to her indoor appearance. Once again I think of myself as being in a play – a play within a dream – knowing the lines that my fellow players are uttering, recognising that they are leading towards lines of my own, and yet not having a clue as to what I am to say or when I am to say it. And so, like a spear carrier or some other minor character, I follow Poppy offstage, while Rosalind, one hand on the banister, the other holding her stick, negotiates the stairs as if mimicking the movements of a slightly weary chaffinch.

US. LIFE

I decide not to beat about the bush. 'Poppy,' I say, as we descend to the kitchen, 'if indeed that is your name, I am very angry with you.'

We are halfway down the stone stairs. She stops, turns suddenly and flings her arms around me. 'I know you are,' she says, and kisses me very hard and long on the mouth. I offer some feeble resistance, then give up. After about a minute I push us apart and pull myself together.

'This is all very well, but you have some explaining to do.'

'I do,' she says, looking slightly contrite. She continues on her way, and I follow. In the kitchen she ambushes me again, using the enormous kitchen table to block my retreat. Her behaviour is outrageous and I can barely contain my outrage. At last she releases me and goes to the sink to wash her hands – not because of anything we have done but because she is about to start preparing food. I take a couple of steps and nearly fall over, my left leg having temporarily died from the pressure her right one was exerting on it against the edge of the table.

'Shall we have a glass of wine?' Poppy says cheerily. 'I think that would help to break the ice. There's a nice pinot noir in the rack over there, that doesn't need to breathe.'

She hands me a corkscrew. I open the bottle while she finds two glasses.

'If I had done to you what you have just done to me, you'd have been furious, and quite rightly,' I tell her.

'No I wouldn't.'

'Well, you should have been. Once again I ask you, what the hell is going on?'

'I will explain, darling –'

'I must ask you not to call me that. I'm not in the mood.'

She disputes this with her eyebrows.

'Douglas,' she says. 'Look, I don't mean to sound insensitive to your legitimate concerns, but I need to get the dinner started.'

'Dinner? You speak of dinner?'

'Yes, a chicken casserole. We killed a hen at the weekend and had it roasted yesterday. What's left will go into the casserole along with some other bits and pieces.'

I am momentarily distracted from the main item on the agenda by this information.

'You killed one of those delightful hens I was talking to?'

'No, the one I killed was dead before you met the others.'

'*You* killed it, personally?'

'It wasn't personal, but yes, I wrung its neck. Rosalind hasn't the strength any more, and it's one of those jobs you shouldn't ask anyone to do if you're not prepared to do it yourself. Don't look so shocked. I like the hens too but there's no point in being sentimental about them. That's what happens to hens – they go in pots. At least here they have a good and useful life first.'

'That must be a great comfort to them,' I say.

'You're not a vegetarian, are you?' Poppy asks, tying herself into an apron and somehow managing to make this simple act sensual.

'No, I am not a vegetarian. I had the Scotch broth the other day, remember? We are getting completely off the subject.'

'No we're not. You can help by preparing the carrots and this leek and peeling some potatoes. We'll talk as we go. You see, right back on subject. Where shall we start?'

'Why don't *you* start, with Xanthe? Or Jezebel or whatever you call yourself when you're not Poppy.'

'Oh, I never thought of Jezebel,' she says, dumping the chicken carcass on a board and beginning to tear it apart. 'That could have been fun, if a little unbelievable. I made Xanthe up some time ago. It's just a name really. I can't remember why I chose it. She's not so different from me, but it's nice to think she could be. When I need to escape – and believe me, sometimes I have needed to – Xanthe comes out to play.'

'How convenient for her. And you. Tell me, does Malcolm know who she is? That is, who you are? I mean, who she *really* is?'

She is not fazed by my sarcastic tone. 'Possibly,' she says. 'He's never been here, and he's not in the least bit curious, but that doesn't mean he hasn't worked it out. Don't be jealous, Douglas. Malcolm and I had our fling but it was ages ago. We're just old pals now.'

'Me, jealous of Malcolm? I don't suppose there's any chance he might be jealous of me?'

She shakes her head. 'No. He doesn't care about anything or anyone but himself, honestly.'

' "Honestly" is a word I'm having some difficulty with at the moment,' I say. It is meant to cut her to the core, in much the same way as she is now carving meat off the chicken carcass with a very sharp knife.

'I can see why that would be,' she says. 'From the outside, everything here must seem a bit off the true.'

'Just a bit. How, for example, do that place of Malcolm's and the Glen Araich Lodge survive?'

'That's two separate questions. Don't just stand there, darling – I mean Douglas.' In spite of myself, I go to the sink, give the leek a good rinse and start cutting it up on another chopping board. Meanwhile, Poppy chatters on.

'The Shira survives because it's not Malcolm's. It's owned by an uncle of his, one of those rich bankers we're all supposed to hate. Well, I do hate them, they won't lend us any money. I can't blame them, though, we wouldn't be able to pay it back. Every August Malcolm's uncle and his wealthy friends take over the pub for a couple of weeks and shoot at every living thing in sight. Sometimes they even manage to wing each other.

The rest of the year Malcolm keeps it ticking over but it doesn't really matter if it makes money or not. He has a cottage a mile away and he spends most of his time there, complaining about the slowness of the broadband.'

'And the Glen Araich?' I can't help noticing we're straying off course again, but maybe this background information is necessary to gain an understanding of Poppy.

'That's more complicated. Corryvreckan owns it. He bought it thirty years ago when I was little and for a while he seemed to make a go of it, but the reality was he couldn't even break even. That's when he started working for us. He uses what we pay him to keep the hotel afloat but it can't go on much longer. He paid off the last of the staff this summer. Give those carrots a scrub, will you, and cut them into quarters lengthwise. Next question?'

'Would you please explain Corryvreckan to me?'

'Ah. That one needs quite a long answer. Can we save it till later?'

'That's what Rosalind said. All right, try this one instead,' I say, sensing a chance to land a few wounding blows. 'Maybe it's more straightforward. How come you turned up at the Shira Inn on Monday? Let me suggest an answer. You needed to get away from here, you adopted your alter ego Xanthe, and then what? You decided to go to the pub and pick up any available man regardless of which side of the bar he was on?'

'That isn't fair,' Poppy says.

'Why isn't it?'

'Because I knew you were going to be there.'

'That's even worse! You knew there would be an available man? Anyway, *how* did you know I'd be there?'

'Because I arranged it.'

Perhaps I shouldn't be surprised, but I am. Surprised and, once again, confused.

'So it was you who put the request in to the train, to get me off it?'

'Yes,' she says. She is hanging her head, possibly in shame but I think she's just looking to see if there's any more meat to come off the chicken bones.

'Why?'

'To check you out. Out of the blue a journalist wants to talk to Rosalind? Nobody's been near her for a quarter of a century. I'm her guardian. Not her legal guardian, but I protect her. I wanted to find out what kind of man you were. If you were going to treat her kindly.'

'And your way of doing that was to seduce me?'

'Oh, Douglas, no, that's not how it was. Honestly.'

'Please don't use that word.'

'Sorry. It's true, though. I didn't plan that part. And if you don't like "honestly" I don't like "seduce". Seduction's one-sided. The seduced may be a willing victim but really it's about power and manipulation. That's not what this is about.' She makes a big gesture that I understand is meant to encompass herself and me preparing food and drinking wine in the kitchen of Glentaragar House.

'How do I know that?' I ask.

'You don't. Neither do I. It's not about knowing, it's about feeling. You just have to feel it, Douglas. And you do, don't you?'

'Well, I –'

'You didn't fight me off just now – not much anyway – any more than you fought me off on Monday. What happened then was mutual. Mutual and mutually enjoyed. Wasn't it?'

'So I thought. Except that you weren't there in the morning to share the memories. That put a slightly different slant on it, for me at any rate.'

'I had to get back here,' she says.

'Aha!' I have her now. 'And so, coincidentally, did Corryvreckan. You left together, I take it?'

'I left in that car, yes.'

'You took your life in your hands, then. Corryvreckan must still have been way over the limit.'

'It wasn't Corryvreckan. It was MacCrimmon. You're right, he wasn't at his best but luckily we didn't meet any other traffic. By the time we reached Glen Araich he was almost sober. Not that you'd have known from anything he said – he didn't speak a word the whole way. He abandoned the car outside the hotel and I imagine he went straight to bed. When he woke up he would have been MacLagan. Why are you laughing?'

'Because the alternative is screaming. And what did you do then?'

'I walked back home up the glen. It was a filthy day but there's something glorious about getting soaked to the bone, don't you think?' She has chopped a couple of onions and is frying them on the range. Some garlic too, if I am not mistaken.

'No,' I tell her.

'Well, I do. I didn't care anyway. I love walking the glen and I was thinking about you all the way.'

'Really? And what were you thinking? Who was that total stranger I had sex with last night? *Did* I have sex with a total stranger last night?'

She gives me a hurt look even as she adds the chopped chicken to the pan. I call that inappropriate multitasking. 'As a matter of fact,' she says, 'I was wondering if you were awake, and if you were following me yet.'

'If you'd stayed a bit longer we could have made the journey together.'

'Do you think I didn't want to stay?'

This strikes me as being a very silly question. 'I have no idea, Poppy. You didn't, though. You left. You could have woken me even if it was just to say goodbye. You could have told me where to find you. You could have told me who you really were. You didn't do any of those things.'

'I was confused.'

'Well, that makes two of us.'

'When I woke up at first I didn't know what I should do. Everything seemed like a dream. I was torn between staying in the dream and running away from it. Then I realised I could put us to the test.'

'What test?'

'The test of fate. Would I ever see you again? I had to leave it to fate. If you actually got here, that would be a sign that everything was going to be all right. And here you are. I feel this is the start of something – something good. It is, isn't it?'

I am chopping carrots vigorously and almost add a fingertip or two to the pile. 'Jesus, Poppy, how would I know? This isn't exactly a normal way to begin a relationship. And I'm not saying it *is* a relationship. Just think about it. You arrange to meet me but not to sleep with me. Then you sleep with me. Then you leave me so that we can get together again, if fate decrees it. And fate does, apparently. And that's the start of something good? Something weird, maybe.'

'You're not so normal yourself.'

'By your standards, I'd say I was.'

'Not beneath the surface. I bet you have a secret life too.'

'And if I do? Does that make me acceptable? Does that mean I'm going to – what was it you said? – treat Rosalind kindly?'

'You already have. You're a decent man.'

'You can't know that.'

'I've been wrong before, but I'm not wrong now. Please be careful with that knife. And can I have those carrots now?'

I put down the knife and hand over the carrots. I sit down at the table and swallow a large mouthful of wine. Then I return to the fray. I have been alone in her company for a while now and am running low on ammunition.

'How on earth did you manage that business with the train anyway?'

'I asked Malcolm,' she says. 'Or rather, Xanthe did. Malcolm knows how to put a request in. When it happens in August about a dozen of his uncle's friends get out, with guns and shooting sticks and a dog or two. Once you'd confirmed which train you were going to be on, I got Malcolm to arrange it.'

'That's why you insisted on that particular train. And the guy on the train said Corryvreckan was supposed to meet me. Are you telling me that you sent Corryvreckan to pick me up but by the time he got to the inn he'd changed personality and was MacCrimmon?'

'No, I just told Malcolm to mention Corryvreckan's name, so you'd be sure to get off. I knew Corryvreckan wouldn't make it.'

'So how was I meant to get to Glentaragar that day?'

'You weren't. Corryvreckan gave me a run down to Glen Araich, at which point I got out and he drove on. I waited for the afternoon minibus to Oban, got out at the junction where the road goes to the Shira Inn and started walking. I told you, that's how I get around. Those women who'd been at a funeral in Oban gave me a lift.'

If my resolve to be stern has been softening, this stiffens it again. 'You mean you left Rosalind alone? How could you? She's extraordinary, but how could you leave her entirely on her own here?'

'You see, you *are* a decent man. Don't worry, Rosalind can look after herself for a night. In fact, she insists on doing so every so often. You've spent the afternoon with her, Douglas – you can see how capable she is. What's the worst that can happen? She dies, aged ninety-nine.'

'That's a terrible attitude!'

'It's hers, not mine, although I happen to share it.'

'She slips when she's getting ready for bed, breaks her femur, and dies alone, freezing and in great pain, on the bathroom floor. You'd feel fine about that?'

'No, but if that's how it happens, so be it. She's not frightened of death, however it comes. She's a philosopher – you should have found that out already. What else can you be at that age? If she were a hen she'd have a philosophic attitude to pots. Anyway, she likes her own company. And it's good for all three of us to have a break from each other.'

I pounce on her inconsistency. 'Five of you, surely? Counting Corryvreckan and his enigma variations.'

'Three. Here in the glen, Corryvreckan is only Corryvreckan. The point is, Rosalind needs her space and so do I. She's not interested in going away, so I do.'

I put my head in my hands but it doesn't help much. 'Can we go back a bit?' I ask. 'You hitched a lift to the Shira Inn and you got there whenever you did that afternoon. You just seemed to appear beside me. Did you tell Malcolm to make himself scarce before you arrived?'

'No need. He has form in that department. It didn't matter if he was there or not. You were going to wait for someone called Corryvreckan, and I knew someone called Corryvreckan wasn't going to come. The only person who was going to turn up was MacCrimmon.'

'Bloody hell, Poppy! This is certifiable behaviour.'

'We don't care much for that kind of label.'

'Again, how convenient!'

She looks at me coolly. 'We're all other people, Douglas, every one of us. Don't think you're immune.'

I know that already but I'm not going to admit it. 'But MacCrimmon *wasn't* the only one to turn up, was he?' I say instead. 'The place was stowed out. If I'd managed to get anyone to give me a lift – and believe me, I tried – your plan would have been scuppered.'

'Yes, that's true. It never occurred to me there'd be all those customers. I don't know where they appeared from. But no one gave you a lift. Maybe that was fate again.'

'To hell with fate. Here's something else. You left me stranded at the Glen Araich last night. Why? Why didn't you come and get me?'

'I don't drive.'

'Ah, yes, you told me that on the phone.'

'I *didn't* speak to you on the phone. I already said, I tried to call the hotel but there was something wrong with the line. Even if I *had* spoken to you and even if I *could* drive, it wouldn't have been any use. Corryvreckan's is the only vehicle here and he'd taken it down to the hotel.'

'Then you could have asked him to bring me up. Or you could have asked MacLagan if that's who he'd turned into by then.'

'*That* wouldn't have worked. MacLagan *never* comes up the glen. My grandmother doesn't like him, and he stays away.'

'So what you're telling me is, I imagined that phone conversation.'

'Maybe you did,' Poppy says.

I remember Ollie saying that the Glentaragar set-up sounded as safe as a bag of snakes. I think he was understating the case.

'Yes, and maybe my head is going to explode,' I reply. 'Maybe I'm having an attack of Brigadoonism. Maybe Glentaragar House and all of you only appear every hundred years and any minute I'm going to find myself wandering around alone in the mist.'

'Now you're getting hysterical.'

'Can you blame me? I seem to have my feet in two different worlds. I don't know who's who, what's what or why anything. I feel there's this big plan and I'm caught up in the middle of it, clueless. The guy on the train said I was going to be like Richard Hannay in *The Thirty-Nine Steps*. I don't think that's how he meant it but he was right.'

Poppy has been adding various items to the pan on the range, including some stock, and now she puts a lid on it, comes over to where I'm sitting, crouches in front of me and seizes both my hands.

'Listen to me,' she says. 'Some of what's happened was planned, and some of it wasn't. You have to believe that or this isn't going to work.'

'What, exactly, is or isn't going to work?'

'Us. Life.'

Those are very wee words with quite a big capacity to frighten. I try not to show it in my face.

'We've only just met.'

'Don't be frightened,' Poppy says. '*I* want it to work. Don't you?'

'What makes you think I'm frightened?'

'Because I am,' she says.

I look for signs but I don't see any.

'Poppy,' I say, 'I don't know whether this is going to work or even if I want it to. I'm not even sure what "this" is. It's all very sudden.'

'That's one way of looking at it,' she says. 'But once you've looked, it's not sudden any more. It's just what it is. You haven't peeled the potatoes yet.'

'No, I got distracted.'

'We'll do them together. The chicken will take about an hour. We'll stick the potatoes in another pan and I'll come back and deal with them later. Meanwhile, we can refill our glasses and take one up to Rosalind.'

'Ah, Rosalind,' I say. 'What does she know about – well, about us?'

'I haven't said anything to her but she doesn't miss much. She knows a lot of things.'

'Does she know that Corryvreckan is insane?'

'That's another of those labels. He's not insane. He's just himself. Anyway, he's not dangerous.'

'He is when he's MacCrimmon. Or MacLagan.'

'But then he's not himself.'

'Now there's another thing. He has a strange voice, Corryvreckan. And for all his tweedy get-up, he is not a mannish kind of man. In his other personae he wears a false beard.'

'So?'

'Would I be right in thinking that Corryvreckan was once – a woman?'

Poppy laughs like a drain. 'What a sweet idea! Oh no, you're very wide of the mark there. The truth is much stranger.' She goes to the door and checks that nobody is outside. 'Corryvreckan used to be – an Englishman.'

'A Friend from the South?'

'Not only that, from the Deep South. From Surrey, I believe.'

'Good God! What on earth happened?'

'He went native. It's not uncommon in the Highlands. Admittedly Corryvreckan is quite an extreme case. Look, we should really go up to my grandmother. Grab the bottle and another glass and I'll take ours.'

I am still very angry with her, but there is something, since I am here for the night, that I need to establish.

'Poppy? Are we going to have some time together? Real, proper time?'

'Oh yes,' she says, and kisses me. 'Most definitely yes. I promise. Honestly.'

This time I do not challenge the word. We gather ourselves together and head upstairs, leaving the chicken casserole simmering.

DIFFERENT FOR TOADS

The cat is padding back and forth at the top of the stairs, meowing piteously. She at once proceeds to rub herself against Poppy's legs.

'What are you doing here?' Poppy says. Sitka meows more loudly and accompanies us down the corridor. I open the door to Rosalind's sitting room. Poppy enters first, followed by me and, finally, Sitka, who seems nervous.

'Hello, Gran,' Poppy says. 'Everything all right? Sitka's lively.'

'I had to put her out,' Rosalind says. 'It's her own fault. If she spent more time in the garden she wouldn't have had such a surprise.'

I fill a glass with wine for Rosalind while the cat explores the room as if she suspects a trap.

'Thank you, Douglas. What an interesting day it's turned out to be! First you, then this.'

'Then what?' Poppy asks.

'I've just been having the most fascinating conversation with a toad,' Rosalind says.

'At this time of the year?' Poppy replies. It's not the first question that springs to my mind. 'Are you sure?'

'Oh yes. I did think it was a mouse at first, crawling along the skirting board, but it wasn't. Sitka thought so too. She was half-awake when she saw it and she actually came off her chair and tried to catch it. Well, didn't she get a shock! Couldn't get close to the creature at all. She tried from all angles, batting at it with her paws, but the toad wasn't having any of that. He stood up and beat his chest, like a gorilla. Sitka ran to the door and scratched and screamed until I let her out. I'm surprised you didn't hear her.'

'It's a long way down to the kitchen,' I say.

'We were busy,' Poppy says.

'I apologised to the toad but he was quite all right about it,' Rosalind says. 'He said he often has that effect on domestic animals. Far from taking offence, he finds it rather amusing.'

'The toad told you that, did it?' I ask.

'He. It was a he. Mungo Forth Mungo.'

'Oh, he told you his name as well?'

'How else do you think I know it? It's a very impressive name. One could go far with a name like that.'

'Like Mungo Park,' Poppy says. 'What was he doing in here, though? Toads hibernate, don't they?'

'They do. He said he was late this year as it was so mild, but he expected to turn in for the winter any day now. As for being in the house, he was just exploring and hoped I didn't mind. Which naturally I don't.'

'Naturally,' I say. 'He's not still here, is he?'

'No. I felt a little drowsy and must have dropped off, and when I woke up he was gone. No doubt he left the way he came in, through some hole or other. It wouldn't be the first time we've had a toad in the house, would it, Poppy?'

'No, but usually the wildlife comes in the summer, and stays in the basement. It's quite a climb up here for a toad.'

'It would be, unaided,' Rosalind says, and she looks at me over the top of her pink glasses as if she and I are supposed to be in on some secret.

239

'What did you and this toad talk about?' I ask.

'Oh, many things. Climate change, diet, folklore, sex, procreation, contraception. He didn't see the point of contraception at all. He was terribly interested in the flora and fauna of the glen. Wanted to know all about the people too, why there weren't any left, and so on.'

'Is that right?' I ask, and check to see how Poppy is reacting. She seems neither surprised nor concerned.

'Yes,' Rosalind says. 'Mungo put it to me that the glen would still be full if there hadn't been so much contraception. I had to put him straight on that but I don't think he understood.'

'Well, it's different for toads, isn't it?' Poppy says.

'Yes, one can't blame him.'

Once again I fear I have fallen among lunatics. Speaking to a toad is all very well – I've done it myself – but being spoken to *by* one is a different matter.

'He seemed to know a great deal about you, Douglas,' Rosalind says.

This is too much. 'Rosalind, how can a toad *know* anything about me? Have you two been eating magic mushrooms or something?'

They both giggle. 'I did once,' Rosalind says. 'It made me dreadfully sick. Did you ever, Poppy?'

'No, Gran. I have lived a sheltered life.'

'Mungo said you're writing a novel,' Rosalind says to me.

'He said what?'

'That you're writing a novel. I told him I'd written a few and he said it was the most extraordinary waste of time he could imagine. Couldn't see the point. Rather like contraception.'

'I'm not writing a novel!'

'Oh well, then, he was misinformed. Think of all the time you won't waste.'

'I don't believe we are having this conversation.'

'Well, we are. Aren't we, Poppy?'

'Yes we are.'

'I mean, having a conversation about you having a conversation with a toad. It's absurd.'

'You were quite happy talking to the hens earlier.'

'But that wasn't really *talking*! And they weren't really *saying* anything!'

Rosalind and Poppy exchange glances. Poppy raises her eyebrows.

'Well, let's not fall out about it,' Rosalind says. 'Is Corryvreckan eating with us tonight?'

'I don't think so,' Poppy says. 'I think he's away to Glen Araich.'

'Then why don't we have our dinner here? The dining room will be cold. You can set up that little table in the window. Or is it too much trouble to bring everything up?'

'It's no trouble at all,' Poppy says. 'Is it, Douglas?'

I shake my head. I can't see the point in arguing.

'If there is a drop more wine,' Rosalind says, 'I would not object.'

And thus the late afternoon slips into the darker peace of the evening.

SMALL SCURRYING ANIMALS

Rosalind retires to bed at nine o'clock, as she promised. She says she is tired after such a stimulating day, and will see us in the morning.

'Douglas,' she says, gathering herself, 'I hope you will stay a day or two longer. I wish we could offer you that job. Thank you, Poppy, that was a lovely meal.'

'What job?' Poppy asks.

'The one we don't have,' Rosalind says.

Her granddaughter goes with her to her bedroom, which is next door, while I take the dinner things down to the kitchen and wash up. By the time Poppy rejoins me I have finished. We stand at the back door of the house for a few moments in a close embrace, which feels to me both dreamlike and a necessary anchoring to physical reality – even if it is the reality of Poppy Munlochy, with whom I am still very angry. The night is chill and calm, the unpolluted sky is scattered with many stars, and owls are hooting in the tall trees. I think of small scurrying animals and wish them well. We go in, find another bottle of wine and return upstairs to the fireside.

I am nervous that Rosalind might reappear but Poppy assures me that she will already be fast asleep. Our only witness is Sitka, who is not really a witness as she is asleep as well, apparently recovered from her ordeal by toad. We make ourselves comfortable. This is a euphemism, though also true. I have never felt so relaxed, which are six words that don't make much sense in the circumstances – the wider circumstances, I mean. Nevertheless, they also are true.

We begin to do that thing that people do when they have been physically intimate – to reveal ourselves, cautiously, in other ways. I talk about my childhood, my parents. I talk about moving back home after my mother's death, and about my father's illness, and this allows me to mention my relationship with Sonya and that it is over. I can say this with a confidence and clarity I haven't felt before, although it doesn't follow that I am starting a new relationship with Poppy. We're probably just ships passing in the night. I talk of the sadness of seeing my father in his present condition: his present absence. This leads us to the male absences in Poppy's life. She doesn't know who her father was or is: she doesn't, she insists, need or want to. Her grandfather – Ralph – died when she was two. Corryvreckan has been around since she was eight or nine but he is not, and never has been, a substitute father figure. Rosalind educated her at home until she was eleven, then she went to the High School in Oban. It was too far to travel to every day so she boarded in the school hostel along with other pupils from distant locations. Her mother and Rosalind both drove, and one of them would bring her home every Friday and take her back on Sunday evening. The teachers and the hostel staff were strict but kind. She learned early to be independent and to do things in her own way. When she needed advice she turned to her grandmother.

And what of her mother, who drowned when Poppy was a teenager? That must surely have been a devastating loss. Yes, she says, it was, but at the same time Georgina was a difficult woman. She had all the determination and intelligence of Rosalind but none of the grace or sense of purpose. She bashed her way through life, landing glancing blows on others along the way, and life bashed back. One day life – or death, which is life in another guise, Poppy says – delivered a knockout blow. Georgina was due to collect her from school one Friday afternoon but she didn't show up. Poppy waited and waited, and still Georgina did not come. Eventually Rosalind arrived. By that time someone walking their dog on a beach had called the police. Georgina, it transpired, had come to Oban on the Thursday and stayed in a hotel. She'd had a few drinks, and then she'd driven to the spot where her grandfather had drowned all those years before, and gone for a swim. Was she tempting fate? In all probability. Was it a deliberate act, to meet death in that way? Perhaps. She was not a contented person. The procurator fiscal concluded that there were no suspicious circumstances, and accidental drowning was recorded as the cause of death.

Does Poppy miss her? In all honesty, she says, no. Life with Georgina was stressful and unpredictable and it was a shock but almost immediately no surprise when it ended badly. Rosalind is and always was more of a mother to her. Does Rosalind miss her own daughter? Poppy shrugs. She doesn't think so. Perhaps she feels guilty, but no, she doesn't miss her either. Rosalind is so old now that if she missed everybody who was dead she would never be done with grieving. Her two husbands, all her siblings and her two younger children have predeceased her, and she has no contact other than an occasional card with her oldest, Gabriella. Gabriella has been in Los Angeles for fifty years, looks from photographs like a Californian prune and will doubtless live to be as old as her mother.

We put another log on the fire and fill our glasses again.

'Do you always drink so much?' she asks.

'No. Do you?'

'Not as a rule. We seemed to drink a lot on Monday, and again tonight. Maybe we're setting a bad precedent.'

'I can go for months without a drink.'

'I expect I could too if I put my mind to it. My mother couldn't. She had a problem with drink. That scares me.'

I think of the outbuilding at Glen Araich, stacked to the beams with illicit whisky.

'MacCrimmon or MacLagan or Corryvreckan or whatever you want to call him has a problem. I don't think you have a problem.'

'You don't know me. And by the way, Corryvreckan doesn't. He hasn't touched a drop for thirty years.'

'Come on, Poppy, he shares the same body.'

'I share the same genes as Georgina.'

'That's different. You share Rosalind's genes too, and I don't think she has a drink problem.'

'Rosalind isn't perfect. Don't imagine she is.'

'I won't. I do understand why you might worry about what you'll inherit. I worry that I'll lose the plot, like my Dad. I had a great-uncle who lost it too, according to family tradition.'

'What happened to him?'

'He drowned in the sea.'

'Oh.'

After that we don't talk for a while. And after that, with the fire reduced to a bed of embers, we pick up our shoes and clothes and creak further along the corridor, away from Rosalind's room and from mine, to Poppy's.

It's a very large, messy room. She has piled clothes and other items, including a lot of books, into a semblance of order, but there is no getting away from the overall impression of untidiness. I am a tidy man. Mess distresses me. On this occasion I find I don't give a damn. There is a table covered in paperwork, and plants in the window, an electric heater in the fireplace, and a big armchair beside it. There are books and CDs on shelves, and a music system, and that is one half of the room, and the other half is where her bed is, with a lamp lit on the table beside it, and the covers turned down.

'And you went to the trouble of making up the other bed,' I say. Poppy's scent pervades the room, making me heady.

'I did that last weekend,' she says, 'and I wasn't so presumptuous as to unmake it when I got home. But it's there if you want it.'

'Thank you,' I say, 'but no.'

A DIFFERENT TUNING

In the middle of the night, apropos of nothing at all, Poppy says, 'So, *are* you writing a novel?'

I put as much authority into my voice as I can. 'No, I am not. I don't know where Rosalind got that idea.'

'From a toad called Mungo, apparently.'

'You didn't seem to think it so odd earlier, that Rosalind should have been speaking to a toad.'

'It wasn't so odd earlier. I just thought your novel might also have come up for discussion when you and Rosalind were in the garden this afternoon.'

'Well, it didn't, for the simple reason that it doesn't exist. I'm a journalist. I deal in facts, not fiction.'

'Ha! Well, you seem like a man who could be harbouring a novel.'

'I confess I have toyed with the possibility,' I say, 'but that's as far as it's gone, toying. And I definitely never said anything to Rosalind about it.'

'How strange. I wonder where the toad picked up the idea.'

'Poppy, can we get one thing straight? I know impossible things do happen – I never thought I would share a bed with someone called Poppy, for example – but toads do not pick up ideas and they do not talk to humans.'

'So you think my grandmother imagined it?'

'Don't you?'

'I don't think it's as simple as that. Is sharing a bed what we're doing?'

'Isn't it?'

'Nothing more than that?'

'No. We're just ships passing in the night.'

'Oh, right. Well, that proves it, then.'

It is very dark in the bed, in the room, in the world. I can't see her properly. I prop myself up on one elbow.

'Proves what?'

'Impossible things happen. And something else.'

'What?'

'I think people who grow very old find a different tuning for the world. They're like small children. Messages come in that the folk in between don't hear.'

'But from a toad?'

'Do you think your father would be able to converse with a toad?'

I don't answer that. I try to imagine it. After a while Poppy yawns and says, 'Are you asleep?'

'No, I'm wide awake. Yes.'

'Yes what?'

'He probably could.'

'And it would make sense to him, whatever they talked about?'

'I don't know. You'd need to ask him.' And this time it is I who yawn.

'You must be tired,' Poppy says. 'Go to sleep.'

'I can't.'

'Then don't go to sleep.'

In spite of myself, I go to sleep.

CONVERSATIONS WITH A TOAD: CONVERSATION #9

Mungo Forth Mungo sat about six inches in from the edge of the huge table that took up much of the space in the kitchen of Glentaragar House, closely observing the other individual in the room. This person wore a predominantly green suit of Harris tweed, a once-white shirt and a knitted tie the colour of dead bracken. Despite being indoors and there being no precipitation, he had a deerstalker crammed down upon his ears, which prevented Mungo from being able to ascertain the extent or texture of hair on his head. His cheeks and jaw were newly shaven and gave the impression of having been buffed with a cloth. Mungo remembered that his name was Corryvreckan. Apart from the absence of beard, however, he bore a startling resemblance to not one but two other men encountered by Mungo in the course of his recent travels.

It was so early in the morning that the night was not really over. Mungo had been pottering about at the rear of the house, working his way through a full Highland breakfast of beetle and earthworm, when he had heard an engine on the glen road, then seen headlights flashing through the trees. By the time the yellow car rolled into the courtyard, Mungo was by the back door. He had followed Corryvreckan into the kitchen and scaled a leg of the table in order to introduce himself.

'What are you doing?' he asked, as Corryvreckan moved between cupboards and stove and sink.

'Oh, it's yourself,' Corryvreckan said, hardly glancing at him. 'I am making some breakfast. Would you care for something?'

'No, thanks, I've already eaten,' Mungo replied. 'What are you having?'

'Porridge. I'm just making some for myself, as I doubt anybody else will be stirring for a while. From their beds, I mean, not the porridge.'

Mungo licked and then raised a digit to indicate his appreciation of this wordplay.

'Are you sure I cannot tempt you?' Corryvreckan said.

The toad gave a sharp belch to indicate that he was full. 'Thanks again, but I'll just watch. I learned recently that porridge is made from oats and water and that oats were a staple of the human population's diet in these parts.'

'They still are,' Corryvreckan said. 'I eat porridge every day and so do the Munlochys. I cannot speak for their visitor. He is from the south.'

'Douglas Findhorn Elder,' Mungo said.

'Yes, him.'

'If he does eat it he probably puts sugar on it,' Mungo said, 'which I gather is an abomination. Porridge should be eaten with a horn spoon from a wooden bowl whilst standing, and it should be liberally seasoned with salt. Or so I gather.'

'Well, maybe,' Corryvreckan said, 'but I'll tell you something, I don't like it that way. I prefer it in a china bowl with a splash of milk and a drizzle of honey, and I sit down with a notebook and plan my day while I am eating it.'

'I like my food salty,' Mungo said.

'Ach well, as the Scotswoman said to the Frenchman, "Some like parritch, some like puddocks."'

'I'll pretend I didn't hear that. What does it consist of, your day?'

'Keeping Glentaragar House functioning. There is never a shortage of jobs to be done. Outside, although the walled garden is not my domain, there are fallen trees to be sawed, logs to be chopped, weeds to be controlled, dykes and fences to be maintained. The house too needs constant attention: fireplaces to be redd out and reset, leaks to be stopped, slates to be replaced, rones and drains to be unblocked. And this is to say nothing of the sweeping and dusting and vacuuming. Do you want tea?'

'Not for me,' Mungo said, as his companion poured himself a strong cup.

'And although much of what we eat is produced by ourselves, it is necessary for me to go to Fort William or Oban periodically, to restock essential provisions. I wish I did not have to – these noisy, overcrowded places are abhorrent to me – but nobody will deliver to us here without making a charge that is prohibitive.'

'Are there not companies that specialise in that kind of thing?'

'They take one look at our postcode and refuse to enter into negotiations. We are not even an island but you would think we were somewhere to the west of St Kilda the way they treat us.'

'Who is St Kilda?'

'St Kilda is an island group far out to sea. Very difficult to get to. Once inhabited, now only visited.'

'I see. When you go to the towns, what are the main items you buy?'

'Tinned food, wine and light bulbs mainly. We get through a lot of light bulbs due to the uncertainties of the electricity supply. And I like to keep a good supply of candles.'

'Whisky?'

'We have enough of that,' Corryvreckan said coolly, lifting the porridge pot.

'You are a busy man,' Mungo observed, observing also the glutinous grey matter that Corryvreckan transferred to a bowl and proceeded to embellish in the manner previously described.

'It is too much, really, for one man alone – or for one man and the very able Miss Munlochy. If she could drive that would help a little. You will not mind me going on with my breakfast?'

'Not in the least. You yourself drive up and down the glen often, to the hotel at Glen Araich. You have just returned from there. Do you assist the manager of that place at all? MacLagan, is that his name?'

Corryvreckan paused with the spoon halfway to his mouth. 'Yes, indeed it is. He is in the same boat as myself,' he said. 'I never see Ruaridh these days, we are both run off our feet. Of course if I am going to town I pick up his messages. He leaves a list at the hotel, and cash as well. But to be honest the hotel is on its last legs, so he does not require much.'

'You don't help him in his other enterprise?'

'What enterprise would that be?'

'His supply of spirits to the licensed trade.'

Corryvreckan lowered his spoon darkly into his porridge. 'Ah, is he at that game still? You are better informed than I, my friend. I do not think I know your name.'

'Mungo. Mungo Forth Mungo.'

'That's an honest true name, a Celtic name. One could go far with a name like that. Well, I wish Ruaridh MacLagan would stay away from that business. It is a bad business altogether, and it will only end in tears. I have told him that many a time, and if he were here now I would tell him again to his face, indeed I would.'

'I've told him too,' Mungo said. 'I think he may have listened to me but who can be sure? I only raised it with you so that, if you were involved, you could uninvolve yourself. As you say, it will end in tears.'

'Tears, shame and imprisonment, most likely,' Corryvreckan said.

'While we're on the subject,' Mungo said, 'I don't suppose you have anything to do with MacLagan's associate, the bard MacCrimmon, have you?'

'Nothing at all,' Corryvreckan said emphatically. 'If I have ever met the creature I have wiped the memory from my mind. I have heard nothing but bad reports about him. He is addicted to drink, untrustworthy, idle and furthermore an execrable singer and musician. Or so I gather.'

'From whom?'

'From MacLagan – and from Miss Poppy too, who has had the misfortune to hear him perform. No, my dear Mungo, you can rest assured that I do not and shall not have any dealings with that character.'

'That's good,' Mungo said. 'I have other questions. Do you ever remove your hat?'

'Only to wash my head.'

'Have you ever had a beard?'

'Not since I was a young man. I was then what was called a hippy.'

'Are you a habitual smoker of cannabis or a consumer of hallucinogenic fungi?'

'Not to my knowledge.'

'Do you speak Gaelic?'

'I am trying to reconstruct the particular dialect of this part of Argyll, from a variety of sources.'

'But do you speak it?'

'Only to myself in private.'

'You are a native speaker? Or a learner?'

'The latter. I am teaching myself. It is a slow process.'

'Do you enjoy the bagpipes, Gaelic psalm-singing, mouth music or other manifestations of Highland tunefulness?'

'No.'

'The pibroch does not enthral you?'

'I prefer Country and Western.'

'You do not admire the musical genius of Kenneth McKellar or Calum Kennedy?'

'Not above that of Hank Williams.'

'Do you have sexual intercourse with Rosalind or Poppy Munlochy, and if so is it with or without contraception?'

Corryvreckan's spoon, with which he was scraping up the last of his porridge, clattered into the bowl.

'What kind of question is that, and me not even finished my breakfast? For heaven's sake, do you have no sense of propriety?'

'No,' Mungo said.

'Your question is offensive.'

'Yes, but will you answer it?'

Corryvreckan gulped down his outrage. 'I will. No such relations exist between me and either of those two ladies.'

'Thank you.'

'Why do you ask?'

'Because Douglas had sex with Poppy earlier in the week and they have been at it again all night. You are correct in your supposition that they will not be leaving their bed any time soon, and I doubt they will want an early-morning cup of tea taken to them. I only mention this because if he behaves remotely like a toad during the mating season he will kick out at any rival who intercedes. I would not advise that you attempt to join in.'

'What they do is their own affair. I do not wish to know about it, far less "join in", as you put it. The concept is an affront to me.'

'Well, now that that's clear, let's talk about something else.'

'Such as?'

'You, for example. Tell me about yourself.'

'There is nothing much to be said. I must be getting on.'

'Och, give yourself ten more minutes, Corryvreckan. The whole day lies before us. It is not even light.'

'You know my name, yet we have not met before. Have we?'

'No,' Mungo said. 'I'm not from these parts.'

Corryvreckan reached for the teapot and poured himself a fresh cup.

'Well,' he said, 'since you mention it, neither, originally, am I.'

[To be continued]

FURTHER EXTRACTS FROM TRANSCRIPT OF
AN INTERVIEW BETWEEN DOUGLAS FINDHORN
ELDER AND ROSALIND MUNLOCHY, CONDUCTED
ON 29TH AND 30TH OCTOBER 2014 AT GLENTARAGAR
HOUSE, GLENTARAGAR, ARGYLL

ELDER: We were talking about survival yesterday. You said that so long as you are here in the glen, or somebody is, the world is here too. And then you said that even if you weren't, something would survive. Don't those statements contradict each other?

MUNLOCHY: Yes.

ELDER: You don't see a problem in that?

MUNLOCHY: No. Something will survive, even if it's a deer sniffing about in the ruins of this house.

ELDER: A ruin is not survival, surely? The deer won't even know it's a ruin. And if nobody is there to see the deer, what does it matter?

MUNLOCHY: I am painting a picture. It is a picture that moves me. It's the same as what I said about going to Canada and feeling a connection with my ancestor. We've been here a long time – not just Strivens, not even especially Strivens, but people. Traces are left. Imprints are not erased. I can't explain it better than that.

ELDER: You also said that if we don't believe there's a future, what good is the past? But what good is the future you describe? It's desolation.

MUNLOCHY: Yes, but it's only one future. I hope for another. What I'm saying is, even if that is the future, something of us will still be here. Our ghosts, if you like.

ELDER: Do you believe in ghosts?

MUNLOCHY: I have no evidence against them.

ELDER: Have you ever seen one?

MUNLOCHY: I'm not sure.

ELDER: I think we are moving into the esoteric. I probably won't keep this in the article. Would that be a lie by omission?

MUNLOCHY (*laughing*): Yes, but I can also see that the readers of the *Spear* will be too far removed to understand what I am trying to say.

ELDER: They would have to be here in person?

MUNLOCHY: They would have to be closer.

ELDER: Not physically, you mean, but in the way they see the world?

MUNLOCHY: Something like that.

   . . .

ELDER: Can we move on to something very personal. If you are still willing to talk about it?

MUNLOCHY: About what?

ELDER: Your daughter Georgina.

MUNLOCHY: Ah, now we come to the heart of the matter.

ELDER: Yes. I'm sorry.

MUNLOCHY: Don't be. It's what you are here for, after all.

ELDER: Is it?

MUNLOCHY: This is what your editor sent you to ask about, surely?

ELDER: Georgina? No.

MUNLOCHY (*becoming irritated*): What burning question did he have, then?

ELDER: He wanted . . . I was to ask you about – the referendum.

MUNLOCHY: What referendum?

ELDER: The one we've just had, on Scottish independence.

MUNLOCHY: What does he need to know about that? He has the result.

ELDER: How you voted.

MUNLOCHY: What business is it of his how I voted?

ELDER: None.

MUNLOCHY: Precisely.

ELDER: That was my position too. He thought the readers would be interested.

MUNLOCHY: In that, but not in my views on ghosts?

ELDER: Well, he didn't really –

MUNLOCHY: It must be obvious to anyone who knows me how I voted. And anyone who doesn't can whistle.

ELDER: When you spoke yesterday of not dwelling on the past, I thought that was what you were referring to, the referendum. That it was over and done with.

MUNLOCHY: Then we were at cross-purposes. The referendum may be over, but the question it addressed is neither over nor done with. How could it be? So long as Scotland exists and England exists, that question will never be over. No, I was thinking of Georgina. And what I said was that there was no point in dwelling on the past if you had a clear conscience.

ELDER: I assumed you had.

MUNLOCHY: Then I wouldn't be dwelling on it, would I?

ELDER: I don't understand. Perhaps you could tell me . . .

MUNLOCHY: The whole story? Very well. It was in the papers at the time. I thought you had done some research on me.

ELDER: Not that much.

MUNLOCHY: This will use up much of your allotted space. Is that recorder on?

ELDER: Yes. Do you want it off?

MUNLOCHY: Absolutely not. There are two reasons why you are here, Douglas, even if you didn't know it before you came, and this is one of them. So listen.

ELDER: What's the other reason?

MUNLOCHY: You know perfectly well. Now be quiet.

ELDER: I won't say another word.

MUNLOCHY: My daughter – Georgina – was never what you would call settled. Perhaps that was our fault, mine and Ralph's. I went away to be an MP when she was barely three, but Ralph stayed. He was a good father to her and Gregory – and to Gabriella too, even though she wasn't his. Life wasn't always easy but this was still a blissful place to be young. It was a permanent adventure when I was a child, and it was still like that for them. But then Ralph had my invalid mother to cope with, so perhaps the children were left too much to their own devices. Schooling wasn't easy either, with them all being at different stages and no secondary school closer than Oban. We made a mistake: we sent them off to private schools and I wish we hadn't. God knows boarding school didn't do me much good. This is why I was so determined to educate Poppy at home and then in the state sector. She had to stay away through the week but I made sure she came home every weekend. Poor Georgina was only eight when she first went off to school – I had been back from Westminster less than six months and she must have felt I was pushing her out of the nest. I couldn't see what else to do at the time but it was cruel, I saw that later and she felt it at the time. So it's not surprising that things became strained between us, and of course as soon as she left school she did exactly what I had done, she went to London, and who was I to say that she shouldn't?

That was in 1959 or 1960. I would have loved London in the Sixties, and I would have thrived there because I always had plans and aims, but Georgina wasn't me. She wandered in like a lost soul and then got more thoroughly lost. There was plenty of fun, endless parties, and lots of drink and drugs and sex and – well, some people come through that and others don't. We didn't realise how badly damaged Georgina was by the experience. It can't have helped when Ralph and I separated. She came here once or twice and fled again, then stayed with him in France for a while but couldn't settle there either. I went to London occasionally and we met, but they were not happy occasions. She ended up in Glasgow – was dropped by one man and took up with another – and then one day she appeared here in an old car with all her worldly possessions and a two-year-old infant, and that was that. The prodigal daughter had come home.

I honestly thought we could make a fresh start, but Georgina was beyond that. She had the drinking disease good and proper. She would stop for a month or two, and then something would trigger her and she would start again. This went on over many years. It didn't matter if I emptied the house of booze, she would take off somewhere else and not come back for days. I lost count of the times I waited for the phone call from the police. When she was sober she went into a black depression. Once she tried to hang herself – or seemed to try. She put a rope round a branch but the branch broke. I think she chose the branch quite carefully. I couldn't influence her – if I said one thing she would do the opposite out of spite or vengeance – so I concentrated on Poppy instead. My reasoning was that if I had failed in my responsibilities to my daughter I wouldn't fail my granddaughter. Sooner or later I would be the only one Poppy could depend on, and vice versa. She kept me going. She still does. She has some of her mother in her, I know she has, and sometimes she takes herself away and lets it out of her system. That's how she deals with it. It's a shame she's stuck here with me, but she won't leave. She's a good girl.

ELDER: Yes, she is.

MUNLOCHY: I am pleased you think so but please don't interrupt or I will lose my thread. Georgina would drive when she shouldn't and I didn't do enough to stop her. I don't know if you have ever had to deal with an alcoholic but it wears you down and you let some things happen because it's easier than trying to prevent them. I let Georgina go off in her car because when she went it was a relief – for me and for Poppy. I used to pray that she wouldn't hurt herself or anybody else and for a long time we were lucky. This was nearly thirty years ago. There wasn't much traffic even then and not a policeman for miles around. It is no excuse but I made it one.

The man who had the Glen Araich Lodge before Corryvreckan took it over was one of Georgina's cronies. She would go down the glen when there was no alcohol here, and he and she would drink together and sometimes she came home and sometimes she didn't but either way it was better than her driving further afield. I didn't like him and the way he encouraged her but if she wasn't at the Glen Araich where else would she go? It's strange to tell you all this now. I thought it was over but I don't suppose it ever is.

ELDER: Do you want to stop?

MUNLOCHY: No. Well, when Corryvreckan bought the hotel – he paid very little for it and thought he was getting a bargain – I had a word with him and he said he would try to get her to moderate her drinking, which just shows you what an innocent he was. One evening, it was this time of year, he telephoned me. 'You had better come down, Mrs Munlochy.' There was something in his voice. I drove down the glen in my own car. Georgina was in the bar. She was very drunk, and very angry because Corryvreckan's manager – he had another manager then – wouldn't serve her. There were two or three local men there who knew us. I said I would take her home. She refused to come until I bought a bottle of whisky and told her we would have a dram when we got back. But when we were outside she wouldn't get in my car. She insisted on taking her own. We had a fight in the car park over the keys, and I nearly left her but I couldn't. I thought if we can just get home she'll be safe, she won't do any more harm tonight. That was all I was thinking. So I sat in the passenger seat and let her get behind the wheel. I let her drive.

All she had to do was drive out of the car park onto the road and turn off up the glen. After that the worst that would happen was she'd put us into a ditch. She pulled out and there was a ghastly thud, a horrible smacking sound against her side of the car. I can still hear it. We got out. There was a bicycle lying under the car and a man on the tarmac about five yards away. He must have bounced straight back off the car. He was all twisted up and very still. I knew right away he was dead.

He hadn't any lights on his bicycle. Otherwise I would have seen him, even if Georgina hadn't. I realised this at once. Georgina realised it too. She started to cry. I can still hear the noise she made too. 'Oh God, oh God,' she wailed, 'he didn't have any lights.' And it was true but that wasn't going to save Georgina, who was well over the limit. She would go to jail and if she went to jail she really would try to kill herself or someone would kill her. All of this flashed through my mind in seconds while we crouched over the dead cyclist. He wasn't wearing a helmet, of course – cyclists didn't then. There was no pulse, no heartbeat, no breathing. Nothing was going to make him alive again.

I did a terrible thing. I got hold of my daughter and I swear she had gone from drunk to sober in the minutes that had passed since that awful thud. I told her that I was driving the car. I was driving the car and she was the passenger because she was too drunk to drive. I shook her while I said it, I was so angry and so frightened. I said it was her last chance, my last chance to save her. We couldn't save the man because he was dead but we could save her. And then I told her to run back to the hotel and get help.

That's what I meant, Douglas, when I said yesterday that people like us could get away with things in the old days. And those days, the ones I'm telling you about now, weren't so long ago. I was seventy-five, the lady of the big house. Corryvreckan and the others came out of the hotel and they tried to revive the cyclist but I was right, he had been killed outright. He was a young forester from Aberdeen, we learned later, going back to his digs at Glen Orach. I told the men what had happened, and they believed me. Why would they not believe me, Rosalind Munlochy, one of the Strivens of Glentaragar? I was taking my daughter home from the pub as I had told them I would do, and the young man came along and he had no lights on his bicycle. We carried him into the hotel and waited. An ambulance arrived, and the police, and they questioned us all, and I was breathalysed and tested negative, and our stories all agreed. And later there was a court appearance, and the sheriff said that it was most unfortunate but that I could not be held responsible because the cyclist had been cycling along an unlit road with no lights, and although there was a moon that evening, so that it was not pitch black, nevertheless how could I have been expected to see him? And I was of sound mind and good character, and my eyesight was fine and I had had a driving licence for fifty years without ever being involved in an accident until then. It was in all the papers, the *Times* – the *Oban Times*, I mean – the *Glasgow Herald*, the *Spear*. I left the court without a blemish on my name. I did not even have points put on my licence, and to prove how competent a driver I was I went on until I was eighty-five.

It was all a lie but I got away with it because of who I was. They might have pressed somebody else harder. They might have found out the truth, but they didn't and I have kept it hidden until now and that is why I thought you had been sent, to prise it out of me, but I had already made up my mind that I would tell you anyway, because it is time to clear my conscience.

So this mother-of-the-nation nonsense, well, that's what it is, non-sense. If Dr Johnson was right about patriotism, then that really would be the last refuge of a scoundrel in this case. Tell your editor that. I wasn't such a good mother and my daughter wasn't such a good daughter.

There's a saying, 'blood is thicker than water'. I used to believe that. The Strivens believed it, they lived by it, but it is an excuse. It's like that other idiocy, 'my country, right or wrong'. Blood is an excuse. It's a reason not to face up to things and it is never a good enough reason.

I kept Georgina out of prison and for a few months I thought that the change had come, I really did. Perhaps I wouldn't have kept up the lie if it hadn't been for that, but that was why I had told it in the first place and it seemed to have worked. She never touched a drop of drink until after the court appearance, she was very quiet about the house and helped in ways that she had never done before. For the first time she did whatever I asked of her. And shall I tell you something? I did not like it. She became somebody I did not know, did not recognise. I did not trust her drunk but I did not trust this new person either. And I was right not to. After it was all over – after it *should* all have been over – she went to Oban for the night, to do some shopping, she said, and to pick Poppy up from school the next afternoon, she said. And I let her go. Again, I let her drive. She didn't kill anybody else this time. She booked into the Royal Hotel where she had a few drinks at the bar and a few more in her room, and then some time early in the morning she drove along the coast a few miles to where my father drowned when he was swimming, and she took off her clothes and left them in the car and went swimming herself. And that was the end of my daughter Georgina.

(Prolonged silence.)

ELDER: Are you all right?

256

MUNLOCHY: It's kind of you to ask. Yes, I'm all right, thank you. It is good, finally, to tell someone all this and know that it cannot be retracted.

You might say, why didn't I go to the authorities *then*, and admit what had happened, tell them who had *really* been responsible for the death of the cyclist. But it wouldn't have changed anything. And of course I really *was* responsible. They might – I don't know – they might have sent me to prison, but I suspect they would have found a way to keep someone like me out. And there was Poppy to consider too. I couldn't abandon her.

ELDER: Does she know?

MUNLOCHY: She suspects. She is not a fool. After we have finished I will go and tell her. I don't want to carry this secret any more.

ELDER: Is that why she doesn't drive?

MUNLOCHY: Yes, it must be. Despite the inconvenience she has always refused to learn, and I have never pushed her to do so.

ELDER: What about Corryvreckan? Does he know?

MUNLOCHY: Corryvreckan is very loyal. It was after all this that he began to work for us. It has been mutually beneficial, especially after I stopped driving. Again, he probably suspects what really happened.

ELDER: It keeps people together, a thing like that.

MUNLOCHY: That's one way of looking at it. Is there anything else, Douglas, that you want me to tell you? I am feeling rather exhausted. And I must go and speak to Poppy.

ELDER: I think we've covered enough for today.

(Interview ends)

CONVERSATIONS WITH A TOAD: CONVERSATION #10

Douglas Findhorn Elder entered the bedroom and took the twelve paces necessary to get from door to bed. The intimidatingly high bed had not been slept in. This did not come as a surprise to Douglas since, although it was the bedroom that had been assigned to him, he had slept elsewhere. He pulled back the coverlet, took off his shoes and launched himself onto the mattress. He was tired, physically and emotionally. It was mid-afternoon and he needed to sleep. He lay back against the mighty pillows.

'The wanderer returns,' said a voice close to his right ear.

Douglas sat up. Beside the bed was a table with a lamp on it. Mungo Forth Mungo was leaning against the stoneware base of the lamp.

'Mungo.'

'Douglas. I had almost forgotten you existed.' The note of sarcasm was unmistakable.

'I'm sorry. I didn't intend to neglect you. I've been . . .'

'Distracted. I know. Don't worry about me. I've been having a rare old time. Have you completed your interview?'

'Aye. I don't think I'll get any more from Rosalind. The second session turned into a confession. It was quite moving. Disturbing too. She wants me to publish it, even though it will show her in an unfavourable light. It won't be what John Liffield's expecting.'

'Have I met this person?'

'He's the editor of the *Spear*. He wanted something celebratory to mark her hundredth birthday. She's given me an admission of guilt.'

'Perhaps that's what he does want. A flawed character. A political butterfly, a bad mother, a liar and deceiver, a relic of privilege and misplaced Highland pride, and an old revolutionary stuck in the past.'

Thought of sleep deserted Douglas. He frowned at the toad, who was positively lounging against the lamp.

'Well, haven't *you* been doing some deep thinking! You don't trust his motives?'

'I don't know anything about them. But I had a good listen when you were interviewing her yesterday and I began to wonder why your editor was so keen to do a – feature, is it? – on her. Have you found out how she voted in the independence referendum? That's what he specifically asked for from you, isn't it?'

'It was discussed briefly but she didn't or wouldn't say. She implied how she voted – in fact she said it was obvious how she voted – but after everything else she's told me I don't think it matters.'

'Mr Liffield might disagree. He might think it would round off the picture nicely.'

Again Douglas was disturbed by the bufonid's acuity. 'Are you comfortable there?' he asked.

'Very.'

'Feel free to hop across if you wish. That's very impressive, Mungo, what you just said. I will have to give it some thought. I'm sorry we've not had the opportunity to catch up. When did I last see you?'

'Here, just before Corryvreckan took you along to meet the old woman. I was in your pocket, remember? I stayed put until you and she had a nap, then I went exploring. You both went outside for a while, and she came back to her room alone. That was when I introduced myself.'

'You what?'

'To Rosalind. And to that cat. Completely irrational. Confirmed what I've always thought about cats. Once Rosalind had put it out we had some peace and that's when I interviewed her.'

'*You* interviewed her?'

'Call it a wee chat if you prefer. Would you like to compare notes? Of course I didn't make any, I just memorised everything. Unlike you, I didn't find it particularly moving or disturbing, but then I'm not having sex with her granddaughter.'

'What's that got to do with it?'

'Quite a lot. Would I be wrong in surmising that there's a nagging doubt in your mind? You suspect that you're out of your depth. You've fallen for Poppy and you're wondering how much of Georgina there is in her. No?'

'No. Well, maybe. Rosalind told you about Georgina?'

'The bare bones, my boy. A kind of rehearsal before the full perform-ance with you. Not that I'm saying it was an act – no, no, I'm sure you were told the truth, the whole truth and very little held in reserve. But she needed to talk it through first with a disinterested but sympathetic listener, and I was that listener. "Get it off your chest," I told her. And it seems she has. As I said, if you think you're missing any salient details, I may be able to fill in the blank spaces. No fee required. Think of it as a thank-you for bringing me along.'

'Well, thank *you*. But she won't have told you anything she didn't tell me.'

The toad made that shrug-like movement that was, in fact, a shrug. 'Perhaps not. On the other hand, you haven't interviewed Corryvreckan.'

'Don't tell me you have?'

'This morning, over breakfast.'

'You are amazing. What did you get?'

'I'd already eaten. He had porridge and toast.'

'Hold the Chic Murray impersonation. What *information* did you get?'

'Do you want the full version or the abridged one?'

'The abridged one. We may not have long. Rosalind's away to tell Poppy the true story of her mother's last days. I'll have to go and com-fort her.'

'Rosalind?'

'Poppy, you idiot. Tell me about Corryvreckan.'

'First, his original name is not Corryvreckan.'

'I'd worked that out. What was it?'

'Ryck Von Carre.'

'*What?*'

'That's an anagram. Don't ever call me an idiot.'

'I'm sorry.'

'Apology accepted. He was born Edward Something – I didn't catch the second part – and he grew up in Surrey. Where's that?'

'In the South of England.'

'Right. He's sixty-two. He first came to Scotland when he was a bearded hippy. Isn't that a breed of dog? Never mind. He fell in love with the Highlands. They were very outré, he said.'

'Outré?'

'I only report the words, I'm not responsible for them. He felt such a profound affinity with the Highlands that he believed he wasn't really Edward Something at all but a changeling insinuated into the Something child's cradle by the fairies.'

'He holds the fairies in high esteem,' Douglas said.

'It was his destiny, he thought, to return to his place of origin. He kept coming back every summer until he found Glentaragar and decided that this was it. One of the things that persuaded him was a book of local folklore which included a fairy legend very like the one he believed about himself. When he discovered that the author, Rosalind Munlochy, lived in the big house at the top of the glen he made up his mind to settle here permanently, but he didn't have the means and his parents wouldn't help him out because, not unreasonably, they disputed the idea that he was a changeling. Then guess what happened?'

'I can't.'

'He won a huge sum of money through having second sight.'

'He could see the future?'

'Specifically he saw the football results one Saturday.'

'You mean he won the pools?'

'That's what *he* said. It was an expression that didn't make any sense to me until he explained about his gift. He wasn't interested in football but one day he saw all the next Saturday's scores as if on a newspaper page so he filled out a form and posted it to somebody called Vernon who gave him all this money. Corryvreckan was quite modest about his success – I understand a lot of people with second sight are, and don't like to talk about it. Sometimes they find it a great inconvenience. Do you remember me telling you about that ancestor of mine who lived

260

with a witch? Well, *she* had second sight. Apparently she was always having to get out of the way of phantom funeral processions and so forth. There was one occasion –'

'Mungo. Not now.'

'Point taken. Unnecessary diversion. Corryvreckan says he's never had a second-sight experience again. Anyway, he won a hundred thousand pounds, which I gather was a lot whenever it was. He did mention the year, but of course it didn't mean much to me.'

'It would just be a number to you.'

'Two numbers. Nineteen and eighty-nine. Springtime, he said. Ah, springtime!'

'Nineteen eighty-nine,' Douglas said. 'Aye, that was a fair sum then.'

'So now he had the wherewithal to do whatever he wanted. He said goodbye to the Somethings of Surrey and headed for here, stopping en route to enjoy the Edinburgh Festival for a few days. He busked – I believe that is the term – with his guitar. It was on this occasion that he invented the pseudonym Stuart Crathes MacCrimmon, although this was purely a promotional device at that time.'

'And then he came on here?'

'Yes. It was where the fairies had taken him from, of course, but it had the added advantage of being remote.'

'Rosalind doesn't like that word. She says it's insulting.'

'Well, that's what he wanted, remoteness. Or did he say "isolation"? Well, anyway, he's a man who finds Oban too thriving a metropolis. Here, he could be what he wanted to be, and what he wanted to be was the complete Highlander.'

'Called Corryvreckan?'

'He had already come up with a name for a wandering minstrel, so now he lighted on another, which represents the untamed, mystical maelstrom that is the Celtic soul, apparently. Fortuitously he arrived just as the Glen Araich Lodge Hotel was put up for sale so he bought it.'

'Why would you buy a hotel if you wanted isolation?'

'He also wanted a long-term income. The cash wouldn't last for ever, so his plan was to live in one part of the building while the rest of it earned him money. He hired someone to be the manager but she was useless, so he sacked her. Then he hired someone else who wasn't much better and he had to sack him too, not long after the Georgina episode. That's when he appointed Ruaridh MacLagan to look after the hotel. Are you with me so far?'

Douglas scratched his head. 'I was until that last item. How could Corryvreckan possibly appoint MacLagan?'

'Listen to me and you shall know everything,' Mungo said, and to Douglas he could have been a wee fat Belgian detective explaining a murder. 'Corryvreckan was already psychologically fragile, given his family background. When the cyclist was killed he suspected the truth of what had happened and felt partially responsible, but he also felt a powerful loyalty to Rosalind Munlochy and to the way of life in the glen. Together they seemed to him to represent the old days. So he created the personality of Ruaridh MacLagan to manage the hotel, while the Corryvreckan side of him did whatever it could to keep Glentaragar House functioning *and* continued to become more Highland than the Highlands.'

'Why not go the whole hog and wear a kilt?'

'Ah, do not ask me to fathom the swirling depths of that mind. It is possible however that a true Highlander eschews such a contrivance as the modern form of the kilt, *non*? Shall I continue?'

'Please do.'

'*Eh bien*, I am not saying that Corryvreckan was unconscious of what he was doing, but over time it became necessary, in order to avoid complete mental collapse, to accentuate the distinction between Corryvreckan and MacLagan. For one thing, the business was now – in Corryvreckan's mind – MacLagan's responsibility, and it was failing. MacLagan felt this too, even though he didn't own the place. Corryvreckan would pay for a few bits and pieces when he went shopping – your breakfast supplies, for example – but not much else. In a desperate effort to keep the hotel afloat and make himself something on the side, MacLagan became involved in the illicit distribution of stolen liquor. He fell in with some bad characters from the Lowlands and they put pressure on him to take ever greater risks. Meanwhile, a third side to his character manifested itself in the revived form of the bard MacCrimmon, who – it transpired – wanted only to absolve himself from *all* responsibilities and wallow in self-pity, alcohol and terrible songs. *Alors*, what do we have? MacCrimmon is an irredeemable drunkard; MacLagan also takes more drink than is good for him – or did until I put in an appearance and showed him the error of his ways; but Corryvreckan does not drink at all – he stopped immediately after the death of the unfortunate cyclist. All this taken together suggests that the young man from Surrey formerly known as Edward Something has vanished and in his place stands a character as divided yet as unified as a block of Neapolitan ice cream. Compare the relaxed, even nonchalant manner in which Corryvreckan received me in the kitchen with the abject terror I induced in MacLagan. If I had shown myself to MacCrimmon he would doubtless have died of fright.'

'Three sides of the same coin? It's a nice theory, Mungo, but it has more holes in it than a lobster creel.'

'Nevertheless the lobster is contained, *mon ami*,' Mungo said. 'It is the sober Corryvreckan who keeps the show on the road.'

'I wish you would stop doing that,' Douglas said.

'What?'

'Dropping in those French words as if you're some kind of Poirot.'

'I think the word you're looking for is *crapaud*.'

'You think you're so smart.'

'*C'est vrai*. Shall I tell you why?'

Before Douglas could answer or Mungo could expand on the reasons for his intelligence, there was a tap at the door. A voice said softly, 'Douglas?'

'That's her,' Douglas hissed. 'Make yourself scarce.'

'Or even uncommon,' Mungo said. 'Very well. I know when I am surplus to requirements.' He slid rapidly down the table leg. Douglas slid off the bed and approached the door in his socks.

'It's me,' Poppy said. 'Can I come in?'

[To be continued]

WE ARE NOT ALONE

Poppy and I embrace. I lead her to the bed and help her up onto it. She has been crying.

'Are you all right?'

'I'll be fine.' She sits on the edge, childlike, her feet well clear of the floor, and I kneel in front of her, clasping her knees. I feel an overwhelming desire to comfort her.

'Rosalind has spoken to you?'

'Yes.'

'And explained everything?'

'Yes. I can't say it's a complete shock. I've thought it through so often over the years. I always knew there was more to it than I was told.'

'Is that why you don't drive?'

'Oh yes. I couldn't. I know it's ridiculous, here of all places, not to have conquered that fear, but I could never get behind the wheel of a car. If I were ever responsible for hurting someone, or worse –'

'It's not ridiculous. It's completely understandable.'

'Rosalind never insisted. That in itself made me wonder.'

'But you never asked her what had really happened?'

'I wanted to, and at the same time I didn't. Why bring it all to the surface again? The longer I didn't ask, the more I questioned what good it would do. The older she got, the less it seemed to matter. There was a time when I felt I was betraying my mother by not demanding the truth. Later I felt it would be a betrayal of Rosalind to interrogate her about it.'

'I don't think you've betrayed anyone,' I tell her. 'Me included.'

'Thank you, Douglas. That's what she told me. She says she's the traitor. She says she betrayed herself and all the things she ever stood for. Truth, justice, equality before the law. It was instinctive, she said.'

'Blood being thicker than water.'

'I don't know about that,' Poppy says, 'but she did it and then she couldn't bring herself to undo it.'

'Where is she?'

'She's gone to her room. She's quite worn out. She'll be all right, but she needs to be on her own. I didn't want to be. Were you sleeping?'

'I was thinking about it,' I say. 'Want to stay?'

'Oh yes,' she says.

'Let's get into bed then.'

Quickly we undress. Not until we are safely under the covers do I realise quite how exhausted I am. We lie very still for a while. Outside, inside, everything is silent.

'Why don't *you* drive?' Poppy asks.

'I do. I just don't have a car at the moment. Sonya, my ex, has it. And I've got points on my licence so I can't hire one.'

'What are the points for?'

'Speeding and a bald tyre. No drink involved.'

'That's a relief. I'm glad you were caught. If you hadn't been, maybe none of this would have happened.'

'Oh, I think it might.'

'There are paths through life. They don't all lead to the same place. So I'm glad anyway.'

'Me too,' I say. 'Although I was very pissed off at the time.'

I think about that incident with the police and it seems a long way away, and then I must drift off to sleep, I don't know how long for – ten minutes or two hours – but it is Poppy's voice saying my name that wakes me.

'Douglas?'

'Hmm?'

'Do you remember the night at the inn, when I said I felt we were not alone?'

'Aye.'

'I feel it again now. Do you?'

'No.'

She sits up and looks around the room. The walls are bathed in afternoon light.

'Ignore me,' she says. 'I must have been dreaming. Sorry.'

'What were you dreaming?'

'There was a . . . a toad. It was sitting on the end of the bedstead.'

I sit up too. 'Where?'

'There. It was so vivid.'

'Well, there's a simple explanation, isn't there? Rosalind told us she saw a toad in her sitting room. That's obviously got into your subconscious. I don't suppose your toad spoke to you?'

'It did, as a matter of fact.'

'Oh dear. What did it say?'

'I can't remember. It was friendly, though. I don't think I said anything back.'

'That was probably the best policy.' I lie down again.

'It had a kind of look about it. As if everything were fine. As if it were telling me not to worry.'

'Well, then. Don't.'

Poppy lies down too. After a minute she speaks again.

'We are not alone, of course,' she says.

'Aren't we?'

'No, not any more, you and I.'

'I don't suppose we are.'

'Love's a kind of madness, isn't it?' she says.

'Maybe,' I reply cautiously. 'Or maybe not. I don't care.'

'Neither do I,' she says, snuggling in.

Darkness gathers. Poppy and I get up and get dressed. She goes out to lock up the hens while I, in the kitchen, prepare an omelette from some of the hens' eggs, and fry some potatoes to go with it.

Corryvreckan comes in and seems surprised to find me there.

'All right?' I ask him. I feel cheerful and magnanimous.

He looks at me with what could be contempt or pity or both.

'I am well,' he replies. He goes to the sink and pours himself a glass of water.

'Thirsty?'

'I am.'

'I should think you would be after all the bevvy you've put away in the last few days.'

He glares at me. 'I do not drink alcohol.'

'Sorry. I must be confusing you with someone else. Would you like to join us for a bite to eat?'

'I would not. I have things to do.'

'We can wait. Poppy's out seeing to the hens.'

'I will get myself something later, thank you all the same,' he says. He turns to go, then stops. He comes towards me until his face is barely a foot away from mine.

'You take care of her.'

It isn't quite a threat, nor do his eyes appear to contain envy or hatred. It is more as if he were delivering a moral instruction.

'I intend to,' I say. 'Sure I can't tempt you with an omelette?'

'Quite sure,' he says, and departs.

Poppy comes in a few minutes later. She has checked on the hens and her grandmother and reports that both have gone to bed. Rosalind is reading, and doesn't intend getting up again. I tell her that Corryvreckan has declined to eat with us. When the omelette is ready Poppy takes a portion, along with some bread and a pot of tea, to Rosalind's room. The two of us eat in the kitchen, then we go back upstairs to Poppy's room, also carrying a pot of tea. Tonight both of us have, for some reason, a strong aversion to alcohol. We spend the evening deep in conversation, filling in knowledge gaps. Among other things I tell her about Gerry and my lift in the hearse, and the stash of whisky at the Glen Araich. She says she is not altogether surprised as the hotel has been in financial trouble for years.

Corryvreckan, she adds, would be appalled to learn that MacLagan has got himself mixed up in such goings-on.

'Poppy,' I say, 'this cannot continue.'

'What?'

'This pretence that Corryvreckan and MacLagan are two separate people.'

'Are you sure it is a pretence?'

'On his part, perhaps not. I'm talking about you.'

She does not speak for quite a few seconds.

'What do you want to do about it?' she says at last.

'I'm not sure. I'll think of something.'

'Well, don't be too hasty,' she says. 'You might regret it.'

A BIG COO'S SHITE

I wake early, much refreshed, before it is fully light. Poppy is sleeping like a bairn beside me. I watch her breathing and a great sense of calmness flows through me. It is fair to say that any anger I have felt towards her and/or Xanthe has evaporated. That's what good sex followed by a good sleep does for you, Douglas, I tell myself smugly. I decide not to disturb Poppy, slip out of bed, return to my own room for a towel and some clean clothes, then go and run myself a bath. By the time I have finished there is still no movement in the rest of the house. It is a fine morning. I go exploring.

I put on my jacket, go downstairs, let myself out of the front door and walk down the path across the lawn and through the gates. The view from here to Loch Glaineach and beyond is even more impressive than it was yesterday. Everything looks washed and clear and new. I remember Rosalind in her smelly coat and woolly hat saying in her ancient voice, 'Behold, the world.'

I have lost track of the days, am under some kind of enchantment. I have no wish to break the spell by leaving but know that soon I will have to. From a professional point of view, there is no reason to delay my departure. I should also contact the Home and make sure that my father is all right.

I set off down the hill towards the loch.

It is autumn but there is a spring in my step. The surface underfoot is firm but not hard, and I find myself walking in big, easy strides. It takes no more than a quarter of an hour to reach the head of the loch. A pile of collapsed stones and timber is all that remains of the building that was once a staging post for goods as they came in from the sea. Birds are chirruping and fluttering, a fish makes a splash, but otherwise I am alone. It is a glorious feeling, especially when I think of Poppy, perhaps waking and stretching between her white sheets, perhaps even at this moment calling out my name. Will she wonder where I am? Will she worry that I might have gone? I don't think so. Because – unlike Xanthe – I will return, the soldier home from the war, the hunter home from the hill. Well, I'll have to, unless I walk right round the house and down the glen without stopping to collect my belongings. I'll have to, but more importantly I want to.

The track continues, more narrowly but otherwise in almost as good a condition, along the north side of the loch, once dipping through a shallow ford at the outflow of a burn, where a line of stones is carefully placed, enabling a walker to pass dry-shod.

There are wet tyre marks on the track on the other side of the ford.

It seems I am not alone after all.

Loch Glaineach is short and fat and in another ten minutes I have reached the far end of it. Twenty yards of fast-flowing black water separate it from Loch Glas, the loch that connects it to the sea. At the head of it stands another old building, which to my surprise appears mostly intact. Parked beside it, where the track finally ends, is a familiar yellow car slumped at a familiar angle. Beyond the car, lying half-sunk against the shore, is the hulk of an old boat, some sixty feet in length. Rusting, and with a gaping wound in her uppermost side, nevertheless the rounded bow, derrick, hold, funnel and engine room together form the almost mythic, dumpy shape of a Clyde puffer.

Corryvreckan is standing at the water's edge, next to two piles, one of flattened cardboard and the other of empty bottles. As if he has been doing it for a long time, in one swinging motion he reaches down, lifts one of the bottles and lobs it through the hole in the boat. *Smash!* Reaches down, lifts one of the bottles and lobs it through the hole in the boat. *Smash!* Reaches down, lifts one of the bottles –

'Corryvreckan!' I shout.

He looks over at me, scowls, pauses only for a second, then reaches down, lifts one of the bottles and lobs it through the hole in the boat. *Smash!*

I walk over to the building. Lamont's old store. Things are blowing about like dead leaves. I catch one: a paper label bearing the legend 'Salmon's Leap'. I let it go and it skips off across the loch.

Smash!

Smash!

Smash!

I peer down into the peaty, salty, weedy water of Loch Glas. I suppose if I am looking for anything I am looking for whisky. But if it's there at all it's a bit too diluted for my taste.

The old store looks as if it could still keep a few things dry, at least temporarily.

I sit down and wait for Corryvreckan to finish.

Eventually he collects the cardboard, carries it back to the car and dumps it on the back seat. Then he approaches me. There is a righteous sweat on his brow and a righteous gleam in his eyes.

'Well, so you are here,' he observes. 'And is it this that you are going to write about in your newspaper?'

'What?' I ask.

'You know,' he says.

'Tell me why I shouldn't.'

Corryvreckan looks at me as I imagine a clan chieftain might once have looked at an ignorant visitor from the Lowlands before dispensing justice according to the old ways.

'I am covering someone's tracks,' Corryvreckan says. 'I am trying to save him from himself. I want him to have another chance.'

There is something so ludicrously heroic about him as he stands before me and says these words that it makes me feel small-minded, and smaller than he is, and not just because I am sitting down.

I rise. 'No, Corryvreckan, I am not going to write about this. I can't deny it would make great copy – there is something deeply ironic about a Highlander pouring contraband whisky into the sea and chucking the empty bottles into the wreck of a boat – but your secret – MacLagan's secret – is safe with me.'

He looks at me with contempt or pity or it could be relief or gratitude or a bit of all four.

'Would you be wanting a lift back to the house?' he asks.

'No, thanks.'

'It is no trouble. I am going that way myself.'

'Thank you all the same, but no. It's a fine day. The walk will do me good.'

'You are right about that,' he says.

I watch the yellow car make its way back along the shore of Loch Glaineach until it is out of sight, and wonder how many times it has made that journey, back and forth in all weathers, day and night, and how often a modern boat may have come up Loch Glas empty and gone away full. I wonder about the arrangements that must have been made, the texts sent and received – if a signal were to be had.

At the very moment that I think this, I become conscious of a vigorous movement in the pocket of my jacket. It's as if something is alive in there. I reach in and extract my mobile phone, which has been dormant for days. The screen has come to life and the message EMERGENCY CALLS ONLY is displayed across it, but suddenly this vanishes. The thing goes into spasm, leaps from my hand and throws itself to the ground where it shakes and moans as if in a state of religious hysteria. This goes on for half a minute before ending in a series of beeps. Perhaps the phone has had a vision, or a message from God. More likely there has been a moment-ary alignment between an orbiting satellite, the top end of Loch Glas and a bunch of digital signals floating in the ether.

When I pick the phone up its screen is displaying nine new messages, none of them from God. They have been sent over the previous three days and the senders are, in order of appearance: Sonya, Sonya, Sonya, Beverley Brown, Sonya, Ollie, Beverley Brown, Ollie and Sonya. They read as follows:

Douglas urgent u call me asap. Have tried 2 phone but either u r switched off or no reception call me asap Sonya

Douglas where hell r u? Phone me urgent Magnus in accident need u here Sonya

Where r u FFS? Magnus in hospital car crash when u get this phone me S

Dear Mr Elder, I don't wish to alarm you and there is nothing to worry about, at least not at this stage as I am sure everything will turn out all right but could you possibly give me a call when you receive this message? As I say nothing to worry about but I would like to update you on the situation. Thank you so much. Yours, Beverley (Brown)

Douglas if u r deliberately ignoring me because I didnt let u have car then stop it now & call me. Car not issue now anyway as write-off. Magnus in hospital call me immediately u get this S

Douglas my old mucker how are you doing well you seem to have stepped right in the middle of a big coos shite my man give me a call on the mobile when you get this not on the office line dont worry ive not said anything and looks like you might walk away with clean shoes but lucky it was me on the desk when the story came in and what a story it is bloody hell theres been nothing like this since that cash dispenser went on the blink in hawick there were queues around the block that time how did your interview go anyway give us a call have kept your name out of it so far ollie

Hello again, Mr Elder, I am not sure if you received my last message but I would be very grateful if you could telephone me so that I can update you on the situation regarding your father. I did contact your partner (?) Ms (?) Strachan and asked her to pass on the details but she seemed quite distracted and perhaps she has not done so? We are of course quite concerned as rain is expected but we are doing everything we can in the circumstances and at least we now know where he is!!! Yours with best wishes and in hope of a speedy resolution, Beverley (Brown)

Douglas have you seen todays front page not bad eh dont know if you are still in the wastes of you know where but give me a call and i will fill you in on the details i assume you are happy with my name on the story well im pretty sure you wouldnt want yours on it for obvious reasons speak soon ollie

DOUGLAS IF U DONT CALL ME IN NEXT 24 HRS I WILL KILL U. MAGNUS IN COMA BROKEN LEG I NEED UR SUPPORT U BASTARD

Having fired off this barrage of incomprehensibility, the phone goes comatose. I pick it up but the effort has clearly been too much for it. Briefly it displays one last message – BATTERY EMPTY – and then expires.

My batteries, by contrast, are fully charged. I set off for Glentaragar House at a run.

My first port of call when I get back is the house telephone. However, when I lift the receiver a mocking hiss issues from the earpiece, which no amount of rattling the equipment can dispel.

I hurry upstairs and find Poppy with Rosalind in the latter's sitting room.

'Douglas!' Poppy says. 'Where have you been?'

'Out for a walk. Look, your telephone –'

'Good morning, Douglas,' Rosalind says, giving me one of her bright smiles. 'Did you sleep well?' And I swear she almost winks. What have these two women been saying to each other?

'Yes,' I say. 'You too, I hope. Look, your telephone –'

'– is dead?' Poppy says.

'Again? How tiresome!' Rosalind says. 'Very well, thank you.'

'What's the matter?' Poppy asks me.

'Something has come up. Several things, in fact. I have to leave as soon as possible.'

'What things?'

'If I could speak to one or two people I'd have a better idea, but none of them sounds good. I've had a lot of messages.'

'Messages?' Rosalind says. 'You of all people, who are so dismissive of the esoteric!'

'On my mobile phone,' I explain. 'I was down at Loch Glas when they all came through, but now the phone has run out of juice and your land-line is out of order and I need to get back to Edinburgh.'

Poppy looks at the clock. 'You'll be lucky now to catch the afternoon minibus to Fort William,' she says. 'And even then you might not make the connection with the last train south. You might have to spend the night in Fort William.'

'You'll be much more comfortable here,' Rosalind says.

'I can't wait that long. I'll have to borrow Corryvreckan's car.'

'Nobody but Corryvreckan drives Corryvreckan's car,' Poppy says. 'Anyway, that would leave us completely stranded. We wouldn't know how long you were going to be away. Or even if you were coming back.'

Neither would I, I admit. I contemplate sneaking down to the court-yard and taking the car anyway (assuming that it made it back up the track from the loch, and assuming that Corryvreckan, like MacLagan, leaves the keys in the ignition – an assumption that worries me as it suggests I am beginning to think like everybody else around here) – but if I do that, is not moral retribution bound to follow in the form of a flat tyre or a complete collapse of the suspension?

'If Corryvreckan could drive me to a main road, I'll hitchhike from there.'

'What kind of way would that be to treat a guest?' Rosalind says. 'Anyway, we're enjoying your company. We like you, Douglas. Don't we, Poppy?'

Poppy's smile is even brighter than her grandmother's. In fact I think she's about to burst out laughing.

'This is serious,' I say.

'I have an idea,' Rosalind says. 'Why don't we *all* go to Edinburgh?'

'Wonderful!' Poppy says, standing up so promptly that I suspect them of subterfuge and collusion. 'I'll go and tell Corryvreckan, and pack a few things for you, Gran. Nothing fancy, just the essentials.'

'I haven't been in Edinburgh since the miners' strike thirty years ago,' Rosalind says, also rising. 'How exciting!'

'But –' I start to protest.

'If you're worried about Sitka, don't be,' Rosalind says. 'She won't even notice we're gone.'

'I'm not the slightest bit worried about Sitka.'

'Good. Poppy, will you leave food out for her?'

'Yes, and for the hens.'

'So you see, there's no need to concern yourself, Douglas,' Rosalind says.

I try again. 'But –'

'But what?' Rosalind says. 'We can be ready to go in half an hour.'

'Forty minutes at most,' Poppy says. 'We can stop at the hotel and you can make your calls from there, if the phone's working. Then we can drive on, and be in Edinburgh this evening. You can tell us all about the things that have come up on the way. It's clearly the best plan of action. And, my darling, what's more –'

'What?'

'– it will be an adventure.'

3

A RELIABLE NARRATOR

There was no sign of life at the Glen Araich Lodge Hotel when a little yellow car pulled up outside the front entrance, some time in the afternoon. A strange collection of people emerged from that car. The driver, a tall, thin individual with a deerstalker crammed down upon the ears, wore a predominantly green suit of Harris tweed, a once-white shirt and a knitted tie the colour of dead bracken. He seemed aloof and separate from the others, and kept glancing around as if expecting a surprise at any moment. He was sixty-two years of age.

From the front passenger seat came a bird-like creature brandishing a thin walking stick upon which, however, she did not heavily depend to maintain her upright position. Her head, brown as an old nut, was topped by a light application of cloud-like hair, and pink, round spectacles accentuated the blueness of her eyes. She was of small build, probably owing to shrinkage, and made to look even more diminutive than she was by a bulky black woollen coat. In one day she would become a centenarian, although an uninformed observer would probably have estimated her to be ten or fifteen years younger.

The third occupant, from the back seat, was a woman considerably less than half the age of the avian one. Larger in size but by no means gross, she had fair, wavy hair that fell over her eyes as she bent forward on leaving the car. Her nose was straight and long, an observer might think disproportionately so for the rest of her face, although someone less critical might think its shape almost classical. She wore a thick grey jumper speckled with other colours, and a pair of blue jeans tucked into brown boots, and moved with a grace and litheness that marked her out from the rest of her companions.

Close behind her came a second man, precisely fifty years and ten days of age. He was of middling height and average collar and shoe size, but was thicker around the waist than he might have been. He wore black trousers of a cotton twill material and a tweed jacket louder in pattern and colour than the suit of the driver. He wore no hat, had a fairly sparse covering of hair on his head and an anxious expression on his face. He had not much to recommend him as a possible athlete, warrior, hunter-gatherer or manual labourer: indeed, the thick belly and a slight stoop suggested a largely sedentary life. It was evident from the glances exchanged between him and the woman with the big nose that they shared a considerable mutual affection.

The names of this quartet were, in reverse order, Douglas Findhorn Elder, Coppélia 'Poppy' Munlochy, Rosalind Isabella Munlochy and Corryvreckan. The author of the present section of this narrative has noted their ages in approximate or specific terms, as humans seem to find this interesting, although, frankly, the author couldn't care less.

A fifth character was travelling with the party, though in a discreet manner. Ostensibly a companion of the said Douglas Findhorn Elder, he was used to being ignored or even forgotten owing to the latter's preoccupation with a number of matters, not the least of these being Poppy Munlochy. Occasionally resident in a pocket of the Elder jacket, this *fifth columnist* also availed himself of other nooks, crannies and means of getting about in order to witness as much of the action as possible whilst still maintaining his low – indeed, all but invisible – profile. In addition to his acquaintance with Douglas Elder, he was known to the other three travellers on a one-to-one rather than collective basis: he had interviewed Rosalind, had had a working breakfast with Corryvreckan, and had appeared in a dream (as she thought) to Poppy. His name was Mungo Forth Mungo, and he belonged, according to human taxonomy, to the species *Bufo bufo*: that is to say, he was an *uncommon toad*. He was a very fine example of his type – large, jowly, brownish-backed, creamy-breasted and well covered in warts – and had no notion as to his age in years except that it was probably greater than he or anybody else might guess. He was, and is, the author of the present section of this narrative, his principal motives being to act as a reliable narrator, recording and offering an objective point of view on events and, occasionally, by judicious and subtle intervention, to influence them. *Now read on.*

Douglas Elder tried the front door of the hotel and found it unlocked. He glanced at Corryvreckan, as if to ask his permission to enter, but Corryvreckan simply shrugged and walked towards the collection of outbuildings across the courtyard. The two women followed Douglas into the hotel but they emerged within a few minutes and began to wander around, passing comments on the poor condition of the paintwork and of the nine-hole putting green.

After some time Douglas came out. He had been making use of the telephone. He invited Poppy and Rosalind to accompany him to the outbuildings, which they did. Corryvreckan, having apparently left by another exit, appeared round a corner while they were inside, and waited by the hotel, looking quite relaxed and even self-satisfied. He was seen to inspect the building, perhaps assessing it for some purpose as yet unknown. A few more minutes passed, and then the entire party reassembled and fitted itself back into the yellow car.

Conversation ensued. As Corryvreckan drove slowly along the narrow road, a substantial amount of information was shared among the company. First, it was acknowledged that the entire remaining stock of Salmon's Leap 10-Year-Old Single Malt Scotch Whisky had vanished from the location where Douglas said he had seen it (and where the present author can vouchsafe it had certainly been) three days earlier. Not a bottle, not even so much as a nip, remained. Poppy indicated that this was a great relief to her, and Douglas agreed. Corryvreckan concentrated on the road. Rosalind said that she had never heard of a whisky called Salmon's Leap and that she suspected it of being an impostor. Douglas said that she was correct in her scepticism and that if he never saw another bottle of Salmon's Leap, or of another whisky called Glen Gloming, he would on the one hand not be sorry while on the other hand he would miss their subtle and enchanting flavours. Corryvreckan, when asked if he could provide an explanation for the disappearance of the whisky, denied all knowledge of its existence and suggested that Douglas must have dreamed or imagined it. Douglas expressed anger that his memory was thus doubted, and made a terse remark at a low volume concerning the strength of Corryvreckan's grip on reality. Poppy instructed Douglas to calm down, reminding him that without Corryvreckan they would be unable to continue the journey to Edinburgh. Corryvreckan apologised for his previous comment and described Ruaridh MacLagan, the hotel manager, as a 'bad lot'. If he had been up to his 'old smuggling tricks' perhaps he had seen sense at last and disposed of every last drop in the nearby river. Douglas asked Corryvreckan if he knew why the hotel was shut up and what had become of MacLagan. Corryvreckan said that he had not seen the latter for several days, and that like the whisky he might well have disappeared for good. What then, Douglas inquired, would happen to the hotel? In Corryvreckan's opinion it would probably be left to go to ruin if a purchaser could not be found. He hoped that it was well insured as it was just the kind of place that, in the event of a fire, would burn to the ground long before any appliances arrived to extinguish the flames. In fact, he had been looking around and could see a number of locations where a fire might very easily start for no apparent reason.

Poppy then asked Douglas to relay to the company the contents of his various telephone conversations – if he had no objections to doing so. He had none. He had first contacted the residential Care Home where his father, Thomas Ythan Elder (aged eighty-three), was incarcerated, and had spoken to the governor or manager, one Beverley Brown (age unknown). After some hesitation, Ms (?) Brown had admitted that the said Thomas Ythan Elder had made a bid for freedom on Wednesday afternoon. An element of premeditation or planning must have been involved, as he had put on clothing suitable for the outdoors, including stout shoes, gloves, scarf, coat and hat. A fire exit, normally alarmed in order to prevent just such an escape as had been effected by Thomas Ythan Elder, had been left ajar by a member of staff to facilitate the indulgence of a surreptitious, or *fly*, cigarette, and it was by this route Mr Elder must have left. His absence was not noticed for nearly two hours when it was time to summon him for his evening meal. (At this point Douglas wryly referred to the home as the Don't Care Much Home, which name shall be used in the present narrative henceforth as the author is ignorant of the correct one.) A search of the building was immediately instigated and the open fire door discovered, but not Mr Elder. Police and other services were then alerted, and Ms Brown attempted to contact the younger Elder, without success. The elder Elder's whereabouts remained a mystery for nearly twenty-four hours.

On the Thursday afternoon (Ms Brown had reported), as the search for the missing man continued, an employee of a roofing company arrived at the Don't Care Much Home, looking for a ladder that he had mislaid. The previous day he and a colleague had been clearing vegetation and sludge from rones, downpipes and drains (a practice which to the present author seems both unnecessary and inconsiderate of other users). They had been called to assist colleagues at another job and had driven off in their van, forgetting to take the aforesaid ladder with them. The roofer went to retrieve it but it had been removed. Supposing that another colleague had already collected it, he went away but was back twenty minutes later. It was then that Mr Elder Senior was spotted, occupying a flat portion of the Don't Care Much Home's roof. A quick assessment of the situation showed that he must have used the ladder to reach the roof and then pulled it up after him. It was not clear how long he had been there. Beverley Brown was summoned, she quickly made a phone call and in a few minutes was joined by a pair of police officers (one male, one female).

Despite having been missing overnight Mr Elder seemed physically unharmed and was in lively spirits. He had established a kind of campsite in the middle of the flat area, and it was later established that, in addition to the clothes he had on, he had brought with him other items from his room, including a rug, a cushion, an extra jersey and his toothbrush. He was sustaining himself with a supply of assorted biscuits, which filled his pockets and which he must have been secretly collecting for several days. When hailed from the ground he responded with expansive gesticulations and shouts liberally seasoned with words that some might deem offensive or unsuitable for broadcast across the rooftops of suburban Edinburgh. He also got to his feet and performed a kind of stumbling circuit around the roof as if marking the boundaries of his territory. A second, shorter ladder was produced by the roofer, and one of the police officers tried to set it in place against the wall. However, Mr Elder became agitated and veered so close to the edge that it was necessary to remove the ladder and withdraw. After some minutes he settled down again, but any further manoeuvres with the second ladder resulted in renewed agitation.

More telephone calls were made, and soon the group on the ground grew to include a doctor, a team of firemen, the roofer's mate and the roofer's boss. A number of idlers, bystanders and onlookers, with their dogs and children, also gathered in the road, and offered various suggestions as to how best to resolve the situation. These included encouraging Mr Elder to jump, hosing him off the roof with a water cannon, and shooting him with a tranquilliser dart or Taser gun. When these ideas began to be loudly chanted by competing sections of the crowd, the police were obliged to disperse it, as Mr Elder was understandably irritated by these insensitive remarks.

Some members of the public objected to the police's attitude, accusing them of brutality and a callous disregard for the fundamental rights of freedom of assembly and freedom of expression. The police showed remarkable restraint in the face of this provocation, and eventually most of the crowd lost interest and went home for their tea.

With the general populace removed, Beverley Brown attempted to persuade Mr Elder into lowering the ladder and either descending it or allowing somebody to go up. He did not approve of these proposals and told her so in robust terms, intimating that he was behind with his work and did not wish to be further disturbed.

It was about this time that the roofer who had forgotten to take away the ladder realised that he had also left some tools, and that they too were in the possession of Mr Elder. These tools were a plastic bucket and a long-handled metal 'scoop' for clearing the rones. The bucket, it was later found, had served as a waste-disposal unit for Mr Elder. His 'work', meanwhile, seemed to be to test the durability and fixings of the bitumen felt on the flat roof, and also to ascertain whether the slates on an adjoining stretch of pitched roof were firmly attached to the sarking boards underneath. He utilised the scoop's handle, which had a hooked end, to prise up the slates and also to check for any slight gaps under the edges of the strips of felt. Although hampered by the limitations of his equipment, he had nevertheless discovered many of the slates and a good proportion of the felt to be inadequately secured. A pile of slates and torn pieces of felt was testimony to the progress he was making.

As rain was expected that evening, it was decided, as much for the sake of the Don't Care Much Home's ability to withstand water incursion as for Mr Elder's health, that he should be encouraged to desist from his labours immediately. While Ms Brown and the police continued to engage him in sporadic conversation, commending his perseverance and attention to detail, the fire crew entered the building and swiftly but quietly gained access to the roof via a skylight on the far side of the pitched section. Waiting until Mr Elder took a break from his work and in fact was engaged in brushing his teeth, three firemen swarmed over the roof ridge and grappled him off his feet. For a few seconds he put up some resistance, and then – according to Ms Brown – he began to laugh, and the firemen joined in, and then Mr Elder began to cry, which the firemen did not, but kindly and gently helped him down to the ground where he was indeed tranquillised by the doctor, though not with a gun.

Since then, Douglas concluded, his father had been back in his room, mostly asleep. On the occasions when he woke he was quite amenable and seemed none the worse for his outing. The roofers were still repairing or replacing the materials that he had so methodically identified as faulty.

The present author confesses to having constructed the narrative of these events not only from the younger Elder's report and responses to numerous questions from the Munlochy women, but also from imagining the scene himself to the best of his ability. He has not, however, added anything purely of his own invention, although he may be guilty of one or two embellishments, as is usual in the art of creative or fictional writing.

Douglas had been astonished and troubled by the story Beverley Brown had told him. Clearly it was a relief to know that the episode was over and that his father was neither hurt nor in any danger. Laughter, some of it from Douglas, filled the car at various points during his relation of events. The general view, in which even Corryvreckan concurred, was that Thomas Ythan Elder had performed heroically, demonstrating fortitude, initiative and commendable levels of *thrawnness*. Rosalind and Poppy both expressed a great desire to make the acquaintance of such a man, and Poppy said that no doubt his influence accounted for Douglas's own independent-minded, self-confident character. Douglas opined that he was not so sure about that.

Douglas's second telephone conversation had been with his Erstwhile Partner or Girlfriend, Sonya Strachan (forty-seven), to inquire after the health of her son, Magnus, a player of the game of Rugby Union, who had been involved in a motor accident. Sonya had been sharp with him at first, accusing him of callous indifference and desertion in her hour of need, and in fact her spinosity did not diminish much during the conversation. Douglas was tempted, he told the company, to remind her that if indeed her son, Magnus, had been in a crash involving their car this was only because she (Sonya) had deserted *him* (Douglas) in *his* hour of need by refusing to let him borrow what was rightfully half his anyway. He felt, however, that this would not be helpful, so instead inquired after Magnus's condition. Sonya became tearful, then regained her composure. Magnus was feeling better, and the doctors were confident that he would make a complete recovery. He had a broken leg, some cuts and bruises, was sore all over and suffering from whiplash, but his physical fitness had helped to reduce the severity of his injuries. When Douglas questioned her about how long Magnus's coma had lasted, Sonya said that he had not been in a coma and wondered where on earth he, Douglas, had got that idea from. From her last text message, Douglas replied. Sonya said that at the time of sending it she had been tired and distressed, and that this had made her confused, and anyway Magnus had been sleeping so deeply at the time that he might just as well have been in a coma, and had Douglas only made contact at last in order to split hairs? Further questioning established that Magnus had actually been knocked uncon-scious when the collision took place, but had come round by the time an ambulance arrived. The hospital was monitoring him to make sure that there was no brain injury, and he would probably be allowed home the next morning (Saturday).

Douglas asked when and how the accident had happened, and Sonya said that for a man who worked, or until recently *had* worked, in journal-ism he was incredibly badly informed. Had he not seen the television news or read the papers? Douglas began to explain why he had not seen any news for three days, but Sonya overruled him. The accident had happened on Tuesday evening. Magnus had been returning from a special training session involving another rugby club in Stirling. He had given a lift to another player whom he had dropped off at his home, a farm a few miles outside Edinburgh, and was driving along a quiet country road when the 'criminal idiot' (Sonya's term) responsible for nearly killing him had come out of nowhere and smashed into the side of the car. What further angered Sonya was that the criminal idiot had been taken to the same hospital as Magnus and because he too had a broken leg was being treated as a patient in the same way, as if he were as innocent as Magnus. A policeman was on duty outside the room occupied by this 'imbecile' (again, her term), which was as well for him or she would have been in there extracting his innards with whatever medical instruments were to hand. Sonya under-stood that he had already been charged with reckless driving and that other charges were likely to follow, but why (she said) such a person should be 'handled with kid gloves' was beyond her. Douglas would have willingly addressed some of these issues but Sonya said she had to go, would be at the hospital in the morning and expected Douglas to be there too, to help transport Magnus home. Before Douglas could ask if there was anything left of his half of the car, or for that matter her half, she terminated the call.

The news of this accident was received in a quiet and sombre manner by the other occupants of the yellow car. Relief was expressed that the young man Magnus was not too badly injured, and Poppy wondered if anybody else had been hurt and who the criminal idiot was who had caused the accident.

To both these questions, Douglas was able to supply answers, as a result of his third telephone conversation, which had been with his Erstwhile Colleague at the *Spear* newspaper, Oliver ('Ollie') Brendan Buckthorn (fifty-two). Unfortunately, the present author is not in a position to provide a full account of this conversation, as at this juncture he fell into a sudden and profound sleep – possibly induced by the motion of the car on a particularly twisty stretch of road – and was only restored to consciousness when the soothing and familiar tone of Douglas's voice was sharply interrupted by a question from Rosalind Munlochy. The present author humbly apologises for any inconvenience to his readers caused by this lapse on his part.

[To be continued]

EXTRACT FROM A TELEPHONE CONVERSATION BETWEEN OLIVER BRENDAN BUCKTHORN AND DOUGLAS FINDHORN ELDER, CONDUCTED ON 31ST OCTOBER 2014. NOTE: THIS IS A RECONSTRUCTED TRANSCRIPT AS THE CONVERSATION WAS NOT RECORDED. CONSEQUENTLY NO CLAIMS ARE MADE AS TO ITS ACCURACY OR AUTHENTICITY. IT IS INSERTED HERE FOR THE BENEFIT OF READERS WHO MIGHT OTHERWISE BE PERPLEXED OR DISAPPOINTED BY THE UNRELIABILITY OF THE SELF-STYLED 'RELIABLE NARRATOR' OF THE PRECEDING ITEM. NOW READ ON

ELDER: Ollie?

BUCKTHORN: Dougie! Is it yourself?

ELDER: It is. Where are you?

BUCKTHORN: At the paper, where else?

ELDER: Can you speak?

BUCKTHORN: What the fuck do you think I'm doing? Where are you?

ELDER: Let's say I'm on my way home.

BUCKTHORN: You are? You took the ball of wool, then?

ELDER: I didn't need it. Ollie, listen, I haven't got long, so I need you to tell me what all this is about me being in the shite?

BUCKTHORN: You don't sound like yourself. You sound forceful and focused.

ELDER: And what's the big story in the paper you texted me about?

BUCKTHORN: There you go again, straight to the heart of the matter. You've not seen the paper? Do they not have paper shops in those parts?

ELDER: They don't have any shops. Not where I am.

BUCKTHORN: Well, I'll keep you a copy of yesterday's edition, but you should try to get hold of it yourself. Can you not get the online edition on your phone?

ELDER: On *my* phone? Not a chance, even if it was working. Just run the essential bits by me. What's been going on?

BUCKTHORN: Right, well, let me see. What day is it?

ELDER: I think it's Friday.

BUCKTHORN: Right you are. So that was Tuesday when it all happened. God, you should have been here, Dougie. It was like something out of a novel, or even a James Bond movie.

ELDER: It was?

BUCKTHORN: No, not at all. I just said that to draw you in. Well, then. It was nine o'clock on an ordinary Tuesday evening at the *Spear*. Nothing much was happening. Oliver Buckthorn, a sub-editor made somewhat cynical after years at the job, though still a romantic at heart, was at his desk tweaking a few bits and pieces on his screen. Through the window he could see the city lights of Edinburgh, or Auld Reekie as it used to be known, owing to the thick pall of smoke –

ELDER: Ollie, I haven't got all day.

BUCKTHORN: I'm scene-setting.

ELDER: Well, cut it out.

BUCKTHORN: Is that really you, Douglas? Where was I? Oh yes, suddenly my phone rang. My *mobile* phone. This is significant. It was a fellow asking me if he was speaking to the *Spear* and in the same breath telling me there'd been a road accident. Two vehicles, one driver hurt but not seriously, the other driver missing in action, which was a little odd; I mean, had he run off or what? I was about to redirect the caller to another line, when he started on about how one of the cars was a hearse and that far from being full of corpses it was stuffed to the gunnels, if hearses have gunnels, with cases of malt whisky. 'The word is out,' he says. 'There's people coming from all points of the compass. You want to see it.' 'What do I want to see?' says I. 'What I'm seeing,' he says. I asked him where he was and he says he's on a little road about halfway between Linlithgow and Broxburn that usually manages to bear the weight of a tractor and a couple of delivery vans every day, but right at that moment it's going like a fair. Those were his very words, 'going like a fair'. 'In fact,' he says, 'it's like yon film, the one with the teuchters in it.' I was about to ask him to elaborate when I heard this other, angry voice in the background asking who the fuck he was speaking to, and then he rang off.

Well, I sat for about ten seconds looking out at the lights of Auld Reekie and contemplating whether life was too short, too long or just about right, and then blow me if my mobile didn't go off again. This time it was a woman, and she'd be the kind of caller you seem to like, Dougie, because she didn't dawdle, she didn't scene-set, she just shouted her information. Hardly needed the phone in fact. 'It's going to be *Whisky Galore!* in Winchburgh!' she yells, and then she was gone. Malt whisky, Douglas, *Whisky Galore!* D'you see a pattern developing, a theme? I did. I looked around for my coat, and I got reception to order me a cab, and I'd hardly done that when the mobile rang again. This time it was a song I got. Do you remember that hit by the Weather Girls, 'It's Raining Men'? Well, this was several men giving me a few bars of 'It's Raining Drams', but they hung up before I could get any details out of them. So I decided I'd better go out there myself. I grabbed the emergency camera from Roy's desk, told him and Grant to hold the fort and the front page, and headed out into the night. Are you still there, Douglas? Are you with me so far?

ELDER: I'm with you, Ollie.

BUCKTHORN: Good. You were so quiet I was missing you. I told the taxi driver to head for West Lothian. 'Can you be a bit more specific?' he says. 'Somewhere in the Winchburgh–Broxburn–Linlithgow triangle,' I tell him. 'Is that near Bermuda?' he says. He was one of them smart fellows that don't know when to just zip up and drive. I told him we'd know when we got there, because I had a suspicion we would, and I was right. As soon as we were off the main roads and into the countryside the heavier the traffic grew, but we just kept going, like a spoon into treacle, until eventually we came to a complete stop and the driver tells me he can't get any closer to whatever it is we're getting close to. There are flashing blue lights and brighter, white ones about a hundred yards away. So I pay the boy and cut off across a big field. And there's this stream of people coming in the opposite direction, all clutching cardboard boxes to their chests and staggering occasionally as they work their way across the muddy ground. It's very ordered, very quiet, and a noticeable thing is that nobody is carrying more than one case. 'Hurry along or you'll miss out,' one of them says to me, so I hurry along until I reach the road at the far corner of the field, and there I see a sight never to be forgotten in the annals of Oliver Brendan Buckthorn. Are you on the edge of your seat, Douglas?

ELDER: I'm standing.

BUCKTHORN: Just as well or you would fall off. There's a crossroads, lit up by several sets of headlights, and in the middle of the crossroads is a red Volkswagen Polo tangled up with a long black hearse. It's like something Eduardo Paolozzi might have thrown together on an off-day. The hearse's bonnet is embedded in the Polo's driver side and to me it looks ominous for whoever's been behind the wheel of that car. The flashing blue lights belong to an ambulance, and the crew are just at that moment taking someone on a stretcher towards it. Well, I haven't worked on a newspaper all these years for nothing. I whip out the notebook and start jotting down details. The hearse's doors, including the one at the back where you slide the coffins in, are all wide open. There's a pile of wet cardboard and broken glass gleaming in the headlights beside the hearse, and the air is so heady with whisky fumes you could get drunk just breathing. I look around for somebody official but all I can see is a few hooded characters around the hearse and I'm pretty sure that whatever they're up to it isn't official.

I bring out the camera and take a few shots, but quite discreetly, because sometimes folk don't like to be photographed when they're doing unofficial stuff. And you'll see for yourself, I think I managed to capture something of the biblical feel that the scene had. There's this queue approaching and then departing from the rear of the hearse, and the hooded ones are handing out not loaves and fishes but whole cases and individual bottles of whisky to the multitude. Are you still there?

ELDER: Still here.

BUCKTHORN: I went in closer, still looking for signs of the police. Then I saw another set of flashing blue lights some distance away and I realised why they hadn't arrived yet. They were stuck in the traffic, or at least their vehicle was. And then suddenly there's a man in a balaclava barring my way, and I'm just bracing myself for a rebuke or even something a little stronger for snapping the goings-on but he doesn't seem to notice the camera hanging round my neck, in fact he starts apologising. 'I'm really sorry,' he says, 'but all the cases are gone. We're just down to bottles now.' I tell him not to feel bad about it, and he says, 'Well, I do, but it's only fair, isn't it? Everybody should get a chance.' And then he thrusts these two bottles at me and thanks me for understanding and I can't help myself, my fingers instinctively close around their necks and I hold them up and inspect them in the glare of the headlights. And do you know what brand one of them is, Douglas?

ELDER: Glen Gloming. And the other will be Salmon's Leap.

BUCKTHORN: It will indeed. You are remarkably well informed, and you don't seem surprised at all. But I am not surprised you're not surprised. As soon as I saw the Glen Gloming I remembered our encounter with it after Ronald's funeral, and I knew something strange was going on. I had a quick walk round the hearse, and a quick look inside. No sign of the driver, as the fellow on the phone had said, but something white lying on the seat caught my eye so I fished it out and wasn't it only one of the fucking calling-cards I made up for you. Only one of the cards I designed with the *Spear*'s logo and your name, DOUGLAS FUCKING ELDER, FREELANCE WRITER, printed on it, and *my* mobile number, the number I'd taken those calls on. So, old mucker, there's something I want to ask you.

[Conclusion of reconstructed transcript]

HALLOWEEN

'Well, whatever have you been up to, Douglas?' Rosalind Munlochy inquired from the front passenger seat of Corryvreckan's car. At this, the present author woke with a jolt.

'That,' Douglas replied, 'is precisely what Ollie wanted to know.'

'Douglas has been bootlegging,' Poppy Munlochy said. The present author discerned a slight note of pride in her voice, as if she approved of this activity. While he forbears to pass judgement in matters that do not concern him, this jarred somewhat with his opinion of her as an uncommonly admirable creature.

There being little point in pretence, Douglas recounted the story of his relationship with Gerry the apprentice undertaker, their journey to Glen Araich, and the loading of the whisky into the selfsame hearse that had collided with Magnus Strachan driving Douglas's own half-car. It was notable that Corryvreckan made no remark at any point.

'And your card was found at the scene of the crime?' Rosalind remarked when Douglas had finished. 'That might be awkward.'

'Ollie pocketed the card and then started interviewing people before they all vanished,' Douglas said. 'He interviewed the police too, when they finally arrived, and was glad to be wearing a long coat with deep pockets, as they were very angry about the removal of the contents of the hearse. Then he cadged a lift off someone going into the city and wrote up a short version of the scoop for the Wednesday paper. He says if we can get hold of yesterday's paper, it has the story in full. But what chance do we have of finding a copy of yesterday's paper around here?'

'We will shortly be passing the shop and service station at Inverawe,' Corryvreckan said, breaking his silence at last. 'They have everything.'

Twenty minutes later the yellow car was on a road wider and faster than any previously travelled by the present author. The place mentioned by Corryvreckan was reached, and everybody got out to perform stretching exercises and to relieve themselves. The present author was able to do both of these in the car park, while the others went inside for the relief.

Before the journey recommenced, hot drinks purchased in the shop were distributed along with food of various kinds, some of the latter finding its way into Douglas's pocket. A copy of the Thursday edition of the *Spear* had been obtained. It was being kept for somebody who had decided not to take it, so the man in the shop was happy to exchange it for cash. To entertain the company, Douglas read aloud the following article, which the present author here reproduces – with an accuracy that will be marvellous only to those who are not toads – from memory:

WEST LOTHIAN FLOODED WITH WHISKY – FROM THE BACK OF A HEARSE!

Man charged with reckless driving and resetting stolen goods after drink-laden death-cab crashes into car

By Oliver Buckthorn

Extraordinary scenes followed a two-vehicle crash on Tuesday night in rural West Lothian, which has left both drivers in hospital in Edinburgh.

Local people who arrived at the site soon after the accident happened, at about 8.35 p.m., helped one of the injured men.

Magnus Strachan (24), who had been at a rugby training session in Stirling, had dropped off a teammate near Torphichen and was returning to his home in Edinburgh when his Volkswagen Polo was in collision with a hearse. The driver of the hearse could not at first be located.

Mr Strachan is understood to have been knocked out and to have suffered a broken leg, cuts and bruises, but does not have life-threatening injuries.

According to one witness, who preferred to remain anonymous, the emergency services were called but before they arrived it was discovered that the hearse was carrying a heavy load consisting entirely of cases of malt whisky. Nearly all the bottles appear to have survived the collision intact. As some people gave assistance to Mr Strachan, and others searched for the missing driver, still others arrived and began to help themselves to the whisky. 'It was obviously under-the-counter stuff,' another witness, who did not wish to be named, said, 'so folk felt it was all right to take it.'

In scenes reminiscent of the Ealing comedy classic *Whisky Galore!* more and more people appeared, with the express purpose of removing the whisky from the hearse. Mobile telephones were much in evidence as acquaintances were contacted to make sure they did not miss out on the unexpected bounty. At one point all the surrounding roads were blocked by traffic. 'It's like wasps round a pot of jam,' quipped one woman, who chose not to identify herself.

Despite the severe congestion a passage was cleared to enable an ambulance to reach the crash site. However, three police cars approaching from various directions found their routes completely blocked, and the officers had to abandon their vehicles as much as two miles away and complete their journey on foot. By the time they arrived, the ambulance, having apparently been guided through the snarl-up by members of the public, had departed with Mr Strachan on board. The police then secured the site, which is being treated as a crime scene.

Detective Sergeant Steven Jephson told this newspaper: 'It is a very serious matter when members of the public deliberately obstruct police officers who are endeavouring to carry out their duties. In this case we are looking at dozens of individuals who collectively prevented officers from reaching the scene while vital evidence was being removed by the same or other individuals. It seems that a large quantity of illegally obtained alcohol was in the back of one of the vehicles and all of it, except for a few broken bottles, disappeared between approximately 8.45 and 9.45 this evening. That in itself constitutes theft and interfering with the course of justice and any individuals identified as having been involved in such behaviour will be charged accordingly.'

When questioned by this newspaper several individuals, some of them wearing scarves around their faces, denied that they were thieves. 'It's the same as things you find washed up on a beach,' said one man, who objected to being photographed. 'If it belonged to anybody, that would be different, but it's fair game in my opinion.'

It was while taking photographs and measurements in reconstructing the cause of the collision, some time after most of the general public had dispersed, that the police heard the sound of groaning coming from a nearby ditch. Closer inspection disclosed a man partially obscured by leaves and other debris. He was suffering from injuries to his back and pelvis and had apparently tried to hide himself in the ditch following the crash. Another ambulance was summoned and he was taken to hospital, accompanied by a police escort. He has not been named, like almost everyone else in this story.

Douglas broke off to express surprise that that last comment had been successfully 'smuggled in'. 'But then,' he added, before resuming, 'Ollie probably subbed it himself.'

The whisky rumoured to have been in the hearse appears to have been of two varieties: the Glen Gloming 12-Year-Old and the Salmon's Leap 10-Year-Old Single Malt Scotch Whisky. When contacted by this newspaper, Julian Parker Gowrie, whisky enthusiast and author of *101 Malts to Die For*, described the Glen Gloming as 'highly desirable, exquisitely balanced, characterised by light herbal notes with an aftershock of badger', while the Salmon's Leap was 'playfully majestic, with an oily nose, a shimmering mouth and a whipped-cream finish'. The whisky expert, bon vivant and raconteur Charles MacLean, however, dismissed these opinions as 'absolute tosh' and 'the usual nonsense from Julian', and said that neither whisky exists outside the realm of fiction.

The article was accompanied by a large, somewhat fuzzy yet atmospheric picture depicting a chain of unidentifiable human beings offloading cardboard boxes from the back of the smashed-up hearse. The photograph, like the written piece, was credited to Oliver Buckthorn.

Douglas's reading was received with a mixture of emotions, ranging from shock and amazement to amusement bordering on hilarity on the part of Rosalind and Poppy. Corryvreckan made throaty noises of disapproval, possibly of a moral kind, but no articulate comment. Many questions, suppositions and speculations followed, and the conversation among Douglas and the two women was enlivened by puns even as the food and beverages were being consumed. Poppy declared that she could neither condemn nor condone the spiriting away of the spirit, and

Rosalind added that it showed a strong spirit of enterprise among the population of West Lothian.

Rosalind then asked what time it was, to which the answer supplied by Corryvreckan was that it was after three o'clock. At this, Rosalind declared that she had not had her postprandial nap and that everybody should close their eyes for not fewer than twenty minutes. Douglas expressed impatience, and wondered why Rosalind could not nap while Corryvreckan drove on. Rosalind replied that the car's motion would undoubtedly disturb her sleep and possibly make her sick. Corryvreckan was reluctant to act against her wishes and furthermore was anxious to protect the interior of his car. Poppy suggested that twenty minutes, in the grand scheme of things, would not make much difference. So four of the car's occupants closed their eyes while the fifth let his glaze over, and the benefit of a short rest was felt, if not by all, then certainly by the present author.

The journey recommenced as the light was fading, and a number of settlements unknown to the present author were passed in near or total darkness. Conversation became sporadic, and Corryvreckan, having received the consent of the others, inserted a succession of discs into a slot in the dashboard, as a consequence of which music filled the yellow car. A variety of compositions sung by the artistes Johnny Cash, Patsy Cline and Emmylou Harris was played, and this did much to relieve the monotony of the journey until, at about the middle of the evening, the outskirts of Edinburgh were reached and Douglas began to give directions to the house and garden from which he and the present author had departed several days before.

Douglas unlocked the door and invited the company inside. He switched on the heating system and with Poppy's assistance set about organising the sleeping arrangements, fresh bedding and towels. It being a small house, any pretence as to the state of relations between Douglas and Poppy was futile, as well as unnecessary. Rosalind was assigned the single bed in Douglas's old bedroom, the happy couple took the bedroom formerly occupied by Mr Thomas Ythan Elder and his late wife, while the living-room couch was to be Corryvreckan's berth. The present author had his own accommodation nearby.

Douglas and Poppy walked to a nearby shop to purchase milk, bread and other foodstuffs for the morning, and also procured four fish suppers from the local 'chippie' as his guests had declared a need for further sustenance. The latest edition of the *Spear* was also brought home, but it yielded little information additional to that which they already possessed. The police were interviewing the driver of the hearse, who was named as Mr Gerald Letham (28), and who remained in hospital under guard and under caution. The police were also carrying out searches in various locations in the West Lothian area, but had so far failed to discover a single bottle of the missing whisky. A Police Scotland spokesperson remained tight-lipped on other aspects of the ongoing inquiries, refusing to confirm or deny any connection between the incident and rumours of irregular activities that had allegedly occurred in recent months at a well-known Speyside distillery.

After the consumption of the fish suppers, Douglas telephoned the Don't Care Much Home to inquire after his father's condition, and was reassured that he was 'sleeping like a bairn' and had been comfortable and calm since Douglas had last called. Soon after this the doorbell was rung by a party of children in masks and costumes intended to represent ghouls, ghosts, witches, zombies and similar supernatural or satanic beings. In return for telling some very feeble jokes, including one of questionable taste ('What do you get if you cross a toad with a dog?' 'A croaker spaniel'), these children demanded payment in cash or confectionery. They were, albeit without much enthusiasm, maintaining the tradition of 'guising', which usually takes place on the last night of October, commonly known as Halloween. Rosalind, who said it was several decades since any guiser had called at Glentaragar House, was pleased to see the tradition continuing but disappointed by the children's lacklustre and cynical performance. She did, however, give them some coins, upon receipt of which they immediately withdrew.

The present author remembers being told by an ancestor that Halloween in ages past was a much more boisterous occasion, and that owing to the association of toads with witchcraft in human folklore it was deemed unwise to be abroad on this night. Indeed, there is even a saying among the bufonidian race, 'Hibernate by Halloween, if in spring thou wouldst be seen', but this is likely to refer to the dangers of the cold rather than to the risk of assault.

Once the children had departed, Douglas recalled another toad joke, which is recorded here only because it touches on matters previously discussed by him with the present author: a man goes to the pictures and notices a toad in the next seat. 'Are you a toad?' the man asks. 'I am,' says the toad. 'What on earth are you doing at the pictures?' the man asks. 'Well,' says the toad, 'I liked the book.'

By this stage everybody was weary and so retired to bed. The present author, after a quick forage in the moonlight, also turned in, happy to be on familiar territory after his Highland excursion. He admits to finding the task of recounting these events somewhat tedious, and is surprised at how tricky an art storytelling appears to be. He suspects that he does not have sufficient imagination to write fiction, if indeed that is what this is, and therefore happily surrenders what remains of the narrative to others. He plans to spend one more evening stocking up reserves for the winter, and then it will be time for a long and, he hopes, uninterrupted sleep.

[Not to be continued]

JUST ED

In the morning, the sky over Edinburgh is laden with rain, and while Poppy and I are getting dressed it begins to pour.

Rosalind is still in bed. Poppy takes her a cup of tea. Corryvreckan is in the kitchen, making porridge.

It seems odd yet familiar, as if we have all lived together in that house – my father and mother's house, *my* house – for years and years.

After breakfast I phone Sonya and ask her what time she intends to be at the hospital.

'Eleven-thirty,' she says. 'Are you in Edinburgh?'

'I am.'

'Good. Do you have a car?'

'Not any more. It was totalled, remember?'

'Not that car, Douglas, any car. Do you have any car at all?'

'I once had half of one, but no longer.'

'Douglas!'

I relent. 'No, Sonya, I do not have any car at all.'

'So how did you get here from wherever you've been?' she says, pouncing like a cat (as she probably imagines herself) on a rather dense mouse. 'Where was it? Argyll or somewhere?'

'That's right,' I say. 'Argyll or somewhere.'

'Well, wherever it was they don't have phone signals so I imagine they don't have trains or buses either. So you came in a car.'

'Your logic is impeccable,' I say, but I don't think she hears the irony. 'I came in somebody else's car. They gave me a lift.'

'So *they* have a car. Can you bring it? To help get Magnus home. Or they can, this somebody without a gender. *They* can bring *their* car and we'll get Magnus back home where *he* belongs.'

In my days away I have forgotten how impressive is Sonya's ability to shift a question into a statement of intent in one breath, whilst simultaneously slipping in some pointed social commentary. She presumably thinks I have attached myself to a female driver and for some reason this irks her. If only she knew the truth!

'They *could*. They *might*. I would have to ask.'

Poppy is washing dishes. Corryvreckan is drying them. They are both hearing my side of the conversation, and probably most of Sonya's too.

'Could you do this one thing for me, Douglas? Could you ask?' she pleads.

'What about a taxi?' I suggest.

Corryvreckan says, quietly, 'We can take the car.'

'*What* about a taxi, Douglas? Have you seen the weather? Even if I can get a taxi, I don't know how long it will take to fetch Magnus from the ward to the exit. I'll have to let one taxi go and then order another while Magnus is waiting around on crutches, probably in agony. I mean, have you thought about that at all?'

'I don't think they'll let him home if he's in agony,' I say.

'We'll go in my car,' Corryvreckan says. 'Tell her that. I'll park as near as I can until everybody is ready, then we'll take her and her son home.'

'You are cruel, Douglas. You have a cruel streak in you.'

'No I don't,' I say. 'And as it happens, my friend Corryvreckan has offered to come with me, collect you and Magnus from the hospital and take you home.'

'Your friend who?'

'Ed,' says Corryvreckan.

'What?'

'Say "Ed",' says Corryvreckan.

'My friend Ed Corryvreckan,' I say.

'Just "Ed".'

'Just Ed.'

'Just Ed? Who is "Just Ed"?'

'A man of honour and integrity,' I say.

'Well, please thank him for his offer,' Sonya says, calling off her inner foxhound. 'Which I gratefully accept. Eleven-thirty. Don't be late.' And she is gone.

I have been instructed: I am not to be the late Douglas Elder. Nor will I be: my choice. All I want is to get this over with.

'She says thank you,' I tell Corryvreckan. 'And so do I. It's very kind of you. Ed.'

'My pleasure,' he says, and I realise that it is not only his name that has altered. All the way down the road last night, I was puzzled by a sense that some subtle transformation was coming over Corryvreckan. The further we got from Glentaragar the stronger that sense was, and again over breakfast this morning I felt it. His voice has shifted, gone down in pitch. Those overwhelming, not quite authentic West Highland intonations have faded, and now his accent is . . . not exactly neutral – for neutral is not a neutral term in this context – but less pronounced. That's not it either, for how can one accent be less pronounced than another? He sounds more southern, more – I hesitate to use the word, for what too does this really mean? – English.

I think Corryvreckan is reverting to his Edward Somethingness. To his original state of being a Friend from the South.

'We'll go in about half an hour,' I say.

'Very good,' says Ed, and retreats to the living room.

'Ed?' Poppy says. 'Who the hell is Ed?'

'It's complicated,' I tell her. As if I should have to!

We return to the parental bedroom. We have both slept well. In the middle of the night we woke at the same time, made love, fell asleep again. There was no talk of anybody else being in the room: no talk at all, in fact. We were alone, together.

Her overnight bag and my suitcase on wheels are not unpacked. She opens a drawer and finds it full of clothes my father no longer needs. She closes it again.

'Sorry,' we both say.

'Don't apologise,' we both say.

There is work to be done, clearly, but not yet.

'We won't be long at the hospital,' I tell her. 'But I do need to see her.'

'Sonya?'

'Yes, and Magnus, and his sister if she's there. Do you mind?'

'Of course I don't. Don't be too hard on Sonya.'

'She's pretty hard on me.'

'Well, she's been under a lot of stress. And you sound bitter and I don't think that's who you are or who you want to be. And maybe, Douglas –'

'Yes?'

'Maybe you weren't the easiest person for her to be with.'

I consider this.

'You're right. I'd have chucked myself out years before she actually did.'

'Well, then. You were incompatible.'

'Like a cheap ink cartridge.'

'What?'

'Nothing. You might find the same thing. That I'm not the easiest person to be with.'

'Perhaps, but there's a difference.'

'What's that?'

'We're compatible.'

'Do you think so?'

'Yes, even if we aren't the easiest people, we'll be all right.'

'Poppy?'

'Yes?'

'What about Xanthe? Where does she fit in?'

'I don't think she will.'

'I'm not sure I could cope with you going off to be her every once in a while. Don't get me wrong, I liked her, but that was before I met you.'

'I'll tell her.'

'Don't be too hard on her.'

She smiles. 'Okay.'

'Right,' I say, 'I'd better go. You and Rosalind make yourselves at home.'

'We will.'

'I'll need to see my father as well.'

'Perhaps we could come and meet him?'

'That would be good. I'll phone you later and we'll arrange it. Here's a spare key. Will you be all right?'

'We will.'

There is somebody else I need to see too, but I don't mention him.

DESTINY

Ed drives me to the hospital. It's a wet Saturday morning, and the city is heaving with revving, hooting, highly competitive traffic, but it doesn't seem to be bothering him. Would it have bothered Corryvreckan, a man for whom Oban is too busy? Ed, I note, is still wearing Corryvreckan's clothes, but *sans* deerstalker.

'How are you doing?' I ask.

'Fine.'

'You seem quite detached.'

'It's my default state.'

This is not something I can imagine Corryvreckan saying.

'Ed, do you ever feel that you're in a dream and want to wake up, but you can't? Or do you ever feel that you *have* just woken up from a dream, even though you know you haven't?'

He taps the steering wheel as we sit at lights.

'No,' he says at last. 'But sometimes I feel I am in a dream but it isn't *my* dream. *That's* an odd feeling. Quite unnatural, in fact.'

I glance at him and he glances at me and there is a sharing of something between us. Horror, perhaps. Then the lights turn green and we are moving again.

There is nowhere to park on the streets around the hospital but to our surprise we find a space in the hospital's own car park, not far from the main entrance. Ed switches off the engine and looks as if he is preparing for a long wait.

'Why don't you come in with me?' I suggest. 'I don't know if Magnus will be in a wheelchair or on crutches or what. There might be things to carry.'

'Happy to assist,' Ed says.

Neither of us has brought a coat but fortunately the rain has eased off. We enter the building and ask at the information desk where we can find Magnus Strachan, then start the long walk to Ward 28 along corridors decorated with children's artwork and posters advertising helplines for obesity, smoking and sexually transmitted diseases. There are lots of people going in all directions, the professional, medical ones marching with purpose and confidence, the visitors and patients looking bewildered or resigned, as if they have entered a maze by mistake and must now see it through to the end, however many hours it takes. It's like walking through an airport. Ed and I swap glances again: clearly he is still detached. Oddly enough, I feel quite detached too.

We come to a kind of concourse. Across it, heading straight for us, is Clan Strachan: Magnus in a wheelchair, holding a pair of crutches and with his left leg sticking out before him in a cast; Sonya pushing the chair; and Paula alongside clutching several plastic carriers, with a sports bag over her shoulder.

'Hello, hello, hello!' I call cheerily. One for each of them.

'You're late,' Sonya says.

'No, you're early,' I reply, for it is not yet half-past eleven. 'Magnus, how are you? Paula, let me take some of those. Ed, this is Magnus, Paula and Sonya. Everybody, this is Ed.'

Greetings are exchanged. Magnus says he's fine, and he doesn't look too bad apart from a few scratches and a neck brace, and the stookie of course. He doesn't even have a bandage on his head, but then, being old-fashioned, I belong to the *Beano* school of picturing what people look like who have had knocks on the napper. He seems genuinely pleased to see me, and even Paula smiles grudgingly and lets me relieve her of some of her bags, but it is the interaction between Sonya and Ed that is most intriguing. Abandoning the wheelchair and ignoring me, the former makes a beeline for the latter. And something happens. It's hard to describe precisely what, but a kind of glow comes over her.

'Ed,' she says breathily. 'I can't tell you how grateful I am. I am *so* grateful.'

'It's not a problem,' Ed says, and a glow comes over him too. His voice has deepened further and his chest seems to swell a little under the green tweed waistcoat and, in a shabby-chic, eccentric kind of way, Edward Something strikes rather an impressive pose there in the middle of the hospital thoroughfare. I have to remind myself that he is in his early sixties. He doesn't look it – but again, what does that mean, not to look your age? It's meaningless.

'It is *so* kind of you to do this for us,' Sonya is saying, launching charm-offensive missile number two. 'We mustn't detain you any longer than is necessary. I'm sure you're a busy man, but if you'd care to . . . That is, if you'd like . . .'

'Let's get Magnus home first,' Ed says, scoring maximum points with minimum effort.

'You're absolutely right. That's our priority. But then . . . but only if you have time . . . some lunch?'

I've never seen her so tongue-tied. It's as if she can barely suppress her desire to offer him hospitality. I am almost persuaded that she means it, she really *wants* him to stay for lunch. At *least* for lunch. What is going on? I may doubt her sincerity, but that's because I'm tired of her. Paula isn't convinced either, judging by the mask-like expression on her face, although that could simply be too much make-up. I can see, however, that to somebody else – like Ed – the full Sonya still packs quite a punch, and that's without taking into account that she is looking at her very best. I have mentioned before her long dark hair, the delicacy of her ears and the slenderness of her fingers; but not the unblemished bloom of her skin, the neatness of her nose, the bigness of her eyes, the fine proportions of her figure and the casual elegance of her dress sense.

'It would be a pleasure,' Ed growls, and Sonya practically expires on the spot. And something else is happening. That age thing: Sonya and Ed both seem to be shedding years by the second. I glance from one to the other, and I even see in Sonya that elusive resemblance to her daughter, and in Ed that elusive resemblance to someone else, as he smiles calmly at Sonya, and as Magnus smiles bemusedly at the pair of them. *What?* I glance again, but this time between Magnus and Ed. Yes, it cannot be denied: Ed carries a shade of Magnus about him, and Magnus carries a shade of Ed!

'Stuart?' Sonya says, wide-eyed.

'Stella?' Ed says, narrow-eyed.

'What is going on?' I say out loud, but to no one in particular.

'Nothing, nothing,' Sonya says. 'I must have . . . You are quite . . . Oh, what were we saying?'

'We were talking about lunch,' Ed murmurs. 'The only problem,' he continues, assessing us through those narrow eyes, 'is how we're all going to get into the car. It's not a big car. Magnus in the back seat, I think, and *one* in the front with me, but . . .'

'I'm not coming home,' Paula says. 'I've got to go to work. Early shift, Mum, remember? I'll catch a bus up the town.'

Sonya gives me a look. Ed, only slightly apologetically, gives me another.

'It's not a problem,' I say, echoing his earlier tone of insouciance but not really bringing it off. 'I'll give you a hand to the car, then I'll leave you to it. You won't need me at the other end if Ed's with you, Sonya. Anyway, I should really go and see my father.'

'Yes, you should,' she says, closing the deal instantly. 'Somebody phoned me the other day from that home you put him in, trying to get hold of you. How they thought I could help I've no idea, especially as they already had your number. And anyway, that was after the attempt on Magnus's life so I had quite enough on my plate.' She is speaking very fast, as if intent on recovering lost ground.

'It was an accident, Mum,' Magnus murmurs, sounding just like Ed.

'Accident? I don't think that hearse was full of drink by accident! The idiot driving it was engaged in criminal activity and everything flows from that. And the worst thing – Ed – is the injustice of Magnus having to share the same ward with the very man who tried to kill him.'

'We were in separate rooms,' Magnus says.

'It's the principle,' Sonya says. 'He only broke his leg too, which seems so unfair.'

'Actually he has a broken pelvis and damage to his back, so I was told,' Magnus says. 'It's quite serious.'

'Well, whose fault is that?'

I watch Ed carefully during these exchanges. I'm looking for signs of hesitation, panic or retreat. There are none. On the contrary, he seems to be quite happily lapping up everything Sonya says, and regarding her with a kind of fond, dreamlike curiosity. And he is eyeing Magnus with almost paternal concern.

But Magnus's father is in Australia. Isn't he?

'Are you okay with that, Ed – if I leave you to it?' I ask, checking one last time, giving him one final opportunity to snap back into reality.

'I'm fine.'

'Very well. On your head be it.' No, I don't say that. I lean in and say, 'You take care of her.'

'I intend to,' he says.

We are now even. He's a grown-up. So am I. I am not responsible for him, nor for Sonya, and he's not responsible for me, nor for Poppy. Nor, it seems, for Ruaridh MacLagan or Stuart Crathes MacCrimmon.

If that makes sense.

Or even if it doesn't.

Sonya reluctantly separates herself from Ed and returns to chair-pushing duties. We continue to the car. On the way, I ask Paula how she's getting on at work.

'Fine.'

'How's Barry?'

'Who?'

'Barry, your colleague at the Lounger.'

'Oh, I'm not there any more. I'm at the Blue Bonnet on the High Street.'

'Is that so? What went wrong?'

'Nothing. I just didnae like it there. That Barry was a tube. He wanted to get off wi me so I told him to stick his job and went and got another one.'

'That's incredibly enterprising, Paula,' I say. 'And quite courageous, if you don't mind me saying so. Was he angry?'

'Aye, but that's just what he's like. When he realised I meant it he just about started greetin.'

'Barry?'

'Aye. He's a big bairn really.'

I am impressed. The cool nonchalance of this nineteen-year-old is amazing.

'And how's the Blue Bonnet?'

'It's all right. It's mostly tourists and students. They're nae bother at all.'

'That's great, Paula. You'll probably end up running the place.'

She laughs. She actually laughs. 'Not for a while, Douglas.'

'Tell me,' I say, 'if it was a tube competition, who would win, Barry or me? Which one of us, in your opinion, is the bigger tube?'

No I don't. I've learned my lesson. I quit while I'm ahead, and Paula and I part on good terms.

With Magnus safely stowed along the back seat and all his belongings in the boot, Sonya installed in the front passenger seat, and Paula having left for a fun-filled shift at the Blue Bonnet, I wish Ed luck and wave them off. Then I retrace my steps to Ward 28, which I manage to do without the aid of either an actual or metaphorical ball of wool.

A police officer is sitting on a chair outside a closed door on the ward. I think about all the kids' comics, Carry On films and other deep springs of life's lessons from which I have imbibed, and recognise that to get past this policeman, even in what appears to be his state of near-comatose boredom, I will have to find a disguise. I retreat, and go in search of a white coat and, if possible, a stethoscope.

I have to report that white coats which aren't already occupied are surprisingly hard to come by in big hospitals, and unattended stethoscopes impossible. I walk for miles looking for staff changing rooms, laundry rooms, store cupboards and other likely sources, until finally, in Haematology I think, I pass an office with its door open and there, draped over a swivel chair, is a doctor's white coat. I lean into the room: nobody suggests I should knock or wait. I step right in: nobody demands to know what the hell I think I'm doing. I swipe the coat, tuck it under my arm and hurry back to the other end of the hospital. Halfway there I nip into a Gents and slip on the disguise. I have noticed that many doctors favour the open-coat look, but my checked shirt and lack of tie are a bit too casual so I button up, noting from the name-badge on the lapel that I am, for the next few minutes, Dr Rodriguez. Not perfect but, I hope, sufficient.

The policeman half-rises from his seat as I stride up in the manner of a confident, busy medic doing his rounds. 'Just have to do a couple of quick checks on Mr Letham,' I say, resisting the urge to put on a Spanish accent. I knock once and open the door as I am speaking. It is so easy! The way 'Mr Letham' trips off my tongue probably helps. The Douglas Findhorn Elder of a week ago would never have dared pull this off, but that Douglas Findhorn Elder is not this Douglas Findhorn Elder. The policeman subsides again, blinded by the whiteness of my coat.

Another reason, I discover, once inside, why the officer is so relaxed is that there is no possibility of Gerry exiting under his own steam. Leaving by the window isn't an option (we're on the first floor) but in any case he is completely immobilised by various straps and pulleys attached to the bed and/or his body. There's a television on the wall facing him, with a cookery programme in progress, but the sound is off. A remote control is lying on the sheet beside his right hand. He is watching the screen intently.

'Good morning, Mr Letham,' I say, quite loudly. 'I'm Dr Rodriguez. How are you feeling this morning?' And then I shut the door behind me, interpose myself between him and the screen, and put my finger to my lips.

Gerry's mouth falls open, then a huge smile breaks across his face. 'Douglas, my man!' he says in a hoarse whisper. 'What are *you* daein here?'

'I've come to see you, Gerry.'

'I'm just watching this shite on the telly. The food's good but I cannae stand the accents. Haud on a minute till I kill it.'

'Keep your voice down. I can't stay long or I'll get caught, which would be bad for both of us. How are you?'

'Could be worse, could be better. What's wi the jaiket? You here tae spring us?'

'Not possible, Gerry, even if that was my plan. Look at yourself. There's more spring in a burst mattress.' I pull up a chair next to the bed.

'Aye, I'm no gaun anywhere fast, am I?'

'Not a chance. Listen, I know all about the crash. What on earth were you doing all the way out there?'

'I thought I'd be smert and come in by the back roads, just in case the polis had been tipped off or something, but then I got lost, didn't I? And it was dark and I didnae even realise I was at a crossroads till I slammed intae the side of the guy in the Polo. Fucking eejit.'

'That's a bit harsh.'

'No him, me! I was that close tae hame, and I fucking blew it. That would have been me sorted – favour done, debt settled. Now look at us. I scrambled intae the ditch and thought I'd lie there till everybody had gone but just as well they found me or I'd be deid. I've fractured my pelvis and they're trying tae work oot whether tae operate or no. They say sometimes it's better tae leave these things tae mend themselves. At least, that's what I think they're saying.'

'Have they said if you're going to be able to walk?'

'They've no said I'll no, but it'll be a while whatever they decide tae dae wi me. Suits me. The longer I stay here the longer I'm no in the jail. Mind you, the longer I'm in the jail the longer I'll no be ootside, which is where I *really* dinnae want tae be the noo.'

'Your pal won't be very chuffed.'

'You're telling me! He cannae touch me here, though, no wi that polis on the door. Thing is, I've a couple of good cairds up my sleeve. So long as I say nothing, he's safe. They'll dae me for dangerous driving, nae licence, nae insurance, stealing the motor, all that, and they'll try tae get me for reset, but there's been a defence lawyer in and he says that might no stick because there's nae evidence of stolen goods. The cops are gaun mental because the folk oot there in bandit country took the lot. There was some broken bottles and cardboard boxes but that's aboot it, and the lawyer says it's no enough. The rain's washed aw the whisky away. He says they're gonnae struggle tae prove it was ever there, let alane where it came fae.'

'Where did it come from?'

'That's another thing in my favour – I hivnae got a clue! Some big distillery somewhere but I've nae idea where, so even if they torture me I cannae tell them. Only thing that's worrying me is if they work oot where I took the hearse, they'll find the rest of the whisky at that Glen Lodge Hotel place.'

'No they won't,' I tell him, 'because somebody's cleared the whole lot out. I was there yesterday. Here, give me your wrist in case anybody comes in.'

He does his high-pitched hysterical laugh, but in a whispery way. 'Ya fucking beauty! Was that you, man? Did you organise that?'

'No, Gerry, and I'm not telling you who did. But, believe me, it's all away. Well away.'

For a minute I think he's going to do a Barry and start crying. But Gerry is made of stronger stuff.

'That's a real weight aff my mind, Douglas. Thanks for coming in tae tell me that.'

'It's not going to make your pal any happier though, is it?'

'Naw, but he's got his ain problems. You see, I was daein him a favour, but he was daein another guy a bigger favour. And I dinnae ken, but I reckon the other guy . . .'

'. . . owes a bigger guy. Gerry, your pulse is all over the place. It's going hell for leather and skipping beats at the same time. That's not healthy. Your pal isn't a big bald guy with a scar on his cheek called Mister G, is he?'

'Jeez, you ken *everything*!' Gerry says. Then he adds, 'Naw, it's no him, but I ken who you mean. Different food chain. Think I should see a doctor about my pulse? A real doctor, I mean.'

'Probably. I noticed it went even crazier when I mentioned Mister G. Is your life in danger?'

'Nae mair than his is, and I'm in a hospital! Look, you stay oot of this. Ye've done loads for me already. I appreciate ye trying tae sort it oot and everything, but there's nae point you getting mixed up in it.'

'Gerry, I assure you, I'm not getting mixed up in anything. Once I'm out of here, that's it for me.'

'Good. Thing is, they'll be tearing lumps oot of each other, which is why the best place for me right now is in here, and then the jail later. By the time I'm oot, wi a bit of luck they'll have killed each other. I'll get five years, the lawyer thinks. I think I'm gonnae study for a degree. May as well make the maist of it, eh?'

'Does the thought of going to prison for five years not depress you?'

'Aye, but it could be worse. I could be deid. Aahaaha!'

'Get them to check your pulse or you might be. I'll say something, Gerry, I admire your optimism. I have done from the first time we met. What'll you study?'

'Dinnae ken yet. History maybe. Or Philosophy. Why is life shite for maist folk? I quite fancy Philosophy. Find oot what the fuck it's all aboot, eh?'

'Good luck with that. Listen, Gerry, I need to ask, have you mentioned my name to anybody? Told anyone you picked me up, that I helped you load that hearse, anything like that?'

If Gerry could move I think he would leap out of bed and kick me, he is so affronted.

'Come *on*, man! You're my mate! You never shopped me. Why would I shop you? Jeesus, Douglas!'

I apologise profusely for even mentioning it. The fact that he left that card at the scene of the crime is neither here nor there. It was an accident. Ollie retrieved it. Even if the police make a connection, it's true that when

I first met Gerry I was attending a colleague's funeral and he was a simple undertaker. I could have given him the card then, if I'd had it. It's not so very far from the truth.

And now is not the time to have a long-drawn-out ethical debate with myself about it. Ten minutes have gone by. The last thing either of us needs is for the real Dr Rodriguez to start making a fuss about his missing coat.

'I better go,' I say, releasing his wrist and standing up. 'I'm sorry it's wound up like this for you, and I hope you get better soon.'

'No too soon,' he says, grinning. 'And dinnae feel sorry for me. It's my ain fault. I should have stopped at that crossroads.'

'That's true.'

'Story of my life, ken. No stopping at crossroads, just breengin on. Ken what, though, if this hadnae happened, something else would have. And anyway, that favour probably wouldnae have been enough for my pal. The bastard would just have said there was interest on it and made me dae something else, probably something worse. So maybe this is, eh, my destiny. A fresh start. A big fucking jail sentence and a degree in Philosophy. Do you believe in destiny?'

'I really don't know.'

'Me neither. That's how I fancy daein Philosophy.'

'There's a need for it, Gerry.'

'Whit?'

'Philosophy. The universities are closing down their Philosophy departments. No demand, they say. I say they're wrong. This country needs new philosophers.'

'You never see notices for them in the job centre, but if you say it, I believe it.'

'How old are you, Gerry?'

'Twenty-nine next month.'

'That's not so old.'

'Aye, plenty time to find oot.'

'I better go,' I say again.

'Aye. Well, thanks for coming in, Douglas. It's made my day. See you around, eh?'

'Probably not,' I reply. ('I hope not,' is what I was going to say, but that would be ill-mannered, as well as untrue.)

'Aye, I will. Years fae now. When I'm an old bastard and you're an even older bastard. We'll bump intae each other, see if we don't.'

'Destiny,' I say. I grip his hand again. 'Cheers, Gerry. Good luck.'

'You too, man.'

And that's it. I exit as professionally as I went in, the policeman does his half-rise-and-fall trick, and I set off in Dr Rodriguez's white coat, breathing more easily once I have gone through the ward doors. At the first opportunity I whip the coat off and dump it in a litter bin, having first removed the name-badge, which I dispose of in another bin. I don't want Dr Rodriguez getting into trouble.

I keep listening out for the sound of boots thundering after me, but nothing happens. I feel like James Bond, or maybe Sid James. Job done. Mission accomplished. Carry on living.

The rain has stopped and the clouds are breaking up. It's a long walk to the Don't Care Much Home but I feel like a long walk. I phone home to arrange things with Poppy. She's been out to the shops, they have had some lunch, Rosalind is having a nap and then they will be bored. I suggest they meet me at the Home in an hour or so.

'How did it go?'

'Fine. There's something going on between Ed and Sonya. They've taken a shine to one another.'

'A shine?'

'More of a glow actually.'

'Well, well.'

'In fact, they seem to know each other, but by different names.'

'You see, it happens all the time,' Poppy says.

'Anyway, they've taken Magnus home between them. I was surplus to requirements.'

'I can see how you would be.'

'Poppy?'

'Yes?'

'Is this okay?'

'What? Ed and Sonya?'

'No. You and me.'

'Absolutely. For you too?'

'Absolutely.'

'Good. See you in an hour.'

'I can't wait.'

Lunch is over and the residents are back in the day room or their own rooms by the time I arrive. Because it's the weekend there aren't so many staff on duty. Beverley Brown isn't in, but Muriel is.

'Hello, David.' I can't be bothered correcting her. 'Come to see your dad, have you? He's doing fine in spite of everything. Gave us all quite a fright though. I'll take you down.'

'It's all right. I know the way.'

'Well, if you don't mind, we are a bit short-staffed today. Your friends are already with him. Do you want a tea or a coffee or anything?'

'No thanks.'

I go past snowy-haired, stone-deaf Jimmy's open door and there he is, watching the muted television just as he was a week and a half ago, just like Gerry in hospital. Maybe he hasn't moved in all that time, or maybe I'm trapped in a time warp. But I can't be, because Rosalind and Poppy are sitting with my father, and they weren't the last time I was here.

Poppy rises and gives me a kiss and an embrace. My father observes this. He does not miss it.

I go down on my knees beside his chair and give him a hug. 'Dad, it's me, Douglas. How are you?'

I receive a powerful, bone-crushing hug back. 'Remarkable,' he says.

'We've been remarking on how remarkable he is,' Poppy says.

'Remarkable,' Dad says.

'He's been giving us his own account of his roof protest,' Rosalind says.

'Is that what it was? What were you protesting about, Dad?'

'Fucking roof. It's in a terrible state. But I chopped it up and . . .' He makes a hammering motion. 'I chopped it up. It's all to hell. Plumbers.'

'What about plumbers?'

'Called them out. Useless. Had to make my own biscuits.'

'You mean "take"?'

'No, *make*. Not biscuits.' He flicks his fingers. 'Things to . . .' He hammers the air again. 'Work.'

'Tools?'

'Aye!' he shouts.

'You made your own tools and then you checked that the roof was secure,' I say. 'Like you did with our floorboards, remember? Only you had proper tools that time.'

'Fucking rotten. But I did it. Got the, eh ...' He does a kind of jerking-upward movement with one hand. It's so vague and yet somehow I recognise exactly what he means.

'The ladder? You got the ladder.'

'Aye, aye. That showed the bastards.' He sniggers and Rosalind joins in. That stops him. He peers at her.

'Who's this? That's not your mother.'

'No.' I wait for the follow-up question – 'Where is she?' – but it doesn't come. 'That's right, Dad. This is Rosalind.'

'Hmm.' He points at Poppy. 'And who's she?'

'That's Poppy. Rosalind is Poppy's grandmother. You've already met them.'

'Hello, Tom,' Rosalind says.

'Hello, Tom,' Poppy says.

'Poppy's a dog's name.'

'It can be,' Poppy says. 'But then, Tom could be a dog's name too.'

'Not sure if that's true,' Tom says.

'Douglas too,' I say. 'Doug the dug.'

He frowns at me. He doesn't say anything, but the meaning in that look is, and this is an approximation, 'Who the fuck do you think you are, patronising me with that bollocks?'

He's more interested in Poppy anyway. 'Who *are* you?'

'I'm a friend of Douglas's. A close friend.'

'She's my *girl*friend.'

'Ah.' He could give Ed lessons in narrow-eyed appraisal. First he looks at Poppy, then at me, then back at her.

'Nice tits.'

'You're very kind,' Poppy says.

'That's a bit rude, Dad.'

'Fuck off.'

Rosalind nearly falls off her chair laughing. 'Oh, I used to swear like that,' she says. 'Haven't done for years. How refreshing.'

'Dad never did,' I say. 'I don't know where he gets it from.'

'You're a late developer, Tom,' Rosalind says, beaming at him.

He beams back. 'Remarkable,' he says.

And so our afternoon chat rattles on. Non sequiturs and the wrong ends of grasped sticks predominate, but there's a weird thread of rationality running through it too: it all just about makes sense, and when it doesn't nobody cares. There's a rapport between Tom and Rosalind which isn't just about their ages, although that helps: when Rosalind says something about the war or the Attlee Government, Tom manages to throw a few loosely connected remarks back at her. But the main thing is, he is relaxed, enjoying himself; happier than I've seen him for months. He laughs and swears in equal measure, and only tries to rise from his chair if one of us is out of reach, because he wants to hold hands, all of our hands. And even when he gets stuck for a while, and gives Rosalind a long, puzzled stare, he comes out of that frozen moment with something really special.

'That's not your mother,' he says.

'No, it's not,' I say.

'I'm your dad. I'm his dad,' he tells the others.

'Yes, you are,' Rosalind says. 'And he's your son. He's a good son.'

'How do you know that?' he says, a slight belligerence in his voice. 'You're not his mother.'

I feel my anxiety rising. Rosalind says calmly, 'No, but I can see he loves you.'

'Can you? Right.'

He's holding one of Rosalind's hands. I'm afraid he might squeeze too hard and hurt her. And I wait for the realisation, the news of Mum's death, and then the tears.

But they don't come. Instead:

'She's dead, you know, his mother. Died a few years ago.'

'Do you miss her?' Rosalind asks.

'Aye, sometimes,' he says. 'What else can you do?'

'I had two husbands,' Rosalind says. 'Ralph died more than thirty years ago. And Guy, the first one, died in the Spanish Civil War. And I miss them both still, but it doesn't hurt any more.'

My father is still staring at her. 'The Spanish Civil War. That was a long time ago,' he says.

'Nineteen thirty-seven.'

He shakes his head. 'Jesus. I don't miss her that much.'

There are smiles all round. No tears. Then he says, 'Ach well. Time for bed. Thank you for coming.'

'It's only four o'clock,' I say. 'You've still to get your tea.'

'I'm tired. Away you go. I'm not hungry.'

'Just sit and have a sleep there. It's not bedtime yet.'

'I'm tired.'

And he is. He doesn't mind us leaving. He wants us to leave. We say we'll come again soon. 'Okay,' he says. And when we do go, he makes no attempt to stand up, to follow, to call me back, as he often has done. He watches us go, and when I wave from the door he waves back.

'Bye, Dad.'

'Bye, son.'

I'm tempted to go back and ask him if he's ever had a conversation with a toad. Then I decide I'll save that one for another day. I don't want to upset the ease of us going. Because it won't always be this easy. It will probably be quite different on the next visit. But mark this down on the card: a good visit, and a good departure. *Man, go forth, man! Go!* Twelve points.

EVERYTHING IS UNREALISTIC

We stop a taxi on the street. As it takes us home, Rosalind says, 'I think your father has benefited hugely from his night out. He was quite at ease.'

'He's not always like that.'

'No, but imagine the good it would do him if he was out of there altogether. If he came away with us.'

'Gran, you're not proposing Tom comes to live in Glentaragar?'

'Don't be silly, my dear. He wouldn't last a week. Mind you, what a week it would be!'

I throw my weight behind Poppy's scepticism. 'It's out of the question, Rosalind. Even getting him there. But once he was – one fall and that would be it. Over.'

'No, it wouldn't. He falls all the time, you've told us. So let him fall. Let him fall until he can't get up again. A week would do it.'

'Gran!'

'It's not realistic,' I say.

'I know, Douglas. Nothing is. Everything is unrealistic until it happens, and then one sees that it always *could* have happened. But if you had a choice between giving him one week with us at Glentaragar – not now, but in the spring, say, with the sun shining and the birds singing and all of us just enjoying each other – or three more years of what he has, would you hesitate for a second? Wouldn't you give him the week?'

'Of course I would.'

'Well, then.'

'Let's see where we are in the spring, Gran,' Poppy says. 'Let's see where we all are, and then we can decide.'

'I'm not serious, really,' Rosalind says. 'He's safer where he is. It's just a thought.'

ALL CLEAR

As we're getting out of the taxi, a fat, familiar figure, with a rucksack on its back, is dismounting from its bicycle outside the house.

'Douglas! Theseus! Ulysses! Whoever the hell you are, you're home!'

'Ollie!' I am as glad to see him as he seems to be to see me. We shake hands. We embrace.

'I was just in the neighbourhood and thought I might catch you. Good timing!'

I unlock the door and he wheels in the bike and parks it under the purple heather and hairy coos. We go through to the kitchen and he dumps the rucksack on the floor. I do the introductions. Ollie and I fill each other in on developments as quickly as possible whilst trying not to exclude Rosalind and Poppy from the conversation. Ollie, always expansive, is in an exceptionally cheery mood. He turns the charm up to full blast and starts rewriting history.

'You're a remarkable woman,' he tells Rosalind. 'It's an honour to meet you. I've been reading up about you ever since Douglas proposed his article. What a life you've had! And Poppy's your granddaughter? You're in good hands there, I can see. And Douglas too. Eh, Douglas?'

I've put the kettle on and Poppy is busying herself with plates and glasses for some reason and we must look very domesticated to him. And Poppy confirms it by smiling at him and touching my shoulder as she goes past.

'Quite right, Ollie,' I say, throwing him a warning glance.

'Aha!' he says. 'Discretion is my middle name,' he says. 'Or it was, but I changed it to Brendan. Discretion sounded too Irish.'

Poppy strikes a match, turns around and produces what she has been discreetly preparing – a chocolate cake, in the middle of which she has planted a single candle.

'I didn't have time to bake, so I bought this this morning,' she says, lighting the candle. Then she brings a bottle of champagne from the fridge and pops the cork.

'What's all this?' Rosalind says.

'*Happy birthday to you!*' Poppy sings, and suddenly I remember.

'*Happy birthday to you!*' (Together.)

'*Happy birthday, dear Rosalind!*' (Ollie adds a rich bass line.)

'*Happy birthday to you!*' (The ensemble.)

'I'd completely forgotten,' Rosalind says. 'Is it today? My goodness! How kind!' She leans over the cake and blows out the candle.

'One candle, one century,' Poppy says. 'And no presents.'

'Thank you,' Rosalind says. 'Who needs presents when there's cake?' She receives kisses from all three of us.

'I completely forgot too,' I tell her. 'Your hundredth birthday – the whole bloody reason for me going to Glentaragar.'

Rosalind gives me a stern look. 'Oh, Douglas, I don't think so.'

'Just think,' Poppy says, 'Harry the postie will have driven all the way up the glen with your telegram from Buckingham Palace, and there'll be nobody there to take it.'

'Even better,' Rosalind says. 'Poor Harry. Never mind, we'll see him next week. You cut it, dear. A small piece for me.'

'A big piece for Ollie,' I say.

'Talking of pieces,' Ollie says, 'I'm not sure how to put this, but . . .'

'What?'

'It's all change at the *Spear*.'

'What, again?'

'John Liffield's gone.'

'Gone?' I say. 'Not – like Ronald?'

'Dead? No, just gone. Fired. That was the editor,' Ollie explains to the others. 'Our Friends in the South didn't think he was taking the paper in the right direction. Told him to clear his desk on Monday, and he cleared it. In on Monday. Gone on Tuesday. That's what it's like in newspapers.'

'But he had all those plans,' I say. 'He'd just survived that big meeting.'

'So *he* thought. The facts would suggest otherwise. Anyway, he's away and there's a new man starting on Monday. Don't know anything about him. It might even be a woman – that *would* be a change. But I'm not sure if that series Liffield planned – what was it, The Idea of Scotland? – I'm not sure if that'll run now. And what I was going to say was, did you nail him down on a fee and a contract for your interview with Rosalind?'

I shake my head.

'I did warn you,' Ollie says. 'Nothing in writing?'

I shake my head again.

'Good. All is not lost. You can sell it to someone else.'

'Rosalind,' I say. 'I'm so sorry. I didn't foresee this.'

She does look crestfallen. The champagne fizz sounds a little mocking. 'I did want to see it in print,' she says. 'I wanted to lay my soul bare to the world. Or, more prosaically, I wanted to correct an untruth.' She smiles at Ollie. 'Douglas knows what I mean.'

'You know,' Poppy says, 'maybe it's better this way. I don't think Douglas can do you justice, Gran, in one newspaper article. Maybe not the truth either. Here today, gone tomorrow. You deserve more than that – a fuller picture, warts and all. Because you are not perfect, you know.'

'One cannot reach a hundred and be perfect,' Rosalind says. 'But I do not have warts.'

'What about you and Douglas talking some more? What about all your papers up at the house?'

'You have papers?' I ask.

'Boxes and boxes of them,' Poppy says. 'There's a whole book to be written about her life and times.'

'Oh, I don't think so,' Rosalind says, but I can see that she isn't entirely dismissive of the idea. 'What do you think, Douglas?'

'It would be a project,' I say. 'I have a bit of spare time.'

'It could be the job I said we didn't have for you. I don't suppose Corryvreckan would mind, would he, Poppy?'

'I'm not sure that Corryvreckan will even notice,' Poppy says. Rosalind raises an eyebrow at this.

'If there was a book in the offing,' Ollie says, 'then maybe the new editor, whoever he or she is, would be interested in a news story. Rather than a profile, I mean. Or maybe that's the hook. What was it you said? "Munlochy to bare her soul through new biography, the *Spear* reveals on her hundredth birthday."'

'That's another thing,' I say. 'I forgot to take any photographs.'

Like a conjurer Ollie draws out the wee sliver of techno-wizardry that is his phone. 'Relight that candle, Poppy,' he says, 'and we'll rectify that at once.'

'Ollie gets my vote for editor,' Poppy says, obliging with a match.

'That's not such a bad idea,' I say, only half-joking. 'You know all about subbing, you can knock off a front-page article at short notice, you've been there longer than most. You could write and edit the entire paper.'

'Piss off,' Ollie says. 'Excuse me, ladies. I'm just about surviving in there. Even football managers last longer than newspaper editors these days. I'll stick with the job I have, thanks.'

'The *Spear* was a very fine paper once,' Rosalind says.

'The *Spear* will rise again,' Ollie says, 'or something will rise in its place if it doesn't. Life doesn't sit still. Neither do you, Rosalind, and I wish you would for a few seconds. Perfect. Thank you. Roy and Grant send you their regards by the way, Douglas. And they'd send them to you too, Rosalind, if they knew it was your birthday.'

The phone rings. I excuse myself and go into the hall to answer it.

'It's Ed,' says Ed.

'Ed, we were just talking about you. Well, actually, we weren't. I assume you are still Ed?'

'I just said I was,' says Ed. 'Sonya would like to have a word. She feels you're owed an explanation.'

'I've been wanting one of those for a while,' I tell him. 'Not from her; from you. But now that I think about it, I'm not that bothered.'

'I'll keep it brief,' says Ed. 'Many years ago I came to Edinburgh during the Festival. I stayed for a week or two. I was a singer and a musician and I did some busking.'

'I know.'

'How do you know?'

'I'm not sure. I just, kind of, somehow, do.'

'I had a stage name, or should I say a street name? Stuart Crathes Mac-Crimmon. Perhaps you heard me play?'

'Not back then; but the name is familiar.'

'Well, it's odd if you do remember it, because I wasn't famous. Anyway, that was how I introduced myself to everybody. For two weeks I had a ball. I made money by day and I spent it by night. I slept on people's floors and I hung out with other musicians and actors and we had a wonderful, liberated time. Do you understand what I mean by that?'

'I think so.'

'And one of the wonderful, liberated people I met was a beautiful young actress called Stella Celeste. That was a stage name too. She was a Business Studies student, but that summer she was playing the part of Felicity in a production of *The Real Inspector Hound* by Tom Stoppard. Did you ever see that play?'

'No, Ed, I never did.'

'I saw it six nights in a row. Stella was brilliant. After the first performance I went backstage and congratulated her. There was a chemistry between us.'

'That would account for the glow.'

'What?'

'Never mind.'

'Well, one thing led to another and for those six nights I slept on Stella's floor. Only not on the floor. Do you understand what I mean?'

'Yes, Ed.'

'We were in love. I'll put Sonya on in a minute. She wants to explain, but I have to explain too.'

'No, you don't. I've worked it out.'

'We were in love but I didn't realise it. I was only passing through. I had this crazy fixation that my destiny lay elsewhere. I felt as if – as if I were –'

'A changeling?'

'What?'

'Never mind.'

'I felt as if I were a Scotsman. More than that, a Highlander. I'd felt it in my blood for years, an overwhelming need to find out who I really was. It's all a mad dream now, but I left Stella on the seventh day and did not return. I felt that if I did not go she would be like a Siren, luring me from my true quest. So I left. I forgot about her and I thought she must have forgotten about me. We were liberated people, after all. We moved on. But she hadn't forgotten me, and she didn't move on, at least not physically, although she did complete her Business Studies degree. And when we met again today, well, I found that I hadn't forgotten her either. Everything came flooding back – the memories, the emotions, even her lines from *The Real Inspector Hound*. I felt as though I had been in another world for twenty-five years.'

'You have. You're breaking up, Ed,' I say, and then Sonya's voice sounds in my ear.

'He's not breaking up, I was just taking the phone out of his hand. It's all right, darling, go and sit down, I'll be with you in a minute. Douglas?'

'Sonya.'

'Do you understand what Ed meant by everything he has just told you?'

'I think so. He was a singer called Stuart, you were an actress called Stella. One summer you and he were together, he fucked off, you both got on with your lives, but what he didn't know was that you were pregnant with his child. Is that about right?'

'Yes, except he did not "fuck off". He went in search of his destiny.'

'Fair enough, but when you realised you were pregnant, why didn't you go after him?'

'I didn't know where he'd gone. And anyway, Douglas, I didn't know I was pregnant with his child.'

'You just said you were.'

'No, I didn't. You did. I knew I was *pregnant*, but not immediately. By the time I did know, I thought it was somebody else's child.'

'Whose?'

'Ben's.'

'Paula's father?'

'Yes.'

'But Paula wasn't even born.'

'Of course she wasn't. Don't be obtuse, Douglas. I met Ben days after Ed went away.'

'You didn't hang around.'

'You wouldn't say that if I were a man.'

'I might. I'm just a bit shocked, that's all.'

'You've lived a very sheltered life, Douglas. Ben and I stayed together when we found out I was pregnant. I thought Magnus was *his* child. And then Paula came along five years later.'

'But Magnus looks like Ed.'

'Yes, he does *now*. But he didn't always. For years he actually did look a bit like Ben.'

'I couldn't say. I've never even seen a photo of Ben. Even though you were together, well, about the same length of time we were.'

'There weren't many photos of Ben. I shredded them anyway.'

I wonder what will happen to any photos she may have of me. Are they, too, bound for the shredder beside her desk at the education consultancy?

'So today,' I say, returning to the fray, 'when you and Ed – are you calling each other Ed and Sonya, by the way, or Stuart and Stella?' I could add, 'When you're not calling each other "darling",' but it would be hypocritical.

'We are calling each other by our real names, Douglas.'

'Ed and Sonya.'

'Naturally.'

'I just wanted to clarify that. When you and Ed recognised each other in the hospital, it must have been as if you had each found your soulmate once more.'

'That's a nice way of putting it, Douglas. Thank you.'

'Not at all. There was this noticeable glow between you. You don't

318

feel resentful about the way he went in search of his destiny all those years ago?'

'We all have to search for our destiny, Douglas. If we're lucky, we find it.'

'Then I take it Ed isn't rushing off again?'

'No. We need some time to talk things through, but he isn't rushing off anywhere.'

'And how has Magnus taken it?'

'In his stride.'

'Metaphorically, obviously.'

'He is very happy. His real father has come home to him. He never liked Ben much anyway.'

'And Paula?'

'She's not back from work yet. She'll be cool about it. She'll take it in her stride, too.'

'Even though her real father hasn't come home to her?'

'Her real father is Ben. She never liked him much either. She'll like Ed, I'm sure of it.'

'She might feel resentful.'

'She'll be fine.'

I think about Paula. Sonya is probably right. She will be fine.

'What about you?' Sonya asks. 'Are you fine?'

'Kind of you to ask, Sonya. I'm fine.'

'Sure?'

'Couldn't be better.'

'Do you have anything you want to explain to me?'

'Such as?'

'Such as, what is your destiny, Douglas?'

I mull that one over for a few seconds. 'Sonya,' I say, 'this is a big moment for you. And for Ed and Magnus and Paula. I don't want to spoil it. Let's save my destiny for another day.'

We exchange a few more pleasantries, establish that Ed will probably not be coming back to the Elder residence tonight, although at some point tomorrow he may pop round for his toothbrush and anything else he's left here, and then – on very cordial terms, I must say – we end the call.

When I return to the kitchen, Ollie asks, 'You were a long time? Who was that?'

'Ed and Sonya,' I tell him. And then I tell them everything that Ed and Sonya have just told me.

'Well, well,' Poppy says.

'Bloody hell,' Ollie says.

'I've been thinking about a birthday present,' Rosalind says. 'I think, when someone attains the great age I have, that *she* should give somebody else a present.'

'That's a splendid idea,' Poppy says.

'So I propose to buy Douglas a new car. Not a *brand*-new one. A second-hand but sturdy and reliable one.'

'You can't buy me a car,' I say.

'I can. There is a *little* money in the bank. *You'd* have to identify the car, of course. One that would cope with the glen.'

'Can I have one too?' Ollie asks.

'Not until I'm a hundred and ten, Ollie. It's just that, whatever Ed's plans are, I think *we* have to make plans that don't include Corry-vreckan. So, really, it would be for Poppy and me as much as for you, Douglas.'

'On that basis, how can I say no?'

'Here's to not saying no,' Poppy says, raising her glass.

'Not saying no,' we all say.

Ollie reaches for his rucksack, and from it produces a bottle of Salmon's Leap 10-Year-Old Single Malt Scotch Whisky.

'This is for you, Douglas,' he says. 'It's a kind of reward for getting me that big story, even though you didn't mean to. There's a bottle of Glen Gloming too, but I'm keeping that for myself, because it's so bloody lovely.'

'I'll tell you a secret, Ollie,' I say. 'Salmon's Leap is exactly the same stuff.'

'Is it? Ah! I suppose it would be. Damn! Ah well, too late now to take it back.'

'It's yours if you want it.'

'I gave it to you. It's yours.'

'I appreciate that. We'll never see their likes again.'

'Here's to singular single malts,' Ollie says, and we all raise our champagne glasses again.

'Cheers.'

'*Slàinte!*'

'Good health!'

'Speaking of which,' I say to Ollie, and with my eyes indicate the bowel-cancer-treatment pack sitting on the counter.

'Ah yes,' he says. 'I almost forgot to say. Results came in yesterday. All clear. Panic over. Not that I was panicking.'

'Brilliant.'

'Well, it's certainly a relief. Don't you be forgetting to do the test yourself now.'

'What test?' Poppy asks.

'Dougie has to take a load off his mind.'

'I'll explain later,' I tell her. 'Mhairi must be happy.'

'She is,' Ollie says, 'and if she's happy, so am I. Bollocks, that's something else I almost forgot. We're going out tonight. I'll need to get home.'

But he stays for another half-hour, a second large slice of cake, a second glass of bubbly, and a cigarette on the sitootery. By the time he cycles off, the Munlochys and Ollie Buckthorn are the best of friends, and there is even talk of getting together with Mhairi and the kids tomorrow. We agree, however, to discuss it in the morning. Because who knows what may happen before then?

TO BE CONTINUED

Douglas Findhorn Elder opens the back door of what is half his and half his father's house – the house in which he grew up, which he has never really left and which, one day perhaps not too far off, will be wholly his – and steps into the blue night. The sky is cloudy and the garden dark with November darkness. His movement triggers a security light set on the wall of the house, and this illuminates the stone slabs of the patio or – as it has always been known in the family – the *sitootery*; or – as his father has sometimes referred to it with a glass of something in his hand – the *wine-cowpery*.

Coppélia 'Poppy' Munlochy, to whom Douglas earlier declared his love, and who returned the compliment, steps out beside him. It is ten o'clock on the night of her grandmother's one hundredth birthday, a day of quiet but heartfelt celebration. Her grandmother, Rosalind Isabella Munlochy (née Striven), has retired to bed half an hour ago, declaring herself worn out with happiness. Whenever she looks at Douglas and Poppy, she says, she feels that one thing at least is right with the world.

They have left Ed's bedding folded up on the living-room couch, just in case, but they don't expect he will need it. Douglas wishes Ed, and all his other manifestations whether gone or just resting, well. He wishes

Sonya well. He wishes Magnus, son of Ed and Sonya, well, and Ben and Sonya's daughter, Paula, too. He wishes Gerry a full but not too rapid recovery, and in the longer term the fulfilment of his desire to study Philosophy. He wishes Ollie and Mhairi and his Erstwhile Colleagues at the *Spear* health, happiness and job security. He wishes Rosalind many happy returns of the day, or even just one or two. He wishes his father, Thomas Ythan Elder, peace and contentment, and likewise Beverley Brown and her staff and Jimmy and all the other care-home residents.

Without getting into lists of the dead and total strangers, that's about it.

Douglas and Poppy each hold a glass of wine as well as one another, but they are not drunk, and neither of them wishes to be so. They have talked a lot about Glentaragar and Edinburgh, and the distance between them, and they are resolved to reduce it. There will be times when they will have to be apart, and there will be times when they will be together. Each has responsibilities. Insofar as they can, they will share them. They will talk much more, no doubt, about how to manage these, but they are practicalities, and practicalities can always be sorted. The decision of the heart is the one that matters, and it has been made. For the moment they are silent, hardly conscious of the background noise of the city as they stand on the stone slabs until the light goes out.

'If we don't move it stays off,' Douglas says.

There is no moon, and this makes Douglas think of his friend Mungo Forth Mungo, and the night they admired the moon together. And he seems to hear – or perhaps he just imagines – Mungo's voice, low, dark, yet sonorous and somehow commanding, coming from beyond the edge of the stones. And Mungo is giving a lecture. Tens of thousands of listeners may be out there in the black night, but only Douglas hears him:

'You think this belongs to you. With all your libraries full of books and universities full of accumulated knowledge, your internet and roads and railways and great cities, you think you are here to stay. You have no idea! You have barely arrived. We, or our ancestors, have been around a hundred times longer than you, a thousand times longer. You may think you have made an impact, but your leavings will be superficial. Fire and ice, wind and flood will wipe them away, but we will still be here. You build buildings that will turn to dust; you make music, art and literature that you think immortal but which will be outlasted by the scream of a gull or the flutter of a moth; you suck the oceans dry of oil and gas and fish; you batter and bleed the land of every mineral and nutrient it holds;

you cut and burn forests and hollow out mountains and drain bogs; and somehow you think you have a plan, a prospect, a future history. You think that you know more than we do, that you have made a storehouse for your children, that you are greater than any other living thing. But the toad, the toadstool, the ant, the blackbird, the deer, the daffodil, the jellyfish – you are less than all of these. That's it really. You know nothing and have nothing and are nothing. You can't help yourselves. You have no moon inside you.'

Douglas smiles at the notion of a toad coming out with such a diatribe. What does a toad, a common toad, know? And to say that humans have no moon inside them is like saying, on a night like tonight, that there is no moon in the sky, when of course there is: you just can't see it.

And although you can't see Mungo either, he is there. It is the end of the first day of November, and he has gone to bed, to sleep the winter sleep of the replete. Do toads dream? If Mungo is dreaming, it is probably of amplexus in the spring.

Poppy says, 'Did you hear Ollie calling you Ulysses this afternoon?'

'I did,' Douglas replies.

'Did you ever read the novel *Ulysses*?'

'James Joyce? Aye, I did once. Skimmed quite a bit of it.'

'Do you remember the last words in it, when Molly Bloom concludes her monologue?'

'Not exactly. She says "yes" a lot, doesn't she?'

'She does. And "I will". She says that too. Well, I was just thinking about it. It's very affirmative. Very life-affirming.'

'It's a good way to end a book. Affirmatively.'

'Yes, it is. It leaves you wanting more.'

'Do you want more?'

'I do. Yes. I want more life. I want more life with you. I want life to go on. To be continued.'

'That's what I want.'

'Can I say something?'

'Anything.'

'Well, we haven't known each other long, but it's just that my biological clock is ticking.'

'I see.'

'In fact, it might be about to chime.'

'What are you saying, Poppy?'

'Nothing. I'm just saying. Does that terrify you?'

'Not particularly. It would have, once. Can I say something?'

'What?'

'Let's not worry about it. Let's just take things as they come.'

'Okay.'

'That way we won't regret anything that doesn't happen.'

'Or anything that does.'

'Absolutely.'

After another few minutes, during which they drink their wine and cuddle very close, Poppy says, 'I'm getting cold.'

'Let's go in then,' Douglas says.

But they stay a while, because it seems to them that the cloud is moving and thinning, and that if they wait they may see the light of the moon, or even one star, coming through to greet them.

He just wanted a decent book to read ...

Not too much to ask, is it? It was in 1935 when Allen Lane, Managing Director of Bodley Head Publishers, stood on a platform at Exeter railway station looking for something good to read on his journey back to London. His choice was limited to popular magazines and poor-quality paperbacks – the same choice faced every day by the vast majority of readers, few of whom could afford hardbacks. Lane's disappointment and subsequent anger at the range of books generally available led him to found a company – and change the world.

'We believed in the existence in this country of a vast reading public for intelligent books at a low price, and staked everything on it'
Sir Allen Lane, 1902–1970, founder of Penguin Books

The quality paperback had arrived – and not just in bookshops. Lane was adamant that his Penguins should appear in chain stores and tobacconists, and should cost no more than a packet of cigarettes.

Reading habits (and cigarette prices) have changed since 1935, but Penguin still believes in publishing the best books for everybody to enjoy. We still believe that good design costs no more than bad design, and we still believe that quality books published passionately and responsibly make the world a better place.

So wherever you see the little bird – whether it's on a piece of prize-winning literary fiction or a celebrity autobiography, political tour de force or historical masterpiece, a serial-killer thriller, reference book, world classic or a piece of pure escapism – you can bet that it represents the very best that the genre has to offer.

Whatever you like to read – trust Penguin.